Bistro La Bohème Box Set

What If It's Love?

Falling for Emma

Under My Skin

Alix Nichols

Other books in the Bistro La Bohème series:

You're the One
Winter's Gift
Amanda's Guide to Love
(coming summer 2015)

Copyright © 2015 Alix Nichols
SAYN PRESS

All Rights Reserved.

Editing provided by Write Divas
(http://writedivas.com/)
This is a work of fiction. Names, characters, places and incidents are the product of the author's imagination or are used fictitiously. Any resemblance to actual events, locales, or persons, living or dead, is purely coincidental. No part of this publication may be reproduced, or transmitted in any form or by any means, electronic or otherwise, without written permission from the author.

Table of Contents

What If It's Love?...5
Part I: La Bohème 6
ONE...7
TWO 31
THREE 50
FOUR.. 73
FIVE 95
Part II: When the Clock Strikes Midnight........123
SIX..124
SEVEN 153
EIGHT 177
NINE 207
Part III: This Funny Thing 231
TEN...232
ELEVEN..252
TWELVE 270
THIRTEEN 298
FOURTEEN 323
Author's Note..343

Falling for Emma 345
Chapter One 347
Chapter Two..355
Chapter Three 364
Chapter Four 372
Chapter Five 378
Chapter Six 386
Chapter Seven...399
Chapter Eight 413
Chapter Nine 419

Chapter Ten	427
Chapter Eleven	441
Chapter Twelve	449
Chapter Thirteen	455
Chapter Fourteen	461
Chapter Fifteen	470
Chapter Sixteen	480
Chapter Seventeen	488
Epilogue	496

Under My Skin 503

Chapter One	504
Chapter Two	528
Chapter Three	551
Chapter Four	573
Chapter Five	585
Chapter Six	604
Chapter Seven	618
Chapter Eight	637
Chapter Nine	657
Chapter Ten	678
Chapter Eleven	690
Chapter Twelve	704
Chapter Thirteen	713

About the Author 735

What If It's Love?

Part I: La Bohème

Two trees are yearning for each other.
My house is across the street.
The trees are old. So is the house.
I'm young—or else I wouldn't stand here,
Commiserating with a tree.

Marina Tsvetaeva

ONE

The man, who spoke mostly Russian, had remained glued to his cell phone throughout his meal. When he finished, he collected his change and placed a ten euro bill on the table.

"*Merci, monsieur*! It's a very generous tip!" Rob grinned.

The service being included by default in all checks in Paris, the locals tipped scantily if at all. With the recession, even the tourists were beginning to heed the advice of guidebooks and do like the French.

"No trouble." The man stood to leave, then turned to Rob, and said in unexpectedly decent French, "Listen, would you like to make some extra cash?"

Has God finally heard my prayers? Rob tried to subdue his enthusiasm. "Depends . . . What's the gig?"

"Nothing difficult. There's this rich kid—"

Rob shook his head. "Sorry, monsieur, but I don't think I'm interested in hearing the rest of it."

On second thought, maybe he should hear it—and alert the police.

The man tut-tutted. "Didn't your mother teach you not to interrupt people when they speak? Let me start again. There's this Russian kid—she lives in this very building. Her father is my main competitor in business. I just want you to make friends with her, be around her as much as you can, and keep me informed of anything that may be of interest."

"Like what?"

"Like when during his phone calls or visits they discuss something related to his business. Or his travel plans. Or any kind of plans."

Rob furrowed his brow. "How often does he call her? And where is he?"

"In Moscow. He calls her every day, and from what I've seen, they talk for at least thirty minutes. She's his only child, so my guess is he's grooming her to join the business."

"What business?"

"IT services." The man arched an eyebrow as if to say, *What did you expect?*

Rob glanced around the room. Things were slow this afternoon, and the other waiters had the situation under control. But he had to get back to work.

The man shrugged. "Basically, I'm asking you to do corporate espionage of sorts."

"But won't this kid be speaking Russian with her father?" Rob's asked. The gig didn't seem to be anything horrible like kidnapping, but it still didn't sound quite legitimate.

The man smiled. "And you can understand it, can't you? I noticed how you smirked at some of my, shall we say, colorful expressions when I was on the phone. Are you part Russian or did you learn it at school?"

Rob sighed. There went his attempt at polite refusal. He might as well admit to this observant captain of industry that he spoke Russian. "School and evening classes. I'm a business student, so foreign languages are a big asset."

"How admirable. Do we have a deal, then? I'll pay you decently, so you can cut down your working hours and focus on your studies."

When the man told him the amount of the "commissions" for each piece of intel, Rob's mouth fell open. *Jesus*. If he delivered a dozen reports over the next few months, he'd be able to pay the school fees in full before the end of August.

And get his MBA.

"Let me get this straight," he said. "You want me to spy on some chick in relation to her father's activity, right? Just pass on whatever I overhear from her in this regard, and no funny business. I need to be sure of it."

"That's right. I'm not a mobster, you know. Do I look like one to you? Where do you think I learned my French? I'm an educated man and a respected businessman."

Rob raised his eyebrows, signaling he needed to hear more.

The man curled his lip. "It just so happens that Anton Malakhov — that's the girl's father — has been seriously hurting my business lately. He's determined to grow even bigger. And he plays dirty: dumping prices, stealing clients, and so on. I'll go bust if I don't get my act together. And this includes taking some ... unorthodox measures."

"Including a little foul play of your own," Rob said.

The man nodded and held out a business card. "My name is Boris Shevtsov. Please go ahead and look me and my company up."

Rob took the card. "Will do. I still have a couple of questions though. First, why don't you have someone spy on the girl's father directly? Why this roundabout approach?"

Boris sighed. "Anton Malakhov is spy proof. He's extremely discrete and not given to excesses of any kind. No wife or known girlfriend. Very few friends. A practically nonexistent social life."

"Have you tried through work? A mole intern is a textbook tactic." Rob tried to hide his sarcasm.

The man raised an eyebrow. "I'm familiar with it, thank you. And yes, I've tried it. But his people do advanced background checks on every recruit, including interns. So I figured spying on his daughter was as close as I could get to spying on him."

"What happens if the girl has no inclination to be friends with me? How long would you want me to keep trying?" Used to girls seeking his attention, Rob wasn't sure how good he would be at making the first steps. Natural-looking first steps.

Boris smirked. "Trust me, you won't have to try for very long. I've watched her from afar for a week now. She's always by herself. Doesn't seem to have any friends in Paris."

"How come?"

"She's new here. She's shy. And here comes a handsome educated boy like you offering friendship? Oh, I think she'll be interested."

"Give me a day to think about it."

Boris nodded and pushed a photo in front of Rob. "Her name is Lena."

Rob looked at the picture, then at Boris. "That's her? I've seen this girl down here a couple of times, with her books and laptop." He paused before adding, "Are you sure it's her?"

"Of course I am."

Rob shrugged. "She just doesn't look like a Russian *minigarch* to me. Where are the oversized sunglasses, tons of makeup, extravagant shoes, and the flashy Louis Vuitton handbag? She looks like the girl next door."

"Must be her Swiss boarding school education. Then again, Anton Malakhov isn't your stereotypical Russian *oligarch* either."

* * *

Stepping out of the cheese shop, Lena eyed the stately—albeit a little worn—limestone building on the other side of rue Cadet.

My new home.

Her gaze lingered on the café, *Bistro La Bohème,* that occupied part of the ground floor. It had all the requisite attributes of a Paris café: red awnings, wicker chairs, and tiny round tables overflowing onto the sidewalk. Over the past week, the bistro had become her stomping ground.

She crossed the street, keyed in the code and pushed the green gate that creaked open onto a cobbled courtyard. Across the way, she had to enter a second code to gain access to a glass door before she stepped into the foyer. The building smelled of old floorboards and something much less enchanting.

Trash.

What a change after her sterile student residence in Geneva!

A few minutes later, Lena and her grocery bags were safely inside her apartment. She went straight to the bedroom and collapsed on the bed, tired after her long walk and grocery shopping. But it was "good tired." She liked the 9th arrondissement, or *le neuvième*, for its diversity. Quintessentially French, *le neuvième* was also Jewish, Armenian, Greek, and Arabic. Its arched *passages* cutting through handsome buildings were lined with antique shops and secondhand bookstores. Its streets ran in wayward directions, forming a web rather than a grid. She would do something celebratory, she resolved, the day she managed to find her way around the 9th without a map.

Originally, Lena was supposed to move into a high-end apartment complex in the posh 16th arrondissement. But having spent the past seven years of her life in Switzerland, she refused to live in a place that would remind her of its eerie neatness.

Not that she'd been unhappy in Switzerland. She'd had absolutely no reason to be. She was the pampered heiress to an oligarch. Like many minigarchs, she'd been sent to one of the best European boarding schools at the age of sixteen. When she decided to continue her education at the University of Geneva, she got her father's full support. She'd been happy in Switzerland, Lena repeated to herself, even as her mind flashed an image of her last picnic with Gerhard. The one that put an end to their relationship.

"I'm moving to Paris," she had announced as soon as they sat on the campus lawn, with their croissants and paper coffee cups.

"Oh," Gerhard had said.

As she waited for him to say something more, she began to feel the dampness of the grass through her jeans. She shifted to sit on her heels. An early morning picnic in April, without a blanket to buffer the dew, had been a dumb idea.

As the silence stretched, and the dark sky threatened to burst out sobbing any minute, Lena wished they'd picked a spot by the wall.

So that she could bang her head against it.

"Why now? It's only a couple of months until our graduation," Gerhard said at length.

"I want to write my thesis there."

"Isn't it easier to write it on campus?"

"It is. But I'd rather do it in Paris."

Come on, get mad. At least annoyed. Anything.

He shrugged. "OK, then."

Her throat hurt. It was amazing she could still breathe given the size of the lump that had formed there. She'd been stupid to think she could provoke him into an emotional outburst. This was Gerhard — a paragon of self-control.

"After I get the degree," she said. "I'll probably go back to Moscow. Or maybe stay in Paris for a year. I haven't decided yet."

He stared at her.

Ask me to stay. Please. Just ask.

"I don't like Paris," he said. "It's noisy and dirty. And polluted."

She gave him a long unblinking stare, and then shifted her gaze to the vast lawn. So much for her brilliant idea to shake him up a little.

This is it — the end.

"I'll visit you," he said with the enthusiasm of a child in front of boiled broccoli.

"No you won't," she said with a sad smile.

He didn't argue.

Over the next week, she packed up, found a place in Paris, and left.

And now look at her!

How could she feel so *content* only two weeks after breaking up with her boyfriend of two years? Must be this city, operating its magic. Even the embryonic state of her thesis couldn't bring her down.

Lena looked forward to her dad's usual seven o'clock call so that she could share her high spirits with him.

When he called, she had just arrived in the downstairs bistro.

"So, how was your eighth day in Paris?" Anton asked.

"Fantastic. But then again, how could it be otherwise?"

"I wouldn't be so smug if I were you. Haven't you heard about these poor Japanese tourists?" he asked.

"I thought they were rather rich."

"Poor as in unfortunate. They arrive in Paris with such an idealized image that they can't handle its dirty streets, rude waiters, and aggressive pigeons. There's a special agency now that repatriates them to Japan before they completely lose it and jump from the top of Notre Dame."

Lena laughed. "I may have arrived here from Switzerland, but let's not forget I'm a Muscovite. I'm sure I can handle dirty streets and rude waiters. As for the pigeons, I already have an arrangement with the ones on my street."

"I'm all ears."

"I share my croissant with them, and in exchange they protect me from other pigeons. You have nothing to worry about."

"Yeah, I wish the pigeons were my only worry, Lena." Anton's tone had grown too serious for Lena's liking. "You're all alone in Paris, with no one to go to if you need help."

Oh please, not again. Next, he'd bring up her heart condition and how she couldn't be too careful. He made a huge deal out of her arrhythmia. Even when her cardiologist didn't. All the good doctor had asked her to do was avoid strenuous effort and saunas.

Anton took an audible breath. "In Geneva, you had Marta and Ivan. They're like family. They know what to do, should you ... feel unwell."

"Dad, I too know what to do, should I feel unwell."

"Of course, you do. But it's not just that. Marta and Ivan had you over for dinner every week, you enjoyed playing with their kids, they took care of you when you had the flu."

All of it was true, and she didn't know how to argue with that.

"I don't have anyone in Paris whom I could ask to watch over you like that," he said.

"I don't need—" she started.

"I'm going to hire someone, Lena. Besides everything else, I'm worried about your safety. There are people who may want to harm me and..."

Anton didn't finish the sentence, but Lena knew it was about his haunting fear that someone might kidnap her for ransom. Or worse—hurt her as a way of hurting him. She didn't want to make light of his fears. But she also knew that if she didn't nip this idea in the bud, she would find herself encumbered with a chaperon for the rest of her stay in Paris.

"Dad, I wasn't yet seventeen when you sent me off to Switzerland," she said patiently. "I'm twenty-three now and I'm capable of taking care of myself."

"Hmm."

Lena chose to ignore that. "Besides, nobody knows I'm in Paris. To anyone outside our closest circle I'm still in Geneva."

Anton didn't argue with that, which was a good sign. Lena continued with as much conviction as she could muster. "I'm perfectly safe here, don't you see? I'm a Miss Nobody. And if I ever get lonely, I can just jump on the train and go to Marta and Ivan's."

Thankfully, her mention of the family friends reminded Anton to give Lena their regards, after which he told her about her grandparents' Black Sea vacation. The conversation ended on an upbeat note, and Lena hung up relieved.

"Ready to order, mademoiselle?"

She looked up. The waiter standing by her table was in his midtwenties and very good-looking. Scratch that, he was jaw-droppingly handsome in that dark, intense and yet wholesome way the ancient gods could be. And it wasn't just his face. He was tall — well, French-tall, not Dutch-tall — lean, and broad shouldered. He was wearing the same café uniform all other waiters wore: a stark white shirt, black pants, and a long black apron tied around his hips. Lena mentally whistled at how it emphasized the exquisite narrowness of said hips.

She ordered her dish and a bottle of mineral water.

"No wine? Are you expecting someone later or will you be dining by yourself?" the black-aproned Adonis asked.

"It's none of your business, monsieur," she said curtly.

His question made her regret she didn't have company tonight. It made her want to tell him she was waiting for her boyfriend—no, her two boyfriends. She itched to wipe that grin off his face and tell him to find another victim for his snobbery.

She composed herself, straightened her back, and said, looking past him, "Would you kindly relay my order to the chef and then tend to your other customers?"

"So much impertinence in one so young." He shook his head admonishingly. "I'll be back with the water as soon as I possibly can. We're very busy today, you see." He smiled.

Was he provoking her? She decided she didn't care, gave him a cursory nod, and pulled out her iPad. She had a more important matter to consider than the shoulder-to-hip ratio of male servers.

She had to figure out what to write to Mom.

* * *

As students began to file out of the lecture hall, Rob turned to Amanda. "Did you have a chance to look at my paper?"

"Yep." She rummaged through her tote bag and handed Rob his draft essay.

He wrinkled his nose. "Your verdict?"

"Much better now, monsieur Dumont," she said in a posh voice, imitating one of their professors. "And those charts you added—they really did the trick."

Rob smiled. "You have my undying gratitude, mademoiselle Roussel."

"It'll fetch you another A, Robby Boy, or maybe even an A plus." She touched his arm. "Mark my words."

Rob's smile grew to a full-fledged grin. "Well, let's hope your crystal ball tells the truth."

"It always does, as you well know by now."

"Would you like me to take a stab at yours?" he offered.

"Nah, Mat already did. Mr. Thorough gave me twenty-five very specific suggestions to work through before tomorrow's deadline." Amanda rolled her eyes. "So, thanks, but no thanks."

"OK. Maybe next time, then." Rob collected his papers and stood. It was the time to bottle up his French pride and go to Starbucks across the street. "Will you at least let me buy you a latte?"

"Sure. Knock yourself out."

As they walked to the Starbucks, Rob whistled a silly tune. When Amanda raised an eyebrow, he just spread his arms as if to say, I can't help it. His life was exactly what he'd wanted it to be. He had a solid chance to graduate top of his class and find a good job. His best friends Amanda and Mat were not far behind. He'd make Grand-papa proud and prove to his parents he'd made the right choice. He'd show them it had been worth it, especially the last two years of all work and no play. But didn't all ambitious young people have to go through a few tough years if they wanted to make it in this world? At least, most of his friends did.

Rob pulled out his cell phone. "Let me call Mat. He may want to join us at Starbucks."

A hint of disappointment flickered in Amanda's eyes, but she schooled her features into a pleasant smile. "I think he has a class right now."

"Does he? I thought he finished before us on Thursdays . . . I'm probably confusing it with Fridays. Anyway, let me try."

Mat answered his phone and said he'd meet them for a mocha.

"See? I knew he'd be free by now," Rob said.

"Great." Amanda turned away from him and pushed open the door to the coffee temple.

Ten minutes later, the three of them sprawled on soft leather armchairs and sipped their brews.

"I wish there were more cafés in this city where you could slouch like this," Rob said.

"As opposed to having to keep your elbows close, so you won't knock over your neighbors' drinks," Amanda said.

Mat looked up from his mug. "Are you describing *La Bohème*?"

Amanda only smiled.

Rob gave a sigh. "Yeah, sounds like it... apart from those two larger tables we have in the back with padded banquettes."

Amanda turned to Mat. "So, Mathieu, have you made up your mind about what you want to do with your MBA? Will you stay in Paris and get a normal job or enter small-town politics in Normandy?"

"I'm still not sure. I keep changing my mind. The thing is, I'm as attached to home as I am to Paris."

"How convenient for me that my home *is* Paris," Amanda said.

Mat brushed his unruly curls from his face and sighed. "It's like asking me to choose between Calvados brandy and Bordeaux wine and stick to that choice for the rest of my life."

"You do realize that you don't *have to* stick with your choice for the rest of your life, right?" Amanda looked at Mat like he was a confused child.

"Yes, yes, of course I do. Anyway, I may end up in neither Paris nor Baleville if I get a job offer I can't refuse in Singapore," Mat said.

"Singapore is the place to be these days. Who knows, you may love it there." Amanda put her drink down and gave Mat a sly look. "But what about Jeanne, your blue-haired muse? You'd be so very far from her!"

"Over the past two years of our unilateral courtship, I've gotten no further with Jeanne than I was on the day I first laid eyes on her lip piercing." Mat's gaze became unfocused behind his thick eyeglasses. "I don't think Jeanne would notice if I left for Singapore this minute and didn't show up at *La Bohème* for a whole week."

"Oh, but she would," Rob said. "You always tip, and there isn't a waiter on this planet who wouldn't notice the disappearance of a loyal tipping customer."

Mat shrugged. "That's all I am to her—a loyal tipping customer."

"Well, at least, you should be happy you can afford to tip, what with our ginormous tuition fees and the payment deadline looming," Amanda said.

And with that little remark, Rob's sense of a benevolent universe vanished, along with his precious moment of self-indulgence. The specter of the tuition fee oozed into his head, chased all his lightness away, and reclaimed its royal share of his attention. His bright future would crumble like a house of cards if he didn't pay the fees before the end of August. No degree, no good job, no prospects.

Amanda looked at him with concern. "Rob? What's wrong?"

"Nothing. Well, no, actually . . . I'm just a little worried about tuition."

"Now, if I know you well, *a little* would be a euphemism for *a lot*, right?" Mat said.

"Well, no, not *a lot*. But maybe just a little more than *a little*. Let's say, if I applied German discipline and precision to my language, I'd say I'm *moderately* worried."

Mat and Amanda both smiled, but Amanda wouldn't let go. "I thought your tuition was taken care of. Didn't you get a waiver?"

"I was sure I would but it didn't work out. And I didn't get the loan, either."

"Are you serious?" Mat asked.

"Banks in this country don't like lending to students whose parents don't act as guarantors."

"Your parents didn't agree to be your guarantors?" Mat sounded surprised.

"I didn't ask them. The banker wanted proof I had a job lined up." Rob smirked. "I gave her proof I had a part-time job waiting tables. Turned out it wasn't the kind of job she had in mind."

"Why don't you just borrow from your parents? They should be able to help you out, yes?" Amanda asked.

"I can't. When I left home six years ago, my parents were mad. They had other plans for me... So they told me not to expect any help from them."

"I'm sure they didn't mean it," Mat said.

"Unfortunately for me, they did. When I ran out of money during the first year—I could only get odd jobs as a busboy back then—I asked if I could borrow a little from them. They refused. During my third year, I was trying to rent an apartment and asked them to act as my guarantors. They said sorry but no."

"I find this hard to believe. They are such nice people," Amanda said.

Rob cracked a bitter smile. "Nice, but pigheaded. They're still hoping I'll give up and return to the farm."

"Why don't you approach your grandfather? He's the one who understands your ambition, isn't he?" Amanda asked, a confused frown on her pretty face.

"All Grand-papa has is his meager pension. He was a crappy farmer when he worked. Brought the family farm to near ruin."

"He did tell me last summer he hated farming," Amanda said.

"Luckily," Rob continued, "my dad was old enough by then to take matters into his own hands. He saved the farm."

Mat gave him a concerned look. "What are you going to do?"

The crease between Amanda's eyebrows grew so deep Rob felt he had to say something reassuring. "Oh, I'll come up with something, I always do. Guys, I take back that I'm moderately worried. I'm not worried at all. I've even got a plan, I swear."

He chose not to reveal that the plan in question was a fishy stint as a spy for a Russian businessman.

That, or an emergency intervention from a fairy godmother.

* * *

Blissful recklessness, my sweet sin,
My companion—and ruination!
You have taught me to laugh at whim,
You have filled my veins with flirtation.

You have taught me to love—and to mend,
Drop the ring, if empty of meaning,
To begin, every time, from the end,
And to end before the beginning.

To be iron—and to be silk
in this world where we are so little . . .
Battle sadness with chocolate milk,
And tend loneliness with a giggle.

Marina Tsvetaeva

TWO

Guidebook, check.

Bottle of Evian, check.

Phone, keys, money, check.

OK, she was all set for today's bit of neighborhood recon. On the program was the *quartier* that stretched from Nortre-Dame de Lorette to Pigalle. Her guidebook recommended starting from the church, but Lena had already seen it during her first two walks. So she took the bustling rue des Martyrs directly to the legendary *boutique* of Père Tanguy.

Or whatever was left of it.

If anything at all.

Her guidebook was suspiciously evasive on that account, and the photo next to the detailed story of Père Tanguy showed no more than a sober white memorial plaque.

During one of her visits to Paris, Lena had discovered Van Gogh's *Portrait of Père Tanguy* in the Rodin museum. She loved the air of quiet serenity the Buddah-like man exuded. Père Tanguy wasn't a random model—he was the best friend of the impressionists.

The jovial fellow sold them art supplies and accepted paintings as payment. He then exhibited the paintings, one at a time, in the window of his tiny shop. On Monday it would be a Renoir, on Tuesday a Monet, on Wednesday a Pissarro, on Thursday a Van Gogh...

She *had* to see that place.

To Lena's surprise and joy, the *boutique* was still there, sold Japanese art, and was called Père Tanguy. After chatting with the friendly manager, she found out the shop had changed hands and was converted into an art gallery a few years ago. Considering Père Tanguy's obsession with Japanese prints, history had come full circle.

Elated, Lena bought a print and headed back home. She'd promised herself to write at least three pages of her theoretical chapter before the end of the day. It was time to get started... After she had something to eat.

It was past lunchtime, but Lena was hoping she could still order a big salad at the downstairs bistro. She took a window seat at the back. It offered a great vantage point from which to observe the passersby. Lena stretched her legs under the table and began to study the menu. She felt mature, self-sufficient, and in charge.

And single, in a good way.

A young woman with dyed pale blue hair approached her table. "Has mademoiselle decided what she'd like to order?"

The waitress's hair, her gothic makeup, and pierced lower lip were in stark contrast to her classical French server uniform: a stiff-collared white shirt, black trousers, long black apron, and elegant black shoes.

She whipped out a little notepad and tilted her head to the side to signal full attention.

"Your Savoyard salad looks interesting," Lena said, looking to her for a confirmation.

"It isn't interesting. It's fantastic — our chef's special. It's the best Savoyard in Paris, if I say so myself."

"Wonderful! Then I'll have it, please."

The waitress shook her head. "I didn't mean to lead you on. We're out of the Savoyard. In fact, the only salad left is the Niçoise."

"That's OK. I'll have the Niçoise then, and a pitcher."

Lena found herself remarkably unperturbed by the salad situation and pleased that she'd remembered to ask for a pitcher. During her previous visits to Paris, she had learned it was local code for tap water. It felt good to showcase that knowledge now, even though she would have preferred to drink Evian.

"Very good choice," the waitress commented with a sly smile.

Lena wasn't sure if she was referring to the salad or the tap water.

After finishing her meal and ordering a cup of tea, Lena turned on her iPad. Thankfully, the café offered Wi-Fi. She checked her e-mails and saw one from Gerhard. He was complaining about his current predicament: how to cut a 200-page mammoth of a monograph down to the seventy required for a master's thesis. At the end of his note he suggested that they critique each other's work.

So Gerhard wanted them to be thesis writing buddies.

All right. It would be part of her healing. Besides, she did need help with her thesis, which at present consisted of only ten pages of theory and about forty pages of poems. The poems were Lena's French translations of Marina Tsvetaeva, her favorite Russian poet. Even though both Lena and Gerhard majored in translation theory and practices, Gerhard was more into theory while Lena preferred the practice.

She wrote back.

> *Gerhard:*
> *I have an idea. How about removing all the speculative bits, historic digressions and unnecessary footnotes?*
> *Try it and I think you'll be fine.*
> *Cheers,*
> *Lena*

It helped that she knew Gerhard and the way he wrote so well. It was also much easier to critique someone else's thesis than to write hers. She attached to her e-mail her own anorexic theoretical chapter and asked him for an honest opinion.

She considered sending Gerhard her translated poems, too—after all, they were part of her thesis. She was curious to see if her translations would stir an emotional response in a person unfamiliar with the original texts. Truth be told, Lena craved feedback on the poems she'd poured her soul into.

And that was precisely why she couldn't send them to Gerhard.

As she packed her iPad away, a nerve-racking sound startled her.

A motorcycle screeched to a halt in front of the bistro, its engine filling the street with a hideous stench and roar. Lena wasn't sure motorcycles were allowed on pedestrian streets, but the biker looked like he wouldn't give a hoot if they weren't. His helmet half concealed his face. He sported a tattoo on each arm, and another one peeked from under the collar of his black T-shirt. He wore black jeans and huge black combat boots along with bulky signet rings on his hands. If appearances could talk, his was shouting that a metrosexual he was not.

A few seconds later, the blue-haired waitress came out and stood next to the biker with her arms crossed over her chest. She said something Lena didn't catch. The biker tapped his helmet but didn't remove it.

"You were gone for more than an hour with some chick," the waitress shouted. "People asked me who she was and if you were coming back to the party, and I had to tell them I had no clue. And then, just as I was about to leave, you show up and behave like nothing's wrong!"

The biker muttered something Lena couldn't make out.

"I don't care that she doesn't mean anything to you!" The waitress yelled, clenching her hands in fists. "I want to know what *I* mean to you. After all this time, do I mean anything at all?"

Lena couldn't hear the biker's reply.

The waitress shook her head. "You know what? Just go away. Right now I can't stand to look at you." She spun around and marched back into the kitchen.

The biker started the engine and drove away, leaving stench, noise, and smoke in his wake.

* * *

From behind a tree Rob raised his gun, took aim at the mobster he had been paid to execute, and pulled the trigger. As he watched the bullet perforate his target's chest, the mobster transformed into a petite young woman with dark hair and big brown eyes. Rob froze. There was no mistake. He'd just shot Lena Malakhova, the girl from the bistro. Suddenly, his head started to ring, the sound getting louder and louder.

He woke up drenched in cold sweat to the deafening peal of his telephone.

"Hello," he rasped, grabbing the receiver.

"Rob, it's Maman. Did I wake you? How's my boy?"

He shook his head vigorously to dissipate the image of Lena Malakhova, sprawled on the ground with a big red stain spreading across her chest. "I'm fine, M'man. What's up? How's everyone back home?"

"We're all OK," Rose said. "Grand-papa is organizing a chess tournament for the Fourteenth of July celebrations. It's put him in a good mood."

"That's great."

"He even went to Besançon to order a special prize from a craftsman for the winner. We've been bugging him about what it is, but he only says 'wait and see.' I fear the worst."

Rob laughed. "I bet it's a chess set with topless mermaids as the queens. That, or topless firefighters as the kings. Or maybe both to make sure to embarrass madam the mayor."

"Oh yes, Bastille Day won't be a success unless your grandfather has embarrassed madam the mayor!"

"How's my little sister? Is she finishing the year well?" Rob asked.

"Caro's been smack in the middle of her class since January. I suspect she's so comfy there she's made it a question of honor to uphold that position," Rose said with a sigh.

"I'll talk to her."

"But there's good news, too. Your sister has declared we're no longer to buy her anything pink, rosy, or purple because it's *not cool*. Her favorite color from now on is black. Please take note."

Rob smiled. Caroline—Caro to friends and family—was an outgoing, happy child. He wondered if she would retain that personality through her teenage years. She loved to be outdoors. As a result her skin was golden and her wild hair bleached by the sun. Being her elder by twelve years, Rob had logged a record number of babysitting hours up until he left for Paris. As a matter of fact, he may have spent more time with his little sister than both his busy parents combined.

"Note taken—pink is *not* cool." He gasped dramatically. "Oh no."

"What is it?"

"I need to replace my entire wardrobe."

As his mother chuckled, Rob stuck the handset between his ear and his shoulder, rubbed his eyes, and got out of bed. "How's Papa? And what about you?"

"Same old. We've been really busy for the past couple of months, but things are calming down a bit."

"Will you visit me then?" He knew there was little chance of that happening, considering how much his parents disliked big cities in general, and Paris in particular. They hated the traffic, the noise, the ubiquitous dog poo, and the weirdoes in the *métro*. He couldn't actually remember a single thing they liked about Paris.

"There's still some urgent work to finish here. Besides, we're both on the organizational committee for the intervillage Olympic Games and the Firemen's Ball. It will be special this year, you'll see."

During his six years in Paris, Rob's parents visited him only three times and complained about Paris for months after each visit. So, he went to them whenever he could. That is, whenever he managed to get a weekend off at the bistro, book cheap train tickets, or find an offer to car pool.

He walked into the kitchen and poured himself a glass of water. "Well, then I guess I'll see you all in Saint-Fontain in mid-July. Say hi to everyone."

His mother promised to do that and made Rob promise to eat well and stay away from cigarettes. It was how they ended each of their conversations for the past six years, and Rob had grown to appreciate the reassuring invariability of that ritual.

He hung up and went to the shower. As warm drops hit his shoulders and back, his thoughts turned to yesterday's exchange with Lena Malakhova. They'd gotten off on the wrong foot. So he'd need to start over... if he were to accept the job.

I can do this.

He would fix their bad start and get Lena to relax around him. And then he'd get close enough to her to eavesdrop on her conversations without raising suspicion. And if he could manage to hold this gig throughout the summer, his little tuition problem would be solved without any need for a fairy godmother.

With a sigh Rob admitted to himself his decision was made. He needed the money, and he was running out of time and options. The gig stank, all right. But after Googling Boris Shevtsov in every language he knew, he hadn't found anything to suggest the guy was involved in criminal activity. So it would be as he'd said — just a bit of corporate espionage.

Nothing more.

Rob turned off the shower, dried himself and got dressed. Then he went to his desk, picked up Boris's card and dialed his number.

Boris answered immediately.

"I'll give it a go," Rob said. "But if she's not interested after a week, I won't pursue her. You'll have to find someone else. Are we agreed?"

"Agreed. I'll talk to you in a week."

* * *

When Lena was eleven, her parents divorced. They didn't fight over her custody in court but resolved the matter amicably after Dad paid off Mom. Lena still remembered every word of that dreadful conversation shortly after the scandal had erupted and turned their lives upside down. She could still feel the lump in her throat as her mother held her by the shoulders and shouted over her wailing. "You can't come along. If you do, both of us will starve." Lena had seen starving children on television. They had huge bloated bellies and vacant eyes. She didn't want to starve.

Then Mom left and Lena stayed with Dad. She cried for a week. For the next year, she waited for Mom to return for her. After that, she waited for Dad to mellow and let Mom visit. After several years, she gave up.

Lena shook her head to dissipate the memories and forced herself to concentrate on the e-mail she'd been writing for the past half hour. It had two sentences. She added a third one, and reread her note.

> *Hi Mom,*
> *I'm in Paris now, settled and very happy with my neighborhood and apartment.*

> *I'll be working on my thesis over the next month and then will travel to Geneva for the defense. After that — we'll see.*
> *Hugs,*
> *L*

Lena pressed send and sighed with relief. It was no small feat to have written such a well-rounded and informative missive to her mother. Those three short lines summarized hours and hours of phone calls with Dad.

Just think of all the time she saved . . .

Rob arrived at *La Bohème* an hour before his shift was to start. He scanned the bistro for Lena. To his great relief she was there, sitting at one of the sidewalk tables with her laptop and a glass of iced tea. He made himself a coffee and settled at the table next to hers.

The moment she stopped typing to take a sip from her glass, Rob made his move. "Hi there. I see you like our little bistro."

She looked at him, recognition flickering in her eyes. "Hi. So you're here as a patron today?"

"Not really. Just getting sufficiently caffeinated to make it through the evening. Saturday nights are the waiter's nightmare."

"I thought they were the best in terms of tips," she said.

"You thought correctly. Which is why we servers accept to work them without coercion. Have you ever waitressed?" he asked.

"No, I haven't. My knowledge is purely theoretical." She took another sip of her iced tea and asked, "Are you a born Parisian? I cannot quite determine from your accent."

Rob smiled. This conversation was going well. In fact, much better than he had hoped, given the other day's calamity. "I've lived here for the past six years, but I come from a small village in the southeast of France. The region is called Jura."

"I know Jura. It borders Switzerland. I even went hiking there on the Swiss side a few times," she said quickly.

"So, I take it you come from Switzerland?" he asked.

She hesitated for a second and then said, "I've lived there for the past seven years."

"I like Switzerland, but I don't think I could live there. It would be like living inside an idyllic postcard."

She leaned in, eyes bright with understanding. "Exactly. Like someone locked you up inside an idyllic postcard and threw away the key."

It was Rob's turn to offer an insight into Swiss life. "It's a very reliable country, just like its watches. The first bus always arrives at your stop at 7:13, as announced on the schedule. The postman delivers the mail at 7:14, and the ducks land on the pond at 7:15 sharp, every day."

"It depends." She arched her eyebrows. "Where I lived, they hit the pond at 7:03. Every day."

He shrugged. "Must be lark ducks. Hey, here's another one: the Swiss won't cross the street at a red light even if there isn't a single car in sight. They'll just stand there and wait."

"If you try it in Paris, people will think you're stoned. Have you ever noticed the big red button you're supposed to press in such situations?"

"When you're stoned?"

The corners of her mouth twitched upward. "No, when the traffic light is red, but there are no cars."

"Ah, that one! Yes, I've seen it. We have them in France, too."

"Well, in Switzerland people actually use them! They press, and wait, and press again several times, and wait some more. There are still no cars, but they won't cross."

Her eyes were now sparkling with mirth. "I used to think the button made the light change to green faster. But then I timed it and realized its sole purpose was to give the law-abiding citizens some form of release. Like a punching bag for fingers."

Rob laughed. "Reminds me of another Swiss quirk. If you inadvertently drop a candy wrapper or a bus ticket, at least three people will notice and tell you in French, German, and Italian to please pick it up."

He held up his index finger and said with a thick Swiss accent, "Keeping our country clean is everybody's business!"

She put her hand over her mouth. "Oh my God—this actually happened to me once!"

The game is on, he thought as he listened to her peals of happy laughter.

* * *

I'm glad that you're in love with someone else,
I'm glad that I'm enamored with another,
And I'm content that never will the Earth
Relax its pull, condemning us to hover.
With you, I can be funny — or a mess,
Let down my hair and abandon caution.
No fierce blushing every time our hands
Brush lightly in an unexpected motion.

I thank you from the heart for being kind,
For loving me so sweetly, so benignly,
For cherishing me, for my peaceful nights,
For the non-kissing in a moonlit alley,
For the non-dates, no passion to confess,
For happily behaving like a brother,
For being charmed — alas! — by someone else,
While I'm — alas! — enamored with another.

Marina Tsvetaeva

THREE

Two weeks after her arrival in Paris, Lena had become a regular at *La Bohème*. She went there every morning for a breakfast of coffee, croissants, and orange juice. After that she either headed to the library or stayed at the bistro typing away on her laptop and refueling on the barista's delicious-smelling brews. On most days, she cleared the premises by noon, when the shop assistants, builders, and white collars working in the neighborhood arrived for lunch. She often returned in the late afternoon for dinner.

Before giving the monopoly over her nourishment to *La Bohème*, Lena had made sure to check out the available alternatives. But her forays into the neighboring eateries turned out to be disappointing.

At the first place across the street, she was served green beans overcooked to a sickly shade of gray. She ordered a medium steak at a more expensive restaurant a few blocks further down the street. The steak was served raw, and then reluctantly taken back to the kitchen to be returned a good half hour later, thoroughly burned.

The last place she tried had decent food and the wait wasn't too long. But as she ate, she became witness to a heart-wrenching scene. An ostensibly pregnant woman had walked in and pleaded with the maître d'.

"I'm sorry, monsieur. May I use your bathroom?"

"Are you a customer?"

"No, but—"

"The bathroom is reserved for our patrons."

The maître d' swirled and walked away, leaving the woman stranded by the entrance. She shifted from one foot to another, her face contorting in discomfort as she scanned the room for a more sympathetic waiter. Lena rushed to the counter and got a token—the open sesame to the toilet door.

"I'm transferring my bathroom entitlement to her," she told the glaring maître d' and handed the token to the woman.

Lena resolved there and then that the establishment didn't deserve her business.

La Bohème, on the other hand, was free of such nonsense. Its food was delicious and its service quick. Its proprietor and staff were friendly for Parisian standards. Better still, they provided a constant stream of entertainment.

There was the Adonis, of course. Lena still didn't know his name—he never introduced himself, and he never asked her name, either. So, she continued to identify him as Adonis, even though the moniker was beginning to sound ridiculous. He had gotten into the habit of stopping by her table to exchange a few words about this and that, which made her feel like a valued patron. At least this was her official explanation of why she enjoyed those little conversations so much.

After a few days, they'd established they were both finishing grad school and writing their theses. Adonis told Lena he was almost done and shared a few time management tricks.

Yesterday afternoon when he threw her a friendly "how's that thesis coming along", she replied with pride she'd written more than half.

"Well done!" he cheered, and Lena felt her cheeks warm with pleasure.

If I were a cat, the entire café would hear me purr, she thought.

He placed a cup smelling of coffee and chocolate on her table. "This cappuccino is on me. You deserve it."

She shook her head, "No, please, you shouldn't do this. I'm happy enough with your verbal encouragements."

"Oh, but it's nothing. If it makes you uncomfortable, I'll rephrase it. This cappuccino is on the house—more precisely, on Pierre, the owner of the bistro."

He winked and added, "Pierre has no clue he just extended his generosity to you, but I can guarantee when he finds out, he won't mind. He values education highly."

"Well . . . I suppose it would be rude of me to refuse a drink offered by the proprietor."

"He would be scandalized."

She raised the cup. "Here's to Pierre—the champion of education, a generous boss, and an all-round good man."

"Amen," he said.

Then, there was the blue-haired waitress. Most of the other regulars called her Jeanne, and she knew their names as well. She'd greet the old lady who came for her daily espresso with a "Mme Blanchard, how is that knee today?" and actually stop to listen to the answer. She'd inquire of the gray-suited office rat, "Did your business trip go well?" She seemed to know about the patrons' families, their work (or the lack thereof), and health. She certainly knew their culinary preferences, which made her order taking remarkably efficient.

Lena couldn't wait for the day Jeanne would greet her with a "Hi, Lena! The usual?"

She had also spotted a goofy fellow who had his dinner at *La Bohème* every day. His wild curls and huge thick eyeglasses—the kind ugly ducklings wore in movies before their transformation—hid most of his face. On top of this, the guy was extremely thin. His T-shirt hung from his wide but bony shoulders in a two-dimensional way, like a shirt on a clothes hanger, with no noticeable relief anywhere along its length. His arms were so skinny that were he a woman, Lena would have bet he had anorexia.

Did men suffer from anorexia?

Mr. Clothes Hanger appeared to be Rob's buddy. He also seemed to be carrying a torch for Jeanne—if his lingering looks and repeated clumsy attempts to strike a conversation with her were any indication. Unfortunately for him, Jeanne didn't take the slightest interest in his person, except how he liked his coffee and his steaks.

The third waiter Lena liked to watch was a black-haired Spanish guy, Pepe. He had the body of a matador—elegant and compact. It was a shame, really, that his shapely frame was too small for today's male beauty standards. He had a goatee, beautiful black eyes, and a charming accent. He flirted desperately with every fair-haired girl who passed through the café, even though the girls didn't flirt back with him.

Once Lena heard him ask three German girls having beers next to her table, "What are your names, lovelies?"

"Brunhilde," one of them said with a sweet smile.

"Irmtraud," the second said with an even sweeter smile.

"Hildegard," the third said, her smile so big Lena worried the corners of her mouth would tear.

Pepe looked from one girl to the next, lips moving as he tried to memorize their unlikely names. This sent the girls into a prolonged fit of the giggles that finally drove him away.

Pepe didn't attempt to flirt with Lena, who was exceedingly grateful this particular gentleman preferred blondes.

* * *

"Having trouble with the writing?"

Lena looked up. Pepe the Matador stood by her table, shaking his head in sympathy. "What if your nails don't grow back?"

"Oh," she said, jerking her hand from her mouth. "How observant of you — Pepe, right?"

"Yes, and you are?" Pepe replaced Lena's empty cup with a steaming frothy blend.

"Lena. I live in this building, as it happens."

"I figured as much. Are you a friend of Rob's? I see him chatting with you whenever he has a spare moment." Pepe smiled innocently and gave her a suggestive wink.

As Lena marveled at how he could accomplish such a paradoxical combo, her brain registered that Rob was Adonis.

"No, I am not a friend of Rob's. In fact, I have no clue why he stops to chat with me."

"Don't you?" Pepe gave her an are-you-dumb look. "Let's see. If I were you, I'd assume he liked me. But what do *I* know?" He shrugged and headed to the kitchen.

Lena's thoughts scattered like beads from a torn necklace. Could Rob really like her? He did chat with her a lot, almost every time he had a spare moment. But what did he find in her? With his looks and charisma he could have any girl—any *gorgeous* girl. Could he have found out she was an heiress? But then, he wasn't the kind of guy to pursue a girl for her money . . .

She blew out her cheeks. This was ridiculous. For one, she had no idea what kind of guy he was. She tried her best to concentrate on her work. But as if on cue, Rob walked into *La Bohème*. He wore a basic white T-shirt and faded jeans. Hidden in her corner, Lena ogled him in a most shameless way. Her gaze feasted on his narrow hips and flat stomach, then traveled up his well-muscled arms to his broad shoulders, caressed his firm jawline, and drank in his intelligent hazel eyes.

Rob sauntered to the counter, his every movement infused with easy masculine grace. When she finally lost sight of him as he disappeared behind the door marked STAFF ONLY, she could feel her heart racing and her cheeks burning. *How stupid!* She should know better than to drool over the first handsome stranger she met in this town.

He's just a pretty boy, offered the familiar sensible voice in her head.

Boy, he is pretty, retorted a voice she'd never heard before.

In the face of such blatant sauciness, her sensible self kicked below the belt. *A pretty boy who will break your heart, given the chance.*

Bingo. Lena blinked as her pulse slowed down and color drained from her cheeks. A broken heart was a messy business. Was the pretty boy really worth it?

Nope. Especially not now. She was finally over Gerhard, really over him. Her soul was filled with a sense of freedom she was beginning to seriously appreciate.

She'd nearly forgotten how it felt to jump at every phone call, and to spend hours debating if she should make a move, or if her boyfriend was still into her. Gerhard had never been given to excesses, but a few months ago Lena started to suspect he cared more for his Labrador than for her. In March she began to wish he'd just dump her and put her out of her misery. But Gerhard was in no hurry to end their relationship. And she didn't have the guts to do it herself. Which was when the idea of a research trip to Paris turned into a plan to move there.

Lena closed her laptop and waved for the check. She wanted to leave before Rob emerged from the staff room and shattered her resolve. This newfound freedom of hers, this unattached bliss—it was too precious to throw to the wind. She should protect it at any cost.

Especially when all she had to do was stay away from a handsome Frenchman named Rob.

* * *

Vanves was one of the Parisian suburbs where Tsvetaeva found refuge during her long French exile. It was residential and dull. Lena wandered through its streets, trying to imagine how they looked in the 1920s when Tsvetaeva lived here. Those years weren't a happy time for the poet. She was separated from her friends and her husband, struggling to provide for her children, and unable to publish her work. She was stuck in French suburbia, too bourgeois to return to Bolshevik Russia and too poor to move her family inside Paris. A fish out of water.

It was midafternoon when Lena fetched her laptop and settled in *La Bohème* to work on the translation she'd started the day before. It wasn't a difficult poem, with one notable exception: the word *careless*. In Russian it implied a bit of recklessness, a touch of irresponsibility, and a dash of sweet silliness. All at once. Lena hadn't been able to find a good French equivalent yet.

She ordered her third café crème — desperate times required desperate measures — opened all her thesaurus apps and dived in.

Rob stole a glance at Lena. She sat at her favorite table, her hair pulled back in a loose ponytail, eyeglasses on her forehead.

He rubbed his neck. Should he finally introduce himself, now that he'd spent over a week blathering to her about everything and nothing?

The dilemma had weighed on his mind for a couple of days now. On the one hand, he and Lena were clearly reaching a critical point in their acquaintance when people learn each other's names—or go their separate ways. Actually, they were already way past that point. Had he spent half that time with any other girl, he would've found out not only her name, but also her phone number, her favorite music bands, and probably the flavor of her lipstick.

On the other hand, this was not a normal situation, at least not to him.

Talking to Lena is a job, Rob reminded himself for the umpteenth time.

Sure, and her being cute as a button is entirely beside the point, a sardonic voice in his head retorted.

He looked at her again. Her hand rummaged through her handbag—no doubt for her glasses—while she squinted at the laptop screen, oblivious to the world.

It's just a job to pay my tuition, Rob repeated his mantra. *I can't screw this up.*

He approached her. "I believe what you're looking for is on your head."

Communication had become so easy between them. One little remark would lead to another, and before they knew it, they would be knee-deep in an animated discussion about polar bears or Daft Punk. This time round, they ended up analyzing the latest twist in a TV show they both liked.

"I must say I didn't find that turn of events entirely plausible," she said.

"I agree, but I don't think the director's goal was to be plausible. It was to take everyone by surprise. Including himself."

"Sorry to barge in on your cozy chat, but your time's up." Jeanne made big eyes at Rob and then turned to Lena. "This young man's coffee breaks have been stretching beyond what's decent since you began to frequent the bistro. He'd better get a grip before Didier tells the proprietor."

She held out her hand. "I'm Jeanne, by the way, Rob's sister in arms—or, rather, in plates. And you are?"

"Lena. Very pleased to meet you, Jeanne." Lena shook hands with her and then turned to Rob. "So you would be Rob, then?"

He tried to sound nonchalant. "Robert Dumont at your service. Sorry for not having introduced myself earlier."

Jeanne rolled her eyes. "Aren't we all incredibly well-bred and courteous? Please accept my sincere apologies for being such a spoilsport, but you are expected inside, Rob. Duty calls. More specifically, the mop."

Rob gave Lena a quick nod and headed to the kitchen. They had officially met now. It was inevitable and perfect for his purposes, but it somehow made his little deal with Boris a touch more unsavory.

* * *

In the cab from the train station to her place, Lena replayed her eventful day. Her meeting with Professor Rouvier had gone well, and she had left his office with lots of good advice on how to revise her thesis. After that she had a coffee with two classmates. Just before she left the university to visit Ivan and Marta, she ran into Gerhard. They greeted each other and then just stood there, not knowing what to say. The thing was . . . she didn't have anything to tell him besides the academic stuff they'd discussed over e-mail. Lena wondered at how just a month ago she thought herself in love with him. Her feelings were so completely gone it was hard to believe they'd been real.

Distance is *a truly powerful medicine,* she thought. A little distance and time was all it took to free her heart of Gerhard and wipe him from her mind. Or was that all? If she was completely honest with herself, could she vouch that a certain Frenchman had nothing to do with it?

By the time she got home, it was around nine in the evening. After the mandatory call to her father to inform him she'd returned safely, Lena went down to *La Bohème* for a quick bite.

There wasn't a single vacant table, inside or outside. She was about to leave when she heard Rob call to her.

"Hey, Lena, over here!" He was having dinner with his scrawny pal and a pretty woman Lena hadn't seen before.

As she approached them, Rob pulled out a chair for her. "Come join us. I'm a free man tonight. Started earlier so I could keep them company for dinner."

His friends smiled, the guy with enthusiasm and the woman tightly. Lena began to say she didn't want to intrude, when Clothes Hanger stood up to exchange a cheek kiss with her. "Hi, I'm Mat, Rob's flatmate. And this is Amanda. We all study together, and these two are poised to graduate top of the class."

"I'm not so sure about that." Amanda waved "hi" without standing for a bona fide greeting. "And you are?"

"Lena. I live in this building." She mouthed *thank you* to Rob and sat down.

"That's it!" Mat clapped his hand on his forehead. "Now I know why you look so familiar. I've seen you here before."

"You've got this tiny *rustic* accent. Are you from Switzerland?" Amanda asked.

Lena smiled. "You have a good ear. I'm from Russia, but I've lived in Switzerland for the past seven years."

"Russia! How exotic. And what brings you to France, Lena?" Amanda asked.

Jeanne arrived to take Lena's order, interrupting Amanda's questioning.

When she left, Rob nudged Lena to look at Mat, whose gaze was locked on Jeanne, lapping her up as she walked away. "Mat here has been desperately in love with Jeanne for—um, let me see—an eternity? But she won't go out with him. She prefers her bad boy biker. It's a very sad story."

Mat turned to face his friend. "Rob, what makes you think I can't hear you when I'm not looking at you?"

"Touché," Rob said.

Mat sighed. "I must sound like a total loser to you, Lena. I guess I am."

"Most certainly not," Lena said.

"Believe me, I've tried to move on, like, a hundred times. I try every day, as a matter of fact. But she's bewitched me. Must be that lip piercing. It does something terrible to my brain chemistry."

"You are so messed up, my friend," Amanda said. "Have you considered seeking professional help?"

Lena was looking for something comforting to say, when she saw the old man sitting at the table next to theirs. She winced. "Oh no, not him again."

Today, he was wearing cream trousers and a well-ironed blue shirt with a silk cravat tucked into its open collar. He had pointy shoes and a thin white mustache. He was dining in the company of a boy in his late teens, probably his grandson. Lena had nicknamed him GLL—the Geriatric Latin Lover. He was the plague of the bistro, the harasser of waitresses, and an embarrassment to whomever he dined with.

Jeanne approached his table, a notepad in her hand. "Has monsieur chosen his dessert?"

"No, monsieur hasn't," he replied, then looked Jeanne over, smiled a sleazy smile, and winked. "Can we ask the chef to put *you* on the menu?"

Lena couldn't believe her ears. This was worse than the previous borderline comments she'd heard him make. And then he winked again, this time at his grandson. The boy looked so utterly mortified that Lena half expected him to dip under the table and put his head between his knees.

"Oh, but there's no need to bother the chef," Jeanne said far too sweetly. "I'm already on today's specials. It's written on the chalkboard over there."

She pointed, and GLL instinctively turned and squinted at the chalkboard.

Jeanne gave him a few seconds then said, her voice full of sympathy, "Is it too far for you to read? Or maybe too close? You must need a new prescription for your glasses."

GLL had now turned to glare at her. His mouth twitched.

Jeanne continued. "What a bummer, old age . . . You hang in there, monsieur, it will all be over soon. You just wink like that a few more times, and poof! No more eyesight issues or any issues at all, for that matter."

GLL looked like someone had hit him with a sledgehammer.

But Jeanne wasn't about to give him a reprieve. "So," she said, all businesslike. "Will you be ordering now, or shall we continue exchanging pleasantries while other customers wait to be served?"

"Canwehavethecheck, please?" the boy mumbled. He cleared his throat and repeated more distinctly, "Can we have the check now, please?"

"Sure—I'll get it right away! No dessert then, I guess." Jeanne produced a disappointed sigh and turned on her heel, finally allowing herself to smirk.

Mat, who'd followed Jeanne's repartee as keenly as he would have watched Jesus walk on water, broke into a triumphant grin. "Did you hear that? Can you see now why I can't put this woman out of my mind?" He began to clap.

Lena found herself wishing she had a friend like Jeanne—ballsy, witty, cool. She expected Jeanne to acknowledge Mat's enthusiasm, but the waitress walked right past him without a glance in his direction.

Lena's phone rang and Rob startled. His stomach clenched when he glimpsed the caller ID.

"Sorry, I have to take this," she said and moved away a little.

The conversation was hushed but not enough to be unintelligible. Lena summarized her Geneva trip and said, "Daddy, how about I don't go to Moscow in July, and you visit me in Paris instead?"

Her father didn't appear to have jumped at that idea, because Lena was resorting to heavy artillery. "The climate here is great for my heart. And the summer is much milder than in Moscow . . . Come on, Dad, please? We can visit the Loire castles."

Either the castles or the heart nailed it, because Lena beamed and said, "You're the best! And early August is perfect."

Rob texted Boris an hour later, after Lena had gone home.

> *Sounds like Mr. M. will be visiting Lena in early August. They are planning to travel in France. That's all for now.*

It wasn't that difficult, after all, was it? He'd just made the fastest money he'd ever made in his whole life.

If only he could get rid of the foul taste in his mouth.

* * *

Why now, so much affection?
These aren't the first caresses
I've known, and lips I've tasted
Much sweeter, my boy, than yours.

I've watched stars light up and dwindle,
Why now, so much affection? —
I've seen eyes light up and falter
Before my still hopeful eyes.

Marina Tsvetaeva

FOUR

The following morning Lena woke up with a sore throat. It was a bad sign. Next, she'd begin to sneeze, by midafternoon she'd get a runny nose, and by the evening she'd develop a fever. Which would lead to at least three days in bed, as was her usual pattern. The problem this time was that she had no one like Marta and Ivan to bring her chicken soup and make sure she didn't run out of tissues. This meant that, unlike in Geneva, her options now were either to handle her cold alone, like the self-sufficient adult she was (hmm), or let her dad fly over and take care of her.

But in the middle of her growing panic she remembered about Martha's favorite herbal remedy. It was a flower extract which, if taken early enough, could thwart a cold. She needed to locate some in this city, pronto.

At the bistro, she greeted Jeanne, who often worked the morning shifts, and ordered her usual breakfast. But she didn't intend to linger. She had an important mission to accomplish. The problem was she had no idea where to look. Would a regular pharmacy carry echinacea extracts? Or would she need to find one specialized in herbal remedies? Or maybe a health food store?

When Jeanne reappeared with her tea and buttered *tartine*, Lena jumped on the occasion to ask a local. "Jeanne, would you happen to know where I could find echinacea around here?"

"Ecki—what?"

"An herbal remedy for colds. Do pharmacies carry herbal remedies?" It occurred to Lena that Jeanne didn't look like someone who'd know about herbal remedies.

But to her relief, Jeanne did. "There's a huge parapharmacy not far the *Opéra*, about a fifteen minute walk from here. They've got aisles and aisles filled with every alternative medicine you could imagine."

"That sounds great. Thank you so much, Jeanne. I'll check it out as soon as I'm finished here."

"I'll come along. My mom asked me to get her some kind of blood pressure regulating bracelet. I'm not sure it will work, but if anyone sells that kind of stuff in this city, it'll be that pharmacy." Jeanne looked at her watch. "My morning shift ends at noon. Do you think your cold can wait until then?"

"Sure. My colds are famous for their patience."

The pharmacy lived up to its reputation. A fresh-out-of-school technician in a crisp white lab coat fetched the echinacea extract for Lena and the bracelet for Jeanne.

"Can I get you anything else, ladies?" he asked, his shoulders back and chin up.

"Actually, yes. I need some tampons, please," Jeanne said.

The technician swallowed hard, blinked, opened his mouth, and closed it again.

"Do you have any tampons?" Jeanne asked.

"Yes, we do." The technician looked as if someone were pulling out his fingernails. "I just need to know... Could you tell me..." He stared at Jeanne, unable to utter another word as his face and ears turned crimson.

Jeanne took pity on him. "Regular absorbency. I need the ones with two water drops drawn on the box. Do you think you can get those for me, please? Or maybe point to where they are and guide me by saying 'colder' and 'warmer'?"

"I'll get them." The technician dashed off as if his life depended on it. Lena and Jeanne looked at each other and burst out in laughter.

They were still chuckling as they walked out of the pharmacy.

"I need to find a place where I can have a glass of water for my first dose of echinacea," Lena said.

"It's lunchtime and I'm hungry. Shall we grab something to eat and get your water, too?" Jeanne asked.

"Back to *La Bohème*?"

Jeanne stopped in her tracks and took Lena's hand. "I'm so sorry to violate your innocence, but it's time someone told you: There are other places in this city that serve food and drink. Some of them even manage to serve edible food and potable drink, and a few of those are still affordable. Come on, I'll take you to one not far from here."

As it turned out, the place Jeanne had in mind no longer served anything remotely edible or potable. It had been replaced, like so many other cafés over the past years, by a trendy, color-block white, optometry boutique.

"I can't believe it!" Jeanne said. "Do the math—one hundred percent of Parisians need food and drink. Only ten percent, maybe twenty tops, need eyeglasses. How come all my favorite cafés and restaurants get supplanted by these lifeless concept stores that sell you a piece of plastic and glass for three hundred euros?"

The question was rhetorical. Jeanne shook her head and then narrowed her eyes as she glanced at Lena's elegant glasses. "Well, I guess it's because there are enough people out there prepared to pay three hundred euros for a piece of plastic and glass."

Lena smiled apologetically. This probably wasn't a good time to reveal that her understated glasses with a logo so discrete it was invisible to the naked eye, cost over eight hundred euros.

"Why don't we go back to *La Bohème* for lunch? You can violate my innocence some other time. I love the chef's cooking, and I want to profit from it while *La Bohème* still stands," she said.

"Knock on wood. I hope *La Bohème* won't go under anytime soon. In all modesty, it's one of the best bistros in Paris. I would throttle Pierre with my bare hands if he ever decided to sell it to an optometrist."

Fifteen minutes later, they were back at *La Bohème*, where the lunch service was in full swing, with the suit-and-tie crowd dominating the scene.

Lena held her palms out in dismay. "All the tables are taken."

"Follow me," Jeanne beckoned and led her to the backyard where a large teak table had been laid for six. "We set this up last week as the staff's private summertime patio. Wait here, I'll go get us food. If you're lucky, I may even return with some chicken broth."

Lena sat down, poured herself a glass of water and counted thirty drops of echinacea. As she drank the bitter-tasting potion, someone walked into the backyard carrying a steaming plate. Without even looking up, Lena knew it was Rob.

* * *

"Lena! What are you doing here?" Rob asked in a strangely coarse voice. He sat down across from her and looked at her attentively.

Lena felt her heart quicken. The effect he had on her was disconcerting. "I was going to have lunch with Jeanne," she said, trying not to sound self-conscious. "And there were no free tables out front, so she brought me here."

Thankfully, Jeanne showed up at that moment carrying Lena's broth and a plate of seafood and mashed potatoes for herself. "Oh, I see we have company. What brings you to *La Bohème* at this early hour?"

Rob let out a heavy sigh. "Pepe is what. Or rather the absence thereof. He was supposed to help out Didier and Laure this afternoon but his noble intentions were thwarted by a plumbing emergency. At least that's what he claims."

Jeanne rolled her eyes.

"Pierre didn't really understand his complicated explanations on the phone this morning. Anyway, your humble servant was called to the rescue and accepted to lend a hand . . . once they told me Claude was serving seared scallops as a lunch special."

Jeanne put her hand over her heart and then wiped off an imaginary tear. "Your generosity knows no limits, Rob. I feel so privileged to be working with you."

"Can you write that down in Pierre's guestbook?" Rob asked.

Jeanne raised an eyebrow. "I'm too shy. But sentiments aside, is Pepe planning to show up at all today? I'd like to know if we're going to be one man short for the dinner service."

"He swore on his great-aunt Dolores's grave he'd be here by four. So I wouldn't worry," Rob said, his tone earnest but his mouth twitching ever so slightly.

They ate in silence for a few minutes before Rob turned to Lena. "I've been meaning to ask you for a while now. What brought you to Paris? You could've written your thesis in Geneva, or Moscow, or . . . Bahamas, for that matter."

Lena put her bowl down. "I fell in love with this city during my first visit a few years ago. So I guess I couldn't resist its pull."

Rob smirked. "People think they come to Paris because they're in love with it, but in truth, they come here because they want to fall in love. And while they're waiting for that to happen, they default to Paris."

Jeanne looked dubitative. "Can you give us an example?"

"Take Pepe. He's in love with Paris while waiting for his legendary Scandinavian blonde to fall into his lap. Come to think of it, I wonder why that genius came to Paris and not Helsinki, which is much richer in blondes . . . On the other hand, I shouldn't be surprised, considering his IQ. But I'm digressing."

"What happens if people don't fall in love with someone here?" Lena asked.

"Well, if they don't, then they just stay on the default option, in the same way a lot of people end up with the same iPhone ringtone. It's elementary, Watson," Rob said.

"And what if they do fall in love with someone, but their heart gets broken?" Lena surprised herself asking. That chicken broth must have gone right to her head.

"Then Paris is still there to step in as a rebound lover." Rob shrugged. Then his eyes lit up and he turned to Jeanne. "Do you remember that old Marc Lavoine song about Paris?"

She shook her head.

"Oh, come on! Jeanne, you must know it. It goes"—he cleared his throat and belted out—*"The Eiffel Tower, she at least is faithful.* Ring any bells? No?"

"I see now why you never sing," Jeanne said. "And I want to thank you for that."

Rob placed his fork and knife on his empty plate. "It's true what Lavoine says, you know. Once yours, it'll always be yours."

Jeanne nodded, but Lena looked confused. "I don't understand. It's also everyone else's—"

"We're talking French faithful here. What counts is that it won't leave you, not how many others it will have," Rob explained.

"Is that your idea of faithful, seeing as you're French?" Lena hoped her defiant tone and saucy smile concealed the quiver in her voice.

"My ancestors on both sides are from Brittany, which makes me a Frenchman of Celtic descent. So I guess the word 'faithful' would have a couple more implications for me."

It was unsettling how happy his answer made her.

Later that day, Lena stopped by the bistro for another serving of broth that Jeanne had set aside for her. As she hugged her comforting steamy bowl, it occurred to her that she now had someone in Paris to give her chicken soup when she was sick. Someone her age, fun, smart, and friendly. A friend?

She drank her soup slowly, looking forward to Rob turning up for their now customary dose of banter. She was downing the last drops, when he finally landed next to her with his coffee.

"I'm going to kill Pepe tonight. At precisely half past midnight," he said matter-of-factly.

Lena smiled. "Oh no, not again! What did he do this time?"

"Emptied a bowl of sugar into my espresso."

"Which is a hanging offense in France, as everyone knows."

He looked her in the eyes. "This guy's been here for three months now, and he still can't remember I take my coffee black, no sugar. So, yeah, I'm definitely killing him tonight."

"I see. He pushed it too far, didn't he?"

Rob bared his teeth.

"Well, that will definitely teach him a lesson." She struggled to keep a straight face. "For the afterlife."

Rob took a sip from his cup and winced.

"By the way, why at precisely half past midnight?" Lena asked.

"It's when my shift ends. You see, I can't kill him while I'm working. And I'm not coming here on my free time to rid humanity of this candidate for Darwin Awards. I'm not as selfless as Jeanne seems to think, after all."

Jeanne, who was wiping a table next to them, said, "Rob, you have to understand that Pepe isn't doing it on purpose. There's no ill will whatsoever. And it's not because he's stupid, either."

Jeanne picked up the detergent and the dishrag and started for the kitchen. She stopped in the doorway to solve the Pepe mystery for Rob. "He just doesn't give a shit about how you like your coffee, that's all."

Lena laughed and caught Rob staring at her.

He didn't look away. "You have the sweetest smile, Lena. And those dimples of yours... they're to die for." He suddenly stood and pointed at his cup. "Can't drink this. I'll have to make a new one. More tea for you?"

"No thanks. I'm going to turn in."

Lena dug into her purse for her wallet. She kept her head low until Rob was sufficiently far, hoping he hadn't noticed her fierce blush. How debutante and embarrassing to blush like that from a casual remark! But there was nothing she could do about it. She was extremely pleased—no, scratch that—she was over the moon. And it wasn't just because of what Rob said. It was also because someone else had said the exact same thing before he did, a long time ago.

Her mom.

She used to say Lena had a sweet smile and adorable dimples. Then she left—and no one else ever told her that. Lena began to think she had lost the smile. The dimples were still there, but when she tried to grin in front of the mirror, all she saw was a smirk, strained and lopsided. Not sweet. Lena finally settled on the theory that the smile had been an invention of her mom's to cheer up her plain daughter and boost her own maternal pride.

A little defeatist voice inside her head told her Rob's remark was just an old pick-up line. But she hushed that voice, because she wanted—she needed—to believe that he'd really seen her famous smile. That it wasn't a chimera. That there was something special about her, after all.

* * *

Lena ran the tips of her fingers across the leather-bound cover, as if to say good-bye, and placed the volume back on the stall. The book was romantically old but it was about bugs. She didn't care for bugs.

Last night, she had mentioned to Rob her plan to pay a visit to the *bouquinistes*, the used booksellers whose landmark green metal boxes lined the banks of the Seine. She wanted to look for original editions of Tsvetaeva's poems translated into French.

"I'm not working tomorrow, and I need a break from my thesis. May I come along?" Rob asked.

This was how they ended up walking by the Seine and browsing through the bookstalls together.

"Your first love, right?" she asked pointing at a tattered electromechanics textbook. "Didn't you say your BA was in engineering?"

"First and only. I'm doing an MBA, so I'm better prepared to start my own manufacturing company one day. I've got lots of ideas."

"Like what?"

He sighed. "Where to start? Like developing a new technology for recycling methane into consumer goods like furniture, for instance."

"Is that possible?"

"It's been done. But the process is still too costly and inefficient." He put the primer back and resumed the walk. "I can spend hours talking about this, which I do with Grand-papa, but I don't want to bore you."

"Just because I study literature doesn't mean I'm not fascinated by technology," she said. "Is your Grand-papa an engineer, too?"

"He's a bit of everything," he said and went on to tell her about his grandfather and then about his mom.

Lena found it endearing how his love for them shone through his droll observations.

And then he asked her about her mom, and she didn't know what to say. She didn't feel like revealing the truth about why her mother had left. It would be too personal. Nor did she want to confess that she missed her, because she didn't really, not anymore. But she wanted to say something about her, share a tidbit that wouldn't mean much but would still define her.

"My mother was beautiful. Well, she still is, unless she's been doctoring her photos."

"Does she look like you?"

"No, not at all. She's tall, racy, and has the highest cheekbones. She used to wear such beautiful clothes. And expensive French perfume at all times, reapplied throughout the day. It made me nauseous."

Rob raised an eyebrow. "Impossible. Must have been a Chinese copy."

"I doubt it. In any event, it really made me sick. But Dad loved it and Mom loved it, so I learned to breathe through the mouth around Mom."

She fell silent. The little tidbit was turning too intimate. Worse still, she was tempted to continue and spill the whole story to Rob. But she couldn't. Things were so complicated and twisted between her parents compared to normal ones. Including the 'normally' divorced ones. She hadn't allowed herself any indiscretions in her seven years in Switzerland, not even with Gerhard. She had no reason to open up to Rob. If only he cracked a joke now and made light of her words! But he didn't. He just gave her a funny look and smiled.

They continued their walk in companionable silence, and Lena couldn't stop thinking about her mom. She had a mane of shiny golden locks that cost her biweekly salon visits to maintain. With hindsight, Lena figured those visits had been Mom's pretext to be with her lover, the man Dad later caught her with. Which meant Mom's hair must have been naturally gorgeous, just like the rest of her. What a shame that the only thing Lena had inherited from Mom was her vulnerability.

Rob interrupted Lena's self-deprecating musings. "Look! Isn't this your poet's book? Marina something?"

Lena focused on the stall before them and gasped. It was a Tsvetaeva book all right. Better still, it turned out to be an early French translation of her poems. Thrilled, she bought it without the slightest attempt at negotiating. She rushed to the nearest bench and began to examine her acquisition. Rob sat next to her, watching her with a smile.

"Oh my God," she gushed. "This is the first French translation of Tsvetaeva's poems by Elsa Triolet, published by Gallimard in 1952. Rob, this is a treasure!"

Rob grinned, pleased about his discovery.

"Triolet has the merit of being the first to introduce the French reader to Tsvetaeva's poetry. Though I must admit, I'm not a huge fan of hers."

"Why don't you like her?"

"She dropped the rhyme and changed the rhythm of the poems like practically all of Tsvetaeva's other translators." Lena frowned disapprovingly.

"And that's *very bad* because . . ." Rob drew out the last word.

"Because those are essential to her poetry. She has only a handful of poems without a strong rhyme and none without a strict meter."

"I don't know much about poetry. But aren't rhyme and meter things of the past?" he asked.

"Unfortunately, yes, and for some time now. But that's the thing. Tsvetaeva insisted on rhyme and meter in an age when most poets wrote in free verse. She produced such delightful trochees and iambs. I wish you spoke Russian to appreciate their beauty! They are so musical; it's almost easier to sing them than to recite them."

"Will you sing one for me?"

"Believe me, you don't want to hear me sing. It may traumatize you for the rest of your life."

"I'm tone deaf, which gives me natural protection against bad singing."

She shook her head. "I have a rule. Never sing in front of another sentient being."

"OK. Then read me one."

Lena leafed through the book, hesitating on some pages, and then closed it. "They are just all so . . . ornate. This is my other problem with the French translations of Tsvetaeva. They are too decorative, too elaborate. Her poetry—like all good poetry—is neither. It's bare human soul."

She reopened the book, traced her finger along the table of contents, and then turned the yellowed pages until she found what she was looking for.

She held the book out to Rob, pointing to a poem. "I finished translating this one last week. It's addressed to Tsvetaeva's daughter Ariadna. I'd like you to read the first verse of Triolet's translation, and then I'll read you mine. And promise you'll give me your honest opinion as to which one you like better."

"Cross my heart," Rob said and took the book from Lena. He read the poem silently, then turned to her. "OK. Let's hear yours now."

Lena closed her eyes to shut out the world and recited from memory.

Don't forget: tomorrow you'll be ancient.
Drive the troika, sing, defy conventions,

Be a blue-eyed gypsy, brightly dressed.
Don't forget: no man's worth your attentions —
And bestow them upon every chest.

Lena opened her eyes. Rob was looking at her in a funny way. His gaze was fixed on her lips, his eyes dark with something primal, fierce, and unbearably intense. Lena's heart quickened in response — and then in panic.

She made herself smile cheerfully. "So. Your honest opinion, please."

He blinked, then a sly grin spread on his face. "Here's my honest opinion: What kind of mother advises her daughter to sleep with every stupid dude who happens to be around?"

"A crazy, wild, passionate Russian poet mother?" Lena wrinkled her nose. "Anyway, I'm not sure she meant it quite so literally. It's poetry, you know. Hyperbole is its second nature."

"Oh. Why didn't I think of that? So, perhaps, what she really meant was: My daughter, you should always be polite to men? After all, it *is* terribly rude when women tell us things like 'not a chance in hell' or 'in your wildest dreams, loser'."

"I think what she meant was that she wanted her daughter to give her body freely—and to take pleasure in it—but to withhold her heart." Lena's eyes darkened. "Because she herself suffered too much from rejection and heartbreak."

Rob grew serious, too. "I like your translation better, and that's my honest opinion."

As she lay in bed that night, unable to fall asleep, Lena thought of how easy it had been to read her translation to Rob. She didn't hesitate for a second before sharing something she had kept from everyone else. Well, not exactly everyone—she did show her translated poems to Professor Rouvier. But that was different. It was a clinical experience, like baring your chest in front of your cardiologist. Reading her translation to Rob was nowhere near a clinical experience. It was electrifying. It was thrilling. It was sensual.

And therein lay the trouble.

* * *

Bittersweet — the taste of passion
On your lips. A siren's call,
Bittersweet — oh, the temptation
To precipitate my fall!

Marina Tsvetaeva

FIVE

The next day, after Lena was politely kicked out of the public library that had to close for the day, she went to the *cinémathèque* and watched an old movie. Then she walked all the way back to rue Cadet, her stomach knotted with anxiety. What if Rob looked at her again like he did yesterday? What if he didn't look at her like that anymore? Good Lord, what a mess.

When she reached *La Bohème*, the dinner service was over and the bistro was relatively empty — not unusual for a Tuesday night. Rob and Pepe were discussing something by the counter. As Lena approached, she heard Pepe say, "Rrrrrrrrr."

"No," Rob said.

"Rrrrrrrrrr," Pepe said again.

Rob shook his head.

Pepe gave Lena a pleading look. "Rrrrrrr?"

"Are you rehearsing for a baby tiger role?" she asked.

"Now that you mention it, he does sound like an angry cat," Rob said, smiling at Lena.

Pepe blew out his cheeks. "Come on, guys — you've got to help me. Rrrrrrrrr. Did that sound French enough?"

"Nope," Rob said, putting his elbow on the counter and leaning his head into his hand.

"Couldn't it pass for a *Midi* accent?" Lena asked Rob. "They roll their *r*'s down in Marseille, don't they?"

"Absolutely. Only Pepe isn't rolling. He's growling."

"Anyway, I don't want a *Midi* accent," Pepe said. "I need those Nordic blondes from the hotel down the street to think I'm a Parisian. You know, a real one. *Authentic*."

Rob rubbed his chin. "It's hopeless, buddy, even if you manage to get your *r*'s right. Even if you learn to say 'mademoiselle' instead of 'made-muethel'."

Pepe's face fell.

"Forget the *r*'s," Rob said. "What you really need to pass for a true Parisian is scorn."

"Scorn?" Pepe's furrowed his brow. "Like in 'humor'?"

"Like in 'contempt'." Rob went behind the counter to make Lena tea. "Look at Didier over there." He nodded discretely with his head.

Lena and Pepe turned to look at the bistro's headwaiter.

"Observe him in action. Notice how he's telling that American couple they're total losers without actually saying it."

The three of them fell silent and watched Didier. The distance was too big for them to make out his words, but his condescending smiles, discrete eye rolls, and impatient finger taps said it all.

"He's good," Pepe said, turning back to Rob.

"Can you do the same?"

Pepe shook his head. "No. And I don't want to, either. I like people. Even the ones who aren't Nordic blondes in minishorts. All customers deserve to be treated nicely."

"That's my boy." Rob patted him on the shoulder. "But you'll never pass for an authentic Parisian waiter."

"So be it," Pepe declared, his expression grave and determined.

"You could find another—" Lena began.

"My r's are definitely getting better, though, I can feel it!" Pepe's face lit up with a grin. "This means I may have a chance with one of those blond angels, God bless their minishorts."

Rob clapped his hand to his forehead. "Oh, for Christ's sake. I was just about to abandon my murderous plans for you, and you have to go and ruin everything."

Pepe snarled at him, then turned to Lena. "You know what I like most about blondes? Their napes."

"You mean the backs of their necks?" she asked.

"You may not be able to understand this, but to me there's nothing more beautiful than the sight of a blonde's hair pulled up, and a few flaxen tendrils coiling down her alabaster nape." Pepe closed his eyes, his index retracing a coiling movement in the air.

Rob shook his head in dismay.

Pepe opened his eyes. "If I was on death row and was granted a last wish, I'd ask to see a blonde's nape one more time before they inject me."

"There's no death penalty in Europe," Lena said.

Pepe raised an eyebrow. "I travel widely. Including to places where it hasn't been abolished. So you never know."

"Right. You never know," Lena said.

"And how was your day, Lena?" Rob asked.

"I—" Lena began, but was interrupted by the ringing in her purse. Must be Dad. "Sorry, I need to get this."

She moved out of the way and answered her phone.

"Still in love with Paris?" Anton asked.

"Absolutely." She tried to convey her enthusiasm while speaking in a hushed voice. "I think I could live here, you know, like forever."

"Easy, girl. This is *not* the plan, remember? The plan is that you stay in Paris for a few months. A year, tops. Then you return to Moscow and start working with me." He sounded disgruntled.

"Dad, I'm not sure . . ." Lena felt the familiar guilt clenching her stomach. She *was* sure. She knew perfectly well what she wanted to do with her life, and it didn't include working with her father.

"Dad, that's *your* plan, not mine. I really don't think I'll be working with you. I'm sorry I'm disappointing you, but I've found my vocation. And you know what it is."

After a long silence Anton finally spoke. "Lena, I've always wanted the best for you. I sent you to Switzerland so that you could get the best education money can buy, a European polish, languages. I wanted to give you the right tools for your future."

"And I'm grateful for all that, I really am!"

"But eventually you have to return home, baby. You belong here. I built this company so that you could take it over one day. You *must* take it over one day."

"Daddy, you're only forty-six! Why all this talk of me taking over the company?" Suddenly a wave of panic washed over her. "Is something wrong? Are you hiding something? What is it?"

"Nothing's wrong, pumpkin. As it happens, I had a medical checkup last week, and I seem to be in perfect health. It's just... I don't know, maybe it's my midlife crisis finally kicking in."

Anton snorted, then got serious again. "My business is my legacy. And you are my only child, who's now grown and about choose a career. This is the perfect time for me to start involving you, mentoring you. Can't you see that?"

"But Dad—"

"No buts. You have a duty toward me. Unlike your mother, I've always been a good parent to you. For the past twelve years, I've been your only parent."

The last statement was grossly unfair, and they both knew it. But Lena was weary of reminding him that the reason her mom had been absent for half of her life was much more complicated than he made it sound.

So instead, she tried another tack. "Anyway, your plan is doomed. You have a hopeless nerd for a daughter."

"Not a problem. In my book being a nerd is a qualification. I was a nerd once, too, remember? I was a computer programmer before becoming a businessman. Can it get nerdier than that?"

"An astrophysicist?"

"It's thanks to my nerdy beginnings that I now have an edge over my competitors."

Lena considered making an observation that being a computer nerd was slightly more relevant to running an IT company than being a translator. But she doubted she could win this argument with logic, if she could win it at all.

"By the way, I've got some news about the negotiations," he said.

"Over Raduga?"

"Yes. I think I finally managed to grind them down."

She was happy to hear it—buying the edgy start-up was a cornerstone of his plan to expand into a new area. "Congratulations, Dad! I know this means a great deal to you."

"They haven't formally accepted my offer yet, but I expect they will in the coming days."

"I'm sure they will. This is big and you worked so hard on it."

"We could work on the next one together . . ."

"Dad," she pleaded. "I study literature and translation, and that's what I want to do as a career. Not use my language skills for business. Can't you understand this? Please?"

Anton paused and then said in an upbeat voice. "Baby, let's talk about this later, OK? For now, you're in Paris, writing your thesis so you can get your master's degree. That's fine with me and, from what I gather, more than fine with you. Talk to you tomorrow."

As Lena hung up, the lightness she had reveled in since last night was gone. She tried to tell herself she still had time — a lot of time — to sway her father and avoid open conflict. But she also knew her chances were slim.

Rob paced his room, trying to get a grip. Good thing he had quit smoking, because this gig he'd signed up for would have warranted a pack before every phone call. The part of the job that required he spend as much time as he could around Lena was a no-brainer. It was like getting paid to watch football and drink beer. Only better. But the part where he had to call Boris and report everything he'd gleaned about her father's plans made him feel dirty and ashamed.

He grabbed his phone and called Pierre to remind him that in three days he was taking two weeks off to prepare for his final exams and thesis defense.

Next, he dialed Boris's number.

* * *

The day was hot, way too hot for early June. Sticky heat permeated the air, dampening people's clothes and pasting them to their bodies. On a day like this, only tourists ventured out midafternoon while Parisians—and Lena—stayed indoors.

Finally, just before nine in the evening, a cool breeze arrived. Lena opened her window and was relieved that it no longer felt like a blast from an oven. Rush hour was over, and she could hear the sounds coming from the sidewalk terrace: clinking of silverware against plates, quiet laughter, and relaxed conversation. Diners filled the bistro and waiters darted between tables, taking orders, bringing food, and opening wine bottles.

Lena grabbed her purse and ran downstairs before the last table was occupied. She took a seat on the terrace, ordered her dish, and opened her book. But she couldn't concentrate on reading. The evening was extraordinarily pleasant—or maybe her senses were unusually heightened. The aromas of fried garlic and fresh coriander from the kitchen mixed with the citrus and sandalwood perfumes of the diners around her. The smells intertwined happily and played backdrop to the sweet fragrance of jasmine snatched by the breeze from someone's balcony. If paradise existed, this is how it would smell, she thought.

Oddly, she also felt as though she could hear every word of every conversation around her. People spoke ever so softly, their voices devoid of urgency, their eyes filled with contentment to be with their loved ones. It didn't matter that they said the most trivial things to each other. Their words fluttered like butterflies with the sole purpose of establishing a connection to share the sweetness of this summer evening.

Lena's pulse ratcheted up as she saw Rob step out onto the terrace. He took a sip of his espresso and looked around. When he spotted her, he smiled and made a beeline toward her.

"How do you feel about Cyril?" he asked.

"Who's Cyril?"

"A rising star of French *chanson*. He's really good." Rob placed two tickets on the table. "The concert is at L'Espace at eleven."

Lena blinked several times, processing the situation.

"Jeanne gave me these an hour ago," he said. "She got them from a friend who's a friend of Cyril's."

"Why isn't she going herself?"

"She was supposed to go with her boyfriend, but he had a motorbike crash this afternoon."

"Is he OK?"

"A broken arm. Jeanne's going to the hospital."

Rob gave her a questioning look.

"Oh. It's nice of you to have thought of me—" Lena began.

"It's for a reason. Remember the song about the Eiffel Tower I massacred the other day?"

Lena nodded.

"Cyril will sing it, and some classic pieces by Brel and Gainsbourg, in the second part of his gig."

How could she say no to that?

They made it to L'Espace a few minutes before the beginning of Cyril's act. The place was a stone's throw from Trocadero. Bigger than a live music bar but too small for a concert hall, L'Espace was packed with a heterogeneous crowd that reflected Cyril's broad fan base. Curious to see the "rising star," Lena stood on tiptoe and arched her neck.

"Urgh. I'm too short." She blew out her cheeks in frustration.

Rob knitted his brows. "Come with me."

He grabbed her hand and began to push their way through the crowd toward the side of the room.

"There's a bench by the wall," he said, turning his head to Lena. "You can stand on it."

Even though the distance to the bench was only a couple of meters, they progressed at a snail's pace. Taking baby steps behind Rob, Lena wished they'd moved even slower. She wished the room had been bigger and the crowd denser.

She wished the wall had been sliding away as they approached.

After telling her about the bench, Rob never turned back, apparently unaware of the effect his firm grip was having on her. He seemed fully focused on getting her from point A to point B with as little shoving as he could manage. She couldn't detect a hint of a caress in the way his palm enveloped hers. His fingers were perfectly motionless. He'd taken her hand for purely practical reasons, she told herself.

But it didn't matter. All that mattered was that he held her. She closed her eyes. His skin was warm—almost hot—against hers, and his hand gloriously big. Ooh, the bliss. It was as if all the nerve endings in her hand had been bared and primed. How else could she explain the intensity of the pleasure that flooded her senses from such a trivial touch?

She opened her eyes—the bench was now within arm's reach.

"Excuse me," Rob said to someone Lena couldn't see. "Could you step aside for a sec, so my friend could climb on top of this?"

He gave her a little push and, once she stood on the bench, released her hand. It took her all her strength not to say, "No!"

When Cyril finished his last encore and the applause died away, the arrows on the clock above the bar pointed at five to two. Lena jumped off the bench and gave Rob a bright smile. "Cyril *is* really good. I liked his songs just as much as the classic hits in the second part."

"I may be tone deaf but I have impeccable taste in music." He grinned. "I'm glad you enjoyed the performance."

"I'll buy his album tomorrow." She began to rummage through her bag. "Shall I call us a cab?"

Rob glanced at his watch. "If we run to Trocadero right now, we can catch the final light show of the day on the Eiffel Tower. It's special."

Lena didn't need much convincing to prolong their evening together.

They got to the plaza just as the sparkling lights on the Iron Lady across the Seine burst into a magical show.

"We can sit over there." Rob pointed at the vacant spot on the steps leading down from the plaza, and they wedged themselves between two groups of camera-wielding tourists.

"Hold your hand out, like this," he said, stretching his own arm. "You see? It looks like you're touching the tip of the Eiffel Tower. I can take a picture of you, if you want."

Lena whipped out her phone. "Let me take one of you first."

She was giddy with excitement. "So how is this show different from the others?"

"During the regular evening shows, the background yellow lighting never goes off. But now it's more like fireworks."

They sat in silence for several minutes watching the lights dance. And then, within a second, the Eiffel Tower was swallowed up by the night. The effect was spectacular.

Lena turned to Rob. "Wow."

She didn't want to go home. Sitting here, in this warm summer evening, so close to Rob that their thighs nearly touched, made her feel acutely alive. It was a wonderful feeling.

"Which one is your favorite Cyril song?" she asked.

"Let me see . . . The one about the stray dog."

"Oh yes. What was the refrain?" She recited, *"Grooming is for poodles. Training is for hounds—"*

Rob joined in, singing off key. *"I traded my leash for dignity. Got any scraps, anyone?"* He smirked. "During my first three years in Paris, that's pretty much how I felt about my life."

Lena didn't dare ask why.

"Which one's your favorite?" he asked.

She stretched her legs. "Hmm. 'Maybe I'm the One'. . . I guess."

"What about 'The Clown'?"

"Urgh. It made me feel uncomfortable. But it's nice to know I'm not the only person on Earth who's scared of clowns."

He chuckled. "I won't be offering you circus tickets then."

"God forbid. I completely freaked out both times my parents took me to the circus when I was little. When I wasn't terrified of the clowns, I was afraid the lions will eat their tamer, or the acrobats will fall off the trapeze and break their necks."

"You should try bungee jumping as immersion therapy," he said.

She made round eyes and shook her head. "Can we change the topic, please?"

"Sure. How about paragliding?"

She ignored his question. "So, what's the plan after you graduate?"

"In the short-term, finding a good job. Preferably, in the energy sector. In the long-term, running my own business."

She nodded, impressed. "You've got it all figured out."

"What about you?"

"I don't really know. Establishing myself as a literary translator... Or maybe an academic career..." She gazed at the shimmering river below them. "But I guess my short-term plan is to just hang around in Paris and try to figure out what I want to do with my life."

"I like your plan," he said.

* * *

Lena was making her way through a plate of garlic butter snails that Rob had recommended, when her phone rang.

Even though Anton sounded cheerful and breezy, something was off. He didn't press her for the details of her day. Lena remembered all too well the last time her dad had shown that kind of neglect. He'd gotten into serious trouble with a corrupt government official and narrowly escaped arrest.

Having ascertained she was fine, he said he had to go and wished her good-night. But Lena's imagination had gone berserk. Five minutes later, she called him back, too worried to wait until they would talk again tomorrow. Anton answered the phone. Lena could hear him apologize to whomever he was with and then it sounded like he was moving. A few seconds later, he asked her if anything was wrong.

"No, Dad, I'm fine. I was worried about you, actually. Are you OK? "

"Yes, I'm perfectly OK. Why?"

He did sound OK and even slightly... amused? Now, this was awkward. In all honesty, Lena couldn't very well reply "Because you were a lot less interested in my life than usual." She would come across as someone immature, which she probably was. Too late to uncall him now, so she'd better come up with an explanation.

"Because you sounded... distracted?" she finally managed to say.

"Did I?"

Lena could hear the smile in his voice and, despite her embarrassment, a weight was lifted off her shoulders. She was about to apologize and hang up, when he said, "You're right, pumpkin, I *was* distracted."

She waited for him to continue.

"I guess I'll have to tell you sooner or later, so I can as well do it now." He cleared his throat. "In fact, I just proposed to Anna and she accepted. I was having dinner with her when you called—"

"Oh my God!" Lena nearly screamed. "Are you serious? I can't believe it! But when did you...? How long have you...?" Lena had trouble finishing her sentences. Her mind raced.

This was big—and she wasn't sure how she felt about it. She had heard about Anna from Grandma but had never met her. Dad had been seeing her for a few months now, at least as far as Lena was aware. He'd never let on how serious the relationship had grown. As far as she was concerned, he still maintained that remarrying wasn't on his agenda for the next couple of centuries. So, Anna was special to him, and Lena had had no clue. That sort of stung.

"I met Anna six months ago. She's a legal assistant, thirty-four, never been married. She's clever, kind, generous—"

"Dad!" Lena interrupted. "You're in love."

"I am? I guess I am." He chuckled. "Anyhow, she's accepted my proposal to become my wife and your stepmother, which is very brave of her."

"We don't bite," Lena said.

"No. But as you're too young and I'm too old to share her taste in music, clothes and movies, she's in for a rough ride." Then his voice became serious. "Lena, darling, can you promise me to be nice to Anna?"

"Of course I will, Dad!" Lena was about to add that she hoped Anna would be nice to him, but she bit her tongue. Somehow, it felt unfair to spoil his moment of joy by alluding to the past. "I'm looking forward to meeting her."

"Me too, pumpkin, I can't wait to introduce her to you. How about we visit you in Paris sometime soon? I'm sure we can find a weekend in the next few weeks when both Anna and I are free."

Lena frowned at his obvious assumption that *she* was free every weekend, before reminding herself that, as it happened, she was.

"Sure, Dad, come any time you want. Just give me sufficient notice to tidy up my apartment. We can't have Anna realize what kind of hopeless pig I am before the two of you are married. By the way, when *are* you getting married?"

"We're thinking end of December. We'll probably have really shitty weather for the ceremony, but then we'll enjoy the honeymoon even more. I'm planning to take Anna to the Caribbean. Remember that hotel in Punta Cana?"

Lena did. But she preferred not to comment.

"I know, I know." Anton read her mind. "It's too tacky, too Russian nouveau riche for you. But, I *am* a Russian nouveau riche, so I have to live up to my image."

Anton Malakhov was positively happy, in a way Lena couldn't remember him, even in their best moments together.

It was strange to hear him chatter away like this. It was also touching and heartwarming. Lena told him December was a perfect month for a wedding and released him to his fiancée.

Her future stepmother . . .

What an idea!

* * *

Lena was on the finish line to her graduation. It was late June and Paris was growing stuffier and stickier by the day. She had no complaints, though. This was nothing compared to Moscow's midsummer hell. The Parisians, however, were beginning to desert the city whenever they got the chance. They went south to the breezy Mediterranean coast or north to the airy beaches of Normandy. As for Lena, she was preparing to go east to Geneva.

She was anxious. Even though her supervisor was happy with her final product, Lena knew she needed to brush up on the theory before the red-letter day. So she studied from dawn to dusk, only breaking for a trip to the bathroom or a glass of water. Her reward was a longer break at dinnertime at *La Bohème*.

But when Rob didn't show up at work for the third day in a row, she began to wonder if something was the matter. Was he sick? Had he taken a few days off? Or had he just quit the job, which would mean she may never see him again? It was disconcerting how much that last thought affected her.

Lena shook her head. *God, this isn't happening. I'm not falling for him.*

She had known him for such a short time! He was still a stranger, too sure of himself, too charming, too handsome. He was the kind of guy she'd always shunned because nothing good could come of it. Then why was she going to the bistro for dinner every day, hauling along her heavy books, and prolonging her meals with several cups of tea, when she had resolved to stay away from him?

As she pondered this question, staring blankly into her course reader, someone sat down next to her. Lena looked up from her book, her eyes bright, but it wasn't who she'd expected it to be.

"Lena, I can't bear seeing you like this anymore. Is it"—Jeanne shut Lena's tome to read the cover—"semiotics that's making you so depressed or is there something else?"

"It's semiotics," Lena said, which wasn't entirely untrue. "If they ask me questions on this topic during the exam, I'll be in big trouble."

"Why's that?"

"I just don't get it. I read and reread the same passages, and I'm still in the dark." Lena shook her head. "I've considered memorizing the main definitions—can't see what else I can do."

"There's nothing wrong with learning things by heart. That's how most learning was done only a couple of generations ago. And it's still the case in some disciplines, not to mention religions," Jeanne said.

Jeanne's comment reminded Lena of something she'd been meaning to ask for a while. "What's your field of study, Jeanne? You never talk about it, but . . ."

"In spite of my blue hair, piercings, and the occasional tough talk, I don't sound like a high school dropout?" Jeanne finished for her.

Lena nodded with a smile. Jeanne was the least touchy person she'd ever met. It was so easy to talk to her.

"I did two years of law in Aix-en-Provence just to prove to my parents and the rest of my family that I could. But I hated it."

"I'm with you on that."

"Then I backpacked around the world for a year, which was great. And then I followed my boyfriend to Paris and got this job. Which I rather enjoy, truth be told." Jeanne took a long swig of her chilled Coke. "So I am, indeed, a dropout, but an extensively traveled and a well-read one."

"Mystery solved. And what about your boyfriend? Is it the biker I saw you... talk to here once?"

Jeanne smirked. "You can say you saw us fight, it's OK."

"So, you've been with him for what—two, three years?"

"Too long. I know he's bad for me, Lena. I left him. Five times at least. And every time, I go back when he asks politely." Jeanne sighed. "I'll tell you more later."

"I'll hold you to it."

Jeanne finished her Coke. "Is there anything else you'd like to ask me?"

"Um . . . nothing comes to mind."

"Well, then I guess I'll just tell you like that, without any specific reason at all, that Rob has taken two weeks off for his final exams. Not that you were asking or anything." Jeanne stood up.

"Oh . . . I did wonder where he'd disappeared to. By the way, I'll be going to Geneva for my final exam and defense the day after tomorrow."

"Good luck! When shall we expect you back?"

"Next Thursday, hopefully with the diploma in my suitcase. I'm so much looking forward for all this stress to be over."

"Hey, I have an idea. Pepe and I made plans to go to Nice for a weekend. Take a dip in the Mediterranean."

"Can you both take the same weekend off?"

"Pierre hired two temps for the summer, so regular staff can take vacations and days off more easily. We could wait until you're back from Geneva, if you'd like to join."

"I'd love to! Thank you so much for inviting me. It would be a great way to unwind."

"Excellent," Jeanne said, turning to leave. "I'll check with Rob if he wants to join in, too."

* * *

Part II: When the Clock Strikes Midnight

In the dark, the world embarks on a migration:

Trees uproot and roam the Earth—in levitation,
Golden grapes go up in foam—becoming wine,
Stars progress from home to home—to rest in mine.
Rivers turn inside their beds—running deep,
And I'm longing for your chest—to find sleep.

Marina Tsvetaeva

SIX

It was done, accomplished, stamped, and signed on a thick sheet of letterhead paper. Lena had passed her last exam, defended her thesis, and received her master's degree. Paris was now hers to enjoy, free of guilt. She had a long list of museums to visit, exhibitions to see, neighborhoods to discover, and shows to watch. And she was going to do all that without the nagging feeling that she should be hunched over a textbook instead.

Lena smiled, pleased about the prospect of an exciting summer, as her cab approached rue Cadet. She was tired and in need of a relaxing bath, but she wanted to see Jeanne or Pepe first to find out about the weekend plans. Jeanne had texted her earlier in the week that they were to meet at the *Gare de Lyon* Friday morning at eight. What Jeanne hadn't told her was whether Rob was coming along.

As Lena walked into the bistro, she spotted Rob and his friends Amanda and Mat having beers at one of the sidewalk tables. She looked around for Jeanne. Her new friend, busy with a group of patrons, waved hi then splayed her fingers to sign "five minutes".

By now Rob had spotted Lena, too. "Over here! Lena, come join us." As she came closer, he offered her a chair. "We're celebrating our graduation."

"Congratulations!"

"Thanks." He glanced at his friends and mumbled, "Even if for some of us it's conditional."

Lena frowned, unsure of his meaning, but he didn't offer an explanation. She sat down and signaled to Pepe hovering nearby for a beer.

Rob pushed the bowl of peanuts closer to her. "Jeanne tells me you went to Geneva for your defense. Did it go well?"

"Yes. And now I'm a proud holder of a master's degree."

"Cheers to that," Rob said, raising his beer.

Mat followed suit. "To no more exams, papers, and late-night cramming!"

"To our future and to beach holidays," Amanda said.

"Speaking of which, I'm going to Nice with Jeanne and Pepe tomorrow," Lena said, hoping she wasn't being too obvious.

"So am I," Rob said and pointed to Amanda and Mat. "And so are these two individuals."

Amanda smiled politely. "It's going to be fun."

"I'm so excited to go on a trip with Jeanne. And *without* her creepy boyfriend. This is my last opportunity to win her over," Mat said.

"I hope you succeed. I don't like her boyfriend at all," Lena said.

Pepe returned with her beer and said, addressing the girls, "Did you know that topless is all the rage at the French Riviera this season?"

"And why are you telling us this?" Amanda asked.

"No reason. Just thought you may want to know what the latest trends are before you pack..." He pulled out a folded sheet of paper from his pocket. "Hey, do you want to see the hotel I booked?"

Everyone looked at the printout.

"It's not far from the beach and it's cheap," Pepe said with pride. "I thought the ladies would like it better than a youth hostel."

"There must be a reason why it's cheap," Amanda said as she perused the printout and handed it to Rob.

"I don't really care why it's cheap. I'm broke, so the cheaper the better." Rob passed the paper on to Lena.

"It looks cute." Lena pointed to the photo that showed a sunny rooftop terrace with a few tables set for breakfast and orange trees in terracotta pots interspersed among them.

Mat took the paper and read out loud. "Welcome to Very Nice, a charming family-run hotel only ten minutes' walk from the city's historic center and the *Promenade des Anglais* beach."

"I booked us three rooms with twin beds. The hotel didn't have any triple rooms, so one of the ladies will have to share a room with one of the gents," Pepe said.

"And I got the train tickets, so you each owe me one hundred twenty euros and ninety to Pepe," Jeanne, who had just arrived with a beer in her hand, said.

"I could room with y —" Mat began.

"Amanda, will you share with me? I promise I don't snore." Pepe said, blocking Mat.

Amanda handed Pepe the hotel money. "It's very kind of you to offer, but I'd rather room with Rob. We hiked for a week in the Jura Mountains last summer, so I know for sure he doesn't snore, grind his teeth, or sleepwalk."

The famed Riviera town unfolded before the Parisian bunch with its palm tree-rimmed squares and boulevards, followed by crooked old town streets. Lena decided she liked it. A lot. The hotel was another matter. Upon closer acquaintance, Very Nice turned out to be a flea-bitten hole flirting with the insalubrious whose only *nice* part was the tiny rooftop terrace. The very same that represented the hotel on its website.

After a few minutes of hesitation, mainly on the part of Amanda and Lena, the group decided to settle in and make the best of it. It was four in the afternoon — the perfect time to go to the beach. Lena and Jeanne were ready within ten minutes. When they came down to the lobby, the boys were already there. Amanda arrived a few minutes later. Her golden hair was braided and pinned above her ears and her camisole barely covered her bikini top. She wore a pair of minishorts that drew attention to her slender tanned legs. Pepe gave a long whistle of appreciation while Mat and Rob emitted wolf calls. She looked smoking hot and very pleased with herself.

"I don't believe we've been properly introduced, madam," Pepe said stepping forward and lifting her hand to his lips. "The name's Bond. James Bond."

Amanda flashed her impeccable teeth. "Pleased to meet you, James. I'm Princess Leia. Shall we?" She pointed at the door, and the six of them headed out of the hotel.

As they neared the beach, Lena could smell the salty ocean and hear the soothing sound of the waves. She felt giddy with anticipation of the sea's comforting embrace and the subsequent sunbathing. Five minutes later, they were all in the water, some of them splashing and screaming their joy and others charging into the open sea, away from the shore, away from the clutter of daily life.

Later, as they basked in the late afternoon sun, Amanda turned to Lena. "Can you hear what I hear?"

"You mean the Russian-speaking group behind us?"

"Yes. And another one to the right. God, they are obnoxious. I have no idea what they're saying, but they sound like they own this city."

Lena tried to conceal her discomfort behind a breezy smile. "I apologize for my fellow countrymen's rustic manners. You could try reminding yourself they are supporting the sluggish French economy."

"One nil to Lena," Mat said.

Amanda pretended she didn't hear that. "Oh, I don't doubt that. I just wish I could understand what they were saying."

As it happened, the Russians *were* being obnoxious, and Lena had no desire to translate their unsavory exchange.

"Ha! I don't actually need you to translate for me. I can ask Rob. He speaks Dostoyevsky's language very well," Amanda said.

"You do?" Lena turned to Rob, unsettled.

If it was true, how come he never told her about it? How come he never let her know that he shared such an important part of her culture? Was it a sign of how little she meant to him?

"Yeah," Rob said, rubbing his neck. He picked up a small shell and began to fiddle with it. "Didn't I mention it before?"

"No, you didn't. Not even when I showed you my translations from Russian." Lena forced herself to smile. She wanted to add that it wasn't a big deal, but the lump in her throat was making it difficult to speak.

Thankfully, Amanda jumped in. "Oh yes, you trained in literary translation, didn't you? Lucky you! You could afford to study anything you fancied, including the most useless stuff, without worrying if you could make a living out of it."

Lena tried to keep cool. "I don't think literary translation is useless, except to those who never read."

"Yes, of course, you are absolutely right," Amanda said before making a dreamy face. "Oh, I wish I could study astrology."

Rob cleared his throat, and Jeanne shifted noisily, but Amanda plowed on undeterred. "Or better still, ufology! I could go around interviewing all those wackos who believe they'd been abducted by little green men. Wouldn't that be a blast?"

"Lena one, Amanda one," Pepe said, but nobody laughed.

Lena turned away and studied the horizon.

After a few moments, Jeanne broke the awkward silence. "I'm getting hungry and a little cold. So, I don't know about you guys, but I'm going to find an eatery away from the beach. The ones around here are just tourist traps."

"I'll come with you," Lena said, her voice barely audible. She stood up, pulled her jeans and T-shirt on, and collected her stuff.

The men did the same.

"Who eats dinner at six?" Amanda muttered, but followed the others nonetheless.

The rest of the evening was a haze. Lena took part in the dinner and the long ramble in the city afterward. She engaged in most conversations.

But she really wasn't there.

* * *

The gang called it a day around eleven in the evening, most of them declaring they were dead tired. Rob had been hoping to have a word with Lena in private, but she dashed to her room as soon as they entered the hotel.

Once he and Amanda were in their room, Amanda proposed they watch a movie on her laptop.

That was when his old pal Thomas called him back to suggest they meet for a quick drink in the old town. As it happened, his timing was perfect. Rob needed a reason to get out of the hotel, breathe the night air, and distract himself.

He hung up and turned to Amanda. "My buddy wants to meet, so I'll be heading out—"

"Now?" Amanda glanced at her watch. "It's almost midnight."

"I'm a big boy, Mommy. I can take care of myself."

Amanda pursed her lips and turned to look out the window. "Have fun."

Rob turned right and took rue Alberti that led straight to the brasserie Thomas had suggested. They hadn't seen each other after finishing the engineering school two years ago. They hadn't been particularly close. But right now, Rob was happy he'd remembered Thomas lived in Nice and texted him from the train. Maybe he could drink himself out of his anger and remorse.

He was cross with Amanda for the way she kept taunting Lena all day. He resented being unable to tell Lena why he'd hidden his knowledge of Russian from her.

But above everything, he hated himself for having hurt her. He winced as he remembered the look of distress and incomprehension in her big brown eyes ... like a wounded Bambi. Had she been wronged by another guy, he'd have taken the a-hole aside and sorted him out in a wink. Rob stopped in his tracks, rapped out a curse, and drove his fist into the wall.

It hurt. *Good.*

A few minutes later, he pushed open the door to the brasserie and walked in.

"Over here!" Thomas waved from the bar.

They hugged and spent the next hour talking about common acquaintances, Thomas's new job, and Rob's prospects.

At one in the morning, Thomas climbed down from his barstool. "Sorry, pal, but I have an early start tomorrow morning, so . . ."

"Sure, it was great seeing you."

Fifteen minutes later, Rob was back in Very Nice. He stopped in the middle of the lobby. Amanda would still be awake, the night owl that she was. He didn't want to talk to her right now. He dropped onto the worn armchair and picked up one of the leaflets stacked on the table next to it. The cheap-looking pamphlet featured the hotel's rooftop terrace on the cover page. *Bingo.* He jumped up and headed toward the stairs. An hour in the fresh night air under the stars, and then he'd sneak into his room and get some sleep.

But someone else had remembered about the terrace, too. Rob walked over to the dark figure wrapped in a blanket that occupied one of the wicker armchairs. It was Lena. She sat hugging her knees, her head thrown back toward the night sky.

She startled as he got closer, squinted at him, then acknowledged him with a small smile.

He smiled back. "I see I'm not the only insomniac tonight."

She adjusted the blanket around her shoulders.

He pulled a chair and sat facing her. This was the perfect opportunity to apologize and clear the tension between them.

"I'm really sorry I didn't tell you about my Russian," he said.

"You don't need to apologize." She searched his face. "I just can't imagine why—"

He looked down. "I wish I could explain."

"Never mind," she said.

He pulled his chair a little closer and leaned in. "I do need to apologize, even if I can't explain why." A deep sigh escaped him. "I'm so messed up, Lena."

Her brows shot up, but she said nothing.

Please, let her forgive me. Please, let us be like before, he surprised himself praying. Why did it feel so vital that they be like before? Was it to make it easier to get intel on her dad? Or was it for a reason that had nothing to do with Anton Malakhov at all?

Jesus, he *was* messed up.

"Can we be friends again?" he asked.

"So you think we were friends?"

He nodded.

She arched her brows. "And you think you can be friends with me and Amanda at the same time?"

"Why not?"

"Can be a health hazard, what with all the sparks that fly."

He grinned. "Never mind Amanda's taunts. She's like that with everyone."

"Nefarious?"

"Spiky. But she's a sweetheart, once you've grown on her."

"I wonder how I could ever accomplish *that*." Lena smiled, a speck of sadness still lingering in her eyes.

He stared, mesmerized. He could never get enough of that smile.

A cloud hiding the moon must have shifted, because suddenly silver light poured over the terrace turning it into an enchanted place.

Lena gasped. "What happened to your hand?"

He followed her gaze and saw that the knuckles of his right hand were smeared with blood. Shit. He could bet there'd been none after he punched the wall.

He covered the abrasions with his other hand. "It's nothing."

She grabbed his wrist and yanked his hand closer to her face. "Have you disinfected them?"

Rob didn't register her question. He looked at her delicate fingers holding up his hand. Then at her face. She was squinting at his hand, trying to assess the seriousness of his cuts. Her gesture was devoid of any erotic subtext. And yet the contact of her skin scorched him, just like when he held her hand at L'Espace. It stirred an impulse inside him that was both feverishly raw and infinitely gentle. It made his heart bump against his ribcage as if demanding to get out.

He gazed at her hands holding his. The urge to run his fingertips over her skin, from her nails down to her wrist and then inside her palm was too overwhelming to resist...

"So have you?" she asked.

Rob blinked and looked up. "Have I what?"

"Disinfected."

"It's just a graze."

"I have a disinfectant in my suitcase," she said. "I can fetch it—"

And release my hand? "Stay," he blurted out. *Shit.* "I mean, I also brought some, so you don't need to bother. I'll disinfect as soon as I get back to my room. I promise."

"OK," she said softly and let go of him.

It took him superhuman effort not to grab her hand and bring it to his lips. *Get a grip, man.* "So, how does it feel to be a study-free person?"

"Great. But also weird. Suddenly, I've got all this time on my hands."

The corner of his mouth twitched. "There may be a sight or two worth seeing in Paris."

"Oh, I've made a huge list. Three lists, actually. One for Paris, another one for France, and a third one for cool places around the world I want to visit or revisit."

"What's the first trip on the list?"

"I wanted to go to New York with my dad, but I'm not sure how that's going to play out in light of the recent scoop."

He raised an eyebrow in question.

"My dad just got engaged," she said.

Ah, *that* scoop. He'd heard.

And so had Boris.

* * *

"Wow," Mat said, whipping his camera out.

Amanda nodded in agreement. "Amazing, isn't it?"

"Reminds me a little of Spain," Pepe said.

Rob grabbed the railing and glanced down. The view was worth the steep climb. From this vantage point at the top of the Castle Hill, Nice was uniquely alluring, its red roofs sandwiched between the blue of the sea and the sky.

"Isn't your hometown somewhere around here?" Pepe asked Jeanne.

"If you mean on the Mediterranean coast of France, then yes," Jeanne said. "But Nîmes is much further west."

Mat stopped taking pictures and turned to Jeanne. "I've been there once, it's a pretty town."

Jeanne beamed. "It sure is. Could be our next trip, by the way. My parents won't be able to host the whole gang, but they'll ensure a constant supply of the best croissants and pastries in town. They're bakers."

Amanda stretched her lips in what was supposed to stand for a polite smile. "That sounds wonderful." She turned to Lena. "And what is it that your father does for a living, Lena?"

"IT services," Lena said, looking wary.

"How exciting! The Russians are famous for their IT skills, aren't they? All those super hackers one hears about . . . Does he run hacking services, too?"

Lena ignored Amanda's question, turning her head to gaze at the sea.

"Hey, why don't we go clubbing tonight?" Mat said. "I spotted a cool place downtown. I think we should check it out."

"I'm not sure—" Lena started.

"Great idea! I haven't danced in ages, what with all the thesis writing and exams. I'm definitely in," Amanda said.

"I never say no to clubbing," Pepe declared.

Jeanne nodded. "Yeah, sure."

"Will you come?" Rob touched Lena's arm. "It'll be fun. You can't visit Nice and not sample its nightlife."

Lena glanced at Rob, then at Amanda, and then at Rob again. "Why not."

He beamed.

By the time they'd made it to the nightclub, it was almost midnight. The place was undeniably trendy. It had the exact kind of lighting, upholstery and sound a self-respecting Riviera club would be expected to have. The decibel level made it difficult to have a conversation, but then again, you didn't go to a nightclub for a conversation.

Rob wedged himself between other clubbers crowding space in front of the bar. "What are you having?" he shouted to his friends.

Once the drinks were bought and downed, Amanda was the first to jump on the elevated dance floor. She began to move in the same competent way she did everything else. She was good, she was hot, and she knew it. The dancers around her stepped back a little so that she could have enough room to execute her sophisticated sequences. After a few minutes, she turned to Rob and hooked her index at him. He joined her. They had practiced their routine at enough parties over the past two years to be the best double act on any dance floor.

One after the other, Mat, Jeanne, and Pepe climbed on the stage and began to dance.

Pepe also sang along, in spite of Jeanne's throat-cutting gestures. Lena was the last one to get on the dance floor. She began to move with the rhythm, and suddenly Rob could no longer focus on anything or anyone but her.

As Lena danced, her silk top shifted in a fluid movement hugging one curve at a time. Her dancing was self-conscious yet strangely free. And it completely mesmerized Rob. She danced unexpectedly well, in perfect synch with the rhythm, as if it was her body setting it. The way she moved wasn't extravagant or studied. Her movements were reserved, their amplitude small, but they were just so... spot-on. Each tiny sway of her hips, each lightest shake of her shoulders was painfully exquisite to him.

When the music changed to Latin, Rob realized he had stopped dancing and stood there gazing at Lena. This kind of behavior was uncharacteristic of him. He told himself he had no business staring at her like that. He reminded himself that Amanda needed him for their salsa routine. But he simply couldn't take his eyes off Lena.

He swallowed hard. There was no denying his reaction to this woman.

I want her.

He turned away, marched over to Amanda, and took her hand to lead her in a perfectly coordinated salsa.

Wanting Lena was the last thing he needed right now.

* * *

The trip back to Paris on Sunday afternoon was uneventful. It contrasted starkly with the boisterous few hours they'd spent on the train to Nice two days earlier. They didn't talk much, preferring the company of their books, tablets, and the landscape speeding by. Even Pepe was quiet with only lips moving as he listened to his music.

After the train arrived in Paris and they said their good-byes, Lena rushed home. She should have been happy and relaxed after that little escapade. Instead, she was in turmoil. There was the lingering hurt over Rob's "omission," a feeling that something significant had happened on the rooftop terrace, and anger against Amanda. And jealousy. Amanda and Rob went back a long way. They knew and understood each other so well. They danced together as if they'd done it for a living.

They had shared a room for two nights.

Once inside her apartment, Lena took a long shower and then started the kettle to make tea. While she waited for it to boil, she resolved that starting tomorrow, she'd stay away from *La Bohème* and spend her time doing all the cool things she'd put on her three lists.

As the kettle went off, so did the entrance buzzer.

She went to the intercom by the door. "Hello?"

"Hi, it's Rob. I have your eyeglasses. Can you buzz me in?"

She just stood there, unable to wrap her mind around the situation. "But . . . Did I leave them on the train?"

"Yep. I noticed them just before I got off, and by then you were already gone. I thought you might need them tonight, so I just . . ." He trailed off. "I was in the neighborhood anyway . . . Can I come up?"

"Yes, yes, of course!" She shook off her bafflement. "Third floor, left of the elevator."

Two minutes later Rob walked in, as sexy and gorgeous as ever. Lena suddenly felt self-conscious about her tangled damp hair, her jersey tank top, checkered boxers, and rubber flip-flops.

Oh, well — too late to do anything about it now.

He handed her the glasses. "As I said, I was in the neighborhood."

"Thank you." She motioned him to the kitchen. "I was making myself some herbal tea . . . if you like that sort of stuff. Otherwise, I've got regular tea, coffee, soda . . ."

"A soda will be fine, thanks."

She gave him a glass and a can of soda from the fridge, and turned away to make tea. As she dropped the teabag into the mug, she heard him take a few steps toward her, then place the soda and the glass on the countertop. Slowly, she poured scalding water into her mug and put the kettle down. Rob was now so close she could feel his warm breath on her bare shoulder.

And then he wrapped his arms around her waist and pressed his chest against her back.

She stood motionless, as her heart raced and her vision clouded. A swarm of delicious sensations overwhelmed her — his head-turning masculine scent, the gentleness of his strong arms, the comfort of his chest against her back. She told herself she had to stop him, right then, before he went too far. But she knew at some visceral level, in every nerve ending under her skin, that there was no force on the face of the earth that could make her stop him now.

Rob's mind had gone completely blank when he followed his crazy impulse and put his arms around Lena. But when Lena froze, he began to panic. He had no idea how she would react to this. Seconds stretched into an eternity. And then she leaned back into his embrace, ever so slightly, but enough to tell him what he needed to know. He wanted to roar with joy. He wanted to see her face. He wanted to remain in that moment forever.

Then she turned around and looked into his eyes. She was radiant. It was one of those charmed instances when everything, absolutely everything was perfect. This universe, this city, this specific spot in the kitchen, and this precise instance in time. And so he cupped her face with his hands and kissed her. Tenderly at first and then passionately, claiming her mouth, sampling the warm softness of her lips, and sweeping his tongue between them.

She responded with ardor, saying yes with her kisses, with her hands stroking the back of his head and with her body pressing into his. Rob was walking on air. He craved Lena, and she left no doubt she wanted him back.

But through his arousal and bliss he heard an admonishing voice. *You don't deserve her trust. You don't deserve this pleasure.* And all at once, he felt like a fraud, like a thief who had acquired something precious through deceit.

He needed her to know the truth.

Lena was light-headed and drowsy when Rob broke the kiss.

"I have to tell you something . . . before we go any further," he said.

She felt like she was falling. *There you go, there's the catch. It was too good to be true.* "So tell me."

"I'm . . . I get paid to spy on you."

She blinked. "By my father?"

"No, by his competitor. He pays me to listen in to your conversations with your dad and pass on anything of interest."

Lena couldn't speak. Her stomach knotted and she had to concentrate hard to hold back the tears. She looked at Rob's hand on her shoulder and then glared at him. He released his grip.

"I'm not proud of what I've been doing. But please believe me that our friendship and . . . and *this*, it's genuine."

She was silent, staring out the window. His words hardly registered. Her mind was too busy replaying the same phrase, like a broken record. *Too good to be true. Too good to be true.*

Rob spoke again. "I got to know you over the past couple of months, and I really, really like you. I wouldn't want to hurt you, Lena."

Her gaze remained fixed on the window. He *liked* her. How sweet. Everyone *liked* her — her mom, her dad, her ex best friend, her ex-boyfriend... Now Rob. And yet they all ended up hurting her, through neglect or betrayal, even if they didn't mean to.

He moved into her field of vision. "If it's any comfort, I've been careful not to cause your dad any real harm."

Does he expect me to thank him for that?

"Lena, I'm so sorry for having spied on you. And I'm even sorrier for having lied to you." He let out a heavy sigh. "I had no idea you'd be this kind, intelligent, lovely person... You were supposed to be a spoiled brat."

She gave him the coldest stare she could manage. She wanted to hiss, *I'm sorry I didn't live up to your expectations*. But she was afraid she'd break down and cry the moment she opened her mouth.

"Which, of course, is a crappy excuse . . ." He gave her a helpless look.

She walked to the door and opened it. "Please leave."

Rob gave her a sad, defeated look. He stepped over the threshold, then paused. "Lena, please, will you give me a chance? I want to be with you. Can you at least think about it?"

He turned around and ran down the stairs. She shut the door and leaned against it, listening to the sound of his footsteps fading away. When she couldn't hear him anymore, she slid to the floor and stopped fighting her tears.

* * *

Oh, I'm so far from heaven!
You — in my reach, so warm.
God, please don't judge — you haven't
Been here in female form.

Marina Tsvetaeva

SEVEN

It was late morning when Lena returned from the grocery shop around the corner. She was unpacking her bags when she heard a knock on the door. *Rob*, she thought. She made a move toward the door and stopped. A few seconds later, she took another step forward, stopped, turned around, and went back to the kitchen.

The knocking became more insistent "Lena, open up, it's me! I know you are there—I saw you walk in!" Jeanne said in her familiar throaty voice.

"Coming!" Lena rushed to the door, taking deep breaths and wiping her damp palms on her jeans. She couldn't tell if the feeling that washed over her was relief or disappointment.

Jeanne walked in and looked around, nodding approvingly. "So, this is the den where you're hiding when you're not at *La Bohème* . . . Cute."

Lena's joy at seeing Jeanne was mixed with guilt. "I've been doing a lot of sight-seeing recently," she said.

"Of course. Sight-seeing." Jeanne rolled her eyes. Then her expression changed to that of an exasperated parent. "Oh, come on, Lena. My coffee break is only ten minutes, so I don't have time for small talk. What's wrong?"

"Nothing. I'm perfectly fine."

"I haven't seen you in days. Make that a week. I'm worried about you! What's going on in your life that keeps you from *La Bohème*?"

Lena racked her brain for a plausible explanation. "I've also been translating a lot. I concentrate better in here. Or in the library."

"Is that so? I thought you concentrated just fine at the bistro."

Lena folded her arms over her chest, refusing to elaborate.

"And I have proof," Jeanne said. "When you're at the bistro, have you noticed how one of the waiters turns up by your side every twenty minutes or so to ask if you need anything?"

"I guess—why?"

Jeanne tapped the side of her head. "Each time we do that, you always order something—usually another tea or coffee or mineral water. The problem is that if no one reminds you, you get so engrossed you forget to reorder. I doubt you'd notice if I'd grown a second head."

Lena smiled. "I'm sure I'd notice your second head."

"You should see yourself staring into space, then typing like a madwoman, and drinking from an empty cup."

"I don't do that!" Lena grinned.

"Which one? Staring into space or forgetting you've finished your coffee? It's bad business for the bistro, you know — a customer who occupies a table for hours with the same drink."

Lena threw her hands up. "You lost me, Jeanne. First you're upset I haven't come into *La Bohème* for a few days, and now you're telling me I'm bad business."

"That's not what I said. You're excellent business, when we give you a little push. Besides, you return for dinner and you tip."

Lena lifted her chin. "That's more like it."

"Lena, we count on you. *La Bohème* needs you. You've become part of the..." Jeanne hesitated, looking for the right word.

"Decor?" Lena offered. "I don't mind. I like it at *La Bohème*."

"Well, if you do, then why don't you haul your nerdy ass downstairs for a nice long coffee between girls? I'll even share with you the last slices of Mom's amazing apple pie."

Lena cocked her head to the side and said innocently, "I thought your coffee break was only ten minutes long—that's what you said, didn't you?"

"What break? Who said anything about a break?" It was Jeanne's turn to fake innocence. "I'm not working until five. I'm here as a patron to have a coffee with a friend."

Lena hesitated. "Is . . . Rob there?"

Jeanne shook her head. "He starts at five today."

Then she put a hand on her hip and delivered her final argument in a deep voice with a terrible Italian accent. "And remember this, *ragazza*: My friends never, ever refuse my offers—unless they have a death wish. You won't disappoint me now, *bella*, will you?"

When the coffee was served and the pie unwrapped, Jeanne repeated her earlier question. "So, what's wrong, Lena? And please don't give me that bullshit about writing and translating. This is about Rob. What's the deal with you two?"

Lena took a bite of the apple pie and gave in to the temptation to spill the beans. Jeanne was a friend, her only friend in this city. With a sigh she told her about their kiss and his confession about spying on her.

Jeanne listened, eyes round, and mouth agape.

"Turns out I've been falling for the wrong guy. So now I just need some time and distance to lick my wounds and try to get over him," Lena concluded her tale.

"Ooh la la—our Rob, a homegrown spy, huh?" Jeanne shook her head, before asking, "Tell me, when was the last time you looked at a price tag?"

"I'm sorry?"

"You know, the little ticket that tells you how much an item you want to buy costs."

"I don't buy expensive stuff—" Lena began to protest.

"I know." Jeanne winked. "I've noticed. So, let's imagine for the sake of the argument you're buying something from that sweatshop outlet down the street. Would you look at the price tag? Not because you're curious to see how much they're charging for that crap, but because you want to make sure you'll have enough money at the end of the month to pay rent?"

"What are you saying, Jeanne? Do you think that lack of money justifies taking advantage of people's trust?"

"No, that's not what I'm saying. I'm saying that when Rob signed up to spy on you, you were nothing to each other. There was no question of trust or affection or anything like that." She glanced into Lena's eyes. "Don't get me wrong—what he did isn't pretty."

"Ah, good. I was beginning to wonder if the French had a totally different value system from the rest of the world."

"But he did come clean after you guys kissed, didn't he?"

That much was true.

"Listen, Lena, I've known Rob for two years now, and I can tell you this: He's a good guy. In spite of this slipup . . . and his looks."

Lena finished her slice of apple pie and licked her fingers. "My compliments to your mom. This *was* an amazing pie."

Jeanne swallowed the rest of her coffee. "I've got to run—have some errands in town. I hope you figure out this thing with Rob pretty soon, so we can all go back to normal." She pushed back the coins Lena had placed on the table. "This one is on the house, honey. I'll tell Pierre it was an investment. *Ciao!*"

Lena was about to leave too, when her phone rang. She glanced at the caller ID—it was her dad. Lena braced herself for bad news: He didn't normally call in the morning.

"Pumpkin, I'm going to have to cancel my Parisian vacation in August. I'm really sorry."

Lena began to panic. "Is something wrong?"

"Not at all. Quite the contrary, I have wonderful news." Anton cleared his throat. "Anna and I decided to advance our wedding date to August. So, we *will* see each other as we'd planned; only it will be in Moscow and not in Paris."

"Oh. OK. I'll come for your wedding then! Wow, Dad, this is moving superfast."

"Sweetie, we advanced the date because Anna is pregnant. You're going to have a little brother or a sister before Christmas."

"Seriously? This is fantastic!"

Lena felt like jumping with joy and giving a bear hug to someone. She wasn't even sure if she was happier for her dad or for herself. Having a sibling had been her number one wish throughout her childhood, and it was finally coming true now that she was twenty-three. *Well, better late than never. Infinitely better.*

She hung up, grinning. As she thought about what it would be like to have a sibling, it hit her that the baby would divert most of her dad's excessive solicitude. What a terrific and unhoped-for boon! She was still smiling when her gaze fell on the couple sitting at the opposite end of the terrace. The woman faced her, and the man had his back to her. She couldn't hear them, but the man must have said something funny, because the woman threw her head back in laughter. The man took her hand, and she didn't withdraw it.

The man was Rob.

* * *

Lena's smile slipped and her muscles tensed. The scene was painful to watch, and yet she did as if hypnotized. She couldn't see Rob's face or hear the conversation, but her imagination readily filled in the gaps. Was he doing this to make his point? To make her jealous? Or was he over her in just one week? Had he ever been into her at all? The last thought made her wince.

But then Rob entered *La Bohème*, gave Lena a nod, and sat at a table not far from her.

Lena's fists unclenched, and her whole body went limp with relief. She looked at the couple again. It was now so obvious that this guy wasn't Rob. In fact he looked nothing like Rob, apart from the similar hair and clothes. His shoulders had a different slant, his back was thicker, and his neck thinner. Lena felt the color warming her cheeks.

How embarrassing.

She glanced at Rob and her cheeks went from warm to burning. He was looking at her in the same dark, nearly palpable way he had done a few weeks ago by the Seine. His eyes bored into hers with stark intent, as if she were the only woman on Earth. As if the world around them had dissolved into nothing.

Her undoing was averted by Pierre, who unwittingly sat next to Rob. "Waiting for someone?"

Rob shook his head. "Just chilling."

"I must be doing something right if my staff comes here on their free time. First Jeanne, now you. Do you mind if I *chill* alongside you for a few minutes?" He waved at Didier. "Two espressos and sparkling water, please."

Profiting from the distraction, Lena stood up and left the bistro. She almost ran the few feet to the building's entrance, up the stairs and into her apartment. Her mind reeled. Rob hadn't forgotten her. He wasn't over her. He wanted her and he wanted her to know it. She thought about their kiss and what it had done to her. In her two years with Gerhard she hadn't experienced anything that could remotely compare to that. Even now, her mouth was hungry for his lips, his taste, and her body ached for him. But could she trust him again? And if he broke her heart—or rather, *when* he broke her heart—would she be able to handle it?

Lena went to her little desk and opened her laptop. She found a file with unfinished translations and scrolled down to the one she had been struggling with for a few months now. As she read the original poem again, the French version poured out of her, as if of its own volition.

Lena began to type frantically, afraid she would forget the words. It was magic—like a locked door suddenly unlatching. When she finished and reread her translation, she knew why the poem had opened up at this precise moment.

Curled up under my fluffy blanket,
I'm summoning that pesky dream.
What was it? Whose triumphant gambit?
Whose loss? Whose win?

You're gone, and both of us are safer.
Except . . . this thing I'm thinking of,
This funny thing I have no name for,
What if it's love?

In our silly competition
Who threw the bull's-eye dart?
And who, on a misguided mission,
Hurled forth a heart? . . .

* * *

Rain poured down in noisy and resolute showers. Lena had planned a trip to the Versailles Gardens for this Sunday, but that plan no longer made sense. According to Météo-France, it was going to be like this all day. She pressed her forehead against the window and tried to motivate herself to get out of the apartment, go somewhere, do something.

After a while, she gave up and admitted that the weather had the upper hand. Dark skies and rain often made her feel lonely. This time round, they also made her nostalgic for the excitement of her first days in Paris and the heady mixture of freedom and possibility they had brought. Why couldn't she maintain that state of mind? How did she let that sense of freedom slip through her fingers? How did she end up with a heart heavy with want and longing—when she had promised herself to keep it uninvolved?

Her phone beeped. It was a text message from Jeanne.

> *Hey, any plans 4 2nite? How about a nite in with a movie & popcorn? If interested, please confirm availability of DVD player/computer & microwave. We'll bring the film & popcorn. 7 pm?*
>
> *Hug, Jeanne*

Lena replied immediately.

> *Computer, check; microwave, check. 7 is fine.*
> *Looking forward to it,*
>
> *Xo, Lena*

It was amazing how a short text message could lift your spirits. Lena didn't feel lonely any longer, and her heart lightened. She was going to spend the evening with a friend.

The friend in question showed up at her doorstep, accompanied by Pepe, at seven o'clock on the dot.

"Nice to see you, Pepe," Lena said, then turned to Jeanne. "I thought the 'we' in your text was you and your boyfriend."

"He's out of town." Jeanne went to the microwave and began to fumble with the buttons.

Pepe made a throat-slashing gesture to prevent Lena from asking further questions, then opened his backpack and took three beers and a bottle of apple juice out.

As they sprawled on the couch, Jeanne introduced the film. "On the program tonight is a French spoof that I doubt either of you has seen. It's called *The Joy of Singing*. Ring any bells?"

Lena and Pepe shook their heads.

"Thought so. It wasn't a huge box office success even in France, but it's one of my favorite movies."

Pepe turned to Lena. "Says the woman with blue hair and holes in her lips. I wouldn't hold my breath."

Jeanne snarled at him before continuing her presentation. "Just remember there's no point in trying to figure out who's doing what, with whom and why. It doesn't matter. What matters is that the movie is hilarious. Especially the leads, Marina Foïs and Lorant Deutsch."

"I know Marina Foïs!" Lena said. "She's so funny."

"They play undercover agents who join a singing class to get information about trafficked uranium. Or something like that." Jeanne started the movie. "You're in for one absurdist, joyous romp, my friends."

Pepe passed the popcorn around, and Lena put on her glasses.

As the movie began, Jeanne raised her index. "Almost forgot: If either of you have a problem with nudity, let me know so that I can tell you when to close your eyes. Which is going to be a lot of the time."

"I thought it was a thriller slash comedy," Lena said.

"And so it is. But remember, it's a *French* thriller slash comedy," Jeanne said. "*Noblesse oblige.*"

The movie was everything Jeanne had touted it to be and more. To the girls' surprise, Pepe did close his eyes a few times. During a particularly risqué love scene, he walked out of the room, ostensibly to get some water.

"In spite of his best efforts to pass for a jaded Parisian, Pepe is a Boy Scout at heart," Jeanne said.

"Well, I'm glad there's more to him than the Nordic blonde obsession," Lena said.

Finally, after the required amount of thrills and chills, ludicrous murders, eccentric lovemaking and deadpan humor, the film ended.

"Wow. This was . . ." Lena paused looking for the right word.

"Indescribable? Weird? Bizarre?" Pepe offered.

"Yes, but also original and very funny. Jeanne, thanks for picking this movie! I don't think I would have ever seen it otherwise."

Pepe furrowed his brow. "And that would have been a great loss for your personal development?"

Lena smiled at him. "Actually, the movie does help to better understand the French and their . . . mores."

Jeanne put the DVD back into its case. "Let's not make sweeping generalizations. I can assure you that in their majority the French aren't this promiscuous. Or this good at singing."

Pepe nodded energetically.

"Take me—I don't sleep around. Or Rob, for that matter." Jeanne turned to Lena. "You may not believe me, but he'd never hit on a customer. That is, except *you*. And he hasn't had a girlfriend since Camille, who he broke up with like a year ago."

Pepe rolled his eyes. "Lena, what Jeanne is trying to say is that Rob is a candidate for sainthood. In fact, he's sworn off women because he's about to be ordained. His business school is just a cover—he doesn't want people to know he's preparing to become a hermit monk."

Jeanne snorted. "Hermit monk, my foot!"

"OK, I admit I let my imagination run wild for a moment." Pepe narrowed his eyes at Jeanne. "Rob is no saint and Lena needs to know it. On numerous occasions, he's threatened to kill me — each time in a more devious way than the last."

"Can you name one member of the staff who hasn't threatened to kill you?" Jeanne asked.

Pepe disregarded her question. "I think I'm still alive only because he's too lazy to execute his plans. Or too busy. Or too lovesick." He pinched his chin theatrically. "Hmm. That's it, lovesick. He's been a sorry sight since Lena quit the bistro."

Lena looked at Jeanne, who nodded vigorously. And that was when it dawned on her.

"Oh my God. This is an intervention, isn't it?"

"What?" Jeanne furrowed her brow.

"Where?" Pepe asked, looking around the room.

Lena shook her head. "The whole movie night thing was a ploy to nudge me toward Rob, wasn't it?"

"It was Jeanne's idea," Pepe said quickly. "She thinks you'd be good for Rob... or the other way around, I can't remember. Anyway, I was threatened with bodily harm if I didn't play along."

* * *

"Amanda! What brings you here?"

Amanda almost squirmed when she heard Jeanne's voice. She had come to *La Bohème* hoping to run into Rob, but he wasn't here. And now her chance of retreating discretely was gone, too.

"I was in the neighborhood, so I thought I'd stop by for a serving of your chef's delicious chocolate mousse."

"Excellent idea. With a cup of café crème and a glass of water?" Jeanne asked.

"Yes, please."

When Jeanne returned, Amanda asked matter-of-factly, "Is Rob working today?"

"Yes, but he arrives later in the afternoon. He should be here in an hour. Have you tried calling him?"

Amanda shook her head. "This wasn't planned. As I said, I just happened to be in the neighborhood."

"If you're not in a hurry, I can join you in fifteen minutes for my coffee break," Jeanne offered.

Amanda brightened. If Jeanne joined her in fifteen minutes, they would chat for another fifteen minutes, and then she could order a drink and send a few e-mails until Rob's arrival.

"That would be really nice."

When Jeanne collapsed onto the chair across from Amanda's, they made small talk, and then Amanda dived in for information. "So, what's up with our common friends?"

"Same old. Pepe is still pursuing his double goal of becoming an authentic Parisian waiter and hooking up with a Nordic blonde. Both with remarkable lack of success. Rob has been doing a lot of double shifts lately. Says he needs the money."

Amanda nodded. "Yes, he hasn't paid the fees for the last school year yet. He told Mat and me he had a foolproof plan, but I'm not sure a few double shifts at the bistro will solve his problem. What he needs is to land a good job so he could get a bank loan."

"I didn't realize Rob needed the money so urgently. That explains why he—" Jeanne bit her tongue.

"Why he what?"

"Um . . . why he's been so out of sorts lately. There's also his . . . situation with Lena, of course."

Amanda raised an eyebrow. "What situation?"

"You know, their falling out. Rob's been very affected by it."

Amanda couldn't bear it anymore. Jeanne knew something that she didn't. And she probably wasn't going to tell her, unless . . .

She leaned in. "Jeanne, I'm going to be frank with you, and I'd like you to be as frank in return. I've had my sights on Rob for some time now. You see, we're perfect for each other in every way."

"Oh. But then why didn't you come forward earlier? He was free for indecently long."

"Well, not really. After he and Camille broke up a year ago, she had a hard time moving on. So she suggested they continue as "friends with benefits" until one of them meets someone new."

"Never a good idea, that."

Amanda rolled her eyes. "You're telling me! But he went with it. And you know Rob—he behaved like he was still *with her*. He wasn't open to something new."

"And you were too proud to declare your feelings."

"It wasn't just that." Amanda sighed. "Once you start as friends—close friends—it isn't easy to . . . to tell your best buddy how you *really* feel about him."

Jeanne nodded.

"And then a few months ago he finally put an end to his weird thing with Camille, and I was beginning to take heart."

Amanda smoothed her hair back. "Jeanne, I need to know if there's something going on between Rob and Lena. You'll understand that I'd rather not tell him about my feelings if he's falling for someone else."

Jeanne shifted uncomfortably. "Wow, Amanda, I had no idea. When you kept badgering Lena in Nice, I thought you were just being mean."

Amanda smirked. "I was *just* being mean. I had no clue Rob and Lena were an item."

"Well, they weren't at the time. Anyway, to answer your question, yes, something happened between Rob and Lena after our trip to Nice, but then Rob... let's just say, he did something stupid, and Lena has been refusing to talk to him ever since."

Amanda would have liked more detail, but it looked like this was all she was going to get.

Jeanne picked up her coffee cup and stood. "Got to go — my break is over. On the subject of Rob and Lena, I think it's a matter of time until they iron things out. So, yeah, you may want to hold any declarations for now."

Amanda opened her mouth to say something, but Jeanne beat her to it. "It goes without saying you can count on my discretion."

"Thanks, I appreciate it," Amanda said.

When Jeanne left, she pulled out her phone to check her e-mails. But she couldn't focus. The letters refused to come together in a meaningful manner to form words and sentences. So she just stared at her phone, her mind processing what she'd learned from Jeanne. She was still convinced that she and Rob were a perfect match, while Lena was wrong for him in every way. But Lena was new and exotic, and so Rob was infatuated with her. It wouldn't last. He'd come around. This was a minor setback, not a defeat. She'd waited for two years, she could wait a few more weeks. Her mom had taught her that the world belonged to those who wait.

* * *

After this sleepless night, I'm awash in lightness,
Poised and serene — a star in the Milky Way.
Rainbows fill every sound, erupting brightly,
Icy-cold streets smell like Florence in early May.

Marina Tsvetaeva

EIGHT

Rob put his hand on Lena's knee and pushed her skirt up. He began to unbutton her shirt with his other hand. Lena cupped his face and leaned in, closing her eyes in anticipation of a ground-shattering kiss.

"We can't," Rob said, leaning away. "We need to find everyone involved in trafficking uranium and apprehend them."

"What?"

Lena woke up, confused, aroused, and dizzy. She blinked a few times, while her mind adjusted to the real world.

The curtains in her bedroom were drawn, softening the summer morning's sharp light. Lena looked at the vacant side of the bed and imagined Rob lying there, gazing at her. The image was so vivid she could almost hear his breathing and feel the warmth of his skin. She longed to touch him. She yearned for his touch. Was she in love? Was it too late to fight her feelings? Or was she merely lusting after him, her mind overpowered by physical need?

She got up and opened the window. The street bustled with delivery vans, bicycles, and pedestrians rushing to their workplaces, dragging their children to day care or walking their dogs.

Lena closed her eyes and listened. Through the cacophony of sounds that included someone's television and a couple of sparrows chirping animatedly, she could hear the vibrant, rhythmic pulse of the city.

She pushed her hair away from her face and sighed in acceptance of what she was about to do. Whether she was in love or in lust was a moot question, really. In any case, it probably wasn't going to end well for her. But the truth was, she had to give Rob a second chance, or else all those what-ifs and might-have-beens plaguing her would soon make her sick, mentally and physically. She wasn't being stupid or self-destructive. She was merely making a rational choice between probable calamity and impending disaster.

After that aha moment, the day dragged as though it had fallen from the normal time-space continuum into a slow-motion black hole. Having decided to go down to *La Bohème* around midnight so that she could catch Rob just before the end of his shift, Lena tried to occupy herself the best she could. She read, translated, read some more, ate, changed into a different pair of jeans, tied her hair up, let it loose, tied it up again. When her dad called at seven, she greeted him with a degree of enthusiasm that made him suspicious.

"Is everything all right with you, Lenochka?" he asked.

"I'm fine, Dad, just a little restless."

She went on to ask him a million questions about Anna and the wedding plans. After they hung up, she tried to read again, but she was too antsy to sit down for more than a few minutes. At eleven thirty, she grabbed her purse, threw on a cardigan, and walked out of her apartment.

The bistro was winding up, but Rob was nowhere to be seen. Probably helping in the kitchen, Lena thought. She sat down and waited for Jeanne, who was clearing up a table, to notice her.

"Look who's here!" Jeanne beamed. "Is it really you or an apparition?" She pinched Lena's arm.

"Ouch." Lena swatted Jeanne's hand away.

"Hmm. Feels real enough . . ."

"Ha-ha. Hey, I was wondering—"

"He's inside. Should be done in a few minutes. Sit tight. Shall I get you a glass of Chablis?"

Lena nodded, realizing that her dream about Jeanne remembering her preferences had come true. Must be an auspicious sign.

Rob walked out of the kitchen, an empty tray in his hand, and looked around. When he saw Lena, he started and then stopped. He looked at her, searching her eyes for an answer to his unspoken question. Lena held his gaze. It took her all her willpower not to stand up and run to him. She wanted him to come to her.

Finally, a smile spread on Rob's face, and he strode to her table. He sat down across from her and took her hand.

"Does this mean I'm forgiven?"

"This means you are on probation for an indeterminate length of time. If I see the smallest sign of spy activity, I'll leave. I'll move out of here . . . and I'll tell your mother."

"Oh no, please, not my mom! She has a really heavy hand." Rob's expression grew more serious. "Lena, you have no idea how glad I am that you came around."

She gave him a long look. He hadn't actually said he'd stop spying. "Can you give me your word?"

"What if we did it together? You'll tell me what I can report. Isn't it a brilliant idea?"

Her mouth thinned. "Is this a joke?"

"Lena, the guy is so desperate he'd take anything." Rob smiled brightly. "The stuff I've been giving him so far was totally harmless."

"And you're the best judge of what's harmless for my family?"

He said nothing, the smile slipping from his face.

She shook her head. "I don't get it. Why on earth would you wish to continue?"

"It's good money. And I need it," he said, a hard edge in his voice.

"I can lend you money or get my dad to lend you as much as you need."

"Out of the question."

"Why?"

"I just can't. Things would become weird between us."

She searched his eyes. "Because now they aren't weird at all?"

He only sighed in reply.

When she spoke again, her tone was firm. "If you want to be with me, Rob, you've got to stop reporting to this guy. The choice is yours."

He nodded slowly. "OK. I'll quit." Then he smirked and added, "And from now on, I'll only accept jobs that don't involve snooping around."

"Will you please consider borrowing from me?" she offered again.

"If you want to be with me, Lena,"—he gave her a sly look, as he echoed her ultimatum—"you've got to stop fretting. By the way, what made you change your mind about giving me a second chance?"

"Curiosity." She smiled, trying to appear nonchalant.

Could Rob see through her? Could he guess that "misery" would have described her state over the past week much better?

He didn't say anything but began to stroke her hand, first gently, then more daringly.

She'd lost herself in his eyes, spellbound, when Jeanne said, "Rob, I can finish up here while you go change. We're nearly done, anyway. And then you two lovebirds can leave, so I can close the shop and go home."

Rob jumped to his feet. "Lena, please wait here. I'll be back in a sec. And thank you, Jeanne!" he shouted already halfway to the kitchen.

When he reemerged three minutes later, having changed into jeans and a T-shirt, Lena was waiting by the exit.

He reached her in three long strides. "I know a cool place just a few blocks from here on rue La Fayette. They're open all night. Want to check it out?"

"No."

She took his hand and led him to the green gate, and then inside her building.

* * *

Rob's heart raced. He had spent so many hours fantasizing about making love to Lena and then reminding himself it would never happen, that the notion migrated to the realm of impossible dreams. Was he really going to be able to touch her, kiss her, hold her the way he'd held her in his fantasies?

When Lena led him into the tiny elevator, and he found himself facing her, their bodies almost touching for lack of space, he could wait no longer. He backed her against the wall and pressed his lips to hers. Dazed by the pleasure of it, he slid his tongue into her mouth and kissed her with an urgency that bordered on desperation. She tasted exactly like she looked — sweet, delicate, and infinitely lovely. He'd been hooked on that taste since their first kiss, hungering for it, craving it. When the elevator screeched to a halt, Rob had to summon all the willpower he possessed to break the kiss and tear himself from Lena.

Once inside the apartment, she turned to him, her cheeks flushed and her lips a little swollen from kissing.

"Would you like a drink?"

He slowly shook his head, a tiny smile flickering in his eyes, and Lena's blush deepened to crimson red. She must have understood his unspoken reply: He wasn't thirsty for a drink—he was thirsty for her.

Without a word, Lena took his hand again and led him to the bedroom. After they entered, she lit two big candles placed on either side of the bed. Shadows began to dance on the walls, and a light scent of jasmine filled the room.

"I know it's corny, but I don't care," she said with a smile that blew Rob's mind.

"Corny's fine. I like corny."

He pulled her to him and renewed the kiss. His hands roamed her back then plunged into her hair. He delighted in its satiny feel, its soft, silky smoothness against his fingertips. She gasped with pleasure. His lips moved down to kiss her neck, and he began to undo the little buttons on her blouse. He was clumsy with excitement. As soon as he managed to open the top three, he bared one of her shoulders and rained small kisses on it, then teased his tongue up along her graceful neck and back to her mouth. He couldn't get enough of her.

In his fantasies about this moment he always went slowly, demonstrating his prowess, driving her to beg him to make love to her. But as her tongue darted into his mouth with an eagerness that equaled his own, he knew that slow wasn't an option this time. Without breaking the kiss, he undid the remaining buttons, removed Lena's shirt and unfastened the clasp of her bra. She slid her thumbs under his T-shirt and tugged it up and over his head. The rest of their clothing flew off in a heated frenzy until they stood in front of each other completely bare. For a few seconds Rob remained motionless, gazing at Lena, completely mesmerized by the play of light and shadow on her small firm breasts, her lithe thighs, and her flat tummy.

Then suddenly he could wait no more. He took a step toward her, flattened his hands against her lower back and pressed the entire length of his body against hers. She moaned softly and threw her arms around his neck. He drew in her intoxicating fragrance and eased her onto the bed.

* * *

Lena woke up and lay still for a moment, her eyes closed. As the sunlight tickled her skin, she listened to Rob's even breathing. By the time they had finally fallen asleep after making love, talking and making love again, it was almost dawn. Lena remembered words, gestures, and movements from that magical candle-lit night. She was afraid that if she opened her eyes now, the enchantment would be over.

When she finally did, what she saw took her breath away. Rob was still asleep, lying on his stomach, his face turned away from her. His arms were raised above his head, hugging the pillow. He had uncovered himself in his sleep, and she could see him — all of him — in his stark male beauty. A ray of sunshine had snuck into the bedroom through a narrow gap between the curtains and landed squarely on Rob's tight, muscled butt. After she looked her fill, her gaze slid upward along his gorgeous torso to his sinewy arms. And then she turned away. For if she didn't, she was going to press her body against his and wake him up.

When she turned back a few minutes later, Rob was still lying on his stomach, but this time awake and looking at her.

"Good morning." His husky morning voice was incredibly sexy.

He shifted, placed his hand on Lena's waist and pulled her close. He smelled deliciously, dizzyingly masculine. She kissed him on the collarbone and the neck, and then trailed her lips along his jawline to his mouth. His lips were soft and warm, and his morning stubble grated a little against her chin.

When she pulled away after a long, lush kiss, Rob's hand that had been holding her waist, went up to cup her cheek. "I don't know how I'm going to manage it, but I've got to go."

Lena drew back a little. "OK."

"I have a job interview at eleven, and I need to get home to change into a suit. The interview is for a junior managerial position. I probably don't stand a chance, but I need to keep trying."

"Go get them," she said.

He placed his hand back on her waist and trailed his fingertips along the curve of her hip. "I'll need all my control to make it through this day before I can be in bed with you again. Or on the couch, a chair, the kitchen table—anything."

Lena bit her lower lip. "Hmm. Let's put a pin on that last suggestion. The kitchen table sounds . . . promising."

She could hardly believe she'd spoken like this to a man—without a hint of inhibition.

Within a second he was on top of her, propping himself up on his elbows, his pupils dilated with desire.

"I'm going to be late for my interview." He bent down and suckled her nipple. "But it doesn't matter." He suckled her other nipple. "Because if I don't get inside you right now, I'll die."

* * *

As soon as he walked out of the small meeting room where interviews were being held, Rob dialed Boris's number.

"Rob, what have you got for me?" Boris greeted him in his businesslike manner.

"I want to call our deal off."

"Oh. You hit the jackpot?"

"I wish . . . I just can't do it anymore."

I promised her.

Rob stepped out of the shiny granite-floored lobby and filled his lungs with warm summer air. It was a relief to put an end to his short-lived spying career and be at peace with his conscience again. Even if, for now, he had no clue where he could get the funds to pay the school fee. Unless, of course, he did "hit the jackpot" by quickly landing a good job. But the chances of that happening, given the current job market, were modest.

"Are you sure about this or are you trying to renegotiate the fee?" Boris asked dryly.

"I'm sure. Besides, I don't see how it's a good deal for you. Lena and her father rarely talk shop, and most of the info I give you is useless."

"Most but not all," Boris said. "Listen. Give me one more juicy morsel like the one about Malakhov's interest in Raduga, then quit. I'll raise your fee sixfold for a scoop like that."

Rob couldn't help doing the math. Six times his current fee, plus what he'd made on the double shifts at *La Bohème,* would free him of debt.

"I'll call you if I hear something," he said.

As Lena emerged from behind the green gate, she spotted Rob approaching the bistro. His grin indicated he had made it to his interview. He'd gone there straight from her place, figuring it was better to show up in an imperfect state than not to show up at all. So he had taken a speedy shower, borrowed her razor to shave, and used his index finger to brush his teeth. On his way out, he'd stopped by the bistro and swapped his T-shirt for one of his starched server shirts.

Already briefed by Jeanne about the reconciliation, Pepe showed them to a small table squeezed between two others. "I am afraid we cannot offer you the private terrace out back at this time. It's currently occupied by the proprietor."

"It's OK," Lena said while Rob glared at Pepe.

After they finished their lunch and ordered espressos, Jeanne joined them during her coffee break. Rob stood up and adjusted the central parasol to make sure all three of them were protected from the midday sun.

"Paris weather rocks," Lena said, taking a sip of her coffee. "It hardly ever rains."

"The past couple of months have been an anomaly, absolutely not representative of Parisian weather," Jeanne said. "If you're lucky, it may last until early September and may even come back for a week in late October."

"Don't you love Indian summer? Like in that Joe Dassin song." Lena hummed the melancholy tune, and wondered if Rob would still be with her in October.

Better not think about it now.

"Yes, yes, it's very nice," Jeanne said. "But the norm in Paris is wet and chilly. Just like London or Brussels. Only for some strange reason, Paris has a better rep. People imagine it as sunny or brightly lit at night. But its true face is gray."

"I've been to Paris several times before, and the weather was nice every time," Lena protested. She wouldn't have the city of her dreams trashed like that.

"When was it?" Jeanne asked. "What time of year did you visit?"

"Well, summer, mostly . . . and spring," Lena had to admit.

"Told you. Wait till you see our real weather. Till you experience the veritable Parisian drizzle—drives you out of your mind."

Lena turned to Rob, but he was busy talking to Pepe who had come to collect the check. Still, Lena was determined to stand her ground. "It's just rain, Jeanne, we have that in Moscow, and in Geneva, too. What's so special about the Parisian drizzle?"

"Oh, it's not just any drizzle, honey. It's this humidity hanging in the air in tiny little droplets, so tiny they penetrate your skin and then your skull and get into your brain."

Lena shuddered at the image... then felt Rob's hand on her knee. He was still talking to Pepe, his face turned away from her, but his hand—concealed by the table—got under the hem of her sundress and began to caress her thigh.

"Rest assured. You'll be able to make your own opinion about the Parisian drizzle soon enough," Jeanne said.

"You're mean, you know? Even if I'm deluding myself about how great Paris is, why *drizzle* on my parade? Can't you just let me bask in my dumb love a little longer?"

"Lena, dear, don't listen to Jeanne," Pepe said. "She's French, so she complains. That's what the French do, always and in any circumstance."

"No, we don't, you silly little—" Jeanne started.

Pepe didn't let her finish. "It's not your fault, Jeanne." He turned to Lena and repeated for extra emphasis, "It's not her fault. It's what they're taught from their tenderest age."

"Says who?" Rob asked, his hand scorching hot against Lena's thigh.

"Imagine this little baby." Pepe made a fish mouth and emitted a couple of high-pitched screams. "So this baby is really, really happy. It just got its first squeeze of breast milk. Life is beautiful, everything is perfect. And then it hears Mommy say, 'Oh shit, I'm so bored' or 'Oh shit, I feel like a cow' or 'Oh shit, this baby is so ugly'."

Encouraged by the girls' giggles, he continued, "I'm telling you, Lena, complaining is a national sport—no, it's a national *value*—in this country. Didn't you know? It's what the revolutionaries stormed the Bastille for. They wanted every citizen to have the right to grumble."

Pepe climbed on a chair, raised his clenched fist in the air, and recited, "*Liberté, Egalité, Fraternité,* Complain."

The patrons sitting within earshot of Pepe cheered enthusiastically. He bowed and climbed down from the chair, looking exceedingly pleased with his deconstruction of the French character. Jeanne narrowed her eyes at him and mumbled something unintelligible.

Rob grinned, obviously too entertained — or too distracted — to defend his compatriots.

Lena smiled, as a wave of pure, unadulterated happiness washed over her.

* * *

By the time they stood to leave, Lena's sole concern was to quickly get someplace where Rob could finish what he had started at the bistro. Without saying a word to each other, they headed straight back to her apartment.

A few hours of lovemaking later—including on the kitchen table—Lena was too exhausted to go out again. Rob said he was happy to stay put. He needed to check his e-mail and send his CV to a few more companies. Lena lent him her laptop and settled on the couch with a book, but she couldn't focus on reading. Too many questions assaulted her mind. She wondered if Rob was going to stay for the night, if he would be prepared to leave France for a job offer abroad, if he'd managed to find the money he needed.

After staring at the same page for twenty minutes, she asked, "What are the jobs you're applying to?"

"All kinds. I'm afraid I'm not in a position to pick my industry or location. I'll be happy if I can negotiate the starting salary."

There, she had at least one of her answers. *Better not dwell on it too much.*

She smiled brightly. "What if the job you were interviewed for this morning worked out? You said the interview went pretty well."

"I hope so." Rob turned to Lena. "And what about you? Any change since a month ago?"

"My supervisor in Geneva encourages me to apply for a PhD program, which means at least three more years of study. I don't mind the study as much as the purpose of doing a PhD. It would be to stay in the academia."

Rob quirked an eyebrow. "Doesn't sound too bad to me."

"Well, it's certainly better than working for my dad in the IT field, which would either drive me crazy or bore me silly. Most probably both."

"But?"

"But . . . I guess what I'd really like to do with my life is translating literary works. I love it and I think I'm good at it. I've decided to do just that during my "gap year" in Paris. I'll translate as much as I can—prose and poetry, from Russian to French and vice versa."

Lena smiled apologetically. "Unlike most new graduates, I can afford to experiment. After all, being a minigarch does offer a few perks."

"I'll take your word for it. Thanks for letting me use your laptop." He stood and ran his hand through his hair. "Lena, I need to go to my place tonight . . ."

"Yes, sure."

He took a step toward her. "Would you like to come with me? I know you're *tired.*" He grinned smugly. "But we could have a *quiet* evening at my place, just watching TV. Mat is out of town, so I have the apartment to myself."

Lena silently counted to five before answering. "OK, let's see what your lair looks like."

The lair was reasonably neat for a place inhabited by two young men. On the way upstairs, Rob picked up the mail and went through it, separating the junk.

"I have a letter from my grandfather. He's the only member of my family who still writes letters using pen and paper. Now that I think of it, he's the only person I know who still does that." He waved a small envelope addressed to him.

"I know. A vanishing art... On the other hand, look at the bright side—all the trees that weren't cut, animals that weren't deprived of their habitat, indigenous tribes that weren't displaced."

"I see your point, but when I read this letter"—he pointed at the two densely filled pages he was holding—"I can relate to the person who wrote it in a different way than when I read a three line e-mail with no caps."

She smiled. "You have a nostalgic side!"

"I hope you still like me." He led her to the kitchen that had a small dining table, a bookshelf, and a wall-mounted TV. "What would you like to drink?"

"Tea would be good."

He turned on the electric kettle and put teabags into their mugs. "You know, my grandfather is the family's maverick. He never wanted to be a farmer, had big dreams when he was young."

"Did he pursue them?"

Rob shook his head. "He gave up on them to stay in the village and marry my grandmother. I think he spent his every waking hour ever since regretting that decision."

"But didn't he love your grandma? Didn't they raise kids together? Live a tranquil life in a beautiful setting?" Lena was inexplicably disturbed by Rob's comment on his grandfather's choice.

"They produced my dad, and then Grand-maman died of cancer. After that, Grand-papa had a pretty long bout of depression. I'm not sure about the specifics, but my father says Grand-papa became too cozy in his depressed state to get out there and face the world."

The kettle started beeping, and Rob interrupted his story to finish making their tea. He placed a steaming mug in front of Lena.

"Thank you. But, please, let me do this next time. I may suck at cooking, but I do know how to make tea and coffee. Isn't it enough that you bring me food and beverages when I'm at *La Bohème*?"

"At *La Bohème*, I'm *paid* to bring you food and beverages. So it doesn't count. Whereas here, I'm free to do as I please, and it pleases me to make you tea." Rob sat down next to Lena and added, "Since I can't very well go and hunt a saber-toothed tiger for you."

Lena raised her eyebrows.

"Because I *would*, you know, if you wanted one. Had they not been extinct." He wiped imaginary sweat off his forehead and blew out his cheeks. "Thank God."

Lena giggled. But she still wanted to hear the rest of his grandfather's story. "Did your Grandpa recover from his depression?"

"Kind of. After my dad took over the farm and married my mom, Grand-papa rented a little studio apartment and developed a routine that still keeps him going. He starts every day with a little exercise session."

"Good for him."

"He also makes sure to always have company for his meals. Usually, it's one of his bridge club or chess club buddies. Sometimes, my sister. Then he goes for a long walk in the afternoon. And then he goes over to my parents' place for dinner."

"This doesn't sound like an unhappy life to me," Lena said.

"It doesn't sound like it, but to him it is." Rob took a sip from his mug. "You see, he measures what he's got against his unfulfilled dreams. He wanted to go to college, travel the world, be a movie director... He didn't do any of that, hence the regret."

"He could've at least traveled once your dad was a grown man, couldn't he?"

"He was broke." Rob gave Lena a strange look, then said, "You see, when you're eighteen and you hitchhike your way around the world, you're an explorer. When you do it at sixty-eight, you're a tramp."

* * *

They spent the rest of the evening quietly in front of the TV, just as planned. The night turned out to be a lot less quiet.

In the morning, when they sat down to coffee and toast in the kitchen, Lena thought it was lucky that Mat was out of town. She would have been too embarrassed to face him now, considering all the commotion she and Rob made during the night.

"You bring me luck!" Rob interrupted her thoughts, turning his phone to Lena.

The company he'd interviewed with the day before had requested a follow-up interview.

"Who knew that having slept for only three hours before a job interview would work for me?" Then his tone became more serious. "This is my first follow-up, and I can't tell you how much it means to me."

"I'm so happy for you." She gave him a playful wink. "Must've been the jeans and server's shirt combo that did the trick."

"How about my superior intelligence and leadership potential? Anyway, I don't want to get my hopes too high yet. It's just a follow-up interview, not a job offer."

Lena was about to ask what and, especially, where the job in question was, when Rob clapped his hand to his forehead. "I almost forgot to tell you: I'll be visiting my family this weekend. Their farm is in a small village called Saint-Fontain, next to Besançon. Have you ever been there?"

"On the Swiss side of the Jura Mountains, yes, but not in French Jura."

"It's the July Fourteenth, so there'll be lots of festivities. My parents extended the invitation to Amanda and Mat. I asked if I could bring a third friend, and they said the more the merrier. So, if you don't have better plans for your weekend . . ."

Lena noted Rob's use of the term "friend" to describe her and it rattled her. On a rational level, she knew he couldn't possibly have referred to her as his girlfriend, considering that they had been together for only two days. She also knew that if she had to mention Rob to her dad, a "friend" would be the word she'd use. But to her dismay, insecurity was once again clouding her judgment, making her doubt herself and others. She was aware of it, yet she couldn't help it.

Rob misinterpreted her frown. "Lena, if you're not too excited about spending the weekend with a bunch of village folk, drinking and making merry, I won't blame you."

"No, that's not it. I'm actually quite curious to get a glimpse of French rural life. It was just unexpected." She fidgeted with her watch strap. "And ... you don't need to invite me just to be polite. I can have a perfectly fine weekend here or go visit friends in Geneva while you're away."

"But I *want* you to come," he said, taking her hand. "Once you know me better, you'll see I don't do things just to be polite. I'm inviting you because I'd like you to come with me to Saint-Fontain."

She searched his eyes.

"Besides, the Swiss side of Jura is a pale sham compared to the French side. Our forests are greener, our skies are bluer, and our mountains are taller."

"Watch out—I may bring my measuring tape."

"Does it mean you're coming?"

"I guess it does."

"Great! You'll see—it's going to be fun."

Lena nodded, trying to ignore her gut feeling that a weekend in Amanda's company was likely to be anything but fun.

* * *

My buzzing city is asleep—tight,
I've walked away into the dim—light,
I may be someone's mother, wife, child,—
But I remember only this—night.

Marina Tsvetaeva

NINE

Jura was beautiful, with its green forests, blue lakes, majestic mountains, and cobalt blue skies. The air was so pure Lena quickly became drunk on it. As they reached Saint-Fontain, she admired the village's central square. As any self-respecting heart of a *commune*, it had a town hall with the tricolor flapping in the wind, a church and a bakery. The streets went up and down, offering breathtaking views, and *every* house had red, pink or white geraniums in its windows.

Rob's parents and little sister greeted them on the porch, distributing warm hugs, handshakes, and kisses. His grandfather, who had picked them up from the station, positively glowed.

"Amanda, you've grown even prettier than the last time I saw you," Rob's mom said, making Amanda color with pleasure. "And you are Lena, right? My name is Rose Dumont—please call me Rose. This is my husband, Jacques, and my daughter Caroline. We are very pleased to meet you."

Her smile was warm and friendly, and Lena relaxed a little. "Thank you so much for inviting me. I hope I haven't caused any last-minute rearrangements."

"Nonsense. The farmhouse is big enough to host a football team—unlike the Parisian shoeboxes you're used to." Rose ushered everyone in. "I'll let you freshen up, and then you can join us for some refreshments in the garden."

She led the girls to their rooms, while Mat followed Rob to the opposite end of the house.

When Lena came back outside, she followed animated voices and laughter to the back of the house, where everyone was already seated around a big table under a sprawling tree. The garden was as pretty and well-kept as the house.

Rob pulled out a chair for her and filled her glass. "You've got to taste this. It's the best lemonade in the universe, produced here at the Dumont Farm by Madame Dumont herself."

Rob's dad pushed a bowl with blueberries toward Lena. "Taste these, too. Organically grown in this very garden. And the cheese cubes in that bowl on your left are cut from the best Comté in the region, produced by your humble servant."

He waited for Lena to taste the berries and the cheese and emit appreciative noises, then continued. "As I was telling your friends, tomorrow night we're having a big event in the village — the Firemen's Ball. Have you heard of it?"

Lena shook her head to humor him.

Monsieur Dumont's eyes lit up at the prospect of educating a foreigner about the French ways. "The Firemen's Ball is held annually all over France to celebrate the Bastille Day and to support local fire brigades. This year, we made a special effort. We're going to have a professional rock band from Lyon, and we're expecting the party to go on until the morning."

Amanda clapped her hands. "How exciting!"

"Jacques, why aren't you telling them there's also going to be madam the mayor making long speeches, Monsieur Pascal playing the accordion. and the Moreau children with their flutes?" Rob's grandfather asked, looking innocent.

Rob snorted, nearly spilling his lemonade.

"Aren't we supposed to buy tickets for the ball, Monsieur Dumont?" Amanda asked, skillfully diverting the conversation.

He cocked his head. "Do I look like someone who lets his guests pay for anything? As far as I know you and Mat are currently unemployed. I am told Lena is a fresh graduate as well, so I guess she, too, lives on pasta and water."

Lena braced herself for a mean remark from Amanda, but the latter took a pass for some unfathomable reason.

Monsieur Dumont turned to Rob. "And as for my son here, he'd rather depend on the crumbs those cheapskate Parisians leave him than return home, take his rightful place at the farm and have a future."

"Jacques, I think these young people are well aware of their financial situations and don't need you to remind them," Rose admonished her husband before turning to Amanda. "So, my dear, I hope you brought a cocktail dress for tomorrow night, so you don't end up having to wear one of my ancient prepregnancy gowns like last year?"

"And what a beautiful gown it was," Amanda said, and then added with a mysterious smile, "But yes, Rose, this time round I've come well prepared."

* * *

Madame the mayor's speech was longish but inspired. The Moreau children, however, turned out to be far worse than Lena had imagined. It was an ordeal to listen to them massacre one tune after another, encouraged by the sympathetic applause of the villagers. Lena began plotting how she could sneak out for a while, when the children finally exhausted themselves and bowed to the audience. The villagers gave them a particularly enthusiastic round of applause—no doubt, out of immense gratitude for having ended their torture.

Compared to the flute players, Monsieur Pascal's accordion wasn't half bad. As a matter of fact, Lena quite enjoyed the classic Piaf and Aznavour tunes Monsieur Pascal spiced up with a hint of rock 'n' roll.

Before the second part of the program began, the fire brigade's courtyard was rearranged for the rock band. The enthusiastic audience dimmed the lights, pushed chairs to the walls, and filled their stomachs with the requisite amount of beer.

"Have you heard of this band before?" Amanda asked Rob.

She wore a shimmering little black dress and strappy high heels. Her golden hair cascaded over her shoulders in artful coils. She was Parisian glamor personified.

Rob shook his head. "Nope. But then again, I haven't lived around here the past six years. My cousin tells me they're big in Lyon and the entire southeast."

The band arrived appropriately late, set their equipment up, and began to play. Their music was rocky, sexy, and loud. The youth raved along in total abandon, while the older audience made a huge dent in the local alcohol reserves.

The ball was undeniably a resounding success.

Just before their well-deserved break, the musicians struck a few incongruously romantic chords. Their bare-chested lead singer shouted into the microphone, "This one is for Lucie who has finally accepted to be Antoine's wife."

The announcement made, he launched into a cheesy slow song.

Among the general cheering and hip, hip hurrahs for the couple, Rob offered a hand to Lena and pulled her into his embrace. As they moved to the rhythm of the song, his strong arms held her close, and Lena felt so happy she wanted to cry.

When the song ended and the musicians retreated for a break, Lena and Rob joined Mat and Amanda who were standing in line for a drink. Amanda gave Lena a strange look, jealous and yet inexplicably triumphant, but Lena told herself not to read too much into it.

"I wish Jeanne were invited, too," Mat said wistfully as the four of them regrouped in a corner of the courtyard. "She would have loved these guys."

He made a sweeping gesture to point at the band and spilled his beer all around. Most of it landed on Lena.

"Shit! I'm so sorry . . ." He put his now empty can on the ground. "Let me go find some tissues."

Lena assessed the state of her dress. "I'd rather change into another outfit. And maybe take a quick shower." She smiled and patted Mat on the arm. "It's OK. I'll be back in twenty minutes or so."

She winked at Rob, spun around, and hurried to the farm house.

Fifteen minutes later, she strode back to the improvised concert hall, humming a tune under her breath. She felt extremely proud of the record speed at which she'd showered and changed. As she turned a corner, she noticed Rob leaning against a tree trunk, tapping something on his phone.

Ha! Didn't expect me to be back so soon, did you?

She began to tiptoe preparing to startle him with a boo, when his phone rang.

"I take it you received my text," he said. "Yeah, this time I'm definitively calling it off . . . Absolutely not. It's got nothing to do with her. I just found a good job, so I don't need to moonlight anymore."

Rob said good-bye and jogged back toward the courtyard. Lena stood motionless for a good quarter of an hour, racking her brain for an explanation to what she'd heard. Other than the obvious one. Finally, she shook off her stupor and walked over to the gang.

Rob grinned happily as she approached and took her hand. She looked away.

"So, have you heard the great news?" Amanda turned to Lena.

"No, she hasn't heard it yet. I was just about to tell her," Rob said.

Lena lifted her eyes to him and held her breath. *Please say something that would explain everything. That would mean I can still trust you.*

"Remember the follow-up interview I went to on Tuesday?" Rob asked. "They offered me a job. It's in the energy sector and it pays decently."

"So, you'll be able to get a loan and pay the school fees?" Mat asked with enthusiasm.

Lena forced herself to say, "Congratulations."

She struggled to remain standing as her mind grappled with the truth about Rob. That truth was so heavy it overwhelmed her, crushed her to the ground. There was no alternative explanation—he had kept passing on intel on her dad in spite of his promise, and he quit only because he'd gotten a well-paid job. Not because of her.

He pretended to like me so he could use me.

"Well, would you believe it?" Amanda jumped in. "They hired *me*, too! We were both invited for follow-up interviews and both got picked over two hundred other candidates."

Mat gave Amanda a pat on the shoulder. "Well done! What's the name of the company? Are their offices in Paris or in one of those horrible northern suburbs?"

Rob shot a look at Amanda as though to warn her against answering and said, "The company is called Energie NordSud. The main office is in Paris, but they're expanding very fast... Lena, the jobs Amanda and I were offered are in their newly opened office in Bangkok."

"Bangkok, Thailand." Amanda expounded. "The hottest city in the world both literally and figuratively, if you ask those in the know."

"When are you supposed to begin?" Mat asked.

Amanda could barely contain her excitement. "In a month. The company's relocation agent has already found a few apartments not far from the office. All much nicer and bigger than what I could ever afford in Paris with the same salary! I can't wait."

Amanda's last words were drowned out by the town hall clock striking twelve. The loud chimes muffled every other sound and reverberated in Lena's head. There it was, she thought, the proverbial stroke of midnight that turned her carriage into a pumpkin and her beautiful ball gown into rags. How symbolic.

"Will you excuse us, guys?" Rob said and took her hand, pulling her away from the others.

When they were a safe distance away, he curled his fingers under her chin, forcing her to look up at him. "Lena, I'm sorry I didn't tell you earlier. We received confirmation e-mails this morning, and I was planning on telling you tomorrow . . . I didn't want to spoil the festive mood."

She looked past him. There was no point in telling him she'd overheard his phone conversation. What would it change?

"We could have a long-distance relationship, like so many other couples our age . . . You could maybe even move to Bangkok. Why not spend your gap year in Thailand?" he asked excitedly.

She forced herself to speak. "I can't. The climate in Bangkok is bad for my heart condition."

He squeezed her hand. "I don't want whatever it is we have to end here. I really like you, Lena."

She gave a ragged sigh. "But it does end here, I'm afraid."

"Don't say that. We still have a month together in Paris, and after that we have the phone, e-mail and video chat. I'll visit you. I'm not planning on staying in Thailand forever. I'll return to France in a couple of years."

"I don't believe in long-distance relationships," she said.

"Lena, please." His voice cracked with emotion. "Will you please take some time to think about it? Yes, we haven't been together long, and yes, I haven't been on my best behavior. But I'm asking you to take a leap of faith now and trust me."

Suddenly it was too much.

"Trust you?" she hissed and jerked her hand free. "I'll never be able to trust you. I *heard* you talking to that guy earlier. I *know* you didn't stop spying on me after we made up. You lied to me!"

Rob swallowed hard. "I did. And I'm not proud of it. But I'm not lying to you now."

She gave him a hard look.

"Lena, listen to me, please. Even though I officially ended it only today, I haven't passed on any info since we made up. It's the truth."

"Of course. If you say so." Her voice was bitter, just like the taste in her mouth. "You also said you wouldn't cause any harm to my family. Well, turns out you have. I didn't want to tell you this, but I will now. Does the name Raduga sound familiar?" She narrowed her eyes at him.

He nodded slowly.

"They refused my dad's offer two days after shaking hands on it, just before they were to sign the papers. Apparently, some guy who'd studied with Raduga's founder turned up at the last minute and proposed a partnership on such great terms, the founder decided not to sell. My dad was livid."

"And what businessman wouldn't be in his place? But, at the end of the day, it's just a business transaction that didn't happen. Nothing more."

Lena shook her head. "It meant a lot to him. But that's not even the point. The point is, you *have* harmed us... God, I was such an idiot to think you were into me, to believe you were so keen for us to make up because you wanted to be with me. But you just wanted to get more intel."

He took a step toward her. "That's not true! Lena, I'm begging you—"

"Please. Enough."

She spun around and ran to the house where she locked herself up in her room and cried her heart out.

* * *

"Come on, Lena, pick up the phone," Rob repeated his silent prayer for the third time.

It wasn't working. When he had entered Lena's bedroom earlier in the morning, after having knocked and waited for what seemed like an eternity, all he found was a neatly made bed and a note on the bedside table.

> *To Rose and Jacques:*
>
> *Thank you so much for your hospitality and your kindness! I am sorry I had to leave without having said good-bye.*
>
> *With warmest wishes,*
>
> *Lena.*

Rob's first impulse was to jog to the train station, catch the first train to Paris, and go straight to Lena's place. But he thought better of it. Lena was too upset with him right now to even accept to talk to him. He should give her a bit of time to cool down. Besides, he was to spend two more days with his family whom he hadn't seen since Christmas. They would be terribly disappointed if he left now. He shoved his phone and Lena's note into his pocket and went down for breakfast.

Everyone was already at the table, including Grand-papa, Amanda, and Mat. Papa was making pancakes and Maman was pouring coffee. Amanda was laughing at someone's joke.

His sister Caro was the first to notice his arrival. "Rob's here! Hello, sleepy head! If you hadn't showed up in another five minutes, I was going to go to your room and tickle you out of bed."

"I'm glad you've assimilated my methods, little sis."

Rob sat down at the table. There was an empty seat next to his, with a plate, a mug, an embroidered napkin, and silverware. Rob braced himself for the inevitable question.

"Is your friend Lena awake yet?" Papa asked. "I don't want her pancakes to go cold."

"Lena had to leave earlier this morning. Something came up and she had to go. She left this for you." He handed Lena's note to his mother.

"What a shame. We've planned a fun day. We're going to hike to Besançon, have lunch there at Michel's Diner, and visit the crafts market, then hike back. Grand-papa is coming, too. Oh well." Suddenly, she frowned. "Amanda, Mat, you're coming, aren't you?"

"Most definitely," Amanda said.

Mat, whose mouth was full, nodded.

Rob could feel his mother's expectant gaze on him, so he looked up from his plate and said reassuringly, "Yes, of course, M'man."

"Good." Grand-papa looked relieved. "I still have lots of questions for you, boy. I don't want to regret having accepted this crazy hiking trip idea."

"You won't regret it, Grand-papa, I promise," Rob said.

The rest of the weekend was a haze of long conversations with his grandfather, pillow fights with Caro, and beers with his cousins and classmates. Mat had left after the Besançon hike, but Amanda stayed on. She took part in most of his activities, and more than one of his buddies told him with glee she was one gorgeous chick — and he, one lucky bastard — in spite of his assurances that they were just friends.

On the train ride back to Paris, Rob wished they still had exams so he could spend the whole trip revising and avoid Amanda's questions. As it was, all he could do was to try and look totally consumed by the book he was reading. Which, of course, didn't deter Amanda from asking questions.

"Is Lena upset about you going to Thailand?"

Rob pretended not to have heard her, but she pressed on. "Why did she leave so suddenly? Did she really have an emergency to attend to or was it about Thailand?"

He continued ignoring her.

She jabbed him with her elbow. "Rob, talk to me."

"It's not about Thailand," he barked. "If you really want to know, I've been an ass. And now she won't pick up the phone."

"Well, I'm sure you couldn't have done something so bad. She's overreacting." Amanda shrugged. "She should grow up."

Amanda means well, he told himself. He had no right to be angry with her. The only person he should be mad with was himself. He remembered how he had asked Lena to trust him. And how she'd replied she couldn't. If only he could make her see into his soul! If only she could read his mind, then she'd know he would never betray her again.

But that neat solution was beyond his reach.

"Poor Rob," Amanda said, bringing him back to the here and now. She patted his arm comfortingly. "She'll come around, like she did last time. Come on, stop looking like a beaten dog, and let's discuss our exciting first job! I'm so happy about it I feel like doing a jig every now and then."

Rob's anger subsided. Amanda was so enthusiastic, it was unfair of him to bring her down with his issues. He shut his book and asked, "So, what do we know about our soon-to-be home base from an economic and geopolitical point of view?"

Amanda blinked, unsure if he was being serious.

He smiled. "By which I mean its public transportation, rent levels, Internet speed, restaurants, and music scene."

When they got off the train in Paris, Rob didn't go to Lena's immediately. He needed to collect himself and prepare for the conversation. He had to bring her around, convince her he wasn't an unscrupulous liar. He had to impress upon her that he truly cared for her and was committed to make the long-distance relationship work.

A tall order for someone who'd never before begged a woman to be with him. Or begged anyone for anything, for that matter.

So he went to his place, unpacked, showered, and did some thinking. When he felt he was ready, he grabbed the neatly wrapped piece of *Comté* his mom had sent with him for Lena and walked out the door. On the *métro*, he recapped his arguments and rehearsed his speech. His spirits higher, he keyed in her intercom code and ran up the stairs. He knocked on her door. Then he knocked again, and again, and again, until his knuckles hurt.

* * *

The cabbie was a frail little woman who looked to be in her seventies. She was elegant, in an inimitable French way, and eccentric. She jumped out of the car and rushed to Lena as if she meant to pick up her huge suitcase. But halfway through, she slowed down giving Lena ample time to realize what was going on—and refuse to let an old lady carry her stuff.

Throughout the trip, she talked and gesticulated with both hands, leaving the steering wheel unattended in a cheerfully cavalier fashion. Her driving was jerky and way too fast. When she ran out of conversation (it was a long trip to the Charles de Gaulle Airport), she rummaged through her bottomless tote bag and retrieved a newspaper. She held it in front of her and began to read, first to herself then out loud for Lena's benefit. When the cab finally pulled up at Terminal 2E, Lena experienced the biggest moment of deliverance in her whole life.

After she boarded the plane and buckled her seatbelt, she felt grateful for that mad ride. Besides giving her the fright of her life, it shot her with enough adrenalin to take her mind off the subject of Rob and stall her budding depression.

She would get over him, she told herself for the hundredth time, just as she got over Gerhard. And Paris... well, Paris was the price to pay. Her favorite city was now tainted, its beauty no longer serene. It triggered memories that had become painful. She couldn't stay there anymore.

Lena closed her eyes and told herself again she was going to be fine. Leaving Geneva had worked remarkably well only a few months before. It had wiped out her feelings for Gerhard so utterly and completely that she concluded she must have finally found her cure for a broken heart. It was an age-old prescription worth more than all the modern antidepressants. Just six short words: *out of sight, out of mind.*

She arrived in Moscow with just one suitcase; the rest of her stuff would follow by freight. A connecting flight took her to Rostov, a town in the south of Russia where her mother had returned to after the divorce. Lena was going to see her, for the first time in twelve years, and she no longer cared that her dad would disapprove. She was twenty-three now, and he could no longer prevent her from visiting her mom.

Anastasia Malakhova was to meet her at the airport. Lena was a little nervous as she walked through the sliding doors to the arrivals area. She hoped they would recognize each other easily thanks to the photos they had exchanged every now and then.

"Lenochka, I'm here!" she heard a vaguely familiar voice.

Lena scanned the crowd until she spotted a tall, youthful woman calling to her. Her mother wore high heels, impeccably cut jeans and a stylish leather jacket, and looked exactly like she did in the photos.

"Come here, darling, and give me a hug." The older woman cooed and kissed Lena's cheek. "My God, how you've grown! Let me take a good look at you."

She circled around Lena, looking her up and down, making her feel increasingly uncomfortable.

"It's striking how much you resemble him," she finally said with a heavy sigh.

After an awkward pause, she shrugged, and flipped her golden mane. "Well, at least you are thin."

"Can we go to your place now, please?" Lena pleaded.

Her mother stopped the inspection and led the way.

Located in the center of town, Anastasia's apartment was spacious, light and professionally decorated. Given her mother's permanent lack of employment, Lena had no difficulty in deducing that the apartment and the expensive clothes were paid for by her dad. It was considerably harder to accept that the said apartment and clothes were the price of her motherless adolescence.

"My dear, I've missed you so much! I am so glad you decided to come visit me."

"I'm glad, too," Lena said.

Anastasia fidgeted with her ring. "Just make sure . . . that your father knows it was your idea, and I had nothing to do with it, OK?"

She smiled sweetly and patted the sofa next to her. "Come here and tell me about everything. What are your plans? Will you stay in Russia or go back to Paris? You must have a boyfriend. I'm dying to hear about him!"

Lena sat down in the sleek armchair on the other side of a designer coffee table. "I don't have a boyfriend at the moment."

"Well, I wouldn't worry more than necessary about that. I'm sure you'll find someone sooner or later. You're still young and you're an heiress."

Lena shifted uncomfortably but didn't say anything.

"Fortunately," Anastasia continued, "there are enough men to go around after the prettiest girls have had their pick."

She winked at Lena, then fingered her phone and held it out. "This is my boyfriend. Isn't he gorgeous? And you know what? He's crazy about me. Says he'd die if I left him. Ha! I should test if he really means it. Don't you think?"

Lena changed her ticket and flew to Moscow the following day. In spite of her complete failure to establish a connection or relate in the tiniest way to her mom, she was content about this visit. It helped her see certain things with more clarity. And it drove away the regret that had plagued her for so many years, giving way to a much less taxing emotion — disappointment.

* * *

Part III: This Funny Thing

Saying your name—a breath of my lungs,

Saying your name—a peppermint on my tongue.
A tiny movement of burning lips,
A single beat of bird's wings.
A glimpse of swallows headed south,
A clink of silver bells in my mouth.

A stone thrown into a pond
Will cry out the name that you are called.

Marina Tsvetaeva

TEN

A Slavic supremacist gang savagely beat up a Tajik immigrant and his four-year-old daughter. The man died on the spot. The girl was hospitalized. Even though at least eight people witnessed the incident, authorities do not appear to have much to go on.

Lena read about this incident in the morning paper and couldn't stop thinking about it ever since. She wasn't the only one, of course. Many of her fellow doctoral students and faculty at the Language and Translation Institute shared her incomprehension and outrage. People shuddered at the horror of the attack, cringed at the brutality of the skinheads and worried about the little girl. Strangely, no one condemned the witnesses who had been close enough to see the crime but did nothing to intervene or help the police find the attackers.

As she walked home from the institute, Lena thought this incident was an extreme form of her home city's ugliest side—its hostility toward the outsiders. Not the rich tourists who bought overpriced souvenirs and ate in expensive restaurants, but the scruffier migrant workers and refugees.

She glanced at the unusually blue September sky, then at her watch, and made a detour to the park. As she treaded on the colorful carpet of fallen leaves, her dark thoughts began to fade away. Soon enough, she lost herself in the childish joy of ruffling the dry leaves with her feet and listening to their soft rustle.

She filled her lungs with air and remembered she had a reason for celebrating today. This morning, before she opened the newspaper, she had realized she could no longer picture the exact shade of Rob's eyes.

At first, she felt shocked and bereft, but then it hit her that this could be the first sign of healing. Since her return to Moscow two months ago, she'd done everything in her power to help the out-of-sight cure do its magic. She had deleted all Rob's photos, avoided social media, and asked Jeanne not to talk about him in her e-mails. But until now, she'd been seeing no results.

Lena reached a five-story building off Tverskaya where she had a small apartment. The location was perfect and within walking distance from both her father's place and her school. Plus it eliminated the need to drive — or be driven around — in Moscow's crazy traffic.

As soon as she walked in, she opened her e-mail to see if she had a reply about the abstract she'd submitted to a conference organizer. With a gasp, she stood up and walked over to the window. She remained there for a few moments, staring at the traffic and counting to ten, then to twenty, then to thirty. When she reached one hundred, she returned to her desk and opened Rob's e-mail.

Hi Lena,

It's been a while since we last talked, and that conversation didn't end well. When I returned to Paris and didn't find you at your place, Jeanne told me you'd left earlier that day to return to Moscow. She also conveyed your request not to contact you, to let you move on.

I'm not a stalker, so when a girl says she's through with me, I respect her decision. Which is why I followed your instructions and let you be. But here's the thing. The more I think about how I behaved over the summer, the more ashamed I am of myself.

I can live with shame. What I can't live with is knowing that I hurt you and didn't tell you how sorry I was, didn't beg you to forgive me. What prevents me from sleeping at night is knowing that you're thinking badly of me.

That's why I'm writing to you now — to say what I should've said during the firemen's ball, what I've said in my head a hundred times. Lena, I'm so very sorry. I wish I had words to convey how much I regret the whole spying business, and, most of all, that I broke my promise and lied to you.

I don't know if you can find it in your heart to forgive me, but I pray to God that you will. And I also pray you'll accept to remain in my life, at least as a friend.

All the best,

Rob

Lena reread Rob's e-mail five more times. Could she forgive him? Eventually, yes. Despite his betrayal, she knew he hadn't meant to hurt her. He'd behaved in a stupid and selfish way. He'd convinced himself that what he was doing wasn't so bad, and downplayed the damage his actions could cause. He'd been irresponsible, but not mean.

So yes, she could find it in heart to forgive him. But she couldn't trust him. Everything she knew about him told her he could hurt her again. He *would* hurt her again. Without meaning to, of course. And when that happened, he might shatter her heart into too many small pieces to reassemble.

And that was why she couldn't let him back into her life. She had torn herself from him in one clean cut, like a surgeon, so that she'd have a better chance to heal. But her wound was still raw. She needed a lot more time before she could envisage even friendship with him.

And by then he'd probably have forgotten she existed.

* * *

Lena made some coffee and sank into the cushy couch. She looked around. The apartment was now nicely furnished, trendy—and impersonal. Just as impersonal as it had been four months ago when she moved in. *Oh well.*

She opened her e-mail and read Jeanne's typically short note.

> *Last night I had an epiphany and discovered my true calling. I want to be a bartender/proprietor. Preferably of La Bohème.*

Lena immediately shot her a reply.

> *How exciting! But what made you see the light? And is there any indication Pierre would want to make you a bartender and then sell the place to you? Please tell me more.*

As soon as her note hit the cyberspace, Lena shut the laptop. She wasn't going to work on her paper or translations. She had established a rule for herself—Saturdays were for relaxing, which was why she was still in her pajamas. The rest of the week she worked almost around the clock, but she didn't want all work and no play to turn her into a bore.

The problem with her seemingly sage rule was that it created a space unoccupied by purposeful activity. A space in which she was alone with her moleskin notebook. A dangerous, murky space in which strange things happened . . . Like now. Feeling as if she were a zombie, Lena grabbed a pen and began sketching portraits of an ancient god—a painfully familiar ancient god. After she filled several pages with drawings en face and in profile, she traced her finger over each line and then tore them into tiny pieces. Next, she began to decorate a blank page with the same tightly strung three-letter word.

Rob, Rob, Rob, Rob, Rob, Rob, Rob, Rob

She couldn't help it and she couldn't stop. She had the impression her hand was possessed, its neural pathways diverted from her brain and plugged into her silly defective heart. After she was done writing and tearing up, she chastised herself and made another useless promise to never do it again.

To distract herself, she turned on the TV. The eleven o'clock news segment was just beginning, which reminded her to stay close to the phone. Dmitry said he'd call between eleven and eleven fifteen, and Lena expected him to call in exactly that interval. The phone rang at eleven oh-three.

"Hello, my dear. I've got great news. I managed to get us front row tickets to the *Swan Lake* at Bolshoi."

"No kidding? The new *stellar* interpretation everyone is raving about? How on earth did you accomplish that feat?"

"I'm not telling. But I'm happy you seem pleased."

"I'm over the moon! Thank you so much, Dmitry, I really appreciate it. When is the show?"

"It's tonight. I hope you don't have other plans, but if you do, you shouldn't feel—"

"I don't have any plans, and even if I did, I would cancel them in a blink. When and where shall we meet?"

"I'll pick you up at six o'clock at your place, so we can grab a quick dinner before the performance. How does that sound?"

"Perfect."

A perfect night with a perfect man, she told herself after she hung up.

Dmitry *was* perfect, in every way that Rob wasn't. Unlike Rob, who was just beginning to build a career, Dmitry was already established. He was a well-respected CPA. Her father's chief accountant, as it happened. He owned a cozy apartment and drove a nice car. He was crazy about literature. He was honest and staid.

Dmitry was also always supportive, even protective of her, but without a trace of machismo. He was keen to know every detail about her work and her workplace, including the names of her colleagues and professors. If she didn't feel like opening her calendar, she could just ask him about her schedule. He knew it better than she did.

When anyone — including Anton and Anna — teased her, she knew she could count on his swift intervention to defend her or to divert the discussion. Which always reminded her of how Rob had let Amanda bully her throughout their Nice weekend without attempting to protect her. He had acted like it wasn't his business to speak up on her behalf. Which would have been fine, had she not been under such a relentlessly taunting assault.

Dmitry would have said something, done something or just ... carried her away. He wouldn't have let her fend for herself.

He was perfect.

* * *

They had first met at Anton and Anna's wedding shortly after Lena's return to Moscow. They had a pleasant conversation and danced together a little. Lena enjoyed Dmitry's quiet intelligence and his undisguised admiration. She forgot about his existence the following day.

She crossed paths with him again three months later. Her stepmother, Anna, who was full of energy in spite of being on the verge of giving birth, had learned that the Moscow City was planning to shut down one of the oldest Children's Arts and Crafts Centers. The center had survived for the past few years mainly on the unflagging enthusiasm of its staff. But it had reached the degree of squalor that endangered the children. The site hadn't been renovated since the Soviet days, when it was called a Young Pioneer House.

During a family dinner one evening Anna banged the table with her fist and told Anton and Lena, "Shut down the center? The hell they will. It's the place where I learned how to make a teddy bear from fabric scraps and dance the *kazachok*. I fell in love with Ray Bradbury's stories in its library..."

She stared at the wall for a few moments, her eyes vacant, and then blinked. "I don't care if the mayor is hell-bent on closing it. I won't let it happen." She winked at Lena and added, "I didn't marry a tycoon for nothing."

"Is that so?" Anton smiled. "Here I was deluding myself that you married me because you were madly in love with me."

"That, too. But don't you think your money is begging for a noble outlet, such as saving a children's art center? Besides, I'm sure your gifted accountants can figure out how to deduct most of it from your taxes."

Anton put his arm around his wife's shoulders. "Anna, my love, you always manage to get me to do your bidding, don't you?"

"Who? Me? I wouldn't dream of it," Anna said.

Anton's eyes fell on his wife's prominent belly. "Well, as long as it's to make children happy . . ." He gave Anna a gentle peck on the cheek. "Do your worst. But promise me to take it easy and not let your enthusiasm interfere with our baby's plans."

Shortly after that conversation Anton donated a substantial sum of money to the center, and Anna organized a fundraiser at a trendy downtown restaurant to collect the remaining capital required for the complete renovation of the building.

It was at that banquet that Lena met with Dmitry for the second time. He took a seat across from her at the long table overflowing with beautifully presented food.

"Lena!" He beamed. "What a pleasure to see you again. You look great."

Lena smiled politely. "Hello. It's nice to see you, too."

Then her smile broadened as she recognized the enthusiastic gentleman. He was the nice accountant from the wedding. If only she could remember his name . . .

Right on cue, he held out his hand. "My name is Dmitry, just in case you were wondering. I've been hoping for a chance of seeing you again ever since we met at Anton's wedding."

Lena didn't know what to say. She had noticed how Dmitry was looking at her, but she found his words a little too forward. She feared the evening was going to be awkward. To her surprise, it turned out to be the opposite. After having unequivocally signaled his interest, Dmitry steered the conversation to completely different subjects ranging from the Russian oligarchs' tentative forays into arts patronage to a comparison of contemporary Russian and Japanese novels.

He was thirty-five, a grown man—a real adult—to her twenty-three. He was well-dressed and good-looking. He wasn't funny or charismatic, but he had impressive erudition, impeccable manners, and that look of adoring wonder that appeared on his face every time he glanced at her.

When the banquet was over, Lena realized she wanted to stay and continue talking to Dmitry. And when he asked if she'd like to visit an expressionist exhibit with him next week, she accepted without hesitation.

* * *

Rob had just finished a complicated financial report when Amanda walked into his office. She leaned against the wall, crossing her arms over her chest. "Shouldn't we be booking our tickets to France? The longer we wait the more expensive they'll get — soon it'll be Christmastime, in case you've forgotten."

Rob shuffled his papers. "I booked my trip this morning."

"What? And you didn't think to tell me? We could have flown together. Now we'll probably end up on different flights!"

"We *will* end up on different flights, I'm afraid." He ran his hand through his hair. "I'm flying with Aeroflot with a twelve-hour stopover in Moscow."

Amanda smirked. "Oh, I see. You must have found a *really* good deal with Aeroflot to accept such a long stopover when you only have ten days of vacation."

"Amanda, I —"

"It's OK, Rob. I get it. You still aren't over Lena, even though she made her position abundantly clear. Are you hoping for a chance run-in while you're in Moscow? It's a small town, after all. Just a dozen million people, give or take a million."

"Jeanne gave me both her home and her school addresses." Rob offered Amanda a lopsided smile. "You think I'm pathetic, don't you? I can't blame you—I *am* pathetic. I'd promised myself to leave her in peace. And yet... here I am, planning to stalk her in Moscow."

Amanda didn't contradict his bitter comment.

He shook his head, as if baffled by his own behavior. "But this time will be the last. Once I've found Lena, I'll do everything I can to sway her. I'll use my *irresistible* charm—it's worked on her before. And if she still won't change her mind, I'll give up on her for good."

Amanda gave him a tired look and turned to leave. She stopped in the doorway and spun around. "You know, Rob, the good thing about this whole Lena debacle is that you've shown a level of constancy I've rarely seen in a man. So no, I don't think you're pathetic."

As she stepped out of Rob's office, she added without turning around, "Let me know how it went, Romeo."

It was three o'clock when Rob finally arrived at Lena's home address, but she wasn't there. So he hurried to her school and waited in the large lobby close to the main entrance. He didn't want to go looking for her inside, afraid she might leave the building in the meantime. He hadn't been to Moscow since student summer camp four years ago, but he'd ascertained that the charming teahouse he'd found at the time was still in business. It wasn't very far, and he could take Lena there for pancakes and a cup of warm chai.

A little after four o'clock he spotted Lena rushing down the central staircase that led to the lobby, a coat folded over her arm, a woolen hat on her head and a big smile on her face.

He grinned and took a step forward. But his smile died and he stopped in his tracks when Lena halted in front of a guy in a suit, standing at the foot of the staircase. The Suit kissed her on the mouth and helped her into her coat. Then he took her hand and led her out of the building.

Rob remained where he was with his jaw clenched while his mind processed the images. Ten minutes later, he walked out of the building. It was getting dark. No longer warmed up by anticipation, Rob could now fully appreciate how freaking cold Moscow was in the middle of winter. The wind filled his eyes with tears that instantly turned into tiny icicles attached to his lashes. He rubbed them off with the back of his hand, took a deep breath of icy air that burned his lungs, and hailed a cab to take him back to the airport.

During their customary after-work drink two weeks later in Bangkok, he filled Amanda in on his missed meet.

"And thus ends my sad tale of foolhardiness and frozen ass. From now on, you are officially authorized to punch me in the face if I ever mention Lena's name again. Oops, I just did. Go on, punch me!"

"I didn't know you were such a drama queen." Amanda laughed, waved at the waiter, and ordered two vodka lemons.

When he raised an eyebrow at her unusual choice, she said with a playful smile, "Seemed appropriate to mark the end of your Russian affair."

A few more vodka lemons later, Amanda declared she was ready to turn in. As it was past midnight, Rob insisted on walking her home.

"You want to come up for a coffee?" she asked just as he was about to leave.

"Sure, why not?"

But he didn't get any coffee, not until the next morning. Once inside her apartment, Amanda began to unbutton her shirt. Rob bent his head and kissed her. She tasted of lemon and vodka.

Amanda put her hands on his chest and leaned away a few inches. "You don't have to . . . continue this, if you don't want to do."

"Oh, but I want to."

He kissed her long neck, admiring its elegance. She was beautiful. She'd always been there for him. She knew him and understood him like no one else.

This was bound to be as good as their friendship.

* * *

In this relentless, laughing city,
I dream of meadows stretching far,
Till laughter fades, and I am giddy
With pain, the escort of my heart.

Marina Tsvetaeva

ELEVEN

"May I also suggest this adorable sleep set that matches with the vests you've picked?" The shop assistant held an apple green item in front of Lena.

"It's lovely. I'll take it."

"And how about this wool cardigan? Cardigans are a must-have for winter babies."

Lena ran a gentle hand over the tiny garment. It was soft and heart-wrenchingly small. "Are you sure it will fit?"

"Our sizes are on the large side, so it will definitely fit."

Lena purchased the items and continued her Christmas shopping. She had already bought a ridiculous amount of presents for Katia, her newborn half-sister. The little thing had arrived a week ago—red-faced, helpless, and adorable. Anton spent all his free time with her, looking acutely happy. Anna was swinging between depressed and ecstatic every half hour or so. Lena had never seen her so moody before.

She walked into a tie shop where she often bought her father his colorful hand-sewn silk ties—the only touch of personality he allowed in his sober business attires. When Lena was younger, she would beg him to wear brighter clothes, but to no avail. Anton's aversion to color had been a mystery to her until three years ago, when she got him a fashionably lilac shirt for his birthday. Two weeks later, she spotted that shirt on his driver. She got upset. That was when Anton asked her to follow him into his walnut and glass walk-in closet.

"Let me show you something." He opened a sliding door at the farthest end of the closet and yanked a hanging garment bag down from the rail.

"Daughter mine," he said as he uncovered a hideous jungle green double-breasted blazer. "You won't remember the nineties—you were too little—but this is what I used to wear back then, like every other wannabe oligarch in Russia. I had more blazers like this one, in different colors."

Lena eyed the jacket. "It's absolutely dreadful. And it looks like it's made of polyester."

"That's because it *is* made of polyester."

"Wow," Lena said.

"When I had my first meeting with international partners, who were all dressed in gray wool, I felt so self-conscious that I made a crappy deal that I regretted the moment we signed the papers. I've never worn color since."

"So why have you kept it during all these years?"

"As a reminder." Anton pulled the garment bag over the blazer and turned to Lena with a mischievous sparkle in his eyes. "Or maybe because I secretly still love it and wear it when no one can see me."

Lena giggled.

Anton said in a more serious tone, "It has to do with who I am. No amount of money can change the fact that I'm a frugal factory worker's son. So I simply can't bring myself to throw away a piece of clothing that isn't worn out."

Anton returned the blazer to its remote corner and drew the closet door shut. "Well, now my dirty little secret is out of the closet, so to speak. But I count on you, Lena, not to reveal it to a living soul."

"Your secret is safe with me . . . but there's a price. I'm going to continue buying you colorful ties, and you'll wear them."

Anton sighed in resignation. "It's a deal. But only the ties. Don't even think about getting me red socks for Father's Day."

Ever since the "closet episode", Lena had respected Anton's sartorial wishes to the letter. If she bought him clothing, it was monochrome. The only the notable exception were the ties. This time she picked vermillion red and magenta. She was about to head to the cashier when it dawned on her that she should also buy something for Dmitry. That's what young women did at Christmastime—they bought presents for their boyfriends.

After Anna's memorable fundraiser, Lena and Dmitry saw each other almost every day. Dmitry was conducting an old-fashioned unhurried kind of courtship that Lena had believed extinct in the twenty-first century. They had spent a month filled with outings, get-togethers and excursions before she'd admitted to herself these were *dates*. He hadn't made the slightest attempt to spend the night with her.

They were past the hand-holding and kissing milestones, though. And a couple of days ago Dmitry stroked Lena's cheek in a way she could only describe as erotically charged. It happened when she read him her favorite Pasternak poem. Why on earth she couldn't bring herself to read her translations to him, Lena couldn't fathom. Dmitry's French was good and his critiques of her academic writing insightful.

The only thing that annoyed her was that Anton wasn't pleased with their relationship. When she asked him why, he initially brought up their age difference. But he stopped after she remarked that he wasn't the ideal person to lecture her on the subject, what with him being happily married to a woman twelve years his junior. So now, he'd just say that Dmitry was wrong for Lena. He couldn't specify why or how — just wrong.

Which was exasperating because the way she looked at it, Dmitry was uniquely right for her. A solid, reliable and open-minded man, he practiced kung fu and meditation. He was a *good* person. He made her feel magnanimous and beautiful — a balm for her bruised heart.

He would cherish her. He would protect her from the world.

* * *

Lena woke up to the ring of her phone that felt like a fire alarm blaring inside her head. She fumbled for her watch—it was past noon. Her mouth was dry and her head was pounding. She had spent the previous night in the company of her father, Anna, and a few other family members and friends celebrating the New Year and Anna's birthday, which fell on January first. Lena had enjoyed herself and had returned to her apartment at three in the morning—an hour Anton would have strongly disapproved of, had she not been partying with him.

She scrambled to her desk and picked up the phone. Her hello came out so husky it was hardly audible.

"Hi, darling, are you all right?"

Lena cleared her throat. "I'm fine—just had too much to drink last night, I guess."

"I see," Dmitry said with slight edge in his voice.

He had told Lena several times he didn't expect to be invited to Anna's birthday party. And he'd made other plans for New Year's Eve, anyway.

"Did I wake you up?" he asked, his voice more cheerful.

"Yes, but it's OK. I don't like getting up late, it ruins the whole day for me."

"Listen, how about I get some fresh croissants and then make us an omelet. We can have an improvised brunch. Do you have any eggs?"

Lena smiled. Dmitry didn't do improvised, which was why his efforts to make it sound as though the idea had just occurred to him were so endearing.

"Yes, I'm sure I have eggs, and butter, too. I may even find some milk. So let's see how good your omelets are."

"I'll be there in forty-five minutes."

Lena would bet anything in the world that he would be, too.

When he arrived, she was fully awake and presentable. He handed her the bag with croissants, went straight to the kitchen, and washed his hands. Turned out his omelets were really good, or maybe Lena was really hungry. She finished her serving in record time and reached for a croissant.

Dmitry took much longer to finish his serving. He was suspiciously quiet and preoccupied. But before Lena could ask what was bothering him, he rummaged in the pockets of his jacket and placed a small black box in front of Lena.

She swallowed hard and stared at the box. *It couldn't be . . .*

"Lena," he said, looking down at his plate. "I . . . I'm going to say this quickly, because it isn't easy." He paused to take a long breath.

Her muscles tensed. She didn't want him to say it. She wasn't ready for him to say it. She'd been expecting Dmitry to make a move to deepen their relationship, but this wasn't exactly the kind of move she had anticipated. And yet . . . how could it be otherwise? Dmitry was so old-fashioned and chivalrous about the whole courtship thing. He probably felt he couldn't sleep with her without having proposed first.

He looked up at her. "I adore you. You are all I've ever dreamed of in a woman. Will you be my wife?"

He opened the box that contained an expensive-looking engagement ring.

"Are you sure about this?" she asked. "Shouldn't we . . . get to know each other better before contemplating marriage?"

"Lena, I'm thirty-five years old, and I've had enough relationships in the past to know what I'm doing. If you feel you need more time, then by all means, take as much time as you need before giving me your answer."

She nodded.

"I just want you to know where you stand with me." He shut the box, put it into Lena's hand, and closed her fingers around it. "Will you keep this while you're considering my proposal?"

She nodded once more.

After he left, Lena began to pace her living room, the velvet-covered box burning her balled up hand. She had been comfortable going out with Dmitry, holding hands with him, even kissing him. She thought she was ready for more, but not so much more. And it wasn't because she doubted he was her Mr. Right. She didn't. It was because she still hadn't been able to purge her heart of her Mr. Wrong.

It had now been five months since she last saw Rob, but he continued to burst into her thoughts every day, unannounced, and usually at most inconvenient times. And each time, she needed all her cool and composure to clear the bittersweet poison that lingered on her tongue after those incursions.

* * *

"Wow, Lena!" Anna sat down and blinked a few times, processing the news. "You're still very young. You need to think about this seriously and take your sweet time."

"That's my intention, but it won't change the fact that Dmitry—"

"Yes, yes, Dmitry may be the perfect man, but you need to be sure he's perfect *for you*." Anna gently wiped Katia's mouth and turned back to Lena. "Did you run the 'last specimen test' on him?"

"Um, I'm not sure I know what that is."

"So, you didn't then. I knew it." Anna shook her head and slid her chair closer to Lena. "My dear, you don't want to marry someone without having run this test, believe me. It's vital."

"OK . . . if you say so. But since I have no clue as to what it is, will you save me from my ignorance?" Lena grinned, expecting a good laugh.

Anna smiled back and rolled up her sleeves. "Here goes. Close your eyes and imagine that humanity is about to be wiped out."

Lena closed her eyes as instructed. "What's causing Armageddon?"

"Nasty aliens. Or an evil genius. It doesn't matter. What matters is that you, Lena, have been marked to be spared."

Lena rubbed her hands. "Because I have secret superpowers?"

"No, your number just came up randomly. But that doesn't matter either. What matters is that you're allowed to save one man—only one—by marrying him."

Lena opened her eyes and gave her stepmother a quizzical look. "Anna, where are you going with this?"

"Stay focused and keep your eyes shut please. Now imagine that the man you'll choose to marry will become the last remaining specimen of the human male on this planet. No alternative. No options. No escape. Till death do you part. Amen."

Lena's smile began to fade. She wasn't finding Anna's extravagant scenario as funny as she had expected. She opened her eyes and glanced at Anna.

The older woman was no longer smiling, either. "What I'm trying to get you to determine is whether you're prepared to renounce all those *other* men for Dmitry."

"There are no *other* men. I'm not seeing anyone else," Lena said, pretending to have misunderstood.

"Of course you aren't." Anna patted Lena's hand. "What I mean is the *possibility* of other men."

Anna gave Lena an expressive look that said, *You know what I mean. And I know that you know.*

"Listen to me, honey. After you're married, there'll be situations in your life when you'll meet someone great. Someone handsome, clever, funny. Someone who's not your husband."

Anna looked straight into Lena's eyes, daring her to imagine that guy. "A square-jawed alpha male with gray eyes?"

"Not impressed," Lena said impishly.

"OK, then a dark, brooding beta. Whatever floats your boat, baby. Hot guys come in different shapes and at most unexpected times. Maybe you'll meet him through work, maybe through friends."

When Lena began to bite her nails, Anna threw her hands up. "I'm not being mean. This kind of stuff does happen in life, Lena. All the time. And what if that hunk developed a crush on you? Would you be prepared to forgo him for Dmitry? Would you be able not to flirt with him, not to encourage him, never to give him the slightest chance?"

Somehow, without any conscious decision on Lena's part, the "hunk" morphed into Rob. And she found herself wondering. Would she indeed?

Anna continued her onslaught. "Would you keep asking yourself what it could be like with him? Are you in a place with Dmitry where there isn't a shadow of a doubt in your mind that you'd give up on this other guy without hesitation and without regret?"

"I don't know. Is it at all possible to be sure about this?" Lena asked honestly.

"Yes, Lena, it is. I was sure when I married your dad. I still am," Anna said with a soft smile. "Can you think of someone in your past, an ex or an unrequited flame, who you'd feel that way about?"

The question gave Lena pause because the answer that formed in her mind immediately was yes. Yes, she could think of someone in her past who would have been enough, for whom she would have given up all other options without hesitation or regret.

Had he not betrayed her trust. Had she not cut him off to protect herself from heartbreak.

"Nope. Can't think of anyone," she finally said and reached over to take Katia in her arms.

"Anyway," she told the little girl, kissing her hamster cheeks and breathing in her ambrosial baby essence. "If those wicked aliens really gave me the power to save a life, it would be yours, my angel, without a shadow of a doubt."

That night Lena phoned Jeanne. She was still planning to give Dmitry's proposal serious consideration, but after having talked to Anna, she needed to know if Rob was still single. She knew that even if he was, it wouldn't mean he still wanted to be with her. It wouldn't mean she'd give him a second chance. It wouldn't mean anything at all... and yet, it suddenly became vital that she know.

Jeanne didn't wait for Lena to finish stammering her question. "He's with Amanda now. I saw it on her recent profile update. I'm sorry, Lena."

"There's nothing to be sorry about. She's a much better match for him than I could ever be."

* * *

As soon as she was married, Lena lifted her Facebook moratorium and posted a few wedding pictures. Congratulations and good wishes began to arrive within minutes of her update. She checked them hourly until she read a short note from Rob wishing her all the happiness she deserved.

She replied.

> *Thank you, and all the best.*

Pepe sent her a warm message full of good wishes and eccentric advice on married life. He ended it with a postscript.

> *After comparing your husband to you know who, I can only assume he must compensate in OTHER areas. Mind you, it will have to be a BIG compensation.*

Jeanne messaged her too.

> *This Dmitry of yours looks like a decent chap. I hope he can make you happy.*

It was a short note, even for Jeanne. Lena wondered if her friend still thought she had made a mistake last summer by running away. She typed her reply.

I have no doubt Dmitry will make me happy. He's the kindest, smartest, and gentlest person I've ever met. Besides, we are from the same country, same city. We have the same mother tongue, we share the same cultural references, love the same movie quotes. I never have to explain anything to him — he just gets it. He gets me.

She pushed send and sat back in her chair. She truly meant every word she had written to Jeanne . . . So why couldn't she shake the feeling that it wasn't Jeanne she was trying to convince?

* * *

You're brave and you're noble, your voice is a spring
Caressing a mountain side.
Shake off this enthrallment, forget how I sing,
Go back to your beautiful bride!
I'm Eva, a witch, dark and shameless and winged —
Your fantasy . . . Wake up, oh knight!

Marina Tsvetaeva

TWELVE

"Lena, stay. Watch this with me." Dmitry grabbed her hand as she stood up from the couch.

"I have a paper to finish."

"Oh come on, you work too much! You did your PhD in two years—can't you relax a little now? Besides, *Going Places* is a great movie. One of the best French films of all times."

"I know. I've seen it."

"Then watch it again with me." Dmitry made a pleading face. "You can translate for me."

"You don't need translation. Your French is excellent."

"But not as good as yours. I'm lost when they talk too fast or use too much slang."

Lena smiled apologetically and pulled her hand away. "I'm sorry, but I really have to finish that paper. Rain check?"

She turned and strode out of the living room, wincing from guilt as she walked. How could she explain to Dmitry that looking at the young male leads in this cult seventies movie was simply unbearable? Watching them, or watching any French male actor for that matter, wasn't just troubling — it was painful.

They all still reminded her of Rob.

Unfortunately for her, Dmitry liked French movies and preferred to see them in the original language.

Even more unfortunate, her telling him some time ago she didn't enjoy French cinema had completely backfired. Dmitry now felt it was his duty to help her gain an appreciation through maximum exposure. *Et voilà* — she was trapped. Because there was no way she could reveal to him the reason why she didn't like to watch French films.

Lena smirked. When exactly did she turn into this mysterious, aloof person? When did she become a woman with a secret? And not just any silly secret, but a big scary skeleton in the cupboard that she couldn't show to anyone, not even Jeanne.

She admired and respected her husband. She counted on him. She loved him—in a grateful, appreciative way. Her only complaints after two years of marriage were that he sometimes crowded her and other times bored her.

But this wasn't her secret.

Lena's shame was to still have feelings for the guy whom she'd known for only a few months nearly three years ago. That guy regularly made wild, passionate love to her in her dreams. And when she woke up in the middle of the night, hot and aroused, she swore she could taste him on her lips and smell his scent . . . She would lie still so she wouldn't wake Dmitry up and ask herself questions to which she had no answer.

Why was it that the imaginary Rob's caresses affected her more than her real-life husband's touch? Why couldn't she feel for this wonderful man a fraction of what she still felt for Rob? Why did her "out of sight" cure that had worked so well on Gerhard fail so completely this time?

* * *

Rob was seriously annoyed. For the first time since starting their company a year ago, he and Patrick—a former Energie NordSud colleague and now his business partner—had run into a hurdle they couldn't solve. It was a technical problem, and a minor one at that. But it could bring their whole enterprise down by delaying the shipment of their first large-scale order of recycled carbon chairs.

The contract they'd signed with the client was ultra-specific on the delivery date. Delay equaled cancellation, which meant a huge loss and a possible bankruptcy for the start-up. The irony of it all was that they were just about to become profitable. Besides, he knew exactly what had gone wrong and how it could be fixed. But they lacked the resources to fix it fast enough to stay on schedule.

A minor miracle was required, which was the reason Amanda, Rob, and Patrick had gathered at Rob's to brainstorm a way out of the crisis.

"I don't understand how neither of us saw this coming, in spite of our careful contingency planning," Patrick said, dropping onto the couch.

"How about we postpone analyzing it until we've fixed it?" Rob handed a printout to Patrick and Amanda. "It's a list of companies that should be able to repair our equipment."

"Have you contacted any of them yet?" Amanda asked.

"All the ones I could reach. I put the results in the comments column." Rob scanned his own copy. "Basically, they are either unavailable within our timeline or too expensive for us. I'll make a second round of calls, but I'm not holding my breath."

Patrick looked up from his copy. "Wait a second. Five or six years ago, Energie NordSud had a similar issue, and my then manager hired these Russian guys . . . what were they called?"

He paused, stared at the wall, and scratched his head. "I remember we were astonished at how quickly they got us sorted. I'm not sure they still exist or how much they charge these days, but why not try calling them?"

"Sure, if you can remember their name," Rob said.

Patrick scratched his head again and closed his eyes. "I have it! Hi-tech Wizards — that's what they're called. The name sounds a bit silly, but they were good."

Rob Googled them on the spot and dialed the number on their contact page. "You never know. Companies often work 24-7 in countries like Russia."

Someone at the other end of the line picked up, and Rob went on to talk in an increasingly confident Russian for over thirty minutes. When he hung up, two pairs of eyes stared at him expectantly.

"This might work. But don't get too excited yet. They want me to fly our faulty piece to them and explain every detail. I think they have an idea on how to deal with that sort of glitch."

Patrick jumped up from the couch, nearly shaking with excitement. "How fast can they fix it and how much are they asking?"

Amanda smoothed her hair. "Do you absolutely need to go there?"

"According to the Wizards, if it is what they think it is, they can fix it within four days. They'll charge between €3,000 and €5,000, depending on the extent of the repair, but no more than €5,000," Rob said.

"It's still ten times cheaper than the lowest estimate we got from anyone else!" Patrick nearly shouted in excitement, not in the least because he'd been the one to suggest the Wizards. "We can afford them."

Amanda cleared her throat. "You didn't answer my question, Rob. Why do you need to go there?"

"Because they won't come to us, and because I'm the only one here who can speak Russian."

Amanda gave Rob a hard look, but didn't say anything.

"How soon can you travel?" Patrick asked.

"I'll leave tomorrow."

Rob could feel Amanda's stare and knew what it was about. But how could he not go with so much was at stake? They had to use every advantage they had — including his Russian.

While in Bangkok, Rob and Patrick had spent countless evenings talking about methane. One an engineer, the other a chemist, they were fascinated by the idea of turning it into plastic and fashioning objects from it — an idea Rob had cherished since his college days. At the time, the technology wasn't yet ready for scalable production. But now it was, as Rob and Patrick firmly believed. It only needed a little creative tweaking.

Well, maybe a lot of creative tweaking.

Gradually, what had been a topic discussed over after-work drinks had become an obsession, then a pet project, and then a solid business plan. A year ago Rob found a visionary Business Angel to help them get started, so they resigned from their jobs and returned to France to set up a lab and launch their company.

Six months later, Amanda managed to get a transfer to Energie NordSud's French HQ and returned to Paris as well. She rented a lovely two-bedroom place in a quiet suburb east of Paris, with a direct *métro* line to her office and Rob's studio apartment. They settled into a routine of spending every second night together, either at Amanda's or at Rob's.

After Patrick left to catch the last *métro*, Rob packed his bags and finally crawled into bed. He could sense that Amanda wasn't asleep. He considered reminding her he had kept his vow to never contact Lena again. He debated telling her he was over his youthful infatuation. He contemplated pointing out that Lena had been married for two years.

But he didn't say any of it. Because deep in his heart he knew he couldn't go to Moscow and not call Lena. And to hell with stupid vows. He wanted to see her, to talk to her, to know how she was doing, to tell her about his crazy year. He wanted her forgiveness. And her friendship.

* * *

Lena looked out the window. April was the best time of year in Moscow. Gone were the heaps of snow and puddles of gray slush from March. It had rained during the night, but by early afternoon the clouds had cleared and the sun came out. Its rays bathed the sodden city in magic light, caressing everything they touched, bouncing off the windows and air-kissing the puddles.

She sat at a small table in a cozy teahouse that smelled of fresh pastry. She'd never been here before, but Rob had insisted they meet here, promising her the best pancakes in the world. He'd arrived in Moscow a couple of days ago on a short business trip and called her to say hello. They had agreed to meet here for chat. Old friends catching up after a long hiatus.

She'd been restless and strung out since that call. She took particular care with her clothes this morning, changing her attire several times before settling on a sky-blue turtleneck and a gray pencil skirt. She wanted to look together, elegant, and classy. But not flirty. Her clothing was supposed to tell a story of a successful woman, fulfilled in every area of her life. She had applied makeup. She had checked several times to make sure she was wearing her wedding band.

And now she was in this teahouse, almost a half hour early, debating whether she should order a tea or go for a short walk around the block. After a few minutes of hesitation, she put on her raincoat, walked out the door, and bumped into Rob.

"Lena! I'm so glad—wait, you're . . . leaving?" He frowned slightly.

He looked as breathtakingly handsome as before. Actually, more handsome, if it was at all possible.

"Hi! I got here too early, so I was just going to take a walk in the neighborhood to kill the time," she said.

He grinned, the familiar twinkle of mischief in his hazel eyes. "Guess what? I'm too early too. Do you mind if I tag along? I've got twenty minutes before my appointment with you here."

"Be my guest."

Lena had spotted a small public garden on her way to the teahouse, so she started in that direction.

"What brings you to Moscow?" she asked.

"We needed someone to fix a piece of rare equipment that malfunctioned, and we found the best people for it here."

Lena gave him a quizzical look. "*We* as in you and your Energie NordSud colleagues?"

Rob shook his head. "No. *We* as in me and my business partner. Didn't you know I'd left Energie NordSud to strike out on my own a year ago?"

"I'm afraid I didn't. I knew from Facebook you had moved back to Paris, but since your status updates aren't usually big on detail, I thought you and Amanda had both transferred to Energie's Paris office."

Rob pointed to a bench that looked dry. "Let's sit down and I'll give you a detailed update."

He dropped onto the bench, and she sat at a safe distance from him.

"Lena . . . I need to tell you something first. I'm not sure you received the apology e-mail I sent you from Bangkok—"

"I did," she cut in. "And even though I didn't reply to it, please know that your apology is accepted. It's been almost three years, Rob. I don't hold grudges that long."

She smiled, seeing how every muscle in his face relaxed with relief. "So, how about that detailed update you promised?"

For the next twenty minutes, he filled her in on his company. She asked a lot of questions. She wasn't equipped to fully understand the process but she loved the idea of converting a polluting gas into consumer goods. And she loved that Rob had the courage to give up a good job and pursue his dream.

"I remember you telling me about this in Paris," she said. "I thought it sounded wonderful but that it was just a beautiful dream. And now you're making it a reality."

He smiled. "Fingers crossed. The dream is now in the hands of five geeks who call themselves Hi-tech Wizards."

"Can they do magic?"

"No, but their combined nerd factor is so high it goes through the roof and into the stratosphere. Nerds of that caliber can do anything."

They fell silent for a little while. Lena was surprised at how comfortable she felt with Rob, just like she had during their short-lived romance in Paris. It was as if three years hadn't passed. As if he wasn't with Amanda now, and she wasn't married to Dmitry. She sighed and lifted her face toward the sun. Her heart was suddenly full to the point of overflowing.

"Lena," he said softly. "Why don't you tell me about yourself now? It's not like you're much chattier on Facebook than I am. All I know is that you're married, have a little half- sister, got your PhD, and became assistant teacher at the Translation Institute."

She turned to him. "You're well-informed for someone who only updates his status twice a year."

He wasn't letting her off the hook. "Come on, I want details. Are you happy in Moscow?"

She shrugged. "There isn't much else to add to what you already know. My sister is two and a half now, and she already has the whole family wrapped around her little finger. She's the world's cutest bossy pants."

"And what about your plans for the future?"

"I've applied for a docent title, which is a sort of associate professor. I've got lots of published articles and a good teaching record, so I should have a fair chance. I even published a monograph." She winked. "A biography of Marina Tsvetaeva."

"Have you been translating?" he asked.

"I translated two contemporary French novels into Russian for a Saint Petersburg based publisher. I also translated more Tsvetaeva poems into French and sent a collection to several French publishers. But I haven't heard back from any of them yet."

"Sounds like you've been busy." He gazed into her eyes. "But what about Moscow?"

Lena hesitated. She could play dumb and tell him about the city, but she knew Rob's question wasn't really about Moscow at all.

"How is Amanda?" she asked.

He stared down at his shoes. "She's fine. She got a big well-deserved promotion recently, so she's happy." He lifted his eyes to look at Lena and repeated his question, this time without prevaricating. "And what about you? Are *you* happy?"

She twisted her wedding ring. Why couldn't she just say, *Yes, I'm happy, thanks for asking, and shouldn't we go eat those pancakes you've been raving about?* It was so easy. And yet it wasn't easy at all.

"I'm doing fine. I enjoy my work and being around my family... It's just that..." She looked away and blurted, "It's the way I feel about my husband. I love him, I do. I admire everything about him. But my body is rejecting him... He's the most wonderful person on Earth, and he worships me, but... he doesn't turn me on. At all."

Lena felt tears well up in her eyes. Her mind was a whirlwind of conflicting thoughts. She should stop right now before she said too much. She'd already said too much. Oh, what the heck. Rob was here for only two more days, and then he'd be gone, taking her secret away with him. She felt as if a massive dam blocking a torrent inside was about to burst. She wanted—no, she *needed*—to tell him things she hadn't told anyone in all this time.

He took her hand and held it in his lap with both his.

And she fell apart. The words that came out of her were painfully honest and raw. "I thought it would change with time. I thought I'd get used to his touch, to his mannerisms. I kept monitoring my reactions to him for hopeful signs. During our honeymoon, there was a moment when I almost believed I was beginning to want him. But I was deluding myself."

She cracked a bitter smile. "It was just a mighty dose of wine and wishful thinking... Oh God. I can't sleep with him unless I'm inebriated. And even after a few drinks, I have to shut my eyes and block my senses out. And then I imagine he's... someone else."

Lena felt Rob's hands tighten around hers. She turned back to him, her eyes glistening and her heart thumping so loudly she was sure he could hear it.

She stood up abruptly. "I'm sorry, I have to—"

Rob stood up with her, still holding her hand. He looked at her in a strange, distressing way and then pulled her to him in one quick, powerful movement. And suddenly, his lips were on hers, his tongue thrust into her mouth, and his arms crushed her to his chest. That taste of his, so masculine and yet so impossibly sweet, intoxicated her. Lena could no longer remember where she was or why she had to leave. She could hardly remember who she was. The only thing she knew, the only thing that mattered was that she was in his arms again. That she could smell him, touch him, feel his strength and revel in his warmth.

He held her and kissed her with a fierce urgency, and she responded to him with every nerve ending, every cell of her body. She ran her hands over the taut muscles of his back, remembering them, remembering him. She moaned her pleasure against his mouth.

His hands descended to her lower back, pressing her to him, and she felt his hardness against her belly. Her pelvis grew heavy, throbbing with need, locking her attention on her own body. On the unrepeatable here and now of it.

She had no idea how long they stood there, when his raspy voice brought her back to reality.

"Please, come with me." He searched her eyes, his expression hopeful. "Let me get a cab to my hotel."

It took her a few moments to find her bearings.

"I can't. I'm hosting a family dinner tonight." She cupped his cheek. "But I'll come to your hotel tomorrow, around three o'clock, if that's fine with you."

"Yes. Yes, it's fine." He smirked. "If I survive until then."

Lena smiled back, releasing him and putting both her hands in her raincoat pockets. "I've got to go now. Text me your address . . . I'll see you tomorrow."

* * *

"Anton, will you please put that child back in her chair so you can eat your soup before it's completely cold?" Anna said.

"You got it, boss." Anton grinned and returned his protesting daughter to her high chair. "Delicious soup, Lena. It's hard to believe that my girl who didn't know how to make an omelet has developed such amazing cooking skills. To be honest, I was secretly worried Dmitry would grow fat eating pasta every night."

"I'm fitter than ever," Dmitry said, patting his abs. "Because my beautiful wife's cooking is as delicious as it is healthy. What more could a man wish for?"

Was that a note of irony Lena detected in his voice? No, it couldn't be. Dmitry looked as candid as ever. Besides, Dmitry didn't *do* irony.

"So, what's going on at the institute, Lena? Are they going to give you that title already? You've been waiting to hear back from the dean for months now," Anton said.

"I believe they will, eventually. For now, they're telling me to be patient."

"Shouldn't I intervene? A little greasing of the wheels to help things move forward?" he offered.

Lena shook her head vigorously. "No way. I've made it this far without your help, and that's how I intend to continue, thank you very much. If they give me the title, it will only be based on merit. Dad, if you ever go see the dean or the rector, you'd ruin everything!"

Anton looked a little taken aback by her outburst.

Dmitry looked up from his plate. "I think we should just be patient. Lena's been working like crazy and defended her doctoral thesis in half the time it normally takes. She now has more publications than some of the established professors. There's no reason for the board to refuse her the title."

As always, Dmitry said the right thing. And, as always, Lena felt grateful for his tactful and sensible intervention.

She added, her tone much lighter now, "Dad, you already did me a huge favor when you stopped browbeating me about working for you. For which I'm eternally grateful."

"If you say so." Anton shrugged. "Anyway, in a few years, I can start browbeating Katia."

"I have no doubt one of you will be browbeating the other in a few years. I'm just not so sure it will be you, sweetheart," Anna said to her husband.

The rest of the dinner went well. Lena received sincere compliments on her baked fish and French apple pie.

After the guests left, Lena and Dmitry cleaned up the worst of the mess and went to bed. Lena was too tired to read, so she turned off her bedside lamp and wished Dmitry good-night.

"Happy dreams, darling," he said.

She suddenly realized they hadn't made love in months. She couldn't even remember how many. It gave her pause. How could she be so frigid with one man—a good man, a man she loved—and so lustful with another, a man she hadn't seen for three years, a man who now belonged with someone else?

She tried to empty her head so that she could drift off. One sheep, two sheep, three sheep . . . eighty-seven sheep. She adjusted her pillow and changed her position. But she couldn't sleep. Guilt, want, more guilt, and more want took turns gnawing at her soul until dawn.

When morning came, Lena was in a haze, torn between what she ought to do and what she ached to do. She made it through the classes she taught on automatic pilot, her mind filled with thoughts and images she wouldn't reveal to anyone.

At lunchtime, her mom called. The occurrence was rare and thus suspicious. Lena apologized to her lunch companions and found a discreet corner to talk to Anastasia.

"Hi, Mom."

"Hello, my dear. It's been such a long time since I last called you! I was wondering what you were up to," Anastasia said cheerfully.

"It's been a week, Mom, and it was me who called," Lena said.

"Was it? Oh well, I've been so distracted lately. So tell me, how are you doing?"

"I'm fine. What about you?"

"I'm so glad you asked. Actually, I'm ... in a tight spot. And I've been feeling so lonely and down."

Lena was at a loss for words. Her mom never felt lonely or down. She always had a boyfriend, a dozen cronies, and an overbooked social life. Did she get dumped? But why did she say she was in trouble? Oh no, what if she had health problems?

"Mom, you're not alone—I'm here. I can fly over in a blink. Just tell me what's wrong."

"You're a sweet girl, Lena, you've always been. Please don't trouble yourself coming here. In fact, you can help me better from Moscow." She cleared her throat. "I need you to talk to your father. He wrote me last week, via his lawyer, that he was going to discontinue my allowance. On the grounds that you are a fully independent adult now, and he can no longer keep you from visiting me."

Lena exhaled slowly. She should have guessed. "I'll talk to him. But I can't promise anything—you know how stubborn he can be."

"I know that all too well. But perhaps you could remind him that your four visits over the past couple of years were entirely your idea. That I never prompted or asked you to come. It's unfair to punish me for something I didn't do!" Anastasia's voice was now full of righteous indignation. "You understand that I can't give up my lifestyle at this point in my life. It's all I've got."

Of course. "I'll talk to him, Mom. I'll do my best to make him change his mind. Give me a few days to handle this, OK?"

"OK, my dear. I knew I could count on you. I'll be looking forward to your call." She sounded relieved.

Lena hung up, but before she headed back to her colleagues, it occurred to her that her planned tryst with Rob was exactly the kind of thing her mother would do. The kind of thing her mother *had* done to her dad. Lena had always wished she'd had her mom's looks, but she was glad she was different from her in character. With time, she had come to secretly pride herself—not without a touch of superiority—that she was nothing like her mom. But when all was said and done, wasn't she about to prove to be exactly like her?

Lena dialed Rob's number. He answered immediately. "Lena, hi! Is everything OK? I'm already back at the hotel."

"I can't do this, Rob, I'm so sorry. I can't do this to Dmitry—he doesn't deserve it."

There was a short silence, and then Rob spoke, his voice thick. "Lena, I've been thinking about what you said yesterday. About us. You're unhappy with your husband... I think you should leave him."

"I can't. It would destroy him."

"He's a big boy. It'll hurt, but he'll get over it. I could travel to Moscow every month, and you could come to Paris." He paused, then added gently, "I'm going to break up with Amanda. I—"

"No... no, you can't—you mustn't. She's loved you for so long... And I care for Dmitry too much to hurt him like that. He's been so good to me. He's the only person on Earth I can trust completely."

"I see. You've forgiven me, but not forgotten." Rob's voice was raw with emotion. "Lena, it may be too much to ask, but I'll ask anyway. Can you give me another chance? I want you to see who I really am. I want to prove to you that you can trust me."

It was so tempting to say yes. He'd let her down once—twice, actually—but maybe the third time would be the charm? His plea was so urgent, so desperate...

But not as desperate as her wonderful, loyal husband would be if she told him she was leaving him.

"I'm sorry, Rob, but I'm done running from my messes. I'm not leaving Dmitry. Who knows, maybe with time I will come to... want him. Two years isn't that long, after all."

"Don't do this, Lena. Not again." He let out a bitter chuckle. "Isn't it time you stopped fighting your attraction for me, and just went with the flow?"

She took a deep breath before answering. "When I ran from Paris and from you three years ago, I made a choice that was impulsive—not perceptive, as I thought at the time."

Saying those words was extremely hard, but she wanted to be completely honest with him. She owed him that. "And then a few months later I topped it with another rash decision. I married Dmitry without having spent nearly enough time with him. If you want to know the whole truth, I accepted his offer within five minutes after learning you were with Amanda."

"But that—" he began.

"Let me finish, please. What I'm trying to say is that it's too late now. I'm stuck—we're both stuck—with the choices we made back then. And I'm not going to further aggravate my case by making another careless choice."

He didn't try to argue this time.

She said softly, "I'm sorry."

There was a long silence before Rob spoke, his voice flat and distant. "Good-bye, Lena."

I did the right thing, she whispered after he hung up. She drew in several breaths, and began to walk toward her colleagues, trying to ignore the dull ache in her heart.

* * *

No thinking, no complaints and no emotions,
No sleep.
No longing for the sun, the moon, the ocean,
Or for the ship.

I'm a befuddled little tightrope dancer,
A humorless buffoon.
A shadow's shadow, an enchanted vassal,
Of two dark moons.

Marina Tsvetaeva

THIRTEEN

"Lena, there you are, I've been looking everywhere for you!" Lydia, a fellow assistant teacher and the closest Lena had to a friend in Moscow, called out from the faculty room.

Lena walked in and exchanged a cheek kiss with her. "What's the urgency?"

"This afternoon's classes are cancelled. Something to do with urgent electricity work or pest extermination."

"Ugh. What kind of pest?" Lena asked.

"Doesn't matter. What matters is that you and I are as free as butterflies on this beautiful day. So, we can either go to the library and finish our conference papers or head to the movies. Your call."

"What's playing this week?"

"No idea. But I'm sure we can find something watchable." Lydia's eyes brimmed with excitement. It looked like she did have a preference, after all.

"I'd rather go to the library," Lena started, but seeing how Lydia's face fell, she aborted her teasing. "Just kidding! Let's go to the movies. I'd love to see a dumb comedy."

It would do her good, she thought, take her mind off yesterday's talk with Rob. And that kiss . . .

Lydia grinned. "How about lunch first? I'm starving."

They went to a nearby eatery and ordered their food. As usual, the conversation turned to conference papers, teaching assignments, and evil Professors.

"Some days I'm convinced Professor Semyonov is the devil himself," Lydia said, biting into her hamburger. She continued with a deep-seated albeit hamburger-tempered ire. "He'sh sho shnobbish and mean!"

Lena tried not to smile. Lydia's expressive face kept switching between anger and gastronomic bliss. The latter prevailed, and halfway through her meal, Lydia wiped her mouth with a napkin, sat back and let out a satisfied sigh.

"I hear yours is nice—lucky you," she said.

"She's super busy and forgetful, and she regularly stands me up. But when I do see her, she's terribly helpful," Lena said.

"Oh, by the way, did you hear the latest?"

Lena smiled. "Probably not. Tell me."

"The institute received a large donation. Apparently anonymous." Lydia gave her a funny look.

"Oh," was all Lena managed to say.

Lydia leaned in. "I hope you realize that... there are people—like me, for example—who've been assistants for ages, slaving for thankless professors, and waiting for the title. You're a rookie by comparison."

When Lena didn't reply, Lydia drove her point home. "We both know that our dean and the board can be swayed with other arguments than merit and length of "servitude." And we both know that your dad is in a position to sway them. I just hope you wouldn't let him do that."

"It couldn't be him," Lena finally said. "He gave me his word. I'll ask him, of course, but I'm sure it's someone else."

"But you have applied for the title, haven't you?"

"Yes, but I don't want any special treatment. No way. I'd rather drop out of the race than let my dad "buy" me the title."

Lena squirmed, her discomfort growing by the second. Her rapport with Lydia had until now been one of easy camaraderie promising to grow into a friendship.

But this conversation changed it, poisoned it somehow.

She dug her nails into her palms as she felt the familiar urge to leave, get away, spare herself the unpleasantness of a broken relationship.

But she wouldn't, she decided. Not this time.

* * *

The following morning Lena woke up early, even though it was Saturday and she didn't have to rush anywhere. Dmitry was still asleep. She was feeling pleased with herself, and deservedly so. Last night after the movie, she had talked to Anton and managed to convince him to keep supporting Anastasia. He had initially balked, but thanks to Anna's deft intervention, he ended up agreeing to a compromise: He would keep on paying but he'd slash the amount by half. She also asked him about the donation, and he vehemently denied having had anything to do with it.

The other reason for Lena's good mood was the way she had handled the situation with Lydia. Lena replayed the previous night's outing in her mind and gave herself a mental pat on the back for not having bailed. After the film, they parted on good terms, in spite of some residual tension. She was hoping that with time she could get her relationship with Lydia back on track. It wasn't like she had tons of other buddies. Come to think of it, Jeanne was her only friend, not counting Anna who was halfway between a parent and a sister.

Even though Lena didn't see Jeanne very often, their friendship survived and thrived. They e-mailed, texted, and phoned each other regularly. They saw each other when Lena and Dmitry traveled to France, Switzerland, or Italy. Their latest meeting dated back only a couple of months when Jeanne had visited Lena in Moscow. During that visit Jeanne had demanded that Lena stop boycotting Paris.

"What's the deal with you and Paris? You travel all over Europe with your husband. When you fly to France, you go straight to Bordeaux or Cannes or Lyon. Now you're suggesting we meet in Brussels this summer. You're circling Paris but won't set foot there. Why?"

"I don't know. I guess I fell out of love with Paris. In spite of what Parisians think of their city, it *isn't* the center of the world."

"Fair enough, but I'm not buying it. I know why you won't come to Paris, and I'm telling you to get over it. It's all in the past now. Water under the *Pont Neuf*. It's been almost three years since you last graced our capital!"

"Shocking."

"I mean it, and I demand that you cease this self-banishment immediately. You can stay with me if you come by yourself. If you come with Dmitry, well, you should be able to find a hotel or two in our shabby old town."

Lena had promised to think about it, but after her encounter with Rob, she doubted she'd be going to Paris anytime soon. She knew she was being irrational. Paris was a big city, and the risk of running into Rob there was negligible. But she didn't want to take that risk.

She got up and began to cook breakfast like she did every morning. Today it would be pancakes with maple syrup—Canadian style.

She was beating eggs by the stove when Dmitry walked into the kitchen. They exchanged greetings, and he sat at the kitchen table.

Lena was a little surprised he didn't kiss her on the cheek as usual. She glanced at him over her shoulder and immediately sensed that something was off. He looked tired and determined at the same time, his gaze fixed on his mug.

"I hope you're in the mood for pancakes," she said brightly.

"Are you seeing someone, Lena?" he asked, his voice even, as if he were inquiring about her afternoon plans.

She put the batter aside and turned to face him. Judging by the cold and expectant look on his face, she hadn't misheard him.

"No, I'm not," she said and then asked in her turn, "Are you?"

He didn't answer immediately—he just sat there staring at his mug. As the seconds passed, she began to feel nausea rising in her stomach. She had asked her question without thinking, almost as a joke—a kind of childish retaliation for his asking her. Dmitry would never cheat on her. But then why wasn't he just saying no, like she had done? Why wasn't he saying anything at all?

After a few long seconds, he took a hearty sip from his mug, looked her straight in the eyes and said, "Yes I am. I've been seeing someone . . . for four months now."

The kitchen began to spin around her. She grabbed the back of a chair, then sat down.

He rubbed his chin. "It started out of frustration with our sex life . . . desperation, you could say."

Lena closed her eyes. This couldn't be happening. Her doting husband, her rock couldn't be saying these things to her. Maybe this man wasn't Dmitry but a stranger who looked exactly like him.

He spoke again. "Then it grew into something more serious. I couldn't help going back to her because she wanted me so much... because of how happy I made her."

He exhaled loudly and continued. "But you didn't seem to notice any of it—my longer hours at work, my new fishing hobby, not even when I stopped begging you for sex. I thought maybe you knew what was going on, but chose to keep appearances to save our marriage. Only that theory had a major flaw—you're too candid to pull off an act like that. And that's when I began to wonder if you too had a lover."

There was an edge to Dmitry's voice that Lena had never heard before. He had paused his confession, and stared at her, but she just stared back. She needed more time to collect her thoughts and to quell her nausea.

"Lena, we haven't made love in six months, and it's not like we'd been at it like bunnies before. I've lost count of your excuses. We live like two flatmates or eighty-year-olds. And it's not just the sex. You're aloof. You don't share much with me. I'm not sure you even like being around me."

"Wait a second," she said, recovering a little. "You've been seeing another woman for months, and you were just... waiting and wondering why *I* didn't notice? Why didn't *you* just tell me that you didn't love me anymore?"

"Because I didn't *not* love you anymore!" His voice was no longer calm. "I was confused. I was unhappy. But I still loved you."

He paused, searching her eyes. "You do all these things for me. You make me breakfast, cook dinner, buy me little presents, but you do all that out of duty, out of some notion of *perfect wifeliness* that you have. And also out of guilt, I think. You're telling me, 'You can't have my heart, but here, have these delicious pancakes instead—I made them specially for you!'"

Dmitry fell silent and looked at her expectantly. But Lena couldn't bring herself to acknowledge the bitter truth of his words. Not even with a nod.

"Who is she?" she asked instead.

"You don't know her. I met her through work. She's my age, a single mom with a five-year-old. He's a great kid. She'd love to have a second one. Can you imagine how I feel every time Aliona asks me to make her a baby? When my own wife has only been finding excuses not to? Can't you see what it does to a man who craves for a child to know that his wife doesn't want the same thing? At least not with him."

Lena began to choke. Her heart beat so wildly she had to cough to help her breathing. She needed more air. More space.

"I can't stay here," she wheezed, and rushed for the door.

* * *

Lena checked her reflection in the ladies' room mirror. It wasn't a pretty sight. Her eyes were red and puffy, with dark circles underneath, and her cheeks were hollow. Well, that's what three days of crying and neglecting to eat did to you. She put her eyeglasses on and headed down the corridor toward the dean's office. It was no small feat to have found the energy to haul herself to the institute this morning, after the dean's secretary called her.

"The dean will receive you now," the secretary said. She bared her teeth in lieu of a smile, stood up from behind her desk, and sashayed to the door leading to the adjacent office.

As Lena stepped into the pompous office, she couldn't help admiring the secretary for her ability to walk in shoes that were higher than they were long.

The dean looked up from his paperwork and nodded to Lena. "Please, come in and take a seat. I asked you to stop by because I have good news for you. The board reviewed your application and okayed it. They were impressed by the number of your publications, by the way. And so was I."

A week earlier, she would have been overjoyed to hear this. Now she felt sick to her stomach. "Does the board's decision have anything to do with the recent donation?"

"The donation was anonymous, Ms. Malakhova." He gave her a long look and pointed to the door. "My secretary will see you out."

Lena nodded and headed for the door. There wasn't much else to say, was there? She would probably never know the truth about the donation, but somehow it didn't matter. If her dad had made it, in the hope that the board would connect the dots, it was out of a misguided attempt to help her. After all these years, she'd gotten used to his misguided gestures of love—almost expected them.

But even if it wasn't him, her docent title would be marred by suspicion in everyone's eyes. Including hers.

She dragged herself home and changed back into her pajamas. At two in the afternoon, she was still in bed, fully awake but unable to get up and face the day. Her phone rang. She didn't answer it. It rang again and again. Whoever was calling clearly knew Lena was home. She tumbled out of the bed and picked up the phone.

"Finally. I knew you were there. What's going on?" Anna asked.

"Nothing, I'm just feeling a little under the weather."

"Oh yeah? I've known you for three years now, and I know that when you feel *a little* under the weather you don't disappear for days and not return my calls. And where's Dmitry, by the way?"

"I don't know."

"What do you mean you don't know? And why doesn't anyone pick up when I call in the evening? I tried both your cellphones, but it's like you and your husband suddenly went undercover. If you hadn't left that voice mail two days ago, I would have broken into your apartment!"

Anna paused for breath. "Lena, what is going on?"

"Please, Anna, don't worry. I'm fine. Really. I just need some time by myself."

"Well, too bad. Because I'm on your doorstep so you have to let me in."

The doorbell rang, making Lena jump. Crap. She'd no time to change out of her pajamas.

"Hang on a minute!" she yelled and went to the bathroom to splash some cold water on her face. After that, she pulled her hair into a bun, and let Anna, now pregnant with her second child, in.

Her stepmother quickly took in the neglected state of the apartment and of its occupant, and headed to the kitchen. "I'm going to make us some tea. Why don't you take a shower in the meantime, sweetheart?"

"Oh God, do I smell?" Lena tugged at her pajama top to sniff it.

"No, not yet."

Fifteen minutes later they sat at Lena's kitchen table, a steaming mug in front of each and a plate with cookies Anna must have brought with her. This was one of the things Lena loved about Anna — her ability to create warmth and a safe haven around her.

"How's Katia? How's Dad? I texted him yesterday to tell him I was fine and not to worry."

"I know. What I don't know is if you really expected it to work. I can assure you that if he wasn't at the other end of the country right now, he would have been here since Sunday night, camping outside your door," Anna replied.

Lena smiled. The image of her dad in a sleeping bag on her landing was improbable, given his aversion to camping. But also likely, knowing how mulish he could be.

Anna pushed a cookie in front of Lena. "Eat. This is just to make sure you can walk home with me to get a proper meal. So, where's Dmitry?"

"We broke up. I'll be filing for a divorce."

Anna's squeezed Lena's hand, her gaze full of sympathy. But she didn't look shocked at the news. Not even surprised.

"Did you know about his mistress?" Lena asked, incredulous.

Now Anna looked surprised. "Dmitry had a mistress? I had no idea. To be honest, I always thought it would be you who'd end up leaving him . . . How long have you known?"

"I found out last Saturday. He's been seeing her for four months now."

Anna squeezed Lena's hand again. "My poor darling!"

"Anna, I'm not heartbroken, believe me. I have been before—and this is not it."

Lena took a long sip of her tea. It was fragrant and unexpectedly comforting. She focused on how it warmed her body. "I'm angry at my . . . arrogant blindness. I was so wrapped up in myself and so sure of his devotion, I missed all the telltale signs of an affair he wasn't even trying to hide."

Anna put her hand on Lena's. "Don't be so hard on yourself. Dmitry was such an *exemplary* husband — it's no surprise you didn't see it coming!"

"I appreciate your solidarity. But here's the truth — I lived in a house of cards for the past two years, and then it crumbled. It happens to houses of cards a lot . . . I wasn't a good wife for him, a wife he deserved. My marriage was a lie, Anna, and it wasn't Dmitry's fault."

Lena felt tears well up again and accepted the tissue Anna offered her.

"It's nothing — just self-pity," she said as she dried her eyes.

"I know what you need to do. You're going to move in with us for a little while, so I can look after you properly. And once you've regained a healthy weight and complexion, you'll dedicate all your time and attention to your career. Aren't you the frontrunner for that docent title?"

Lena sighed. "It's complicated." She suddenly felt drained of the little energy she had left, too tired to recount her conversation with the dean to Anna. So she went for the bottom line. "The truth is I'm no longer interested in it. I'm quitting my job."

"What? But you love translating. You live for translating. You breathe translating."

"That's right. That's exactly right. You see, I'm a translator, not a theoretician. Even the papers I published talk about concrete, practical translation problems. I guess my academic aspirations were as much of a lie as my marriage."

"What will you do then?" Anna's voice cracked, telling Lena her stepmother meant more than just career choices.

"That's the thing," Lena said, looking up from her now empty mug. "I wish I knew."

* * *

As soon as Anton and Anna were out the door, Lena crawled back under the sheets. A month after the breakdown of her marriage and her career, she still spent way too much time in bed. In her more optimistic moments, she tried to look to the future, to pick herself up. But her life was scattered in so many pieces, the enormity of the task paralyzed her every time.

On top of that, she grew increasingly uneasy about her last conversation with Dmitry. She regretted the things she'd said and the things she hadn't. When she returned home on that fateful Saturday, after having aimlessly wandered the streets for several hours, Dmitry was gone. He'd left her a note saying he was sorry about how things had ended between them.

She was sorry, too. It was a strange kind of sorry — the kind that blended grieving, remorse and relief. As for her anger about his affair, it was completely gone. After all, how could she blame him for having opened his heart to another woman, when she'd never opened hers to him?

On an impulse, she grabbed her phone and typed a text.

Can we meet? I have something to tell you.
L.

After a moment's hesitation, she took a fortifying breath and pushed send.

He replied ten minutes later.

Can you make it to Karaway at 1 pm?

She could.

Dmitry showed up in jeans and a T-shirt. He had grown a neat beard that made him look different. More virile and older. It suited him.

"Where do you live now?" she asked after the maître d' led them to their table.

"I'm renting a two-bedroom in Zamosvorechye," he said before adding in reply to her unspoken question, "with Aliona."

She smiled and wrung her hands. It wasn't easy to find the right words.

He studied her face. "I found a job with a company that has nothing to do with IT services. So Anton shouldn't worry I'd leak any insider info."

"He isn't worried. He's convinced of your integrity."

Dmitry nodded before adding, "Yeah, I know. Unfortunately, he was never convinced of my suitability as your husband."

It was hard to argue with that.

"Well, time proved him right," Dmitry said with a smirk.

"I guess he knows me better than I do," she said.

Dmitry gave her a long look. "So, what is it you wanted to tell me?"

She stared into his eyes. "That I'm sorry."

"I was the one having an affair, as far as I recall . . ."

"And I was the one to practically push you into it. I had no right to walk out on you that morning, as if I was the only wronged side."

He shifted slightly in his seat, then rubbed his face. His eyes remained trained on her.

Lena drew in a heavy breath. "I'm truly, profoundly sorry for having wasted two years of your life."

"It was your life, too."

"Yes, but the blame for our failed marriage is mine alone. I want you to know that I can see it now."

Dmitry gave her a tired smile. "I don't think the blame is only yours, Lena."

She shook her head. "The truth is, I haven't done much to make our marriage work. You tried so hard for so long, but I didn't. I cared for you, and I wanted to love you, but I . . . wouldn't let go of my past. I didn't do what it took to empty my heart, so I could give it to you."

"My dear, it's a delusion to believe you can "empty" your heart at will. With hindsight, I don't even understand why I accepted to live like that. Why I hid from this truth you're talking about. I should have known better..." He shrugged. "Love, as they say, makes us stupid."

"Blind," she corrected automatically.

"Thank you." He smiled before becoming serious again. "Had I not been in denial about your feelings for me when we married, or had I asked you a year later, we could've cut our losses."

"Had you asked, I would have told you how much I cared for you, so I don't see—"

"But you wouldn't have told me you were *in love* with me." He tilted his head and paused, giving her a chance to disagree.

She didn't.

He exhaled slowly, looking tired. "You've never told me that. You've never told me you dreamed of me, or wanted sex with me, or wanted my baby."

She turned her head away as her eyes began to well up with tears.

He spoke again. "I appreciate this... initiative, and the intention behind it. I do. But you're definitely not the only one to blame."

"Are you in love Aliona?" she asked.

He nodded.

"I wish with all my heart you'll be happy with her."

"I *am*." He suddenly grinned. "I can't even begin to tell you how good it feels to be with a woman who's mad about you."

* * *

That night Lena went to her desk and logged in her Facebook account, for the first time since her meeting with Rob in April. She checked out his personal page. He hadn't updated it in months. She went to his company page and learned that they'd successfully shipped their first big order, then a second one, and then a third. The company was flooded by new orders from all over the world. The page contained dozens of links to rave reviews in the French and international press. She opened and read every one of them.

Next, she went to Amanda's page. After some scrolling she found what she was looking for—and dreading. It was an update posted in early May.

Rob and I are moving in together. Yay!

She stared at that post for over an hour, until her eyes hurt and her head began to pound.

* * *

Two trees are yearning for each other.
My house is across the street.
The trees are old. So is the house.
I'm young—or else I wouldn't stand here,
Commiserating with a tree.

Two trees—in the dry heat of summer,
In sopping rains, under the snow—
They bend, they reach—toward each other.
That is the law: toward each other,
The only law: toward each other.

Marina Tsvetaeva

FOURTEEN

Over the next week, Lena no longer bothered to get out of bed for Anna's and Anton's visits. They would let themselves in, leave some nice smelling food in her kitchen, talk to her, and then let themselves out.

Today, Anton brought Katia along.

"Why are you in bed when it's light outside?" Katia asked.

Anton tousled his daughter's hair. "Lena isn't feeling very well."

Katia looked worried. "Are you sick? Do you have to eat medicine? Can I take your temperature?"

Her eyes lit up. "Daddy, did you bring my doctor's kit? I need to examine Lena."

Anton spread his arms apologetically. "Sorry, baby. Your doctor's kit is back at home. But I brought your favorite car."

He turned to Lena. "I wonder if I should be worried or thrilled that she prefers cars to dolls."

"Hmm. I think that you think you should be worried but in reality you're thrilled," Lena said.

"Am I that transparent?" Anton asked.

Lena just smiled and cupped Katia's plump cheek. "I'm not sick, sweetie. I'm just . . . tired."

Katia frowned, thinking hard for a few seconds before delivering her diagnosis. "It's because you ate too much candy and didn't take your nap. That's why you're tired."

She pursed her lips and turned to Anton. "Daddy, shall we take all her candy away?"

Without waiting for an answer, she turned back to Lena. "You can have half of it back when you aren't tired anymore."

"Why only half?" Lena asked.

"Because . . ." Katia stretched the word until she ran out of breath, and then went for honesty. "Because we haven't got any at home! Mommy gives me fruit instead. But I want candy."

Lena threw her hands up. "I'm very sorry, sweetie, but I agree with your mom on this. Besides, I haven't got any candy around here."

Katia's eyes became round. "You ate *everything*?"

When Lena nodded, Katia's face fell with disappointment. Lena couldn't bear to see the little girl's hopes crushed like this. She mouthed *ice cream* to Anton and he nodded.

She turned back to Katia. "Cheer up, candy patrol. I might have something else of interest for you. How about vanilla ice cream?"

Ice cream was definitely of interest, so Lena was obliged to get out of bed to retrieve it from the freezer.

After Anton and Katia left, Lena picked up her phone to text Lydia who'd left her several alarmed voice mails. She told her she was fine and she'd be away for a while. And, in a manner of speaking, she was. Her mind was in another dimension, trying to find a reason why life wasn't a waste of time.

In particular, her comfortable, charmed life, shielded from misery, need and pain. Shielded so well that most of her essential experiences and emotions were secondhand, derived from the novels and poetry she translated. They were a little stale and a little musty, those secondhand emotions, but one hundred percent risk free. As for her heart, she'd locked it in a safe box and thrown away the key. She had hoped it would shrivel and dry up, but instead it was beginning to rot. Lena knew it because she could smell the putrid odor.

She stared out the window and thought about the man she'd loved, all this time. How her love had bellowed and done somersaults right under her nose—and yet she'd failed to notice it, or to acknowledge it for what it was. How she found excuses to dismiss it and words to diminish it, by calling it a crush or a flame. At best, she called it an infatuation. But mostly, she avoided naming it, so that she could pretend it wasn't there.

Because I'm a coward.

Lena pushed her blanket aside and walked over to her massive bookcase. After a quick scan, she pulled out the biography of Marina Tsvetaeva she'd written. Curling up in her favorite armchair, she opened it on page one and began to read. When she closed the book a few hours later, she had the answer to her existential question.

Throughout her life that ended too soon, Tsvetaeva had excelled at taking ill-advised decisions, making bad choices, and falling for the wrong men. But she had never hidden from anything. She had faced life head on. She had *lived*.

Lena opened her e-mail and sent Jeanne her shortest note ever.

Is your offer to visit you in Paris still on?

* * *

"What a jerk!" Jeanne said, for the third time in one hour.

As soon as Lena had arrived at Jeanne's place, they'd all but glued themselves to the couch while filling each other in. Jeanne had trouble wrapping her head around the fact that Dmitry had been having a secret affair for months.

"Will you stop calling him that, please?" Lena begged. "I'm not an innocent victim in this story. In a way, I've been asking for his infidelity."

"Please don't tell me you had a secret lover, too." Jeanne cocked her head.

"I won't—I haven't. But I haven't exactly been a loving wife to him, either." Lena sighed, exhausted from the topic. She preferred to talk about Jeanne again. "So, are you currently on or off with your boyfriend?"

"We're back on, even though I'm not sure how much longer I can do this. We argue all the time. I've changed over the past three years. I think I've grown up, but the problem is that he hasn't. If anything, he's regressed."

Lena smiled. Jeanne was well aware of what she thought about her boyfriend, so there was no point in repeating herself. "And what about Mat? He was so hopelessly smitten by you three years ago. Is he still in Paris?"

"Who's Mat? Oh, that malnourished friend of Rob's from Normandy? No, he left Paris. I think he went back to the boondocks. But to do what? I'm sure Rob has told me—I just can't remember."

"And how is our favorite Spaniard? He left Paris a couple of years ago, didn't he? Have you heard from him since?" Lena asked.

"You haven't heard? Pepe is doing great. He works for an international real estate agency now. And he did end up finding his Nordic goddess."

"No kidding? I want to know everything about her!"

"I haven't personally met her, but I've heard so much about her from Pepe over the past year that it feels like I have. I couldn't make it to his wedding, so I was strongly encouraged to comment on every single wedding picture they posted on Facebook. And they posted *tons* of them. I remember commenting and commenting, until I was at my wit's end for things to say. And then I realized I'd just finished the town-hall batch and hadn't even started on the church and the party pictures. I hope Pepe appreciates the extent of my goodness."

"But who is she, what's she like?" Lena pressed, expecting a twist—something like the Nordic goddess turning out to be a raven-haired Inuit from the *real* North.

Jeanne only smiled, her fingers scrolling and tapping on her phone. When she found what she was looking for, she held the phone out for Lena to see. It was one of the famous wedding pictures—a close-up of a blue-eyed blonde with a smile full of teeth whiter than her bridal veil. She looked as Scandinavian as they came.

"Oh my God! Pepe found exactly what he'd been raving about! She looks like somebody cut and pasted her from his daydreams," Lena said.

"Apparently, she adores him. She looooooves that he's so full of color and spice, I am told. She calls him something like *scoot*, which is supposed to mean *treasure* in Danish. Oh yeah, her name's Nana. She's from Copenhagen, and that's where they live now."

Lena chuckled. "I can't believe it. Not only did Pepe find his blonde, he ended up living in a country where there's one at every corner. He must have done something really good or suffered greatly in his previous life. Or both. Maybe he fought against Franco and was tortured to death?"

"I don't know what he did in his previous life to deserve this, but he sure didn't do much in his present one, apart from wanting it really, really badly. Maybe that did the trick—who knows?"

Jeanne grinned. "Oh, and you should hear this—do you know what he calls her when he isn't calling her *mi amor*?"

"No. What?"

"Snow White! He calls her 'my Snow White'." Jeanne started laughing. She held her hand up to signal that she wanted to add something but her every attempt was thwarted by fits of laughter that rocked her whole body.

She finally calmed down, wiped off her tears, and pulled up another wedding picture on her phone. "Can you see why now it's so funny?"

The photo showed Pepe and his Danish beauty standing next to each other in front of the priest. The bride was a full head taller than the bridegroom.

Lena snorted. "Our Pepe looks positively *dwarfed*," she managed to say before both of them burst into another fit of hilarity.

It was just like the old times. Lena was immensely grateful that Jeanne was there for her, that she hadn't changed—well, except for the color of her hair, which was now a more realistic copper red.

She mustered all her courage and asked Jeanne about Rob.

"I haven't seen him in a couple of months," Jeanne said. "Last time we talked he was working like crazy trying not to screw up his first major order."

"I saw him two months ago in Moscow," Lena said. "He was still with Amanda. I have the impression they've moved in together by now."

Jeanne searched her eyes. "Lena, are you trying to give yourself a reason not to call him? Cut that crap, honey, and give the guy a call. You know, just to say hi."

"I will . . . when I'm ready."

It would have to be soon, she thought, or else she'd lose the nerve. If she didn't lose her mind first from not knowing.

* * *

With its statues, ponds, and colorful metal chairs, the Luxembourg Gardens were a magical place, as beautiful in summer's green as in autumn's yellow or winter's white. That is, if you managed to meditate yourself into a deep state of denial of the hordes of tourists strolling up and down its sandy alleys and producing a multilingual bedlam while dropping blobs of ice cream on the ground. Lena finally spotted an unoccupied chair hidden behind a rectangular-shaped shrubbery. She sat down and searched her contact list for Rob's number. She had no idea what she would tell him.

When he answered, she blurted out in a single breath, "Hi, it's Lena. I'm in Paris."

"Hi, Lena," he said.

Did he sound happy to hear her voice? Indifferent? Annoyed? She was too nervous to tell, nor did she have a clue what to say next. Why on earth didn't she prepare for this call?

Rob broke the long silence. "So, what brings you to Paris?"

"I had a date . . . with the Eiffel Tower," she said, finally recovering her speech capacity.

"Ah! So now you're OK with its *open* approach to love?"

Oh God. She opened her mouth to say, *No, I'm not. Sorry about this call — it was a mistake*, and hang up. But then it occurred to her this was what the old, cowardly Lena would have done.

She would see this conversation through, even if all she got was closure. "Yes, I am. But only as far as the Eiffel Tower is concerned."

"I see. Then I guess you're just calling to say hi to an old friend," he said, his voice cold.

Amanda. This could only mean he was still with her. And why wouldn't he be, having moved in with her only a month ago? What was she thinking, coming to Paris, calling him like this?

But wait — Rob didn't know she and Dmitry had split up. Only . . . what was the point in telling him now? What would it achieve except making this huge letdown even bigger? Better end this quickly.

"Yes, I just wanted to say hi," she began and stopped.

She couldn't make herself say *to an old friend.* And . . . Rob hadn't actually *told* her he was with Amanda. She had filled this information in for him, which meant there was still a tiny flicker of hope. And Lena chose to go with that flicker.

"Dmitry and I split up," she said, not bothering with a smooth transition.

"What? When?"

"Shortly after you left Moscow. He told me he had a mistress, and I . . . I was relieved. And so was he, I think."

There, she'd said it. Lena closed her eyes and tried to take solace in the knowledge that this conversation would be over in a moment. As soon as Rob expressed his sympathy and wished her good luck.

After a short silence, he asked, "So why are you in Paris now?"

"I . . . I'm visiting Jeanne."

"I see."

She waited for him to continue, but he didn't. As the silence stretched, she realized he wasn't going to say anything. If only she could see his face now! But as it was, she was in the dark — and he wasn't putting on the lights for her.

I can do this. I must do this.

She squeezed her eyes shut. "I'm here because of you. I wanted to see if . . . if there's still any hope for us."

Her hands began to tremble. She felt like she was in one of those nightmares where she stood naked before a crowd. It was terrifying. She hadn't allowed herself to be this vulnerable in ages.

"Amanda and I broke up, too," he said.

Lena didn't dare speak, afraid she had imagined his words and was loath to clear up her misunderstanding.

"Lena, we broke up."

"But . . . but you just moved in together."

"No, we didn't."

"I don't understand—"

Rob didn't let her finish. "Where are you calling from?"

"Luxembourg Gardens, the Senate end."

"Can you take line 4 at Odeon and get off at Château d'Eau? I'll be there in twenty minutes. Please, I need to show you something."

Half an hour later, Rob invited Lena to step into a minimalist studio apartment off Boulevard de Strasbourg.

"This is where I've lived since I moved back to Paris. By myself."

Lena looked around.

"I never moved out," he said.

She looked into his eyes and smiled.

He took a step toward her. "I can't believe you're here."

He was so close now. Close enough for her to feel the heat of his body. He took a handful of her dark hair and brought it to his face. Then he closed his eyes and inhaled. Lena stood still, her head tilted up and her eyes shut.

Oh, how she had missed him! She ached to put her arms around him, run her hands through his hair, and kiss him with all the ardor she was capable of. But she also wanted to savor every moment, every second of this delicious reacquaintance. Unlike in Moscow two months ago, it was just the two of them now, without the distressing presence of Dmitry or Amanda at the back of her mind. She delighted in being with Rob like this, free of guilt and misgivings, free to let him take things as slow as he liked.

He kissed her ever so gently. Her hands went to his chest, his neck, his hair. He continued to softly kiss her lips, taking his time and teasing her. Then his big, warm hand cupped one of her breasts. His touch was as gentle as his kisses—and incredibly erotic. His thumb brushed her nipple through the thin fabric of her dress, and she quivered.

"Rob," she whispered into his ear. "I want you."

He cradled her face in his hands, his eyes intense as they searched hers. And then his mouth came down on hers, hard. His tongue pushed inside with so much pent-up hunger that all rational thought fled from Lena's mind, leaving behind only liquid fire. Her whole body became a vortex of excruciating need. She needed the feel of his bare skin against hers. She wanted his hands all over her. She craved the weight of his body.

Rob knelt before her and pressed his face into her tummy. His hands began to stroke her thighs, pushing her skirt up as he progressed. Lena closed her eyes and threw her head back. A moan escaped her lips. She couldn't wait another minute. He let out an unintelligible groan and pulled her down to him, easing both of them onto the carpet. And then he was atop her, around her, in her, giving her what she hungered for, holding nothing back. The world exploded into a billion shiny pieces — then slowly came together again, in perfect congruity and peace.

* * *

"There's something I still don't understand," Lena said as she lay on the couch, her head on Rob's lap. "What about Amanda's Facebook update from early May? She announced you were moving in with her."

Rob stroked her hair. "Oh yes, that update. After I returned from Moscow, I spent two weeks working around the clock. I rarely talked to anyone unrelated to the company. I hardly slept or ate until all the merchandize was manufactured and shipped. During that time, Amanda started telling people we were moving in together . . . Imagine my surprise when I got a text from Mat congratulating me on the big step."

"What did you do?"

"I finally took an honest look at my relationship with her. I couldn't be with her anymore. I didn't want to live the way you were living with Dmitry—a lie. Amanda and I . . . it wasn't working, in spite of all the reasons why it should have worked. In spite of us being 'perfect for each other' as you once told me."

Lena covered her face with her hands.

"It's OK. Everyone thought we were perfect for each other. *I* thought we were perfect for each other. In fact, I still do. We *are* perfect for each other, but only as friends."

"I was stupid—stupid and blind," she said.

"You think you're wiser now?" he asked, a smile in the corner of his lips.

"I think I'm braver now." Her expression was earnest.

"So you won't run away next time I stumble?"

"Why, are you planning to?"

"Of course not." He traced the outline of her mouth with his fingertips. "But it may happen. Nobody's perfect—not even your ex-husband, as it turned out. Are you now brave enough to stick around and work things out?"

Lena sat up, tucking her legs under her, and took Rob's hand in hers. "I am."

He gave her a long intense look, then smiled and drew her closer to him.

After a little while, he continued his unfinished story. "When I went to Amanda's to break up with her, I was so clumsy. I started by saying I had to tell her something. She jumped in and told me she wanted to start a family."

He grimaced and stared at the wall in front of them. "That was when I told her we were through. It was the most difficult conversation in my whole life."

Lena felt sorry for him, but she couldn't help imagining herself in Amanda's place. It must have been awful for her.

He turned to look into her eyes. "I hated myself every second of that talk, and then some. I delivered all the clichés people say in such cases. I told her she deserved better. I also told her I wasn't worthy of her. I might've even mumbled 'it's not you, it's me'."

"How did she react?"

"With dignity and composure. She was so cool." He smiled bitterly. "The best part—or shall I say, the least awful part—was when she gave me that hard look and told me to go screw myself."

"That *does* sound like Amanda. I mean the message, not the particular choice of words."

"Yep. That's why I wish I could keep her friendship. I love her frankness, her wit, her determination. I just could never love her . . . the way I love you."

He broke off, panic flickering in his eyes. "Can we please rewind the last ten seconds? I didn't mean to hit you with it yet. I wanted to wait till you were ready."

Lena felt like she was in one of her daydreams. Only this time it was real and utterly unexpected. And glorious beyond anything she'd ever experienced.

She brought his hand to her face and pressed her cheek into his palm. "I love you, Rob. With all my heart."

<<<<>>>>

Author's Note

On Tsvetaeva

Marina Tsvetaeva (1892-1941) is one of the greatest Russian lyrical poets of the twentieth century. Critic Annie Fitch describes her work: "Tsvetaeva is such a warm poet, so unbridled in her passion, so completely vulnerable in her love poetry [...]. Tsvetaeva throws her poetic brilliance on the altar of her heart's experience with the faith of a true romantic, a priestess of lived emotion. And she stayed true to that faith to the tragic end of her life." (Source: *Poetry Foundation*).

On poems and translations

All the poems included in this novel are by Marina Tsvetaeva. The translations are mine.

My initial intention was to use existing translations, but after checking out every volume I could get my hands on, I had to review my approach. I had found the translated poems so thoroughly *altered* in form (i.e., rhyme and meter) that I could no longer recognize Tsvetaeva's unique voice. So I had no choice but to translate them myself from the Russian-language originals.

A couple of other things you may be interested in

The *Bistro La Bohème* is fictional. It's an amalgamation of several favorite haunts located in different parts of Paris.

Rue Cadet, however, is real and very charming, indeed.

I borrowed the idea of the carbon recycling technology developed by Rob from a newspaper article about two young geeks, Mark Herrema and Kenton Kimmel, founders of *Newlight Technologies*. Which is to say that what Rob is doing in France isn't science fiction—it has already been done in California. (Source: Wendy Koch, USA Today, 12.31.2013)

Falling for Emma

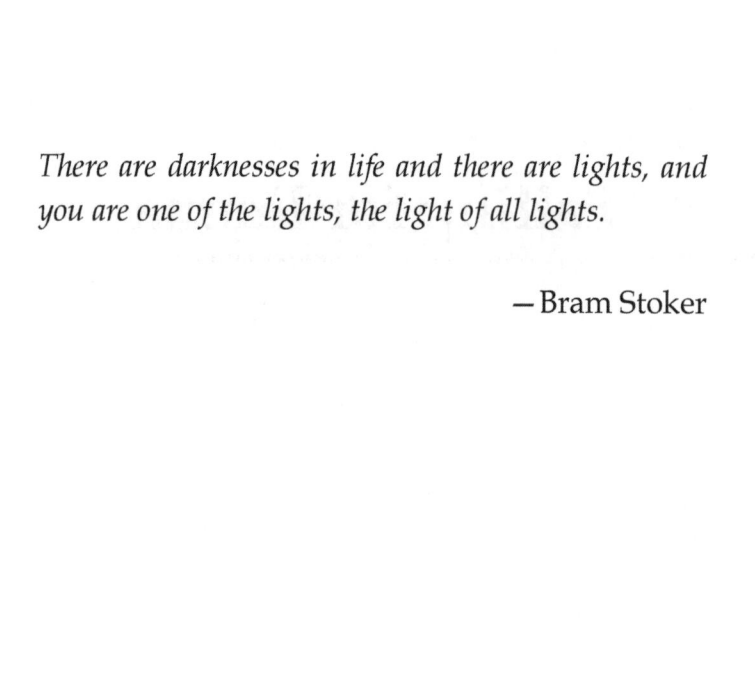

There are darknesses in life and there are lights, and you are one of the lights, the light of all lights.

— Bram Stoker

Chapter One
Emma

"I'm in love with my sister's boyfriend," Emma said in one breath.

She didn't dare look up at Manu, keeping her gaze on the ancient fan-shaped steps they were climbing.

"Wow." Manu turned around to glance at her. "Cyril, right? The musician?"

She nodded.

"OK." He returned his attention to the corkscrew staircase. "So what's your question? You said on the phone you needed to ask me something."

She remained silent for a long moment, struggling to put years of hope, shame, secrecy and self-loathing into a question. They continued climbing the north tower of the Notre Dame Cathedral, their steps synchronized and their breathing increasingly pained. When they reached the walkway leading to the open gallery, Emma was too hot inside her coat and out of breath. But she'd come up with a question.

"Does it make me a contemptible person?"

Manu pointed at one of the formidable stone monsters watching over Paris, its pensive mug propped on its elbows. "Meet Stryge the Immortal, chimera extraordinaire. Isn't he gorgeous?"

She surveyed the winged creature. "He is…in a creepy half-human, half-demon sort of way."

"Chimeras are the guardian demons of the cathedral. Notre Dame wouldn't be the same without them."

Emma pointed to the less intimidating gargoyles perched atop both towers. "I think I prefer those. They're less intimidating."

They stayed at the chimera gallery long enough to feast their eyes on the intricate iron lacework of Eiffel's Grande Dame, the gilded dome of the Hotel des Invalides, the white cupolas of the Sacré Coeur and all the other magnificent vistas the gallery offered. A native

Parisian, Emma had enjoyed these views countless times, but the beauty of her city never failed to move her.

"Ready for the second leg?" Manu asked.

She consented with a nod.

"Emma," he said as they ascended the south tower to the upper viewing platform, "I'm not sure I'm the right person to answer your question."

"You're the most spiritually inclined friend I've got." She gave him a pleading look. "Manu, it's either you or a shrink. I prefer you."

"How about a priest?"

"I don't know any. My parents are chemistry teachers that don't believe in 'spirits.'"

"Do you?"

She hesitated. "I don't know… But you do! You're a Buddhist monk, for goodness' sake!"

"Please." He shook his head. "Dabbling in Buddhism doesn't qualify me as a man of the cloth."

"If 'dabbling' is how you describe your daily practice and your two-year stay in a Sichuan monastery, then fine, you're no monk."

Emma tightened her grip on the handrail as she scrambled up the steep staircase. Manu didn't seem to struggle as much as she did. She smiled to herself. Must be his daily meditation practice. Who knew it could build muscle and stamina?

"To answer your question," Manu said, turning around, "you're not a contemptible person."

She gave him a long stare, unsure how to ask her *other* question.

He raised his index finger. "That is not to say your feelings for Cyril aren't morally dubious or that you shouldn't fight them."

She swallowed, processing his words.

"Can you go away for a while?" he asked. "Chances are, you'll forget him in a few weeks."

"Been there, done that." She paused to take off her coat and catch her breath. "When you met me in Sichuan three years ago, what do you think I was doing there?"

"Really?" He gave her a sympathetic look. "When I suggested you go away for a while, I only meant a vacation in Europe. But, wow. You actually spent a whole year in China just to get someone out of your system."

"And I'm prepared to do it again. I'd go even further than China, to some island at the other end of the world."

His lips quirked. "I hear Samoa is fun."

"Samoa it is then." She sagged against the wall. "Only I don't think it would help. He's stuck too deep in my heart."

Emma let out a long breath, relieved to have finally spoken of her feelings, shared her secret with someone. She should've done it earlier. Manu was the perfect agony uncle — compassionate, wise and kind. He wouldn't judge her. He might not understand her, but he wouldn't judge.

"Is Cyril in love with your sister?" he asked.

"Yes." She smirked. "You wouldn't be asking this if you'd seen Geraldine. She's... sparkling."

"Does he have any feelings for *you*?"

She shook her head, her expression resigned.

"OK. Does Geraldine love him back?"

"I...I don't know." Emma sat down on a cold step and hugged her knees. "Gerrie and I never discuss personal matters. Besides, no one ever knows what she's thinking or feeling...or if she's even capable of feeling."

"Has something significant happened or changed recently?"

She looked up at him. "Why are you asking?"

"In the three years we've known each other, you haven't said a word about this. Why now?"

She tucked a loose strand of hair behind her ear. "I think he's going to propose to Geraldine."

"Are you sure?"

"It's a hunch. But my hunches are uncommonly reliable."

"I can help you let go of it, Emma. You can use the power of your mind to silence regret and sadness. You can train your heart to accept their happiness with equanimity."

"But they won't be happy together!" Emma shouted before clapping her hand to her mouth. "They can't be happy together," she repeated quietly.

"Why not?" He sat down a few steps below her.

"I can't explain it… You see, Geraldine already dumped Cyril once, when she met a guy who she thought was even cooler than him."

He stroked his chin. "Then come out. Tell him how you feel."

"I can't."

"You can."

She furrowed her brow. "It would be awful."

"Why?"

"Because it's doomed. He's crazy about her."

"Still, you should tell him."

She chewed at her lower lip, hesitating. "If I do, I'd ruin any chance of a normal relationship with my sister and my future brother-in-law."

"There's a risk. But your love for him…it won't go away by itself, not even after they're married. It'll stay, turn ugly and corrode your heart."

"I know."

"Then don't let it."

"How?"

"By telling him. Tell Geraldine, too. Put it out there, and then go Samoa, if you need to."

"They'll despise me."

He shrugged. "I don't think so, but even if they do, you'll get over it."

"If you were in my shoes, would you tell a nearly engaged man you loved him? Would it be Buddhistically kosher?"

He smiled. "The Buddha said, 'If one acts or speaks with a pure state of mind, then happiness follows like a shadow that remains behind without departing.'"

"Pretty," Emma gave him a lopsided smile. "But that's the thing: I'm not sure how *pure* my state of mind is."

Manu stood and offered her his hand. "Come on. There can't be more than fifty steps left till the top."

She let him pull her up.

When they reached the top, he filled his lungs with air, looked around and then turned to her. "You wanted the Buddhist view on your dilemma, right? Here it is: to love another being isn't a crime or a sin. It's not what you *feel* but what you *do* with it, how you act on those feelings that can cause suffering... Or set you free."

Three months later...

Chapter Two
Cyril

Cyril Tellier swigged his beer.

His third one, to be exact.

To be even more exact, he was downing his third beer before noon.

It wasn't like he had better things to do on this balmy September morning, considering the circumstances.

"I worry about you, buddy." Adrien's voice brimmed with sympathy. "You've been through a lot."

Cyril pictured his friend's kind eyes peering at him in concern.

"Life's been a first-class bitch," he agreed. "But as long as I'm capable of drinking craft beer as fine as this, I'll hold on to it. You have no reason to worry."

Adrien snorted but didn't comment.

Cyril extended his hand in front of him and fumbled for his glass, his fingers catching nothing but air. Then he heard something slide across the table. Had to be his tumbler inching toward his hand with a little help from Adrien.

Good man.

There. Cyril felt a cold, smooth surface touch the back of his hand. He grabbed the glass and carefully lifted it to his mouth. His nostrils caught the bittersweet smell. Then the foam coated his lips. He took a long, appreciative sip, savoring the passage of the delicious liquid over his tongue and down his throat, and delighting at how it quenched his thirst and cooled his whole body.

The brew he'd favored for years without knowing why now offered a new sensory discovery every single time. It was still the same smoked malt but infinitely richer in subtle smells, tastes, and aftertastes—things he hadn't noticed before the accident. In his previous life. A life so different and so far away that he sometimes wondered if he'd dreamed it up.

"So," he finally said, interrupting the awkward silence. "Why did you bring me here? What's so special about this café?"

"Several things." Adrien perked up, obviously happy Cyril had asked that question. "For one, it's an easy walk from your new apartment."

I'll be the judge of what's easy.

"Remember our itinerary?" Adrien asked. "Two right turns, then about twenty meters down rue Cadet, and you're at the entrance of *La Bohème* on your right. It doesn't get more straightforward than that."

"Easy," Cyril said, doing his best to conceal his sarcasm.

"Second reason," Adrien continued. "The food here is amazing—the best you can get in a Paris bistro. And on top of that, Jeanne—one of the waiters—is a friend. She'll take care of you."

"Perfect." Cyril smirked. "So next time I send my soup to the floor and my ravioli across the room, I won't need to call Mom or Gerrie."

Not that he'd asked Gerrie for help with anything lately. She'd made it crystal clear she didn't want to be his "nurse."

He doubted she still wanted to be his girlfriend.

"I'm sure your mom and Geraldine are always happy to give you a hand," Adrien said a little too cheerfully. "But you can be autonomous here with Jeanne around to keep an eye on you."

Right. Of course.

If by "autonomous," one understood switching from dependence on people in your inner circle to people outside it.

But Adrien had meant well. And when Cyril needed him most, he had left his wife and infant back in Bordeaux and cancelled important tournaments. He had basically put his life on hold to be by Cyril's side in those dark first weeks after the accident. And now he traveled to Paris every Thursday, covering hundreds of kilometers each way, just to spend some time with him.

Shame warmed Cyril's ears. A bit of indulgence was the least his friend deserved for his dedication. "I appreciate—"

"Speak of the devil." Adrien interrupted him. "Hi, Jeanne. How have you been?"

Cyril heard what sounded like cheek kisses, pats, and chairs moving.

"I'm great, but *La Bohème* isn't the same without you and Fritz," a throaty female voice said.

"She's referring to my computer chess program," Adrien explained to Cyril. "I used to play here against *Fritz* every afternoon."

"You're Cyril, right?" Jeanne asked. "Adrien tells me you've moved to rue Buffault. You should know that none of the bistros on your street are as good as this one."

Cyril smiled. "I don't doubt it. Your judgment is obviously unbiased."

"Don't be a smartass," Jeanne said. "Besides, I wasn't finished. You see, half of the staff at *La Bohème* are fans of your music. I own both your albums. Rob, whom you'll meet soon enough, adores *The Stray Dog* and fully identifies with the dog in question." She lowered her voice. "A word of advice—if you hold your eardrums and your mental health dear, don't ask him to sing it. Or anything. Ever."

"I don't know about my mental health, but I hold my eardrums very dear indeed. I will *never* ask anyone who's called Rob to sing," Cyril said.

"Good." Jeanne chuckled. "What I'm trying to say is you're one of our favorite musicians and a friend of Adrien's, to boot. You're guaranteed special treatment here that you won't get elsewhere in the neighborhood."

Cyril nodded. "I see."

And nearly clapped his hand to his mouth.

How much longer until he would stop saying "I see" all the time? Sounded stupid coming from him.

"And what's up with you, Adrien?" Jeanne asked, thankfully turning her attention back to his pal. "How's Natalie and baby Lucas?"

"They're doing great. Nat says hi."

"Hi back. Will you guys be ordering lunch later? Today's special is bouillabaisse. Claude's bouillabaisse is better than what they serve in Marseilles, if I say so myself."

"I seem to recall you're from Nîmes, not Marseilles," Adrien said.

"And so what?" Jeanne countered. "It's still better than what they serve in Marseilles."

Cyril's mouth quirked.

"I'll leave you to mull over it," she said. "Duty calls."

Adrien touched Cyril's arm. "Do you have any plans for lunch?"

"Nope." He had no lunch plans until Sunday, when his mom would come by to help him clean and cook. She visited every Sunday and Wednesday, spending almost the entire day at his place. She knew he could afford a cleaner—along with a cook, if he wanted—but she wouldn't hear of it. He suspected her overflowing solicitude was her way of coping with what had happened to her son.

"Want to try out the famous bouillabaisse?" Adrien asked.

"On one condition." Cyril turned to Adrien. "Can you describe this place? I'd like to have an idea of my surroundings."

"It's a regular neighborhood bistro, nothing fancy. The one impressive feature is the bar—antique wood and copper and a floor-to-ceiling wall rack with every wine you can think of."

"Sounds right up my alley. Anything else worth mentioning?"

"Hmm. Let me see. The waiters wear white shirts, black pants, and black aprons."

Cyril nodded slowly and then tilted his head to the side. "Ties?"

"No ties."

"Aha. Interesting." Cyril pressed his index finger to his mouth. "*Very* interesting."

God, it was frustrating to no longer be able to read people's facial expressions. Unless they laughed out loud, he had no way of knowing if he was being funny or a bore.

Adrien didn't laugh. One could only hope he was smiling.

Suddenly, a wave of melancholy came over Cyril, turning the corners of his mouth down. "Just three months ago I was giving concerts, preparing a new album, and scouting for the perfect engagement ring."

"And now you're eating the best bouillabaisse in this country with your oldest friend."

"You make it sound so... normal. Like nothing's wrong with me."

"I'm not trying to make light. It's just... I know it's cliché, but you have to focus on the positive stuff."

"Like what?"

"Like music, for one. You don't need your eyes for it."

Cyril sighed. "I'm too full of bitterness."

"Work that bitterness into your songs. You've done it before."

Cyril shook his head. "In small quantities, it can make for a good song, but... I got nothing else. If I write a song, it'll be crap halfway between a rant and a screech."

"You should write anyway," Adrien said. "As a form of therapy."

"Oh, it's *therapy* we're talking about." Cyril clapped his hand to his forehead. "Stupid me."

Adrien began to say something, but Cyril wasn't listening.

"This"—he pointed to the tumbler in his hand—"is the best therapy for my *affliction*. Works like a charm."

He brought the glass to his lips and emptied it in one long gulp. Ah, the incomparable flavor, the spicy tang. It took his mind off the darkness around him for a few seconds.

Which was the longest he'd managed so far.

Chapter Three
Emma

She walked down rue Cadet, squinting against the sun to read the names of the cafés and restaurants. *La Bohème* had to be somewhere around here, unless its webpage had the wrong address, which would be strange. Then she saw it—a cozy-looking bistro with a sidewalk terrace nestled under classic red awnings.

Emma slowed down, feeling the blood rush to her cheeks and her heartbeat ratchet up. Which was unnecessary. Cyril wasn't on the terrace, and she couldn't discern anyone that looked like him through the windows. But even if he was inside the café, she had no reason for anxiety. He wasn't going to rebuke her. How could he? He wouldn't be able to *see* her, for Christ's sake.

She took a few fortifying breaths, stepped over the threshold, and went straight to the most strategically located table. A uniformed waitress with pale blue hair smiled from behind the bar. Her eyes were lined with black kohl, her nails were painted dark blue, and she looked to be in her early twenties. Emma smiled back, mouthed "coffee, please," and pulled out her phone to keep herself busy.

When the waitress brought her coffee, Emma looked up from her email. A ping-pong sized ball snaked in through the door. The white cane attached to it followed. Emma dragged her gaze from the cane to the person holding it—Cyril.

Unseeing.

Unsteady on his feet.

Scarred.

She covered her mouth with her hand and choked back the sob threatening to erupt from her lungs and give her away.

"Hey there!" The blue-haired waitress cheek kissed Cyril and accompanied him to the table opposite Emma's.

She couldn't have chosen a better spot.

Recovering from her initial shock, Emma studied Cyril's face—every inch, every detail of it.

He wore dark eyeglasses, even though, according to Geraldine, his eyes were unharmed. His blindness was a consequence of the brain trauma he'd suffered during the accident, not direct damage to his eyes.

The glasses had been Geraldine's idea because his vacant gaze made her uncomfortable.

Next, Emma studied the close-cut beard he'd grown to hide some of his scars.

The ones that could be hidden.

Emma blinked several times to push back the tears and turned away. She needed to stay calm and act normal. Otherwise someone might ask her if something was wrong and attract Cyril's attention. She didn't want his attention.

Not yet.

The blue-haired waitress reappeared with a beer for Cyril. "The usual breakfast?"

He nodded. "Yes, please."

"I'm sorry I can't sit down and chat today. I'm filling in for a colleague who's home sick. But Rob is taking his coffee break in ten minutes, so—"

"You don't have to entertain me, Jeanne. And neither does Rob."

Jeanne put her hands on her hips. "Honey, do I look like someone who does things out of obligation?"

Cyril pointed to the smartphone and earbuds he'd pulled from the pocket of his jacket. "I have my audiobook. And a friend will join me here shortly."

Panic crushed Emma's chest. Could the friend be Geraldine?

Her sister had been putting off that drink with Cyril for a couple of weeks now. What if she'd finally made the time for it? What if she walked through that door and gave Emma a tongue-lashing for ogling her boyfriend?

Or ex-boyfriend.

Or whatever he was to her now.

The image of Geraldine's entrance was so vivid that Emma could hear her sister's polished voice. And every bit of mockery in it. Cold sweat beaded her forehead and her palms grew clammy. She rummaged in her purse for her wallet. She had to get out of here ASAP.

And then she remembered something. The friend Cyril had referred to couldn't be Geraldine. She was in Montreuil right now, pitching their new concept to a potential client. Emma pulled out her phone and checked their shared calendar. The meeting had just started, and there was no way Geraldine could make it to the 9th arrondissement in the next couple of hours. The friend Cyril was expecting had to be Adrien, Romain, or Kiki. Emma had heard about them but never met them in person. She was safe.

She returned her attention to Cyril and Jeanne, who continued bickering.

"Trust me, honey, nobody's trying to entertain you," Jeanne said. "We're simply taking advantage of your unfortunate circumstances to get the inside scoop on your songs."

Cyril's mouth quirked into a smile. "Oh, I s— I understand. That's OK, then."

"Good," Jeanne said and sauntered away.

Emma watched her go behind the bar, butter a lengthwise-halved baguette, place it on a plate, and hand it to a waiter whose most remarkable feature was his utter unremarkability. If God had blended every human male together to mold a new specimen, the result would have been this man.

"For table three," Jeanne said.

The statistical derivation glanced over his shoulder. "The disfigured guy with the sunglasses?"

"Didier, for Christ's sake, can you lower your voice?" Jeanne hissed. "He's blind but not deaf."

Emma cringed. As a matter of fact, Cyril *was* deaf. The head trauma that had caused his blindness had damaged his eardrums, too. He now wore discreet hearing aids in both ears. According to Geraldine, the devices worked perfectly, even if Cyril complained they distorted voices beyond recognition. This piece of intel, incidentally, was the cornerstone of Emma's plan.

And perhaps her future.

The insensitive Didier shrugged and added in a quieter voice. "People who drink beer at eleven in the morning don't give a shit about what others think of them."

Jeanne gave him the stare. "He isn't like that."

"I'm just saying, sweetheart." Didier took a step toward the front room, then stopped and turned his head to Jeanne. "Mind you, if I looked like him, I'd make sure I was *never* sober, too."

When he finally delivered the buttered tartine to its destination, Cyril's mouth was pressed into a hard line. He must have heard everything.

He took a swig of his beer, lifted his smartphone to his face and said, articulating every sound, "Call Gerrie."

No.

Emma felt every muscle in her body tense up.

Don't call her. She's not coming. She won't even pick up right now.

But she did pick up, judging by the smile spreading across Cyril's face.

"Hi. When do you think you'll be here?" he asked.

Emma slid to the edge of her chair with her hand on her purse, ready to take off at any moment.

Cyril's smile faded.

"Oh," he said. "Yes, of course... I can hear that... No, you didn't promise anything. It's just... when we talked on Sunday, you said your Thursday morning was free, so I expected you'd meet me here." He swallowed. "I must've gotten the day wrong."

Emma's body went limp with a mixture of relief, shame, and heartrending pity. Her snow queen of a sister had just blown Cyril off without as much as an apology.

As if it was a perfectly fine thing to do.

As if he wasn't broken enough already.

Chapter Four
Cyril

Over the past two weeks, Cyril got in the habit of eating breakfast at *La Bohème* every day and extending it with a coffee or a beer. Or two. But he made it a question of honor not to overstay Jeanne's hospitality, especially during the busy hours between midday and three in the afternoon when the bistro sounded like a beehive on Prozac. Besides, it made him uneasy being in the midst of a small crowd emitting all kinds of noises and talking all at the same time.

But excepting the lunch-hour madness, *La Bohème* was a pleasant enough place to be, even at dinnertime. Besides Jeanne, another waiter looked out for him there—Rob, the tone-deaf fan she'd warned him about. He loved to quote from Cyril's lyrics, of which he had an impressive knowledge. Rob had just finished grad school and received a job offer abroad. He was friendly and upbeat, even if Cyril could detect unmistakable notes of sadness in his voice every now and then. But Rob denied having any defensible cause for complaining about his life.

A couple of days earlier, when Cyril pressed him about the indefensible causes, Rob took some time to consider his reply. "I'll tell you a story," he finally said. "Once upon a time, there was a penniless knight. Actually, he wasn't even a real knight. He was a commoner pretending to be a knight so they'd let him compete in tournaments."

"You're shamelessly plagiarizing *A Knight's Tale*," Cyril cut in.

"Only the setup. Great movie, by the way."

"I agree. But go on."

"So this fake knight signed up to slay a dragon for a briefcase of gold."

"A satchel," Cyril corrected. "For the sake of period detail."

"Period detail, huh? It's my story, remember?"

"A little historical accuracy can go a long way, *mon cher* Passepartout." Cyril held up his index finger, imitating Phileas Fogg from Jules Verne's classic.

Rob snorted. "OK. You want accuracy? I'll give you accuracy: It was a pouch of gold. Now stop distracting me." He tut-tutted. "Where was I? Ah yes, the knight slays the dragon and frees the damsel—"

"You didn't say anything about a damsel."

"That's because she didn't matter to the knight at the beginning. He was only after the gold."

Rob shrugged. "Anyway, the knight and the damsel travel back to the capital, and it turns out she's amazing—you know, fun and kind and... sweet. The journey ends way too soon, and they bid each other farewell in front of her parents' house. The next day, the king tells the knight, 'Dame Elena—the damsel you rescued—likes you. You may marry her if you renounce the gold.' "

"And the knight?"

"The knight says, 'I'll keep the money, thank you.' "

"I suppose he later regretted that choice?"

"Something like that."

Other than this allegorical confession, Rob never discussed personal matters. Most of the time, he shared well-observed tidbits of the goings-on at the bistro, which invariably brought a smile to Cyril's face. Unlike everyone else in his life, including his best friend, Adrien, Rob didn't go out of his way to avoid subjects that might upset him.

It was refreshing.

Last night Cyril went to *La Bohème* on a fact-finding mission. He intended to secure an objective description of his appearance from Rob.

During the first two months after the accident, he'd hardly given any thought to the issue, the enormity of his blindness occupying all his available gray matter. Until a few weeks ago, he'd believed he didn't care what he looked like. He'd had no plans to grow obese or scruffy, of course, but his scars hadn't been a concern.

That was before Gerrie started avoiding him.

As expected, Rob turned up during his break. "I'll be leaving for Thailand in ten days," he said, pulling up a chair. "This week is my last at *La Bohème*."

"*Bonne chance.*" Cyril paused and then took a long breath. "I want you to tell me if I look creepy."

"Wow. You don't bother with smooth transitions, do you?"

Cyril shrugged. "I can assess the size of my scars, but I have no way of gauging how bad they look. How bad I look."

"Um... Well..."

"Listen, I need you to be completely honest and describe what you see without choosing your words. I can't trust my family or friends to do that, you understand?"

"Yes."

"So tell me."

"OK. Fine." Rob went silent for a brief moment. "Here goes. Your forehead is a mess. Big purple-red scars all over, curving and crisscrossing. How did you manage that?"

"Hit the windshield."

"You should consider growing bangs. Thick and long. And sideburns. And maybe combing your hair forward at the temples? You know, Beatles-style."

"It's that bad, huh?"

"Bad, but not creepy. Believe me, you don't look scary."

Cyril nodded.

"Will the scars fade with time?" Rob asked.

"Somewhat."

"But I'm sure modern medicine can do something, right? What did the doctors tell you?"

"They told me they could diminish the redness with lasers and they could thin them surgically."

"So?"

"The surgical revision has to wait until a year after the accident. But the laser can be done in a few months, as soon as the scars are 'mature.'"

"That's good news," Rob said. "Hey, the other good news is that the bottom half of your face is totally presentable. Whatever scars you may have there are hidden behind that neat beard you've got going. Who trims it for you?"

"My dad. He's had a beard most of his adult life, so he's really good."

"Aren't you lucky?"

"I *know*. It's crazy, right?"

"And there's more good news. Your mouth area looks good. I'd say you have a sexy mouth, man."

Cyril snorted.

Rob cleared his throat loudly. "Correction. I *would have* said it. If I were gay."

Chapter Five
Emma

"And here comes mademoiselle's *petit noir*." The server gave her a fleeting smile as he placed her espresso on the countertop and rushed off to another customer.

Emma swallowed the scalding coffee, counted to ten to calm her breathing, and walked over to Cyril's table. "You're Cyril, right?"

She hoped the doubt in her voice sounded convincing.

"That's correct. And you are?"

"Laura."

"What can I do for you, Laura?"

She expelled a long breath. *Say it.* "May I sit down?"

He shrugged. "Sure. I can autograph an album, if that's what you want, but no photos. And I mean it."

"I'm good," she said, pulling out a chair to sit across from him. "I already have your autograph, and I don't want a picture."

"Oh. OK."

During the silence that followed, Cyril cocked his head as if to ask, *What is it you want from me then?* But Emma was dumbstruck. All last night's preparations had been in vain. She couldn't remember any of the icebreakers she'd come up with.

As quietly as she could manage, she opened her purse, retrieved a folded sheet of paper, and read out the first line from her list. "I love your songs."

"I don't," Cyril said. "But thank you. If it weren't for you and the likes of you, I'd be blind *and* poor."

If it weren't for me… Oh God.

Cyril raised his beer glass. "To your good health." He moved it toward his mouth and paused. "Are you having a drink? Can I buy you one?"

"I don't drink alcohol in the morning," Emma said, unable to redact disapproval from her voice. "But thanks."

"Good girl. Don't you let decadent assholes like me sway you from the path of righteousness." He closed the remaining distance to his mouth and took a sip. Gingerly, he lowered the glass to the table in front of him.

"I get tipsy off one beer," Emma said to soften her earlier admonishment.

"Not me. Unfortunately. But I *never* drink anything stronger than beer before lunch. I, too, have principles."

Principles, my foot.

"So tell me, Laura, how can I help you?"

"I was hoping for a chat... about your music. As I said, I'm a huge fan and this is a fantastic opportunity."

"As *I* said, I'm not a fan of my music... but I've got time to kill, so sure. What is it you'd like to know?"

"I've always wondered about your creative process. Where do you get your ideas? Where do the lyrics and tunes come from? Which one comes first?"

Cyril sighed. "Have you checked out the F-A-Q section on my website?"

"Of course I have. But it's useless. You don't really answer your fans' questions in your F-A-Qs. You just goof around and show off how funny you are."

Cyril spread his arms apologetically. "One has to goof around *somewhere*."

She wasn't done. "It's like you're two different people. In your songs, you're someone who feels deeply, someone sincere and relatable. But you turn into a superficial smartass in... the website."

Emma cringed. She hadn't meant to say these things, at least not now during the first meaningful conversation she'd ever had with him. What if he suspected something? What if he realized this was too personal and figured out who she was?

She stared at him, trying to read his expression. To her surprise, Cyril's mouth stretched into an amused grin. "You don't take prisoners, do you?"

"I'm sorry. I didn't mean to be unkind—"

"You weren't unkind. You were honest, and I appreciate that." His face grew thoughtful. "I guess... I guess when you routinely bare your soul before people, it's hard to maintain the same level of naked intensity in other aspects of your life." He wrinkled his nose. "I'm not sure I'm making sense—"

She leaned in, praying for him to continue. "You are."

He nursed his glass with both his hands. "Suppose I wasn't a superficial smartass. Then you can think of my stupid jokes and my cynicism as... clothing. Something to cover my untanned nudity when I'm not exhibiting it on stage."

She swallowed. "I never thought of it that way."

"Laura, may I ask you a question?"

She nodded — and rolled her eyes, realizing the pointlessness of her gesture. "Yes, of course."

"Why do you sound like you know me?"

Cold sweat gathered under her hairline. *Stay calm.* "Beats me. Maybe because I know all your songs and have played them daily since your first album came out? Which, using your metaphor, is the same as seeing you in your birthday suit. Many, many times."

He opened his mouth and roared with laughter.

Oh, how she loved that unrestrained laugh of his. It was better than a bowl of rum raisin ice cream or a scented hot bath in the middle of January or an afternoon on the beach with a great book. It was simply the best thing in the world.

"Wow," someone behind her said. "How did you do it?"

Emma turned around and saw Jeanne, the blue-haired waitress, gawking. A chubby middle-aged man stood next to her.

"Hi, I'm Jeanne." The waitress extended her hand.

"I'm Laura." Emma shook it, surprising herself with her flawless reply. A full week of practice had paid off.

Jeanne turned to Cyril. "Hey, Cyril. I need your friend here to tell me how she managed to make you laugh like that. In all the hours you've spent at this bistro over the past three weeks, the most anyone could wring from you was a lopsided smirk. So, I *must* know."

"She said she liked the sight of me in a particular *suit*." Cyril pursed his lips to contain his hilarity.

"I said no such thing," Emma protested.

Jeanne winked. "Being cryptic, are we? Anyway, I just want you to meet Pierre, my boss. He's standing next to me."

Cyril nodded. "Monsieur."

"Bonjour," Pierre said. "I'm the proprietor of this establishment."

"Let me guess—and a huge fan of my music. Everyone at *La Bohème* seems to be."

"Not everyone. Just me and Rob," Jeanne said.

Pierre gave him a toothy smile. "I must say I don't know your songs. You're too young for me. But I am a big fan of soft rock and the French chanson, and I'm told you're the new generation's face of it."

"I certainly hope not," Cyril said. "It would *not* be a pretty face."

Jeanne coughed and Pierre's smile drooped.

Cyril broke the awkward silence. "I suppose your love of the French chanson is the reason you called the bistro *La Bohème*?"

"Right on the button." Pierre grinned again. "When I bought this place from the previous owner, the first thing I did was rename it after my favorite piece by Charles Aznavour."

"It's my favorite, too," Cyril said.

"Well, in that case, this beer is on me." Pierre turned to Emma. "And whatever mademoiselle is ordering, too, of course."

After he left, Jeanne swapped out the empty peanut bowl in front of Cyril for a new one. "You have a fresh supply of peanuts next to your left hand." She turned to Emma and smiled. "What shall I get you?"

"A Perrier, please, or any other sparkling water."

Jeanne nodded. "I'll leave you to your conversation, then."

Emma stayed at *La Bohème* for the rest of the morning and chatted with Cyril about all sorts of things, forgetting she had a huge amount of work and a tight deadline. She wouldn't have budged if someone had called her to say her apartment was on fire. What did it matter if her home or all of Paris burned down when she was finally talking — really talking — with Cyril?

Chapter Six
Cyril

Gerrie called at the worst possible time: he was in the shower. Hearing her ringtone sent his brain into a frantic dilemma-solving mode. Safety required that he ignore her call and carry on with his shower. But Gerrie had been so difficult to reach lately. His calls would go straight to her voice mail, and it took her days to call him back.

He pushed the faucet handle down, toweled his hands and ears dry, and grabbed the wall-mounted receiver. "Hey."

"Hi there! Thought I'd give you a quick call between appointments."

"How's business?"

"Not bad," she said with a tinge of pride in her voice. "Old clients come back for more and recommend us to new ones. But the downside is that Emma and I are swamped. I get up at dawn, and she toils at her computer until one or two in the morning. Every night."

"She's really good at what she does," he said, and he meant it. Emma produced the most original and handsome images he'd ever seen. She'd created the covers of both his albums. He loved them.

"Yep," Gerrie agreed. "She's a fantastic designer. And I run around like a headless chicken, taking care of everything else from accounting to contracts to customer service."

"Why don't you hire someone to help you out?"

"We're thinking about it. But it's a big step for a small, family-run company, you know?"

"Yes, of course."

Only... she had worked just as hard before his accident and yet had found time to see him every day.

"Gerrie," he said. "I need you to be honest with me. It's not just the work, is it?"

"What do you mean?"

"After I came home from the hospital—over two months ago—we've hardly seen each other... I hate to be a pain, but something has changed." He paused, giving her a chance to protest.

She didn't.

He waited, heart sinking with every passing moment.

"I... I can't do this, Cyril," she finally said. "I care for you and I want us to remain friends, but... I can't be your babysitter."

He'd expected something along those lines, but it still hurt like hell to hear her say it.

"I'm so sorry, baby," she continued. "But I'm not a Mother Teresa type. Self-sacrifice isn't in my nature."

He could tell her he didn't want or even need her self-sacrifice. He could give her countless examples of his growing autonomy and enumerate all the smart gadgets that allowed a blind person to do almost everything sighted people could do.

But this wasn't just about his autonomy. He'd given the matter a good deal of thought. The accident had forced him to become someone else. Someone Gerrie didn't seem to like anymore. His appearance, his social status, his lifestyle—all of it had changed, and not in a good way. Who could blame her? He was no longer the man she had been in an on-again-off-again relationship with since high school. Even his so-called soul had morphed into something different.

Angrier.

Uglier.

A lot less fun.

"That's OK," he said. "I understand. Take care of yourself."

He hung up and stepped back into the shower stall.

Stick to the routine.

Thank God for the routine. The daily planner app on his phone had been his lifeline since the accident. He tried to have a task planned for every hour, including things like *go to La Bohème for a drink* and *listen to the radio*. Marked down like that, those activities stopped being a pastime and acquired a vague purpose. He didn't go to the bistro just for the beer. He went there so he'd have a reason to leave his apartment, familiarize himself with his neighborhood, and maintain a semblance of social life.

Today's list contained his usual activities and two tricky tasks—pasta cooking and grocery shopping. He was going to do both things on his own this time. Like the big boy he was.

Cyril dried himself, got dressed, and headed to the kitchen. Two days ago, a *Darty* technician had come by to swap his touch screen ceramic hob for a basic one with hand turning knobs. Which meant he could now prepare his favorite spaghetti al pesto. At least theoretically.

Before the accident, spaghetti had been his go-to dish, the easy and filling meal he'd cooked so often he could make it with his eyes closed. Or so he used to claim. Well, he had the ideal conditions now to put that claim to the test. After all, what better way to test a theory than a *blind trial*?

Something jabbed his thigh, making him flinch. His fingers came into contact with the corner of his fashionably rustic dining table.

"You have arrived at your destination," he said out loud, mimicking the polished robotic voice of the GPS in his adored MINI Cooper.

Which was now as much of a wreck as its owner.

OK. Spaghetti. He skirted the table to get to the pantry. Mom had stocked it with all kinds of foodstuffs, organized and labelled in Braille. Finding a spaghetti box shouldn't be too difficult. Over the past months, the good people at Mobility Help had taught him lots of food-related tips and tricks. He was now able to brew his own java, spread jam on his toast without losing half of it on the floor, and press orange juice.

Cooking pasta would be his next milestone.

Grabbing the box, he walked over to the cooking area, where he put it on the worktop. Now, if he could locate a saucepan, fill it with water, and get it to the stove, he'd treat himself to a good swig of beer.

He opened the cabinet where he kept his pots and pans and groped. But all he dug up was skillets. Five of them in different sizes—and not a single saucepan. Mom must have moved the saucepans to another place that made more sense to her. But where? He could call her and ask, of course, but then this undertaking would become *assisted*.

Cyril sighed. His cooking adventure would have to wait until he found the energy to turn his kitchen inside out.

For now, he would tackle the next item on his to-do list: grocery shopping. He rushed to the foyer, grabbed his cane, and walked out of his apartment, spurred by determination. But once inside the convenience store, his confidence evaporated. He'd studied these aisles with Mom several times. So why couldn't he remember where to start?

Concentrate.

OK. Beer and milk were at the back. Bread on the left. What about coffee? And cheese? This was a lot more difficult than he'd expected.

He was about to call for the shop assistant, when he heard a familiar voice. "Cyril, hi! What are you doing here?"

He turned toward the voice. "Hi. Who is this?"

"Stupid me! It's Laura. From last week at *La Bohème*?"

"You didn't mention you lived in the neighborhood."

"I don't. I just have some business here this month."

"What sort?"

"Stalking you."

He lost his tongue for a second.

"I'm kidding," she said, laughing. "I'm a photographer, and I'm doing shoots on rue du Faubourg Montmartre for a magazine."

"Oh, good. Stalkers are creepy."

She cleared her throat. "So, what is it you need to buy?"

"The basics. Coffee, beer, licorice candy, milk, bread—"

She giggled. "I hope that list doesn't reflect your order of priorities."

"Of course it does."

"Can I help you? I finished today's shoot earlier than planned, so I have time on my hands."

"Sure," he said, trying to conceal his relief. "You're very kind."

She hooked her skinny arm through his. "All right, then. Let's go hunt down some licorice."

When they'd marked off the last item on his list, Laura offered to help him carry the bags to his apartment.

Cyril silently thanked the god of vanity for having made sure he'd left home without the granny-style shopping cart his mom had gotten him.

"There's no need," he said without a trace of conviction in his voice.

"I insist."

"OK. Follow me."

* * *

"Can I get you something to drink?" he asked her as soon as they'd finished transferring the contents of the bags to the pantry and refrigerator shelves.

"One of those beers you bought would be nice now."

He motioned to the kitchen table. "Please, have a seat."

As he opened the fridge door, he itched to demonstrate his recently acquired skills to this woman. He'd become good at pouring liquids, rarely spilling a drop. You could actually do without sight to measure the fullness of a glass. He'd learned to rely on nuances in sound and weight and on a judicious use of his index finger when the liquid approached the top.

Hmm. Perhaps no finger this time.

"What do you look like?" he asked as he held her glass out for her.

"Who? Me?" She took the glass, brushing her fingers against his.

"I know you aren't obese," Cyril said. "But other than that, I'm in the dark."

"OK. Let's see. I'm foxy. I wear my platinum blond hair in a wavy bob. My waist is narrow, and my hips are full. My boobs are size D. Oh, and I have a gorgeous little beauty mark above the left corner of my mouth."

His lips twitched. "You sound amazing, Marilyn."

"Pardon me? I have no idea who you're talking about."

"Don't you? So you just described *yourself*, what you really look like, and you weren't at all poking fun at an optically challenged person?"

"Uh-huh."

He sat down next to her. "I demand to verify."

"And how will you do that? You have no way of gauging how blond my hair is."

"Wrong. I have a color-detecting app in my phone."

"Really?"

He nodded. "But even without it, I can assess the veracity of the beauty mark, the D cup, the thinness of the waist and the fullness of the hips."

"By *groping* me?"

Cyril threw his hands up and schooled his features into a look of misunderstood innocence. "A blind man's got to do what a blind man's got to do."

"Yeah, right." She was silent for a few seconds and then said, "You can check the beauty mark. But that's it."

He lifted his hand to where he expected her face to be. She shifted a little, and then his fingers came into contact with smooth, warm skin. Her cheek. He stayed there for a moment, reveling in the feel of it, then cupped the side of her face and ran his thumb across her sweet chin and her elegant jawline.

"So far so good," he said with a satisfied grin.

She didn't speak or move.

He slid his fingers to the area above her mouth, looking for the famous mark. Finding none, he went up to her cheekbones and then down to her soft lips.

After a good three minutes of brushing her mouth and cheeks and acquiring a substantial hard-on in the process, he pronounced his verdict. "You have no beauty mark."

Her reaction came with a suspicious delay. "Don't I?"

Was she out of breath, or was it just his imagination?

"Nope. At least none detectable with the naked thumb."

"Darn! I was sure I'd glued one on this morning."

He laughed. "Maybe it fell off. You should use stronger glue next time."

"I sure will."

Now, if he could come up with another excuse to touch her, everything would be fine in the finest of all possible worlds.

Think, Cyril, think!

"I've got to go," she said suddenly.

Shit. Damn his anachronistic cockiness! This was what happened when a *visually-impaired person* with a scarred face acted as if he were still a heartthrob.

He swallowed hard. "I scared you. I'm sorry."

She fumbled with something and shifted in her seat.

"I promise to keep all my digits off you in the future," he said in a last-ditch attempt to salvage the situation. "Please stay."

"It's not you," she said. "Really. I just... I remembered an important appointment."

A chair scraped lightly against the floor tiles, followed by a short silence, and then her voice. "I'll see you around."

"Bye."

He listened to her retreating steps. Then the door clicked shut, and his apartment became unbearably quiet.

He remained seated, frozen in a stupor at his kitchen table, while his mind replayed both of his encounters with his fan Laura. After a long moment, he admitted to himself she had stirred something in him.

Then he made peace with the idea that he would never see her again.

In any sense of the word.

Chapter Seven
Emma

"And then I said, 'Sure, no problem. If you think you can find a better designer who'll meet your deadline and charge less than us, be my guest. I promise no hard feelings.'" Geraldine tilted her head to the side and spread her lips into a disdainful smile, reenacting her standard *killer punch* for Emma's benefit.

Emma smirked. "I bet they said, 'OK, you win, let's discuss the color palette.'"

"Believe it or not, they didn't! Those cheapskates made a new offer, higher than the first one but still below our quotation."

"That's unusual. So you delivered the *death blow*?"

"Oh yes, I did—and took immense pleasure in it. I looked at the new figure and pushed the sheet back across the table. I flashed them my Smile Number Three and said, 'Messieurs, it's been a pleasure, but my time is too expensive to be wasted on useless haggling. Good luck with your launch.' I picked up my purse and began walking toward the door..."

Somewhere in the middle of Geraldine's account, Emma tuned out. She was having a hard time concentrating on her sister's self-congratulatory chatter. She'd had a hard time concentrating on anything lately since the beauty mark episode in Cyril's kitchen. God, how she'd wanted him to continue touching her! Her body had gone all gooey and hot, and her brain... her brain had rearranged all its neurons to form three short words: *Yes. Please. More.* The only thing that made her pull back and leave was her fear of destroying the fragile little sprout between them with an excess of zeal.

She couldn't risk it. Not now, not when she finally had a chance with him.

It was important he get to know her a little better before they became lovers.

Sweet Lord.

The mere thought that making love to Cyril had moved from the realm of fantasy to the domain of possibility was enough to send her pulse into the stratosphere. Was she freaking out? Was she scared she'd disappoint him in bed? After all, he'd dated none other than Geraldine—the woman who claimed to know every trick in the Kama Sutra and emit pheromones during sex that messed with men's heads. Which was, of course, one hundred percent pure Geraldine-grade bullshit. Unlike Emma's easily verifiable lack of experience and prowess.

The thought gave her pause. Was this the *real* reason she had run away from Cyril the other day? Because she'd realized he might touch her like that again and kiss her and... who knew? So she left, afraid to disappoint the man of her dreams—the man she'd loved for so long it had become part of her identity.

Emma had fallen for Cyril at thirteen, on the day sixteen-year-old Geraldine came home with her cute new classmate. The two of them stayed in Geraldine's room for hours, admittedly studying. But Emma's room was next door, and she could hear them talk and laugh and fool around. Cyril strummed the guitar he'd brought along and sang songs she'd never heard before. They were funny, sad, silly, superficial, and wise. All at once. They moved with ease from the importance of doodling to bonds of friendship and from there to the meaning of life. They were so melodious she couldn't help tapping her foot to the beat.

She loved them.

And before she knew it, she loved him.

But Cyril only had eyes for Geraldine. And who could blame him? Unlike most kids her age, Geraldine sailed through her teens without so much as a medium-size zit to tarnish her angelic face. She was confident, witty, luminous, and immensely popular.

As for Emma... At the time, she'd been hopelessly self-conscious. She hid her face behind her hair and wore baggy sweatshirts and loose-fitting jeans to conceal her lack of curves. She was still the family's baby—someone to watch over, patronize, tease, and never take seriously.

And that was exactly what Cyril had done, taking his cue from her parents and Geraldine. He called her Boney Em, as a nod to her thinness and the famed '70s disco group. Considering how much time he'd spent at their place during the two years he and Geraldine dated in high school, the conversations he'd had with her were remarkably short and few.

The most frequent situation when they talked was when he would ring the doorbell, and she would open the door. He'd smile and say, "Hey, Boney Em. What's up?" But his gaze would slide over her and travel to the dark hallway leading to Geraldine's room. He'd peer, trying to decipher if Geraldine was coming out to meet him. His feet would point in that direction. Emma knew it because she always looked down when she talked to him. He would stay put just long enough for her to say, "Hi Cyril. I'm fine. Geraldine's in her room." Then he'd nod and head there, offering a polite, "Bonjour, Madame Perrin," when he passed by the kitchen where Mom lingered.

Had Geraldine been in love with him back then? It was hard to say. One thing was sure: her sister enjoyed having him around. Cyril was undeniably cool, and Geraldine liked everything that was cool.

Then the two teenage lovebirds finished school and went their separate ways. For six years, Emma only saw Cyril when she went to his concerts. Initially, he performed in small bistros and neighborhood cafés. After his first album became an overnight success, he began to sing at trendy places like Chez Luke and L'Espace and lately at Le Zenith and the Olympia Hall.

She had attended his every Parisian performance and a great many concerts in other parts of France. She'd traveled to Belgium and Switzerland when she could. She had even invented a boyfriend in Lyon to explain her frequent trips out of town. Her mom and dad were still upset over her refusal to introduce said boyfriend to the family.

After all, he was the only one they'd ever heard about.

* * *

Emma arrived at the bistro at seven thirty. It was still half-empty and relatively quiet, the dinner service having barely begun. Cyril was already at his usual spot, biting into a delicious-looking hamburger. She stepped in and marched toward him, anxious to cover the short distance before she lost her nerve.

When she halted by his table, he put his hamburger down and turned in her direction, his expression uncertain.

She exhaled, refilled her lungs with air and opened her mouth. But no sound came: Her tongue simply refused to move.

"Can I help you?" he asked.

She gripped the back of the chair in front of her. "Hi. You're here. What a surprise."

Her words tumbled out, rushed and clumsy—not casual and unaffected as she'd intended. Emma rolled her eyes skyward, the temptation to bang her head against the marble tabletop almost too powerful to resist.

He narrowed his eyes. "Laura?"

"Yes."

"I didn't expect to see you again after... last time."

"I just—" She swallowed. "I just stopped here for a quick bite before heading home... after my photo shoot... around the corner."

Get a grip, woman.

"Did it go well?" he asked politely.

"Yes, thank you."

Emma was about to inquire if she could sit next to him, when the room erupted in loud noises, high-pitched screams and a few select curses. She turned around. What she saw was the most spectacular case of indoor flooding she'd ever witnessed.

Water had breached the ceiling and cascaded down, showering the unfortunate guests sitting under the crack. Judging by the amount of it, a pipe must have leaked for a long time in the apartment above the bistro. As the customers leaped to their feet and scrambled to get away from the downpour, another hole opened up above the bar area. A second jet gushed down, hitting the counter, knocking the neatly stacked glasses to the ground and soaking the baskets of sliced baguette.

"What's going on?" Cyril asked.

"The Deluge."

"Everyone out, please!" Jeanne yelled as she zoomed by with a bucket that she placed under the first leak.

Another server put a big saucepan on the counter to collect the water from the second hole.

"Messieurs-dames, please leave immediately!" the proprietor bellowed. "It isn't safe for you here. All checks are on the house."

"I'm not leaving," Cyril said loudly.

"You're in the mood for a cold shower?" Jeanne shouted.

He shook his head. "I just received training at Mobility Help on how to respond to home emergencies, including leaks and flooding. I know exactly what to do."

"That's great." Jeanne turned to Emma and gave her an emphatic look. "But you heard what the man said. Out, both of you!"

"You need to shut off the water supply," Cyril said, unflustered. "Can you locate the valve?"

"Already did." Jeanne nudged the bucket with her foot. "And Rob called an emergency plumber and the fire brigade. There isn't much else we can do, apart from praying there won't be another hole."

"You better turn off the electricity in the building as an additional precaution," Cyril said. "Do you know where the main switch is?"

"Must be in the basement." Pierre cut in. "I'll take care of it. Rob, come with me. You'll hold the torchlight."

When both of them were gone, Jeanne turned to Cyril. "Thank you, honey. But you must leave now."

"What about the furniture?" Cyril's voice was full of concern. A little too full. "The wooden chairs, the marble-top tables... I bet they're vintage."

"How did you know?" Jeanne asked.

Cyril ran his fingertips over the back of a chair. "The shape. The texture..." He stroked the tabletop then gripped its edge and tipped the table a little. "The weight."

"They're from the 1920s and 30s," Jeanne admitted. "Pierre's been buying them for the bistro over the past twenty years."

"Well, then he wouldn't want them damaged, would he?" Cyril paused, then added, "I could help you take them out..."

If his last words weren't a desperate plea, then Emma didn't know what was. She peered at Jeanne, praying the waitress would understand what this meant to him, how much he needed to feel useful, competent, in charge.

Jeanne threw her hands up in resignation. "How do you propose to do that?"

Thank God.

"If someone—you or one of the other waiters—could give me a hand, we'll push the furniture away from the water." He leaned in, enthusiasm palpable in his voice. "And then we'll carry it all out to the terrace."

"I'm in," Emma said. "The artist in me can't bear letting such fine pieces be ruined."

He smiled. "Thanks, Laura."

"OK," Jeanne said. "I need to help Claude

and Didier take care of the electrical appliances and empty the pantry under the bar. So I'll let you guys salvage the furniture."

"Don't touch anything that's plugged in until Pierre is back," Cyril warned.

"Yes, Mom," Jeanne said and winked at Emma.

When she was gone, Emma touched Cyril's hand. "Follow me."

For the next thirty minutes, they pushed dozens of chairs and tables toward the entrance door and then evacuated them outside. During that time, the firefighters and the plumber arrived. Pierre and Rob returned from their mission and started explaining the situation to the professionals. Men in uniform ran to and fro, carrying toolboxes, equipment and ladders. A group of onlookers gathered around the terrace, watching the show.

Emma registered all of that in a strangely detached way, as if she were watching a 3-D movie. Her immediate reality was the hot jolts of pleasure that shot through her body each time her hand brushed Cyril's. It happened when she guided him to a piece of furniture that needed moving, when they lifted a table together or when she handed him a chair to be carried outside.

As they shuttled between the front room and the terrace, Cyril looked concentrated and purposeful. But Emma noticed—unless her heightened senses were messing with her brain—how his expression changed when they touched. And how he didn't rush to break the contact.

When they transferred the last chair to safety, she found comfort in the hope that he'd suggest they have a well-deserved drink at another cafe or at his place. They would talk. She'd be sure to encourage him to touch her again like he'd done last time. And she wouldn't run, no matter where his exploration led them.

Jeanne emerged from the kitchen, shook Emma's hand and then Cyril's. "Thank you, guys! Your selfless heroism will become legend, like Claude's 2006 tiramisu. It'll be passed on from one generation of servers to the next."

"It was fun," Cyril said. "What's the story with the tiramisu?"

Jeanne took a theatrical pose. "On July 27, 2006, Claude made a tiramisu that gave all of the female guests a deep, multiple orgasm at the first spoonful." She paused for effect. "Unfortunately, he never managed to find the exact same proportions of mascarpone, coffee, brandy and ladyfingers. And that is how the

2006 Orgasmic Tiramisu became legend."

Emma giggled.

"When do you expect to reopen?" Cyril asked.

"In a couple of days," Jeanne said. "As soon as the ceiling is patched up and the apartment upstairs drained."

"I'll hold you to it." He smiled at Jeanne and then turned to Emma. "Thank you for supporting me! Jeanne wouldn't have taken me seriously if it weren't for you."

"I'm glad I could help," Emma said.

He picked up his cane. "I'd better be going. See you around, Laura."

"See you around," she murmured, doing her best to hide her disappointment.

He walked down the street, disappearing behind passersby and reappearing for brief moments, until his distant silhouette completely dissolved into the evening crowd.

Chapter Eight
Cyril

He wished they would stop the rumpus and go home. He wished they had never started in the first place. The initiative was no doubt well-intentioned and looked great on paper. It should have made him happy and grateful.

But instead it annoyed him to no end.

He was now forced to fake enthusiasm to indulge the proactive trio that had gone to great lengths to organize this surprise. They'd researched, purchased, and arranged for the delivery of a custom-built recording studio. It had all the necessary hardware and software and even a vocal booth to keep the noise pollution out.

Every piece of equipment was accessible for the blind. The hardware was simple and tactile. The software was intuitive and talking. It included programs to convert conventional scores and to transcribe his own compositions in Braille.

And now his three meddling buddies and a technician dispatched by the manufacturer were busy setting up his magical studio in the nook of his living-room. Louis, his agent and unrepentant gadget buff, oohed and aahed every time the technician demonstrated some cool functionality. Adrien—a certified geek—rivaled Louis's excitement. Adrien's wife, Nat, emitted appreciative uh-huhs and ooh la las and kept asking Cyril what *he* thought about it.

The trouble was Cyril couldn't tell her what thought. Because he thought the home studio idea was a huge waste of their money and time. They should have checked with him first before deciding to play Santa. Had they asked, he would've told them he had no need for the studio, didn't want it, and wouldn't use it.

He didn't compose or sing anymore. His guitar was collecting dust on top of a wardrobe. None of his many sleepless nights had begotten a tune, a verse, or even a line of lyrics.

Music was simply no longer a part of his life.

"So what do you think?" Nat asked again.

"Sounds cool," Cyril finally said, choosing not be a party pooper.

"How about we try one more thing?" the technician asked for the hundredth time over the past couple of hours.

He itched to say, *I'd rather not*. But he just nodded.

"Put the headphones on. Now press the big button labelled *record* and plug in the headphones here. OK?"

"*Oui,* monsieur," Cyril said with a smirk.

But his sarcasm was lost on the guy, who gave him a hearty pat on the shoulder. "And voilà! You're recording! To stop, just press the other big button—the one marked *stop*."

Cyril dutifully executed. "Amazing."

"We'll send a programmer next week to customize the workstation to your specs and teach you to use the more advanced software. But for now, you can play with the recorder and use the basic functions I just walked you through."

"Great," Cyril said. "Thanks."

An hour later they were finally gone—first the upbeat technician, then Louis, and then Adrien and Nat. Cyril savored the blissful silence for a few minutes before deciding he needed a drink. He put his shoes on, picked up his cane, and headed out the door.

On his way to *La Bohème*, Kiki called to ask if he felt like joining forces to drown their sorrows in alcohol. She had recently been dumped by her boyfriend and was going through a rough patch. When they met for drinks, he was the one to do the cheering up, which was refreshingly different from almost every other social situation he'd been involved in of late.

When Kiki arrived, he'd just finished his first beer.

"Feeling better?" he asked her.

"Depends. You need to be more specific."

"Feeling better today than last time we talked?"

"No."

"A glass of Chablis?"

"Yes. Please."

He ordered her wine and another beer for himself.

"What about you?" Kiki asked.

"Same old. Still blind as a bat."

"Is there a chance your eyesight might return?"

He nodded. "Oh yes. The only problem is that it's lower than my chance of being struck by a lightning."

"Well, it's probably still higher than my chance of getting back together with Romain." She snorted humorlessly and rummaged through her purse from the sound of it.

Something tiny hit the table.

"Next to your beer," she said.

He felt the surface of the table until his hand brushed a small round object. He placed it in his palm and stroked it with the index finger of his other hand. "Hmm. A pill with a smiley face etched into it. I think I know what it is."

"It's magic," she said. "Aka Ecstasy."

"Since when have you been doing drugs?"

"I don't *do* drugs. It's just... an ad hoc measure. A friend of mine got me these babies to see me through my blues."

"Kiki—"

"I'm not saying you should do like me. But I can tell you when I popped one of these smiley faces last week, I felt great for three days. All my despair, darkness, hopelessness—it all went away. It was amazing."

"Yeah, and next time you pop one, you'll OD."

"No chance. I'm going to take only one pill per week, just so I can feel better for a while until time blunts the pain."

"And that's your friend's genius plan for your recovery?"

"Why, you have a better idea?"

"Sure. Pack three kilos of chocolate and go to Tahiti."

"You forget I'm not as rich as you are. Besides I can't take vacation until Christmas." She grabbed his left hand and folded his fingers over the pill. "This one's for you. Keep it for the day you hit the rock bottom."

"There are lines I won't cross no matter what."

"If I were you, *mon pote*," Kiki said. "I would never say never."

Chapter Nine
Emma

She'd gotten up at five in the morning to make as much progress with her work as she could before heading to *La Bohème*. Having watched him from afar over the past week, she'd figured out his schedule. It looked like he went to the bistro twice a day: first for breakfast and a beer and then for dinner and more beers.

At around five in the afternoon, Emma grew so restless her concentration eluded her. She packed her sketches and her laptop with the unfinished design and walked out into the golden afternoon.

The *métro* ride was crowded and much too long, and when she jostled her way out of the train at Cadet, it was already six. Which was OK, she told herself as she raced the escalator to the exit. She still had at least an hour's head start — enough time to complete her project and rehearse her little speech before Cyril arrived.

To her surprise, he was already at the bistro. She spotted his thick brown hair as soon as she crossed rue LaFayette onto rue Cadet. He sat outside on the sidewalk terrace, lounging in a red and cream wicker chair, his nape leaned against the glass behind him and his face turned up to the soothing September sun.

Emma's pulse quickened. For a brief moment, she was tempted to go up to him and say, *Hi, it's Laura, but my real name is Emma Perrin.*

She pictured the look on his face. He'd be shocked, for sure. Probably angry. Possibly disgusted. No, no, it was too soon. In spite of Geraldine's assurances, Emma feared that Cyril hated her. She hated herself, after all, for the suffering she'd caused him.

She approached him. "Hi, it's Laura."

At the sound of her voice, he broke into a big smile and yanked the earbuds from his ears. "Laura! What are you doing here?"

She had intended to feed him another lie about her fictitious photo shoot. But her mouth refused to deliver it. Emma hesitated then made up her mind. Even if she'd resolved to continue her charade for now, she could at least tell him the truth about her motives.

"I was hoping to find you here," she said.

Cyril's smile grew bigger, but he remained silent.

"A little help, please?" she pleaded.

"Apologies. Where are my manners?" He pointed to the chair next to his. "Would you like to sit down?"

"Thank you." She took her seat and dropped her backpack on the ground between her feet.

"Sounds heavy," he commented.

"My laptop's in it. I was planning to finish some work before you arrived."

"Is it urgent?"

"Kind of... Actually, yes."

"Go ahead, finish it. I'm not going anywhere." He raised his empty glass above his head and continued speaking. "I'll have my second beer while you're finishing your work, and then I'll invite you to dinner. If that's agreeable."

"That's very agreeable. Thank you." Emma opened her backpack and pulled her laptop from its protective case.

They spent the next hour in companionable silence. Cyril didn't ask her what she was doing and how well she was progressing. He let her concentrate on her work, which was terrific. The only time she lost her focus was when she felt the sun tickle her face as it was about to disappear behind the building across the street. She touched the spot on her cheek where it had kissed her and stole a glance at Cyril, who sipped his beer, listening to something on his smartphone.

She felt ridiculously content.

Dinner turned out to be a different story. Not in terms of contentment but with respect to the number of questions Cyril had for her. He wanted to know everything about her: where she'd grown up, if she had any siblings, if she liked her job, what her favorite books, shows, and movies were, and the lowdown on her first love and first heartbreak.

She attempted to reply as truthfully as she could, given the circumstances. The questions about books and movies were the easiest.

"You're the first female science fiction buff I've ever met," Cyril said.

"Then you haven't met a lot of women. How unusual for a musician."

"I had the same girlfriend for many years. And I'm only twenty-six."

"Do you still love her?" Emma's voice was composed even as her hands trembled.

"I don't know." He furrowed his brow. "I do miss her. But it may be that I just miss the company of... a woman."

"Arthur C. Clarke," she said.

"I beg your pardon?"

"My favorite sci-fi author. If you haven't read him, you absolutely should. Start with *Rendezvous with Rama*."

"Will do." He touched her forearm. "You didn't answer my earlier question."

"Which one?"

"About your first heartbreak."

"I'll tell you only if you tell me about yours." She rolled her eyes at her cheap stalling trick. Oh well, desperate times and all.

"OK," he said, surprising her. "It was Gerrie, my girl—um, *ex*-girlfriend. We were eighteen. We were finishing school, and she told me she wanted to date another guy. I was devastated."

"But you took her back again later, when—" Emma shut her mouth, realizing she had said too much.

Luckily, he didn't seem to notice her slipup. "And so I did, yes."

Would you do it again, if she came begging?

Emma didn't dare voice the question. What if he said yes?

"Now you," he said.

"OK, fine. It happened when I was thirteen."

"The little bastard dumped you?"

"No."

He cocked his head. "What, then?"

"He didn't do anything wrong, actually. He was simply in love with someone else. And I broke my heart all by myself."

"Well, I hope you're over him now," Cyril said with an amused smile.

You have no idea. "Yes, of course. Ten years is enough time to lick a wound."

One of the waiters approached their table. "I don't want to rush you guys, but we're closing a bit early tonight. It's my going-away party."

"Thailand, right?" Cyril asked.

"Right. Listen, if you aren't otherwise engaged, would you like to stay for the party?"

"I'm in." Cyril said. "Laura? You emailed your project off, didn't you? So you're free as a bird now... unless you have other plans for tonight."

What other plans?

Even if the President of the French Republic had called to invite her to a reception at the Elysée Palace, she'd have declined without a moment's hesitation.

"I happen to be free tonight," she said and turned to the waiter. "Thank you for the invitation."

"My name is Rob." The waiter held his hand out. "The blue-haired Goth over there is Jeanne, and I'll introduce you to the others as soon as we've closed the place."

"I have a condition, though." Cyril said.

Rob grinned like he knew what was coming. "Shoot."

"You won't play my songs."

"Fine."

"And you won't try to sing them, either."

"Who told you about my singing?"

"Nobody."

Rob turned to the bar where Jeanne hovered and narrowed his eyes. "Then *nobody* will pay dearly for this act of treason."

Cyril sighed. "*Nobody* is innocent."

"As for you, Cyril," Rob said, snarling theatrically. "Your 'tortured genius' status doesn't entitle you to repress my freedom of song."

"I wouldn't dream of it," Cyril said.

Chapter Ten
Cyril

Rob kept his word and didn't play any of the forbidden songs. He didn't try to sing anything either, which secretly disappointed Cyril, who'd grown curious to hear just how bad Rob was. Instead, Pierre regaled everyone with good old Duran Duran, Les Rita Mitsouko, and Indochine, accompanied by an endless supply of pinot noir. Rob's colleagues and friends took turns toasting his bright future and betting on the number of years it would take him to emerge as a global energy mogul.

At each prediction, Cyril clinked glasses with Laura, who stood next to him at the far end of the bar.

When it was Jeanne's turn to play the oracle, she started with a long and loud sigh.

"Is that all you got?" Rob teased.

"My impatient brother in trays," she said. "I'll miss you. We'll all miss your indomitable optimism and witticism. As for *La Bohème*, it'll also miss at least a dozen female patrons aged sixteen to sixty-five who only come here in the hopes of catching your eye."

"Unless they get real and start hoping to catch *my* eye," someone cried out amid catcalls and laughter.

Judging by the accent, it was Pepe, the Spanish waiter.

Cyril turned to Laura. "Why did Jeanne say that about Rob?"

"I guess it's because he's handsome."

"Oh." Cyril leaned close and whispered in her ear, "Is that the reason you started coming here? To catch Rob's eye?"

"No," she said.

He knew it already, but it didn't diminish the pleasure that rushed through his veins from her unequivocal response.

"Why, then?" he asked, pulse drumming in his ears.

"I started coming here to catch *your* eye," she said before adding with mirth, "or rather, ear."

He chuckled as a sensation of warmth enveloped him and made his body light. "Consider your mission accomplished. For the past couple of weeks, I've only had ears for you."

Now, if he could somehow figure out where exactly her hand was, he'd take it into his and hold onto it for the rest of the evening.

He heard her shift. Was she moving closer or farther from him?

"OK, folks." Rob's bright voice carried over the music. "I think everyone's heard enough eighties rock for the night—or a lifetime, as the case may be. How about something a little closer to the present day?"

"Yes, please!" a few guests pleaded.

After some fumbling, Rob's playlist took over, and Cyril recognized the signature four-count introduction to Pharrell Williams's *Happy*.

And then he felt Laura's hand on his.

She gave it a little squeeze. "Shall we dance?"

"Um… I'm not sure I—"

"Hey." Laura laughed. "I'm not suggesting we go out there and do pirouettes."

"No?"

She laughed again. "We stay by the bar and just groove. Do you think you could manage it?"

He nodded. Whether it was the pinot noir, Pharrell's irresistible beat, or the lure of the legitimate excuse to hold Laura, he would've agreed to pirouettes, had that been the only option.

Clasping Laura's hand, he took a step away from the bar and began to nod in synch with the rhythm.

She placed her free hand on his chest, and soon they were moving to the music. Laura softly sang along to Pharrell's falsetto. Cyril led their unobtrusive dance, guiding them with the hand that held hers and with his entire body. Somewhere in the middle of the song, she pulled her hand away from his and gripped the back of his neck. Whatever this initiative implied, he approved of it. He placed his hands on her shoulders and slid them down her slender back, palms flat, reveling in its sensuous curve.

"Can you describe yourself, Laura?" he asked softly. "Not Marilyn Monroe. You."

"OK," she said. "My hair *is* blond. Ish. And my eyes are greenish. Other than that, I'm quite ordinary. No D-cups to speak of, unfortunately."

He trailed his fingers over the clean lines of her forehead, nose, cheekbones and jaw. His other hand slid down her back to rest on her softly rounded hip.

"You're anything but ordinary," he said.

It was amazing how he could picture her—face and body, even the way she danced—through his hands. They translated into images the contours, size, and shape of her torso, the pattern and cadence of its little shakes and twists, and the rhythmic rocking of her hips.

The song ended all too soon. He refused to let go of her, hoping the next piece would be something danceable. Thank God—or, rather, Rob—it was.

He continued exploring her delectable curves for a few more songs while his hunger for her grew by the minute until somebody stopped the music to make another speech.

Reluctantly, he broke contact with her, praying the party would never end.

And then he heard her soft voice. "How about we sneak out and party on our own terms... at your place?"

Of the thousand different suggestions she could've made, this was the indisputable, hands-down winner.

In every category.

When he pushed open the door to his apartment, he could hardly wait to put his arms around her and claim the kiss he'd been craving for several hours now. But she marched right past him, and he heard her drop her backpack further down the hallway.

"Will you give me a tour of your apartment?" she asked.

"Sure."

The bedroom would be a great place to start.

She placed her hand in his. "Let's begin with the kitchen."

Argh, the minx. "Your wish is my command."

Once in the kitchen, she flooded him with questions. How did he find stuff? How did he go about cooking? How did he make sure not to eat expired foods?

He explained all the tricks and techniques he'd learned over the past weeks. After that, he operated his expensive talking machines. She tried his Braille labeling gun and the food thermometer. When he thought he would explode with pent-up lust, she announced she was ready to continue the tour.

"Would you like to see the bedroom?" he asked, heart thumping.

"Yes, I would."

He nodded, all businesslike. "Follow me."

Thank you, God. I take back my complaints against you. All of them.

As he led the way to the bedroom, he tried to recall if he had made his bed this morning. Not an easy task, given that most of his blood had pooled in his crotch. Hmm… he may have left a pair of socks on the floor. He wasn't sure. Oh well. Laura didn't seem to be one of those cleanliness maniacs who would whirl around and leave at the sight of an untidy bedroom.

His gut feeling proved to be right about her lack of fanaticism, but he hadn't factored in her rampant curiosity.

"How do you make sure to wear socks of the same color?" she asked.

Merde. He must have left those socks lying around, after all.

"The trick is to keep them tucked together in the wash." He sighed before adding, "It's a good method if you remember where you keep the tuckers."

"And do you?"

He shook his head. "Another method is to use the color-detecting app. But I found a better strategy a week ago. I gave all my old socks to Dad and had Mom buy me twenty identical dark gray pairs."

She laughed her contagious laugh.

"You're allowed one more question," he said.

"Why's that?"

"I won't be able to fight the urge to kiss you for more than thirty seconds."

"And if I ask two questions?"

"You'll have to watch me swell with suppressed longing until I turn into a human bubble and blow up in your face."

"Yuck."

"My point precisely."

She took a step toward him, and he could smell her exquisite scent again, just like during the party. It was delicate, sweet, and sensual, all at the same time. It made his body ache with desire.

"Musk rose?" he asked, his voice coming out so winded he wasn't sure she would hear him.

She placed her hand in his. "Old-fashioned, I know."

"It's perfect. It's absolutely perfect."

He stroked her graceful fingers, brought her hand to his mouth, and pressed a soft, intimate kiss to her palm.

She inhaled sharply.

He jerked her to him, savoring every sensation as his hands roamed her already familiar back and her breasts brushed against his chest. He cradled the back of her head, playing with the fluffy wisps at her nape. Her hair was gathered into a high ponytail, and he itched to set it free. But that could wait—he had something a lot more urgent to do. He bent toward her and tilted his head, preparing to sample the taste and feel of her lips. His heart pounded in anticipation.

"Cyril, I—" she began.

"Don't worry about a thing, *mon ange*," he cut in, his words rushing out hot and hungry. "We'll only go as far as you'll want us to."

"I know," she said. "It's something else."

"I have condoms," he whispered in her ear, hoping he had decoded her hesitation.

"That's... great. But it's something else."

He didn't like the anxiety in her voice. He didn't like it at all. "Is it something... upsetting?"

"Possibly." She drew in a long, heavy breath. "Probably."

He had to lighten things up.

Now.

Clearing his throat, he gasped in feigned shock. "Are you a man?"

"What? No!"

"Phew. Good. That would've been a deal breaker."

She chuckled.

His hand went to cup one of her little breasts. "As real as they come," he commented, kneading it. "Could that thing you want to tell me... could it ruin this night for us?"

She hesitated. "Yes."

"Then don't tell me now. You'll tell me tomorrow."

"OK," she said quickly and raked her hand through his hair.

He gently tugged at the rubber band restraining her locks. He wanted it off now—he needed to bury his hands in her hair, to feel its weight, its texture, to bring it to his face and inhale its scent. But the contraption wouldn't give in. He was silently cursing and fighting the urge to yank at it when her nimble fingers joined his. She removed the elastic, and her feathery strands spilled over his hands.

Pure bliss.

He stroked her nape and the back of her head, his fingers delving into her hair, scooping it up, and letting it slide between his fingers.

"I love how sleek your hair is," he said.

"I believe the appropriate word is *silky*," she murmured.

"To hell with appropriate words," he rasped, lowering his head to brush his lips against hers.

So soft.

As he kissed her, his awareness of her breasts, abdomen, and thighs pressed hard against his body intensified, building to a fever pitch. He penetrated her mouth, stroking her tongue with his and tasting the sultry-sweet flavor of pinot noir. A wave of heat jolted through his veins, warming his face and shattering his control.

Three steps.

Three small sideways steps and he could lower her to the bed.

She slid one hand under his T-shirt and splayed her palm over his stomach. Her other hand tugged at the hem. "Take it off."

He removed it in a wink and dropped it to the floor.

"Your turn, *mon ange*," he whispered, pulling her to him and pushing her T up and over her head.

She snapped open her bra, and her deliciously soft breasts spilled against his chest. He palmed and fondled them with total abandon until he heard a crisp sound. She had unzipped his jeans.

"Oops," she said saucily.

He pushed his sneakers off, lowered his jeans and kicked them aside, then removed his socks but kept his boxer briefs on. Hands clumsy with impatience, he undid the zipper of her shorts and dragged them down her hips and thighs, kneeling before her until her shorts were around her ankles, and she stepped out of them.

He dropped hot kisses on her tummy along the waistband of her low-cut cotton panties, hesitating to go further.

Not yet.

When he pictured her standing in front of him, naked but for her panties, it took all the self-control he possessed not to tear them with his hands and teeth.

He rose, scooped her up, and took those three sideways steps to the bed.

After he lowered her on it and positioned himself between her legs, he drew back, trying to calm his ardor so he could slow things down a notch. All his past experience and confidence couldn't stop him from feeling like an overexcited first-timer. He hadn't made love since the accident. Not even a proper kiss, except Gerrie's fleeting smooches that held nothing sexual. Three months wasn't such a long time, of course, but to him it had been an eternity. It had been the entirety of his new life.

Laura ran her hands over his pectorals and abs. "You haven't let yourself go."

"Dad got me a rowing machine." His hand traveled to her lower abdomen and slid inside her panties. "I use it when I'm bored,"—he sucked in a sharp breath as he found his prize—"which happens a lot these days…"

As he caressed her there, she gasped and whimpered and writhed under him.

If only he could see her face now.

About a year ago, Gerrie had made him wear a blindfold during foreplay. It had been fun, lying on his back, guessing what she'd do next, and being constantly surprised by her inventiveness. But when things had started heating up, he'd torn the blindfold off. He needed to see the woman he was making love to.

Now his blindfold was permanent.

As if sensing his frustration, Laura slipped her fingers under the waistband of his briefs and tugged. He hurried to remove them while she shifted under him, pulling her own panties off. When they were done, he lowered himself on top of her, bringing every inch of his skin into contact with hers. She wrapped her arms and legs around him.

"I want you so much," he whispered against her mouth.

"How fast can you get that condom?" she asked.

* * *

After they climaxed and their muffled groans ceased, they lay still, legs entwined and arms draped over each other, basking in the drowsy afterglow of their release. He pressed a gentle kiss to her temple, inhaling her head-turning perfume heightened from the heat of her skin, and listened to her breathing grow quieter. As she snuggled to him, he closed his eyes and let the rhythmic beat of her heart lull him to sleep.

Chapter Eleven
Emma

She woke up with a diffuse sense of happiness. For a moment she lay still, eyes closed, trying to figure out where that feeling had come from. Had she been flying again in her sleep? When she did, she rode the wind wherever it took her, zooming out on magnificent landscapes—ragged mountains, lush forests and crystal blue lakes—and then closing in on people's faces and smiling as they looked up and waved. That recurrent dream was the most inspiring, most beautiful experience in her life, and whenever she had it, she would spend the whole day in a state of unsinkable benevolence.

But this time, she couldn't remember flying. It was something else, something… Oh God. Oh, dear God. Images of last night flashed in her mind as she remembered where she was and what had happened. Suddenly, she became aware of a large palm splayed across her tummy. She opened her eyes and turned her head to gaze at the owner of said palm.

This was real. She was in bed with the love of her life.

And he was smiling.

Her hand went to his face, and she stroked his chiseled cheekbones, his trim little beard, and his scar-slashed eyebrows.

This was better than flying in her sleep.

"Good morning, *mon ange*," he said.

She loved the endearment, the husky voice that delivered it, and the crooked smile that accompanied it.

"Good morning," she replied, hesitating to give him a pet name of her own.

Soon.

"I slept like a baby," he said. "Haven't slept like this in months."

He moved closer to her and propped himself on his elbow. "Will you promise me something?"

"Depends what."

"That you'll sleep here tonight. And tomorrow night. And the night after that."

"OK," she said.

"How about the rest of the week?"

"Granted."

"And the rest of the month?"

"Aren't you rushing things?" she teased.

"Absolutely not. But I'll take the week for now." He pulled her close and combed his fingers through her hair. "Renewable upon tacit agreement."

She laughed.

"Laura," he murmured, running his fingers over her face. "Laura. What a beautiful name."

Oh no.

She winced as her little bubble of unadulterated joy burst apart, leaving her to grapple with the truth of her situation.

He kissed her shoulder. "I dreamed I was playing my guitar."

"Will you play for me now? I'll get it for you."

He shook his head. "I'm not ready." Then added with a smile, "Yet."

"I can wait," she said. "I have all day."

"It may take longer than that, *mon ange*," he said, a tinge of sadness coloring his handsome voice.

"I'll wait as long as it takes."

I can wait a lifetime.

He gathered her to him. "The thing you wanted to tell me last night—does it still apply?"

"Yes."

"Oh. I was hoping... It doesn't matter." He sat up, leaning his back against the headboard. "Tell me then."

Already?

She couldn't possibly. She needed to stock up with more of this connection, this baggage-free trust between them, before she emptied a bucket of water over her sand castle and prayed it would resist.

"I'll tell you over breakfast."

"Agreed. Which means you're coming to *La Bohème* with me."

"Why?"

"That's where I eat breakfast."

She laughed. "A man of habit."

When they stepped out of his building into the bustling Parisian morning, Cyril paused and turned to her, a smile dancing on his face. "Can I ask you a small favor?"

"Ask away."

"On our way to *La Bohème*, do you mind describing the surroundings and... holding my hand?" He stretched out his left hand for her, the right one holding his cane.

"Sure." She walked over to his left side and placed her hand into his. "For your balance?"

"Not at all." He extended the cane in front of him. "For my sense of wellbeing."

Her mouth twitched. "It won't hurt mine, either."

"You see," Cyril said as they walked down the street, "I used to live in the eleventh before, and the twelfth before that. I know the area around Opéra Garnier, but I have trouble picturing what this part of the ninth is like."

She looked around. "Your neighborhood is perfect."

"In what way?"

"You know how some parts of Paris are handsome but insanely boring? And some are so ugly you wonder if you've been transported to the outskirts of Brussels or a Moscow suburb? Well, your neighborhood is a perfect mix of elegance, grit, and hipness."

"That's good to know." Cyril smiled. "But I want details. For instance, I can sometimes smell fresh bread around this spot. Is it a baker? What does the shop look like?"

"It's called 'Boulangerie Châteaudun.' The front is art nouveau—curvy wrought iron painted pale mint green. Reminds me of Ladurée. Rather well maintained. Lots of customers inside, so I guess their croissants must be good."

"Mental note number one."

"Take another one while you're at it—right after the baker there's a garage entrance. You should watch out."

Crap. She hadn't just said "watch out," had she? Yep, she had. Emma rolled her eyes. *What an imbecile.*

"I know about the garage, but thanks for the warning. Anything else of interest before the convenience store?"

"Let's see. Oh yes, there's a fishmonger further down the street. But you may have figured it out already."

The corners of his mouth turned up. "I kind of suspected there was something *fishy* going on around there."

"And *crabby*, too."

He chuckled. "Now tell me about the passersby."

"Why? You don't think it's always the same people, do you?" She stood on tiptoes and whispered into his ear, infusing exaggerated gravitas into her tone. "Your life isn't *The Truman Show*, believe me."

He narrowed his eyes. "Remind me why I should believe the woman who just popped up out of nowhere?"

She knew he had meant it as a joke, but it still turned her stomach. Emma clenched her jaw. That was it—she would confess as soon as they ordered breakfast.

And then come what may.

"OK," she said. "The passersby. I spy with my little eye… a white-haired monsieur with a little boy—must be his grandson—who keeps jumping up and down."

"The old man or the boy?"

"Take a wild guess."

He puckered his lips, feigning intense mental effort, and shook his head. "I give up. OK, who else do you spy?"

"A new couple, madly in love. They're cute."

"How do you know they're new? And how do you know they're in love?"

"I don't know that, of course, but it's the way they hold hands, the way they look at each other… And here's the most telling detail: They stop every ten seconds for a smooch."

He stopped in his tracks, pulled her to him, and gave her a searing kiss.

As they resumed their walk, she asked, bright-eyed, "Were you trying to make a point?"

"Absolutely."

Inside the bistro, Emma picked a cozy window table, a little removed from the others. Cyril ordered croissants, buttered tartines, scrambled eggs, orange juice, and coffee for both of them.

Emma smoothed the napkin on her knees.

Time to fess up.

She glanced behind her to check if a particularly speedy waiter was heading their way with the croissants.

But it wasn't a waiter she saw advancing toward them with the inexorability of a falling tree.

It was Geraldine.

Chapter Twelve
Cyril

The click-clack of sharp heels against the floor tiles grew louder until it stopped somewhere near their table.

"Hey, Cyril," a woman said.

Funny how she sounded exactly like Gerrie.

"You told me I could always find you at this bistro…"

It *was* Gerrie.

Her voice trailed off, but when she spoke again, her tone was completely different. "And what are *you* doing here?"

"Hi," Laura mumbled.

"You texted me you were home with a cold today," Gerrie said.

"I… lied," Laura said under her breath.

What is going on?

"Do you two know each other?" he asked.

Silence.

A wave of nausea clutched his stomach. "Do you guys know each other?"

"Sometimes I doubt it," Gerrie said, her tone pensive before it changed to shocked. "Oh my God! You have no clue who's sitting across from you, do you?"

Please, let this be just another one of Gerrie's stupid jokes.

Jaw clenched, he turned to Laura.

"My real name is Emma," Laura said. "Emma Perrin."

No. It couldn't be.

He swallowed hard and said with as much calm as he could muster, "Lau... Emma, care to explain?"

"I will. I promise... as soon as... we're alone."

"I suppose this is what you wanted to tell me last night?"

Jesus. He'd spent the night with Emma. Gerrie's little sis. The woman who—

"Cyril, please," Emma begged before her voice broke off, choking on a sob.

He could feel the nausea in his throat now.

"Please, let me explain this," Emma said, her voice raw.

He turned to Gerrie. "And what is it you want from me, darling?"

"Nothing," Gerrie said quickly. "Well, it's just a trifle. Remember *Melchior*, our biggest corporate client? I've told you about them."

"Vaguely."

"Well, turns out Jean-Thomas, the CEO, is a huge fan of yours. He thinks you're one of the best singer-songwriters of this century. The future of the French chanson. Aznavour, Gainsbourg, and Brel rolled into one."

He smirked but said nothing.

"When I told him our company designed your covers, he was tickled pink. And when I said that you and I were close friends, he became delirious. Begged me to get you to autograph a CD for him."

"Do you have it?" Cyril asked drily.

"Yes, right here." Gerrie thrust a CD insert and a pen into his hand.

He put the insert on the table. "Where should I sign?"

"Around here would be great." She guided his hand to the right spot.

As he scribbled his usual autograph, it struck him that he was writing on a piece of art created by Emma. He pushed the thought away.

"Here." He held the insert and the pen out to Gerrie. "You're all set."

"May I join you?" she asked. "I could do with a strong coffee right now."

"No," Cyril and Emma said in unison.

Cyril took in a breath before adding, "I'll be happy to catch up another time. But right now I need to talk to Emma. Alone."

"No problem. I'll leave you to it, then." Gerrie sounded as cool and nonchalant as always, but he knew her too well to miss the hurt undertone in her voice.

Well, right now, he didn't care.

As soon as the sound of her shoes faded, he turned to Emma. "I'm all ears."

"I was... I needed to talk to you after the accident. I wanted to tell you something." She drew in a ragged breath. "Something important. But I was afraid you'd be too upset to hear me out."

"So you opted for deceit."

"Yes... I don't know what I was thinking. I can see now it was a dumb idea. But at the time, I thought—"

"What did you think, Emma?" he cut in, barely containing his anger.

"I thought that passing for an anonymous fan would give us a chance to be strangers who'd just met and could talk to each other without the baggage of who we are and what happened... a chance at a clean slate."

"Only we aren't strangers, are we? And at some point that truth was going to come to the surface."

"It was supposed to come from me!" She sniffed, and then more words poured from her. "I was going to tell you. Right now, during this breakfast, just before Geraldine showed up and ruined everything."

"Emma," he said, the calm in his voice a contrast to her emotion. "Why? Why did you want to talk to me 'without the 'baggage,' as you call it?"

"I... I..." she mumbled.

"I know why. You think it was your fault. You think you're responsible for my blindness. And you seek some kind of redemption."

"No! That wasn't the reason." She must have leaned in because he could feel her breath on his face. "Well, I do feel guilty, that much is true, and I do hope to earn your forgiveness—"

"There you go," he interrupted her. "Hey, I have great news. I don't hold you responsible for what happened."

"Cyril—"

"Let me finish. There's something else you need to know. I don't want pity. Yours or anybody else's. Pity friendship is bad enough, but pity sex..." He shook his head. "And lies. The last thing I need now is lies."

Couldn't she see? Couldn't she put herself in his place—in a *handicapped* person's place because that's who he was now—and imagine how it felt to find out he'd been tricked?

"Don't you see it, Emma?" His voice cracked. "I'm so easy to fool. I'm blind and I'm deaf without my hearing aids. I've become so... vulnerable. You should've known better than to fool me."

"I'm so sorry! I'm so very sorry." She began to snivel.

"OK," he said, placing his left hand flat on the table. "OK. I accept your apology, but I need you to leave now. Can you do that? Please?"

She grabbed his hand with both hers and wheezed between sobs, "Don't send me away."

He slowly peeled her hands off.

After a moment's silence, her chair moved, and she ran away.

Chapter Thirteen
Emma

It's over! Emma thought when she bolted from the bistro. She'd taken her shot at a relationship with Cyril and missed the mark.

He had rejected her as soon as he found out who she was.

He must despise me.

An elderly woman stopped and touched her arm, a mix of concern and pity in her eyes. "Are you all right?"

Emma wiped her eyes with the back of her hand and managed a lopsided smile. "I'm fine, thank you."

Choking back a sob, she lowered her head and scurried down the street. She marched for a good half hour, her mind vacant and her gaze fixed to the ground. When she finally looked up, she was already on rue du Louvre. The Seine would be no more than ten minutes away.

Relieved to have found a tiny purpose, Emma crossed rue de Rivoli and hurried to the waterfront. She needed to sit down somewhere by the river and contemplate its steady flow. It would calm her, dull the crushing pain in her chest to an endurable soreness.

It always did.

Emma picked one of the roomy stone benches on the Tuileries Quay not far from her favorite bridge, *Pont des Arts*, kicked off her sandals, and hugged her knees to her chest. She watched the breeze ruffle the river's surface and the quaint *péniche* barges float by. Barge spotting had been one of her favorite pastimes since she was a kid. She had missed that most about Paris during her self-imposed Chinese exile.

Three years ago, when Geraldine and Cyril got back together, Emma was twenty, a student at the prestigious *Ecole des Beaux-Arts*, and still a virgin. As the couple's relationship deepened, being around them became too hard, so she resolved to leave Paris. The ideal solution was to find an exchange program that would let her spend a year abroad before she'd return and finish her studies.

Of course, seeing how long she'd been in love with Cyril, a year wasn't guaranteed to solve her problem. But it was a long time. Who knew what could happen in a year?

She applied to a bunch of arts schools and fine arts departments, and the first one to admit her was the Sichuan University in Chengdu. She looked it up. The province of Sichuan boasted spicy Tibetan food, a peaceful coexistence of Buddhism, Taoism, Confucianism, and giant pandas. Its capital Chengdu was a smallish city for Chinese standards, even though it was the size of Paris and other European metropolises. Dynamic, unpretentious, and open, Chengdu sounded like a fun place to be. It was also very, very far from home.

She didn't wait to hear from the other schools.

In Chengdu, Emma met Manu, a quiet Frenchman studying Buddhist philosophy in one of the local monasteries. She also hooked up with Lino, a dashing fellow art student from Italy. Like her, Lino had come to China with a knowledge of Mandarin that boiled down to *ni hao* and *xiexie*. They attended after-school language classes every weekday and waited tables at the same high-end pizzeria off Jinli Street in the evenings. On Saturday nights, they went clubbing in Lan Kwai Fong, and on their free Sundays, they scoured the city's flea markets in search of bizarre objects.

Two months into their friendship, Lino rid Emma of her virginity. He had been gentle and considerate—the almost perfect deflowering a woman could have.

When the man of her dreams wasn't scrambling for the honor.

"Be careful not to fall in love with me," Lino had warned her the morning after.

"You're as safe as if I were gay," Emma said. "This was just a one-off never to be repeated."

He gave her a funny look that was both surprised and a little hurt. "Was I that bad?"

"No! No. You did everything right, just like it's done in books and movies. It must be me." Emma held her palms up as though to say, *What can you do?* "I guess I'm just not a sexual being."

"Shit happens," he said, as the last traces of hurt vanished from his eyes.

In the weeks that followed, Emma's mind obliterated the details of that night, only retaining a diffuse sense of satisfaction that a long-delayed chore was finally over and done with.

By Christmas, which she and Lino celebrated in Chengdu with Manu, Lino and a few other friends who couldn't afford a round trip to Europe, she had nearly convinced herself that the story she'd fed Lino was true. Her love for Cyril must have been no more than a platonic admiration for his talent. She didn't fancy anyone. After all, even a first-class hottie like Lino hadn't managed to stir any kind of longing in her. From there, it wasn't so farfetched to conceive that she was, indeed, an asexual woman with no need for a boyfriend or even a fuck buddy.

When she returned to France, just in time for the start of her final school year, she was certain the libido-free persona she'd fabricated was her true self.

Until she saw Cyril again at her homecoming party.

He greeted her with a bear hug. "Welcome back, Boney Em."

"Thanks," she breathed, her head spinning from the caress of his velvety baritone, his intoxicating male scent, and the snug haven of his strong arms around her.

She nearly collapsed to the floor when he released her, stunned by the intensity of her reaction. Luckily, others stepped forward to hug her, providing the necessary props for her body and time for her senses to regroup.

The rest of the party was a haze, dominated by dizziness and regret. It had been a huge mistake to come back to France. She should've stayed in China—and to hell with finishing her fancy school and getting the degree.

Emma rubbed her forehead as if to drive away those memories and tried to focus on the river again. But her mind refused to obey this time, disregarding even the most picturesque barges that passed by. Some critical pathway in her brain got stuck on the same refrain as at that disastrous party two years ago.

I should've stayed in China. I shouldn't have come back.

Chapter Fourteen
Cyril

At one in the afternoon, Cyril flicked his portable radio on and slumped into the sofa.

"It's thirteen hours in Paris," the radio said, "twenty-eight degrees Celsius. Traffic is heavy on the *Boulevard Périphérique*…"

Cyril tuned out, his thoughts wandering off to his calamitous morning. He still struggled to wrap his mind around the fact that Laura, the charming stranger who had tumbled into his life two weeks ago, was Emma. And that Emma, the sweet, withdrawn girl he'd known for ten years, had tricked him so unkindly. Why would she do such a thing?

His lips stretched into a sardonic smile. What a poor judge of character he'd turned out to be! He used to think Emma didn't have a cruel bone in her body. He'd also believed Laura was a Heaven-sent angel... a kindred soul who sought him out because she appreciated his music... a beautiful creature who liked and desired him as he was and didn't find him pitiful or lacking in any way.

A few hours ago he had practically asked her to move in with him. She'd been a virtual stranger, but he figured he'd glimpsed enough of her soul to know she was a keeper. Maybe even the woman of his life.

What a schmuck.

He was a vastly admired and allegedly wise schmuck.

Why was it that people equated fame with intelligence? Fans were persuaded their favorite singer or actor was smart and knew something about life that ordinary folks didn't. The public emulated celebrity styles, workouts, diets, and political opinions—including the most ridiculous ones.

The worst thing about this uncritical reverence was that the "stars" ended up believing that they had, indeed, tamed the universe. Cyril pictured himself a year ago, when three of his songs hit the Top 20 in France and Belgium. Had he fancied himself special back then? Smarter than others? Had he — despite all his clowning around and self-mockery — actually bought into the myth of his superiority?

Absolutely.

Well, as far as rude awakenings and cold showers went, his had been Niagara Falls. In the space of three short moths, he'd lost his eyesight, hearing, looks, girlfriend, and his passion for music.

And then Emma came along and finished him off.

Cyril startled at a familiar sound and his attention zeroed in on the radio. It was airing his guitar intro to "Maybe I'm the One" – the song he'd written for Gerrie two years earlier.

Then came his voice. He hated the sound of it, hated the lyrics, hated the music —

Enough.

He grabbed the radio receiver and turned it off. *Must get up and do something.* Preferably something challenging enough to keep his mind occupied. Why not cook spaghetti? The saucepans had turned up, so he had no excuses.

He dragged himself to the kitchen and opened the pantry doors.

His phone emitted Louis's ringtone.

Cyril sighed. He was in for another pep talk from his upbeat agent.

"Hey," Louis said. "The weather is beautiful today. How about a trip out of town?"

"Whatever for?"

"Fresh air, greenery, birds?"

"I'm in the middle of something."

"Listen, I'm under your windows and I'm double parked. Hate Paris for that. You need to come down."

"I'm cooking spaghetti."

"I'll get us some from that fantastic Italian place next to the *Bois de Vincennes* Park, and then we'll picnic. How's that?"

Oh well, his pasta-cooking feat could wait until tomorrow. "Fine. I'll be down in five minutes."

On the lawn, Cyril paid more attention to the beer he had insisted on buying than his spaghetti tub.

Louis babbled on about the future. "The sales of both your albums are still strong. Which is great, but you shouldn't rest on your laurels. Have you tried out your new home studio yet?"

"Nope. I haven't even touched my guitar. And I'm not sure I ever will."

"Come on, of course you will. You just need to finish your… grieving and adjustment."

"Could you pass me another beer?" Cyril held his hand out. "My banker tells me that if I'm prudent, I can live a very comfortable life with what I've made so far. Even if my albums stop selling."

"That's great news. But you never did this for the money. I don't believe you'll last long without writing new songs."

Cyril shook his head. "I'm dry, Louis. My mojo's gone. And it has nothing to do with grieving. It's… I need to *see* the world around me so I can spit it out as music."

"Bullshit. Your mojo will come back. You just need time. Stevie Wonder did it, Ray Charles did it, Andrea Bocelli did it. So will you."

"You're a great agent, Louis, and a good man." Cyril sighed.

"But?"

"You have to move on." His shoulders sagged as a bout of monumental fatigue came over him. "Can you drive me home now?"

On the ride back, Cyril cringed from a throbbing headache. If only he could stop thinking for a while. If he could just forget—snap his fingers and make the hurt crushing his chest and the anger stuck in his throat go away. If he could shut his emotions off and turn into a zombie that walked and talked and felt nothing.

Before Laura's—Emma's—cataclysmic incursion into his life, he'd been well on his way to that coveted state of apathy with the help of substantial amounts of liquor. But she gently shook him out of his stupor and gave him something precious. Affection. Hope. *Joie de vivre*.

He became borderline happy... until her gifts turned into poison.

He'd always considered himself strong and resilient, but this was too much.

More than he could bear.

More than alcohol or any other distraction could ease.

Except maybe... the little smiley pill Kiki had thrust into his hand a few days ago. He had intended to throw it in the trash, but he didn't. Which meant—unless the pill's magic properties involved mobility—it still sat on the countertop where he'd left it.

For the day you hit rock bottom, Kiki had said.

Looked like that day was today.

At home, just before he put the pill on his tongue, a little voice in his head whispered he should abort this stupid act. Taking a drug was a bad idea. Taking it for the first time in his life, alone, after half a dozen beers, was a terrible one.

But he silenced that voice. This wasn't even a hardcore drug, right? Just a little shot of lighthearted oblivion. It had lasted Kiki a few days. Imagine that. Not just hours, but days of being at peace with the world, of not feeling any pain or anger.

He swallowed the pill.

The next few hours zoomed by in fast-forward. His spirits rose, and his energy level went off the charts. He played his rock 'n' roll CDs and pranced around until he collapsed to the floor, gasping for air, in the middle of his living room. He remained there for a while, enjoying visions of Martian landscapes. Then he zipped to the bedroom and climbed on his rowing machine, where he rowed and rowed until he was hot, sweaty, dry mouthed, and half-conscious.

And then he rowed some more.

The last vision he had before darkness swallowed him up was a memory.

He was at the wheel of his car. Emma in the passenger seat. He fumed that she'd gotten so pissed at her friend's party and insisted on going home in the middle of the night instead of sleeping over. Thank God, she'd had enough sense to call Gerrie, who then called him. And now here he was, driving her home in this downpour when he could have been in bed asleep or watching his favorite show. Emma mumbled something about Gerrie. He couldn't make out her slurred words. And then she puked into her hands. The vomit spilled over onto her clothes and the cream leather seat of his brand new car.

"Shit!" Cyril started groping for the paper towel roll in the glove compartment before remembering he'd left it on the backseat.

He stretched his arm as far back as he could and felt the seat. The roll must have fallen down. With a quick glance to the road, he unbuckled his seatbelt and groped the backseat floor. His index finger touched the roll, so he bent farther, reaching a little more as he tried to grab it.

And then the car skidded, nose-dived onto its bonnet, and flipped over. There was sharp pain before he sank into darkness.

Just like now.

Chapter Fifteen
Emma

Emma spent the afternoon around the Seine, wandering along the quays, watching the boats, and crossing the bridges from the right bank to the left and back again. She hung around until the setting sun gilded the roofs and kissed goodnight to the river. With twilight, the turmoil in her mind finally subsided, making room for meek beginnings of clarity.

The night she'd spent at Cyril's place had meant the world to her. And it had meant *something* to him, too. Something more than a bit of fun with an enthusiastic groupie. She was sure of it. She knew it in her bones. Even if he had believed her to be a stranger, what they had shared was real. That connection, that sense of having finally come home was real.

And it was beautiful.

Emma threw one last look at the now dark water and crossed the *Pont Neuf* back to rue du Louvre.

On rue Montmartre, she realized she was returning to the 9th arrondissement, which was in the opposite direction from her apartment southeast of the city.

Too late to turn back now.

She might as well drop by *La Bohème* on the off chance Cyril was there.

She sucked in a long breath, visualizing that possibility. Suppose he agreed to hear her out. What would she tell him?

The one thing that really matters.

In all these years, she had never told him about her feelings. She'd written him at least a dozen love letters, chickened out, and ripped them to pieces, rationalizing that he must have known or suspected how she felt.

But what if he didn't? What if he had no clue?

Cyril wasn't at the bistro.

Emma went to his building and buzzed his intercom. He didn't answer.

She tried his landline and his cell phone. Same luck.

Her hands began to tremble.

Calm down. He's just out with friends.

It was what people did to take their minds off a disappointment.

But what if he wasn't out? What if he'd had too much to drink and tripped over something and hit his head? What if right now he was lying on the floor of his apartment, bleeding to death?

Her knees wobbled.

She keyed in the code he'd given her last night and ran to his door. She rang the doorbell again and again before banging on the door with her fists.

"Are you a friend of Cyril's?" someone asked from behind.

She whirled around. An old lady stared at her from her doorstep across the landing.

Emma nodded. "I'm worried about him."

"Wait here." The woman retreated inside her apartment, pulling her door shut behind her. A few minutes later she reopened it. "He left me his spare keys in case he locked himself out."

Emma snatched the keys from the woman's hand, unlocked Cyril's door, and rushed in.

He was in his bedroom, slumped on the floor next to his rowing machine.

Please.

No.

Kneeling next to him, she took his pulse, and her whole body sagged with relief. He was alive.

She carefully rolled him onto his side, thanking God for that first aid class she'd taken in Chengdu, and dialed the emergency number.

The *sapeurs-pompiers* promised to be there in less than five minutes.

Emma sat on the floor next to Cyril and fixed her eyes on her watch. She reminded herself how well trained and competent the *pompiers* were. Everyone knew that. They were the country's superheroes.

They would fix him.

He's going to be fine. He's going to be fine. He's going to be fine…

She kept murmuring these words like a conjuration as she waited. She still murmured them as she jumped up at the siren, let the *pompiers* in, and watched them carry Cyril's limp body out of the apartment.

* * *

"I just couldn't stop. I kept at it until my body overheated and I passed out." Cyril pulled himself up against his cushion and grimaced in pain.

Emma moved closer to his bed. "Are you OK?"

She ached to touch him, to take him in her arms and press his head to her chest. But she didn't dare.

"Yeah, don't worry," Cyril said. "The doctor said I'll be discharged tomorrow. I'm just hurting everywhere right now, but I'll live."

"Good."

He smirked. "What's good? That I'll be going home, that I'll live, or that I'm hurting? Mind you, I deserve the pain. I might've died from dehydration had you not found me."

She shook her head to drive away the scary thought. "No, you wouldn't have. You're too strong."

"I just lucked out, Emma." He sighed. "Did you know that some people are chemically sensitive to MDMA? They can actually bite the big one from their first dose. It doesn't apply to me, apparently, but I wish I'd looked this up before I—"

"What's MDMA?"

"The official name of Ecstasy—the little pill I took yesterday afternoon. No doubt one of my smartest moves yet. Comes second only to unfastening my seatbelt while driving."

"About that..." Emma's hand went to touch his arm, but she pulled it back just before her fingers came into contact with the sleeve of his hospital gown.

"Yes?"

"I know you don't blame me for the accident, but I can't help thinking that if it weren't for my stupid actions, you wouldn't have lost your sight."

"Emma—"

"Please let me finish. I need to say this. I need to tell you why I got so drunk that night." She wrung her hands. "Let me unburden myself, and then I'll never mention it again."

He crossed his arms over his chest. "OK."

"I don't usually..." She took a long breath, trying to compose herself. "I never drink more than a few sips of any alcoholic beverage. Can't hold my liquor."

"No kidding."

"But just before I left for that party, Geraldine told me she knew you were going to propose."

His mouth twisted into a sneer. "And it rubbed you the wrong way?"

She hesitated.

"Emma?"

"Yes," she admitted. "But what was even harder to take was that Geraldine intended to accept you."

She held her breath, expecting him to ask why.

And then she would tell him.

After which, there'd be no more hiding behind Cyril's having no clue.

"Gerrie called me earlier this morning," he said. "Told me she wouldn't be able to live with herself if I did something silly again." His lips curled. "She seems to be under the impression I was trying to kill myself."

"Because you totally weren't."

"Absolutely not. Trust me, if I had, I would've done something a bit more... permanent."

"Did she say anything else?" She hoped he couldn't sense the panic in her voice.

"Only that she still cared for me and wanted us to get back together."

Of course.

She scrutinized Cyril's stony expression and then turned to stare out the window. "So, you and Geraldine... you're on again?"

"I declined her kind offer of reunification." His voice was as unreadable as his face.

"You think she offered out of pity?"

He nodded. "She keeps saying altruism isn't in her nature, but looks like guilt got the better of her." He gave Emma a wry smile. "But that wasn't the reason I said no."

Her breath caught in her throat. Could it be? Could his reason be *Laura*? "What was it then?"

"I just don't feel the same way about her anymore." He shrugged. "I guess after all this time I finally fell out of love with Gerrie."

Emma shut her eyes and plunged. "Cyril, that night in the car, I was trying to tell you—"

"As for *your* guilt and penance, you need to get over it. I was the one driving, remember? It was my responsibility to keep my eyes on the road, no matter how much you puked."

"But—"

"I'll say this again. I don't blame you for what happened that night, Emma. I never have. Hell, I could've gotten you maimed or even killed. It was just your dumb luck that you got away with only a few bruises."

"But you're angry with me," she murmured.

"Oh yes, I am. For what you did over the past weeks. For lying to me and taking advantage of… my situation."

"I'm so sorry, Cyril!" She gripped his hand. "Tell me what I can do to earn your forgiveness. Please, I'll do anything."

"There's no need. You saved me yesterday — so we're even. You're absolved." He sagged against the headboard, his hand limp in hers. "I mean it. You can go and live your life with a clear conscience now."

She chewed at her lip. "My seeking you out... it wasn't about penance."

"*Ah bon?* What was it then? Curiosity?" His nostrils flared. "Because you've always wondered what it would be like to sleep with a blind man?"

"No!"

"Did it live up to your expectations? Was it good?"

She jutted out her chin. "Yes, it was good. As a matter of fact, it was the best sex of my life."

"Phew." He feigned wiping sweat off his forehead. His face was livid.

"But that's not why I did what I did."

"No?"

"I..." Her voice cracked. God, it was hard to get those words out. "I fell in love with you when I first saw you and heard your songs... I went to China three years ago hoping to cure my feelings... but I failed." She swallowed. "There's no one else for me."

A deep frown creased his brow. "What?"

"You dimwit!" Emma shouted, giving up on controlling her voice. "If you could just set aside your bitterness for a sec, the truth will glare at you. Can't you see it? Can't you see how much I love you?"

He smirked. "That's the thing, baby—I can't. I can't see shit."

Chapter Sixteen
Cyril

The recorder beeped twice and fell silent. It was a good sign. Cyril expelled the breath he'd been holding and slowly pulled his hand away from the stop button. He removed his headphones, leaned his guitar against the wall, backed his swivel chair from the mic, and stepped out of his vocal booth.

It had been a week since he'd returned from the hospital.

And a week since he picked up his guitar and began to play. He hadn't stopped since then. Getting reacquainted with his faithful Taylor 814ce had been as painful as it was sweet. Like rekindling with an estranged lover. The instrument felt different, and yet it was the same. Cyril spent a few hours on the first day just pressing its shapely body to his chest, stroking its rosewood sides, and caressing its strings.

He strummed through his favorite riffs and licks for all of the next day.

Three days ago, he played his songs.

Yesterday, he began to compose.

And today, he could no longer fathom why he'd sworn off music in the first place.

He also marveled at how his unflinching fascination for Gerrie had vanished so quickly. And how he couldn't stop thinking of Emma, not even for a short while. Not even when he played.

Especially when he played.

He was no longer angry with her. How could he be after what she'd told him in the hospital? True, she had deceived him, but solely because she'd thought there was no other way. As he pondered her words, he recalled episodes from the past when she'd acted weird toward him. He'd ascribed her behavior to teenage gawkiness. On occasion, he suspected she didn't like him. The real reason never crossed his mind.

Was it because sometimes being sighted prevented you from *seeing*? Ever since he had started performing for his friends, and then for unknown people, there had been too much glitter and shine in his life. And he had let it distract him. He'd noticed only what was skin-deep, unable to focus on the things that really mattered. Maybe that was why he'd been so enamored with Gerrie. She was, after all, unequalled in the glitter department.

Cyril opened the well-used case he'd retrieved from the hallway closet and placed his guitar in it. Then he checked the time: His taxi would arrive in fifteen minutes.

He'd ordered it during his breakfast at *La Bohème* just after he called Emma, whom he hadn't talked to since their conversation in the hospital ward. It had taken him a whole week to admit that he'd been hoping—longing—to hear her voice every waking moment since then.

And now that he had, he trembled with anticipation. His whole body reverberated with a thought as imbued with the promise of wonderful things as the Christmas trees of his childhood.

Emma loved him.

There was profound comfort and immense joy in knowing this. And freedom. Freedom to move on, forgive her deception and claim her as his lover, his muse, his very own two-faced Janus. Because sometime during the past week the mysterious belle who'd taken his breath away and the quirky artist he'd known half of his life had clicked into one.

Laura became Emma.

Once that transformation was complete, he could no longer deny how he felt about her. Not just the part where he craved her right down to his bones, but also the part where he had let her take up residence in his empty heart and was still reeling from the glow that filled it.

When she met him in front of her building, he prayed that she would take his hand.

She did but released it as soon as they reached the high counter that served as an all-purpose table in her apartment. He remembered the large loft-style room with a cooking area, a bar, a lounge corner, and a huge desk with two computer screens.

"I don't have any craft beers, but I can offer you a *Seize*," she said.

"A *Seize* will do just fine."

Cabinet doors squeaked open, heavy glasses hit the countertop, and the beer fizzed up.

She thrust a glass into his hand. "Chin-chin."

He raised it to his lips. "*Santé*."

"So what did you want to tell me?"

He placed his glass on the counter and rested his hand next to it. "That I was dating the wrong sister."

She put her glass down, too, but said nothing.

"There's this woman," he continued. "Her name is Emma… on most days. Except when she feels more like a Laura. She's talented, kind, and charming."

She kept silent.

"She's gorgeous."

Emma started to protest, but he interrupted her. "You can't say I don't know it because I'm blind. I've seen you, *mon ange*." His mouth curled up. "And I've touched you everywhere... Did I mention you're sexy as hell?"

He waited, but she didn't emit a sound. None whatsoever.

Since when had his inability to gauge her reactions become the hardest part about being blind?

Touch my hand, love.

She laid her hand on top of his. "So you're not angry anymore about... the whole Laura business?"

He shook his head and smiled, savoring the warmth of her palm.

She moved closer—so close he could hear her breathe.

"Besides," he said, putting his free hand on her arm, rubbing her shoulder, and then cupping her neck. "You did try to tell me the truth before we made love. It was me who asked you to wait 'til the morning."

"I shouldn't have listened," she whispered against his throat.

He breathed in the scent of her hair mixed with her musk rose perfume. Memories of his night with her rushed in, followed by memories of *Emma*.

He could see her in his mind's eye, all of her, even the things he hadn't realized he knew. As his hand raked through her shoulder-length hair, he pictured her disheveled strands with enough clarity to distinguish the ash-blond highlights in the darker mass. He stroked her heart-shaped face, his thumbs tracing the lines of her eyebrows and brushing over her soft lashes.

As he cupped her face with both hands, his brain brought up an image of her dark green eyes full of kindness and intelligence. He remembered how she screwed them up in the most adorable fashion when she laughed.

And then he pictured her mouth.

It wasn't the kind of mouth one would call voluptuous or glamorous, but it was… alluring. Just like the rest of her. He savored its tantalizing proximity and the promise of its honeyed taste that he had craved for a whole week. With a guttural growl, he bent toward her and crushed his lips against hers, hungry and a little rough, but he couldn't help it. Her lips parted, and his tongue penetrated her mouth with a thrust so powerful and urgent she gasped and clung to him as he drank in the sweetness he had hungered for.

For the next fifteen minutes, he held her in his arms and made love to her tongue, stroking it, sucking on it, diving in and out of her mouth. As he reveled in the precious intimacy of the moment, he knew he would want this again very soon. And then again, and again, and again. He could never have enough of this.

Or her.

Chapter Seventeen
Emma

She drew away and took a ragged breath.

When Cyril leaned in to renew the kiss, she planted her hands on his chest and pushed gently. "Let me look at you for a moment."

He straightened and gave her a panty-dropping smile.

His unseeing eyes were as handsome as ever. His complexion had darkened with desire, and the bulging muscles of his chest flexed under her touch. Through the thin cotton of his T-shirt and through the air between them, she could feel the heat coming off his body. There was something feline—graceful and hard—about his posture.

Like a wild cat before a bound.

He was magnificent.

Cyril bent toward her, angling his head for a kiss. "Your time's up."

And she abandoned herself to his demanding mouth and hands all over her.

When he drew back, it was to yank his T-shirt off. She took in the expanse of his chest, sculpted muscles everywhere. Giddy with excitement, she stepped closer and pressed her lips to him, trailing hot kisses on the bulges and hollows of his chest. Her hands caressed his upper back then slid down and found his firm buttocks. He had a fantastic ass—tight with muscle and rounded just so—a treat to stroke.

And to squeeze.

He tugged her T-shirt and pulled it up and over her head. Buckles clinked undone, zippers came open, jeans slid down and thumped to the floor.

Thank God it was still warm and she hadn't yet started layering her pullovers or wearing pantyhose. She would have died from an excess of lust before her winter getup came off.

He reached down between her legs, stroked the sensitive skin of her inner thighs, and cupped her through her panties. A wave of pleasure shot through her and stole the strength from her legs. She gripped his shoulders and threw her head back as his skilled fingers drew heat to her core.

When she felt herself nearing the edge, she grabbed his wrist and pulled it away from her.

He leaned forward, a plea in his raspy voice. "Emma."

She searched for words to tell him she didn't want to climax this way, not now. It was their first time as Cyril and Emma. On some deeply significant level, it was their real first time together. And she needed him to be with her — in her — when she came.

But words failed her, so she laced her fingers through his and led him to her bedroom. They toppled to the bed, kissing and removing each other's underwear in a heated frenzy. An unbearably long intermission later, caused by too much eagerness and a stubborn foil packet, he finally entered her with one delicious thrust.

Dear God.

She moaned her pleasure, straining with anticipation, but no other thrusts followed. Instead, he captured her hands in his, yanked them up, and pressed them into the pillow. She kissed his chin and whispered his name, her voice breathless with desire. Her legs wrapped around his thighs, and her hips rocked under him, urging him to resume his lovemaking. But he lay perfectly still, only his rattled breathing and flushed skin betraying the effort it cost him.

He held her hands for a few moments, his palms pressing into hers, fingers interlocked. Then he brought her hands closer together.

She panted with the sweet torture of it. He clasped her wrists with one large hand and tongued her earlobe while his free hand traced the contours of her neck, clavicles, and shoulders. Then it slipped between their chests and cupped her right breast.

She whimpered softly as he kneaded and fondled it, applying just the right amount of pressure, rubbing the pad of his thumb across its peak. Then his fingers slid down to her tummy, caressed her hip, and dug into the yielding flesh of her bottom. She tilted her head and kissed him again, this time full on the mouth. He groaned and began to tease her tongue with light strokes. When he pulled out of her mouth, her tongue followed him into the warmth of his, and she shivered when he caught it between his teeth and bit lightly.

As their tongues danced their fevered tango, his hand returned to her breast, and he gently rolled her nipple between his thumb and index finger. She gasped against his mouth and thrashed in another desperate attempt to get him to do her bidding. He wanted her to beg, did he? Was that what he was after? Very well, she'd beg because right now she didn't care if she did something wrong, if she was awkward or ridiculous. She didn't care about her lack of sexual prowess anymore. She didn't care about anything except how badly she needed him to start moving again.

Inside her.

"Please," she rasped. "I can't... I need you to..."

He stopped stroking her breast and smiled. "Yes? What is it you need, *mon ange*? I'll do anything. Just say it."

Just say it? "You fiend," she growled. "You know very well what I need."

His face grew serious. "Yes, I do."

And so he did.

An hour later, he rummaged through the pile of discarded clothes they'd left on the floor and found his boxer briefs. He pulled them on and rose from the bed. "Which way is the entrance door?"

Emma burst out in laughter. "Wow. You're really in a rush to leave."

He chuckled. "No chance. I won't leave here until you kick me out. I just need the bag I left there."

"I'll fetch it." She padded to the door and back in her bare feet and handed him his bulky duffel bag.

He unzipped it, took out a faded black guitar case, and opened it.

She held her breath. Could it be? Was he playing again?

"I wrote a song last night—"

"You what? Oh my God, Cyril, that's fantabulous! Can I hear it? Please?"

He nodded. "Just keep in mind that I haven't had time to polish it."

"I'm sure it's good."

"I hope so." He shrugged. "But it doesn't matter. This song isn't for the public. It's... private."

He strummed a few chords and cleared his throat. But instead of singing, he smiled self-consciously and said, "It's called 'Falling for Emma.'"

It took her a few seconds to register his words. As soon as she did, her eyes began to cloud over. She blinked ferociously to hold the tears back. Being with a blind guy had its perks—no need to worry he would see her cry and think she was a cornball.

He was still strumming, his expression betraying a mix of concentration and nervousness.

She wiped her cheeks with her palms and sat on the bed, tucking her knees under her chin. "Let's hear it. With that kind of title, I'm sure I'll like your song no matter how terrible it is."

He grinned, his facial muscles suddenly relaxing.

And then he began to sing.

Sweet Lord, that voice. So intense and yet perceptive. So quintessentially masculine — deep, velvety, a little ragged on the edges. It always had the same effect on her ever since she heard him sing for the first time in Geraldine's room all those years ago.

In fact, "hearing" didn't even come close to conveying what his songs did to her. They enveloped her, penetrated every inch of her skin, every muscle and tissue held under it, and went straight to the twenty-one grams of mysterious substance people called a soul.

Epilogue
Cyril

Emma's palm is clammy when I take her hand. We've been here for a full day and a night. Seems like a lot longer. I've stepped out a few times to use the bathroom or have a bite. Emma isn't allowed to eat. My poor darling has gone without food for twenty-four hours.

The nurse tells me it's not a problem; she'll be fine; it's normal for women to go through prolonged labor these days. I know—something to do with the way the human race has evolved. Babies' heads have become bigger to accommodate their smart brains, but women's pelvises have remained the same. Which means that difficult childbirth is now the norm rather than the exception.

Thankfully, Emma's had an epidural. They

injected an anesthetic into her spine, just the right dose for her to be fully conscious but feel nothing below the waist. She's exhausted, but she isn't in pain.

I don't think I could handle this whole experience otherwise.

"Would you like me to fetch the iPad?" I ask. "You could watch an episode of 'Friends.' It helped distract you earlier."

"Thanks, *mon chou*, but I'm too tired for that." Her voice is small, almost a whisper.

Someone enters the room and goes directly to the corner where the nurse is monitoring the screens. Sounds like the obstetrician's heavy stride. I'm glad he's come to check in on Emma again.

"Sorry to wake you up so early, *Docteur*," the nurse says. "But the baby's heart rate is too fast. Looks like the cord got wrapped around its neck."

What? No. *No, no, no.*

I hold my breath.

"Not to worry, parents," the doctor says. "This happens a lot and is rarely life-threatening. But we need to act fast. We'll move madame Tellier next door for the C-section."

"A C-section?" I repeat like an idiot.

Emma gives my hand a squeeze. "Phew. I

thought they'd let me rot here forever."

I try my best to sound cheerful. "You'll be fine. You're in excellent hands."

"I know. This is going to be over soon."

She withdraws her hand, and they roll her away.

This is going too fast.

"Monsieur Tellier, you can stay and wait here, if you want," an unfamiliar voice says.

I nod. I cannot speak.

As soon as the room's gone quiet, I begin to pray. I'm not sure God pays attention to my prayers, though. Why would he want to listen to someone who only prays in emergencies... and who isn't even sure he exists? And if he does, I doubt he likes what he's hearing or approves of what I'm asking him to do.

Thing is, I suspect he's cross with me for some yet undetermined reason. I also suspect I wasn't meant to survive that car accident two years ago, or the desperation that followed. But here I am—the blind and scarred SOB who refused to give up. I've adapted to my loss of sight, rebuilt my life and begun to make music again. People love my new songs. And as if that wasn't enough, a woman like Emma loves *me*.

When we got married, I didn't want her to take my name. I told her it brought bad luck. But she just laughed and said she didn't believe in superstitions.

I should've insisted.

I shake my head and go back to praying.

God, let them be fine. Let them both make it. If you need a sacrifice, take my voice, my hearing, my legs, my arms, anything. And if you're determined to reduce the number of Telliers on this planet, will you please take me? I'm ready to go any time. Just spare Emma and the baby. Please. Amen.

I concentrate all my energy on this prayer and beam it up to the stratosphere, trying to outshout millions of other prayers for a chance to be heard. Suddenly, an image fills my brain, and I break into a cold sweat. It's a vision of the doctor cutting Emma's belly open. I can't see the baby in my mind's eye. I don't care about the baby right now. All I want is for Emma to make it through this ordeal.

Because she's the kindest, sweetest, most beautiful human being there is. Because I love her more than words or music can convey.

Breathe, Cyril. She'll be OK.

I'm well aware how low maternal mortality rates are in this country. Emma has excellent odds, a thousand times better than she would have had a century ago. But I'm scared shitless.

So I pray some more.

Dear Lord, if you absolutely must take one of them, then spare Emma. Please spare Emma.

I cringe, half-expecting a bolt of lightning to fry me on the spot or a huge divine fist to flatten me for what I just wished. As I said, God and I aren't close, so I have no clue how he would react to the brutal honesty of my prayer. I don't have the foggiest how he'd take my admitting that, if I had to choose, I'd pick my wife over anyone, including myself and our baby.

Another fear creeps into my feverish mind: What if the problem isn't my honesty but my love—too much of it—directed at another person? Doesn't religion tell us to only love God? Or was it God in all things?

A little voice in my head—must be one of the scattered remains of my sanity—whispers that how I *feel* or what I *think* cannot change the course of Emma's life. She has her own destiny. And right now it's in the hands of the obstetrician and of God—or Randomness—but definitely not in mine.

The voice calms me down a little. I take several deep breaths and try to concentrate on the faint noises coming from the hallway. But then I notice that my hands are trembling. And so are my legs. The world is slipping out of control, and there's nothing I can do about it.

A shrill cry comes from the operating room.

It's a baby. Our baby.

Someone walks in. I recognize the nurse's light shuffle.

"You can touch your boy," she says. "He's beautiful."

"How's the mother?"

I can't—I won't—touch the baby until I hear her reply.

"She's fine. Docteur Prouvost just finished sewing her up."

I breathe, processing the information.

"You're pale as death," the nurse says. "You shouldn't've worried, poor thing. This is one of the best labor wards in Paris, and Docteur Prouvost is one of our most experienced obstetricians."

I take a deep breath. "Can I talk to her?"

"In about half an hour. We'll transfer her to her room, and then someone will come and get you. Do you think you'll survive the wait?"

I nod and hold out my hand. The nurse lowers the baby—we're going to name him Leo—and my fingertips come into contact with soft, warm skin. It's his foot. An inconceivably tiny little foot with minuscule toes and microscopic nails on them. I stroke it, wrap my index and thumb around the plump ankle, caress the sole. On an impulse, I lean forward and press my lips to it.

And that's when I see God, right here beside me, smiling.

It's a humbling sight.

"Thank you," I whisper.

"You're welcome," the nurse says, and takes Leo away.

A grin spreads across my face. After a while, my cheeks start to hurt, but it won't go away, won't shrink even by a millimeter.

Emma lives.

And I'm a dad.

<<< <> >>>

Under My Skin

Chapter One
September

A tall well-dressed guy entered the bistro, dripping rain and hotness. He stopped by the door and surveyed the room.

Must be looking for Rob.

Jeanne tried to peel her gaze off him and focus on the conversation around her. Easier said than done. Aside from his general attractiveness, the stranger was full of contrasts that mesmerized her.

He had long legs and narrow hips, yet his upper body was deliciously brawny. *The poor fellow must have a hard time finding suits that fit.* Speaking of suits, his was a sleek number cut from the finest, smoothest wool to grace *La Bohème* on her watch. The trendy jacket overlaid the lines of his V-shaped torso as if it were tailor-made. Which it probably was. On top of all that, his friendly, clean-shaven face sported a masculine nose and a firm jawline.

Just as the mysterious hunk turned to survey her side of the room, Rob approached him and gave him a big hug.

"I'm so glad you made it! It wouldn't have been a proper engagement party without my best man."

"It's a matter of having one's priorities straight," the hunk said. "I told the boss I was leaving at five thirty, whether we were finished or not."

His crooked smile sent a couple of Jeanne's internal organs into a happy little somersault.

"That's the spirit, man." Rob grinned.

The guy winked. "Having Mom as my boss does have its perks. Where's Lena, by the way?"

"Fetching her folks. They should be here in half an hour." Rob patted him on the shoulder. "Now, why don't you give me your wet jacket and get yourself a drink. The party doesn't officially begin until eight thirty, so you can chill and talk to the people you know."

The hunk removed his jacket, uncovering an expensive-looking shirt—and a better view of his broad chest.

Jeanne swallowed. Was this guy real?

Rob took the wet garment from him and walked away. And then something weird happened. The hottie remained by the door instead of walking toward the guests or the bar. He looked around the room as if searching for someone—his gaze lingering on the females until it met Jeanne's. He beamed and walked toward her, his eyes trained on her and full of warmth.

Does he know me? Do I know him?

It was downright impossible she would forget a stud of this caliber, even if she had met him during her wild teens.

"Hi, Jeanne. Don't you remember me?" He was close enough for her to discern the hint of five-o'clock shadow on his chiseled jaw.

"I'm sorry . . . Are you sure we've met?"

"Every day for almost two years."

Righto.

She tilted her head to the side. "Next you'll tell me I used to go out with you."

"Unfortunately, you didn't." The dreamboat sounded genuinely sorry. "But it wasn't for my lack of trying. I spent most of my money eating at this bistro just so I could see you."

She gave him a puzzled look. Who *was* he?

"OK, you really don't remember me." He bowed ceremoniously. "Mathieu Gérard, also known as Mat. I'm a friend of Rob's. We studied together here in Paris a few years back."

"Mat?" There was no way this guy was Mat. "You can't be him. Mat was . . . he was . . ."

"Nothing like me?" he prompted, the corners of his mouth twitching.

To put it mildly.

"Thin," she finally said. "Anorexic thin. And his hair was like an explosion in a spaghetti factory, and he had these bulging eyes—"

"Ah, so you do remember me." He smiled that crooked smile again. "I'm reassured because I often wondered if you'd even registered my existence."

There was a sudden commotion at the entrance, and Jeanne turned in the direction of the noise, happy for the distraction so she wouldn't have to react to Mat's remark.

The bride and her family had arrived. The ambient music Jeanne had compiled for the occasion was no match to the decibels produced by Lena's little half sisters. It was amazing how much noise a toddler and a baby could make.

"If you'll excuse me,"—Jeanne stood—"I'll go greet Lena and her tribe."

"Of course," Mat said. "I'll do the same."

After endless hellos, hugs, kisses, "pleased-to-meet-yous" and "how-are-yous," everyone settled into small groups, chatting and sipping their predinner aperitifs.

"Jeanne took care of everything," Lena told her dad. "I'm so lucky to have a professional restaurateur for a best friend!"

"This place is cozy," Lena's father said. "But I would've preferred to celebrate such an occasion at a more ... upscale restaurant. If you and Rob had let me handle things, of course."

"Have you tried the food here?" Mat asked him.

Anton shook his head.

Mat gave Jeanne a lingering look. "Is it still the same chef as three years ago?"

"Yep."

He turned back to Anton. "He's one of the best in Paris. Believe me. You get better food here than in a Michelin-starred restaurant, for a fraction of the price."

"I wouldn't go that far, but our chef *is* good," Jeanne said, not without pride. "You'll tell me what you think of him after the dinner tonight."

"Besides, there's no way Rob and I are celebrating our engagement anywhere else." Lena turned to her father. "This is where everything began, Dad."

"Ah, *oui*?" Anton gave his daughter and her fiancé an amused look.

"I used to work here with Jeanne and Pepe," Rob said. "And Lena used to come here to write her thesis. This is a special place for us."

"How's Pepe, by the way?" Mat asked.

"Pregnant," Jeanne said. "I mean his Danish wife. They live in Copenhagen now."

The exchange was interrupted by the chef, who peeked out of the kitchen and signaled he was ready to send in the first course.

His special menu turned out to be everything one could hope for.

Three hours later, the guests had finished their meals, downed an impressive amount of wine, and begun to order their *petit café*. Lena's youngest sister was fast asleep and the older girl was nodding off in her chair.

"I apologize for what I said earlier this evening. The food is so good, I would've licked the plate if I were less inhibited," Anton declared.

Whether because of the drinks, the amount of food or simply the fatigue, Jeanne began to feel sleepy and a little lightheaded, too.

"Who's the DJ?" Lena's stepmom, Anna, asked.

Jeanne raised her hand. "Me. Are you tired of this music?"

"It's a great playlist. Perfect for the aperitifs and dinner." Anna winked before adding, "And getting the girls to sleep. But now we need something we can dance to. I don't know about France, but in Russia, a party isn't a party without people dancing until they drop."

"I thought it was more like *drinking* until they drop," Jeanne said with a sly smile.

"That too," the older woman agreed, unfazed. "So, do you mind if I play my dance list?"

"Be my guest."

Lena's dad carried the sleeping girls to the staff room where two portable cots had been set up. In the meantime, his wife changed the music and enlisted helpers to move some tables and chairs around for an improvised dance floor.

"I'm curious to hear Russian pop," one of Rob's friends said.

"It's not only Russian and not only pop," Anna countered. "I've got a nice mix of everything, including a couple of slow songs so we can catch our breath."

At the first notes of the first slow song, Mat walked over to Jeanne, who was downing a big glass of water by the bar after a string of exhausting Latin dances.

"Shall we dance?" He offered his hand.

"Sure," she said nonchalantly.

Yahoo! her body sang.

She put her hand in his, and he led her to the middle of the room. Lena and Rob were already on the dance floor, and so were Anton and Anna. Both couples held each other close, and Jeanne wondered if Mat would do the same.

When he went for the classical ballroom position, she exhaled in relief—or was it disappointment? They began to move to the music, sliding their feet on the floor tiles. He maintained a polite distance, and their bodies touched only in the prescribed places—his hand on her mid back, her hand on his shoulder, and his other hand holding hers. All very *comme il faut*. Except for the way Mat looked at her lips . . . and then at her chin, her neck, her bare shoulders, and her cleavage. And then at her lips again.

Had Jeanne been shy, she would have blushed and lowered her gaze, but as it was, she stared right back, feasting on his handsome features and savoring the effect she had on him. His light gray eyes darkened, burning into hers. His lips parted slightly, and his chest heaved as if he'd been running.

And all at once, the pressure of his hand against her back and the soft grasp of his other hand felt intimate—a motionless caress that raised hairs on her body. In some spectacular trick of Jeanne's mind, everyone except Mat vanished, leaving them alone, weightless, outside time and space. When she caught a whiff of his musky male scent that his cologne could no longer contain, her hand shot up from his shoulder and cupped the back of his head. She took a tiny step closer.

Then she moistened her lips and whispered, "Kiss me."

* * *

The music stopped, breaking the spell. As they held each other for a few more seconds, Mat looked at her with a mixture of regret and relief. Jeanne could definitely understand the regret, but why the relief? Hadn't he been the one who ogled her during the dance?

She pulled her hand from his. "All good things must come to an end, I guess."

He gave her a funny look. "I need a drink. What about you?"

"I've had too many already . . . Oh well, one more won't make a difference. Your table or mine?"

He threw a quick look at both. "Definitely mine. We still have a bottle of that terrific Château-Grillet."

"So, what do you do for a living these days?" she asked, filling their glasses.

"I work for my mother's PR company, and I'm the Green candidate for mayor of Baleville."

She gave him a quizzical look.

"My home town in Normandy," he explained.

"Green, huh?" Jeanne raised her glass. "Here's to your success. Is it looking good?"

He touched his glass to hers. "Fifty-fifty. I need to work hard over the next months to convince the good citizens of Baleville that my youth is an asset rather than a handicap."

"You have a good team?"

He smiled. "I'm not running for president, remember? The regional Greens are helping as much as they can, but I'm basically on my own."

"What, not even a private chauffeur for the future mayor?" She tut-tutted. "Where is this country going?"

"Well, my biggest helper—and mentor—is my girlfriend. She's an environmental litigation lawyer, a great strategist, and a perfectionist to boot."

Ah. Now she understood why he'd been relieved when the music stopped.

He continued. "Cécile is my Pygmalion."

"No less?"

"I'm not exaggerating. She's molding me into a winner. She corrects my speeches, picks my suits . . . I couldn't do this without her."

"Why isn't she here?" Jeanne asked.

"She had to prepare for a court case she's pleading on Monday."

Jeanne took a big gulp of wine and closed her eyes to savor it. "Oh yeah, it *is* good. I'm glad I insisted on Château-Grillet over Rob's choice."

"Rob is from Jura, remember?" Mat swept his hand in a *need-I-say-more* gesture.

"Why, the region has a couple of excellent—"

"Cheeses," he cut in. "They may know a thing or two about cheese over there, but not much about wine."

"Whereas in Normandy, I'm told, wine education begins in the nursery." Jeanne gave him a wink. "Jokes aside, you're discerning for a *green* politician."

"I'll take it as a compliment, coming from a professional waitress."

"I'm no longer a waitress," she said.

"What are you then?"

"A barista by day and bartender by night. Oh, and bit of a sommelier, too."

"Wow—a one-woman band. Sounds like you're working double shifts."

"On most days." She emptied her glass. "I'm hoping to take this place over when Pierre retires."

"More?" He asked, and after her nod, refilled both their glasses. "I remember him. An easygoing chap with a beer belly, right?"

She nodded.

"What about the headwaiter?" he asked.

"Didier? Still here, still the headwaiter. Also interested in buying the bistro, by the way."

"Well, I hope it goes to you and not to that jerk." Mat banged his fist on the table. "He never missed an opportunity to show how much he despised me and most of the other customers."

"He's not that bad. He learned to look down his nose at everyone from his mentor. Now it's a habit."

"Hey, guys." Lena approached their table. "We'll be heading home soon. I can't feel my legs anymore."

Jeanne looked around. Everyone had already left except Mat, Lena, and Rob. The rest of the bistro staff was gone, too.

"Thanks again, Jeanne, for helping us put this together," Rob said.

"My pleasure." Jeanne stood to say good-bye.

"I hope you're not staying to clean up the mess," Lena said as they hugged. "Remember your promise to forget you're hosting this party, and behave like a regular guest? A *special* guest—my maid of honor and my best friend!"

"I've kept my word so far, and I intend to stick to it. I'm going to finish my drink, close the place, and go home. Scout's honor."

Rob grinned, hugging her in his turn. "Says the former Goth."

"Oh well, Goth's honor then. Come on, off with you now." Jeanne nudged him toward the door.

"What about you, Mat? Need a lift to your dad's place?" Rob asked.

"No, thanks—I'll walk. Besides, I won't leave as long as there's a drop left in here." He pointed to the last bottle of Château-Grillet.

Jeanne raised her brows. Why wasn't Mat leaving with Lena and Rob? He'd just told her he had a girlfriend who meant the world to him. This was very confusing.

After Lena and Rob left, Mat picked up the bottle. "Shall we finish it?"

She held her glass for him to fill. Her cheeks felt warm, and all her muscles were blissfully relaxed.

"I've often wondered if you'd changed over the past three years," Mat said.

"And?"

"Well, the hair's no longer blue and the lip piercing's gone. But other than that, you're the same."

As he spoke, his deep, velvety baritone enveloped her, caressed her, added depth to the scorching heat of his gaze. They sat a good two feet from each other, and yet she felt as though he was stroking her. Her skin prickled and a heavy awareness began to build in the pit of her stomach.

"You, on the other hand, are thoroughly transformed," she said.

"I guess I'm one of those guys whose puberty is so delayed it kicks in at twenty-five."

She shook her head, summoning her no-nonsense persona. "OK, I can buy some of it. The hair is easy to crop. The muscles—I suppose you took to weight lifting?"

He nodded.

"And this whole"—she pointed at his chest—"*Vikingy* virility thing . . . hormonal change?"

The corner of his mouth quirked. "Must be. By the way, a lot of people in Normandy have Viking ancestry."

"OK. But what about the eyes? Plastic surgery?"

"What do you mean?" He gave her a perplexed look. "Why would I need plastic surgery on my eyes?"

"Your eyes used to make me think of a . . . toad."

He frowned for a second, and then burst into laughter.

"It wasn't my eyes; it was my cheap eyeglasses. I'm farsighted, which means I need a plus prescription." He pointed to his elegant glasses. "These ones are thinner and hi-tech, so they don't magnify my eyes. See?" He drew closer until his face was only a few inches from hers.

Jeanne told herself to draw back, but her body refused to obey. She glanced at his eyes as he had requested and tumbled headlong into their stormy depths. Her breath caught in her throat, and she quivered as her body began to ache for his kiss, for his touch—for any form of physical contact with him.

How weird to burn like this for someone I barely noticed three years ago.

Someone who was no longer free.

Mat's world spun like a top, round and round, faster and faster, until it concentrated into a single spot... which happened to be a luscious female mouth. Jeanne's mouth. In a last bid for sanity, he reminded himself that he wasn't a philanderer, that he'd never looked at another woman since he'd been with Cécile. But when the tip of Jeanne's tongue darted to moisten her lips, he didn't stand a chance.

The crush he'd thought long gone was alive and kicking.

Right where it hurt.

A primal hunger surged in him, thickening the blood in his veins, assaulting his senses and robbing him of his free will. There was no fighting it.

As if hypnotized, he brought his hand to Jeanne's face and traced his thumb across her lower lip. He moved slowly, pressing lightly enough not to hurt her, but with sufficient force to miss nothing of the texture, warmth, and fullness of her lip.

Her chest heaved as she closed her eyes.

"God," he rasped, hardly recognizing his own voice. "You have no idea how often I've dreamed of doing this. I'm crazy about your lips, Jeanne. Even without the piercing."

When his thumb reached the corner of her mouth, he trailed it across her upper lip, savoring every sensation and growing so aroused it hurt. It was much too soon when he completed the circle, but no force on Earth could make him break the contact or make him stop touching her. His thumb slid down to her chin, his palm cupping her cheek. Oh, the sweetness of her, the long-forbidden treat he was finally about to sample. It was heavenly. It made him want more.

His gaze traveled down her graceful neck framed by auburn hair, to her shoulders. He bent down and began to cover them in hot kisses as his hands wandered across her back, bared by the figure-hugging dress she wore. And what a clever dress it was—specially designed to drive him out of his mind. Its skirt reached the middle of her thighs, revealing most of her shapely legs. Its seemingly demure neckline skimmed her collarbone and then plunged in the back, descending all the way down to the two sweet dimples in the small of her back. Which was exactly where his hand was going... until she opened her eyes and pulled back.

"This is wrong," she said.

He stared at her, disoriented.

She sighed. "I've been here before, Mat, and I got burned. I can't... I won't... fool around with a man who's taken."

He swallowed hard and released her. As his heartbeat slowed and his breathing evened out, his speech capacity returned.

And so did reason.

"You're right. I'm so sorry, Jeanne."

"I'm sorry, too," she whispered.

He gave her another long look. "Let me walk you home."

She shook her head. "I live five blocks down the street. Really . . . Just go."

She spun around and rushed away, leaving him no choice but to grab his jacket and bolt out the door.

* * *

"And then she told me I was too old and too ugly for her." José, a regular at *La Bohème*, smoothed the long-gone hair on his shiny skull.

"Her loss." Jeanne shrugged. "Are you coming back for lunch today?"

He shook his head. "I have another date this afternoon, in the park. I'm tired of paying for drinks and dinners only to hear I'm too ugly."

"Honey, you're not ugly, and don't give up yet. You started this Internet dating thing only a month ago." She wrung out the dishrag and wiped the copper surface of the bar.

A newly retired *vieux garçon,* José was a little chubby and seriously grumpy. But Jeanne didn't mind his ranting, especially on days when she didn't want to be alone.

And on this beautiful Sunday morning she needed company more than ever. The brunch crowd would provide a welcome distraction, but it was still too early. So thank God for José whose stories took her mind off what had happened last night.

"What's the name of today's date?" she asked.

"Clementine. I know—terribly old-fashioned, which makes me think she probably lied about her age."

Jeanne smiled. "You'll find out soon enough. Besides, would it be so terrible to date someone your age or older?"

"Hmm," José said. He took a sip of his brew. "Your coffee's better than the previous gal's."

"You've already told me that. And don't think I didn't notice how you changed the topic." She turned away to empty the filter basket. "But thanks—I'm flattered."

Somebody else spoke from José's right. "Can I have one, too, since it's so good?"

Mat.

She hadn't seen him come in. Why was he here?

"Espresso?" she asked without turning to look at him.

"A double, please," he said.

As she began preparing his coffee, she sneaked a peek at him. He looked even hotter than last night. No expensive suits today—just a pair of faded jeans and a navy blue V-necked sweater over a white T-shirt. He propped his elbows on the counter, a tiny smile wrinkling the corners of his eyes.

Jeanne looked away, flabbergasted. One quick glance at him had been enough to make her pulse quicken and her hands grow clammy. How was this possible? After all, she had happily snubbed this same person a few years ago. Granted, he was more masculine now than in those days. A *lot* more masculine, what with those biceps and pectorals he hadn't showed the slightest inclination for in the past. Besides, his general demeanor was more confident. Even his voice was deeper. Sexier.

But people couldn't change so completely, could they? Somewhere deep inside this gorgeous male was hiding a mild, nerdy guy with unruly hair and eyes like a toad's. If she could only spot one or two telltale signs of that guy, she'd be able to shake this spell and forget about his existence.

"I'll be off. See you tomorrow, Jeanne." José paid for his coffee and plodded away.

"A regular?" Mat asked.

"Nine o'clock every morning," Jeanne said, placing his steaming espresso on the counter.

"Are mornings a busy time?"

"Not really. A half dozen builders and drivers who come for an espresso and a cigarette outside. Another half dozen white collars pop in for various blends and croissants to go, and then José and a gang of moms."

"What do the moms order?" Mat asked, looking vastly entertained for some mysterious reason.

"Café crème or tea."

"And after they leave?"

Jeanne shrugged. "I make myself a nice strong coffee and read my paper."

"Still loyal to *Le Monde*?"

She nodded, absurdly pleased that he remembered.

"What about the cig that always went with the coffee?" he asked.

"A thing of the past."

"So you gave up smoking then?"

"It's been two years now." She smiled. "I quit after Lena started emailing me horrible photos of blackened lungs. Daily."

"I quit, too, thanks to Cécile."

He looked down at his cup, and Jeanne suddenly needed to occupy her hands with something. She grabbed the dishrag and started wiping the spotless countertop.

"I'm so sorry about last night," Mat said.

Jeanne stopped wiping and stared at the dishrag, noting absently that it was dark green and had too many holes from overuse.

"I behaved like a jerk... like one of those sleazebags I enjoy feeling superior to." He gave a heavy sigh. "This isn't who I am, Jeanne. I don't know what came over me."

"Château-Grillet. Too much of it," she said, trying to make light of the situation.

He shook his head. "Anyway, I just came to apologize and... to say good-bye."

Why did it hurt to hear him say those words? Had she expected him to announce he was changing his life after an evening with her? Had she actually entertained the idea he had come to tell her he was dumping his girlfriend because of their ground-shattering moment? She was such a pathetic fool.

"*Bonne chance* on your election." She turned away to fumble with the coffee machine.

She heard coins clank against the countertop and then Mat's retreating steps.

It's over, she told herself. *Just a bit of drama that came and went.*

She'd forget him in no time.

***

Chapter Two
October

They were ready to start the job interviews. Pierre and his two lieutenants—Jeanne and Didier—sat next to each other on one side of the large teak table that dominated the bistro's tiny backyard. On the other side of the table, they'd placed a lonely chair for the applicants. *La Bohème* had been a man short for a couple of weeks now, which put an extra strain on everyone, but especially on Manon and Jimmy, the front of the house servers. This was why Pierre had lined up four interviews for this afternoon and was determined to hire one of the candidates on the spot.

"I hope it doesn't rain," Jeanne said puckering her face at the uncertain sky.

Didier shrugged. "It was your idea to do this outside."

"It's not like we can't move back in if it starts raining," Pierre said, browsing through the stack of paper in front of him. "The first candidate arrives in ten minutes, so I suggest you both take another look at their CVs and the questions I asked you to prepare."

Jeanne scanned her copies. None of the four candidates had waited tables before, but then, everyone had to start somewhere. Two of them were students, so they'd probably be only interested in evening shifts, which was fine.

"We'll have to train whoever we hire from this batch." Didier shook his head disapprovingly.

Pierre put his papers down. "And so we will. Regardless of how much pride we take in our trade, let's face it—rocket science it is not."

"I disagree." Didier gave him a disgruntled look. "I did three years of specialized school before applying for my first serving job. I was a *professional* compared to these greenhorns."

"Well, there aren't enough *professionals* to go around," Pierre said. "So we have to make do with amateurs."

Manon appeared in the doorway, bowed ceremoniously and said far too politely, "Excuse me for interrupting, *messieurs-dames*, but the first candidate has arrived. Shall I show him in... um, *out* here?"

Pierre smiled. "Please."

Manon stepped sideways, making way for an elegantly dressed young woman. She walked slowly toward the empty chair and greeted the trio with a bright smile.

One point for style.

Jeanne remembered the hardcore Gothic look she'd been sporting when Pierre hired her six years ago. He must have been feeling brave that day. Or desperate.

"Please, sit down." Pierre pointed to the lonely chair.

"You study communication and marketing," Didier said, scanning the woman's CV. "Why are you applying for this job?"

"I need more pocket money than my parents are giving me," the woman said.

"Do you realize this is hard work?" Jeanne asked.

The woman shrugged. "I'm sure I'll manage."

Jeanne was beginning to find her slightly off-putting, but told herself not to jump to conclusions. Before she could ask her next question, a phone went off in the woman's purse.

"Excuse me," she said with the same polite smile and opened her handbag to retrieve a latest iPhone. "*Salut*," she purred into the phone. "I'm fine. What about you? ... No kidding? When? ... What did she say exactly?"

Didier cleared his throat.

Jeanne tapped her pen on the table.

"Shall we give you some privacy and return in twenty minutes?" Pierre asked.

"Thank you, it's very kind of you." The woman beamed, the irony of Pierre's words completely lost on her.

The interview panel exchanged amused looks, marched inside the bistro, had a coffee and returned twenty minutes later.

The woman had finished her conversation.

"You're really nice, you know? I'm sure we'll get along famously," she said.

"Thank you for your time," Pierre said.

"Is the interview over already?"

"We'll be in touch," Didier said, poker-faced.

"Or not," Jeanne added, reluctant to give her false hopes.

The second candidate was an accounting student who told them he was a "numbers person" and hated dealing with people. The third one was a middle-aged woman who, within the space of fifteen minutes, managed to tell them about her epic divorce, her landlord's refusal to repaint her apartment, the mistress of her former boss, and her recent thyroid surgery. She blew her nose every thirty seconds using paper tissues she pulled from her bottomless tote bag. She then neatly folded each used tissue and put it next to the previous one on the table in front of her.

Jeanne crossed her fingers by the time the last candidate lowered himself on the chair. The combination of his name, face, and zip code on his CV suggested he was a son of North African immigrant workers.

"Why have you applied for this job, Amar?" Jeanne asked.

"I'm a pro football player, but I sustained a nasty knee injury six months ago, and had to give up on football."

"Are you saying that waiting tables is the only alternative to professional sports?" Didier asked.

"No. But until I figure out what I want to do, it's a better alternative than many others I can think of."

Well said, Jeanne thought.

"Waiting tables requires a lot of walking," Pierre said. "Would your injury allow it?"

"Without a problem. There's a big difference between walking between tables and sprinting around a football field."

"You're only twenty-one, and this would be your first proper job. How can we be sure you'll manage?" Didier asked.

"I guess you'd have to trust your judgment," Amar said with a small smile.

But Didier wasn't finished yet. He opened his notebook and read, "Please describe your best professional quality using *just one word*."

"I'm very good at following the instructions I'm given," Amar said gravely.

Jeanne frowned, until she noticed the corners of his mouth twitch. A second later, a sly grin spread on his face.

She burst out in laughter.

"You're hired," Pierre said, smiling. "Can you start tomorrow?"

A little after midnight, Jeanne closed the bistro and headed home. She was dog-tired. Working double shifts for the past three weeks had affected her physically. On one level, at least, it was a good thing. The more her muscles ached and her head pounded, the less she thought about Mat. She'd discovered this effect shortly after the unfortunate incident at Lena's engagement party and was determined to exploit it fully until she purged him from her system.

Stepping into the lobby of her building, Jeanne walked past the concierge's loge and stopped in front of the door to her apartment. Lucky thing she lived on the ground floor. She couldn't imagine climbing even one flight of stairs right now. As she fumbled with her keys, she focused on one thing: a hot bath—a steaming, bubbly, foamy bath, with an old Sting album in the background and a scented candle flickering on the shelf above the tub. She'd soak until the last bit of tension, the last ache, left her body and then she'd turn in. This was the best way to fall asleep as soon as she hit the bed.

The apartment felt stuffy, so Jeanne opened the window to the inner courtyard and began to run her bath. As she browsed through her music collection, a thumping sound and a shrill female scream pierced the air. Then a male voice shouted something unintelligible.

"Get out of here!" the woman yelled.

More racket followed, something heavy hit the floor, and then a kid — a boy by the sound of it — shrieked, "Stop it, please, stop it!"

Jeanne turned off the tap and rushed to the window. The voices came from the concierge's loge. The concierge, whose name Jeanne couldn't remember, had been hired by the condo a couple of weeks ago after the previous one retired. Jeanne tried to remember what the woman looked like. Small, frail, curly-haired, late twenties maybe? Her face was a blur. Did she have a child? And who was she was fighting with? Should she intervene?

Someone slammed a door and a female voice said soothingly, "It's over, baby, he's gone now. He's just had too much to drink. He didn't mean any harm."

Jeanne waited a little longer to make sure the man wasn't coming back before she closed her window and went back to the bathroom.

***

Amar jogged over to the kitchen pass-through. "Table three want their steaks cremated."

"Got it," Claude replied.

Amar nodded and hurried back to the dining room.

Jeanne smiled privately. They'd made a good choice. In less than three weeks, Amar had learned an incredible amount, improving his waiting skills and picking up the bistro jargon as he progressed. The boy was a natural.

After another hour of hustle and bustle, the last lunch customer left the bistro, and time slowed its pace from furious gallop to a leisurely amble. Jeanne glanced at her watch. She had about three hours until things got hectic again. Enough time to make a coffee and finish the novel she'd started last week. That is, unless Didier wanted to chat.

A couple of weeks ago he'd become uncommonly chummy, which was weird. They'd worked together for many years now, but they'd never been friends. Now was hardly a good time to develop a friendship. Had he forgotten they were rivals competing for the same prize—*La Bohème*?

Jeanne sighed. Pierre hadn't yet given any indication as to whom he favored. He and Didier went back a long way and saw eye to eye ... But Pierre was also known to have a quasi-paternal affection for her.

Jeanne pulled her book from her purse and hurried to the coffee machine. If she was quick, she'd be out of the bar area and engrossed in her book by the time Didier showed up. And if she was lucky, he wouldn't intrude on her down time. Unless his sudden friendliness was part of some diabolic plan to get her to withdraw her bid.

Like that *was ever going to happen.*

Jeanne picked up her fragrant cup and her book and strode to her favorite corner by the window. As soon as her butt touched the padded bench, she opened the book and started reading.

Someone cleared his throat above her. She looked up expecting to see Didier, but it wasn't him.

"I need to talk to you, Jeanne, if you can spare a minute," Pierre said.

"Sure." She shut her book. "I'm all ears."

"Just a second, let's wait for Didier to join us," Pierre said. "I want to talk to both of you."

Jeanne cocked her head. "Are you sure?"

Pierre nodded.

As soon as Didier arrived, the two men sat across from Jeanne.

"I'll cut straight to the chase," Pierre said.

She glanced at Didier. He was leaning in, his jaws clenched.

"As you know, I'm retiring in a year," Pierre said. "Both of you have approached me about the bistro."

Jeanne nodded.

"That's correct," Didier said.

"I've known you both for years, and love you almost like my own children." Pierre smirked. "And probably more than my nephews."

"Are you going to tell us one of your children has finally expressed an interest in the bistro?" Didier asked, his eyes narrowing.

Pierre waved his question off. "There's no hope of that. My children think running a restaurant is too much work for too little money. And they're right." He let out a heavy sigh. "But you both love this place—love this job—you're competent, capable and motivated. It's breaking my heart to have to choose between you two."

"So, what do you propose?" Jeanne asked.

"I don't know," Pierre confessed. "I just wanted us to put it out in the open. I wanted the three of us to talk about it . . . but I don't have a solution yet. I've got a year to figure it out—unless one of you changes their mind in the meantime."

"Not me," Jeanne said.

"What if you didn't have to choose?" Didier asked mysteriously.

"What do you mean? Are you forfeiting?" Pierre gave him a puzzled look.

"Not a chance," Didier said. "But what if Jeanne and I came to some sort of . . . understanding about this affair?"

"What, like partnering to buy *La Bohème* together?" Jeanne asked.

"Something like that," Didier said.

Well, this explained his recent friendliness.

The idea appeared great... but only on the surface. First, Jeanne had savings and several loan options: her parents, Lena and Rob, her bank. She certainly didn't need a partner to help her buy the place. Second, even though she'd never had any quarrel with Didier, she had no particular affinity for him either. So, no, she wasn't thrilled about the idea.

"That would be brilliant!" Pierre looked so relieved it was touching.

"Wouldn't it?" Didier turned to Jeanne.

"I don't think—" she began.

"Listen, Jeanne," Didier said, placing his hand on her arm. "You don't need to decide or even say anything now. Give yourself some time to process the idea. You may change your mind and find it as appealing as I do." He gave her a long look that made her uncomfortable.

"I hope you will, girl," Pierre said. "I hope you'll do us all a huge favor and change your mind."

***_

Jeanne glanced at her watch for the third time in five minutes. She had to make a decision, and quickly. One option was to wait ten more minutes and elbow her way through the crowd to get on the next *métro* train. The risk associated with that option was if she failed, she'd be stuck here for another twenty minutes. At least. According to a well-established Parisian tradition, the *métro* workers were on strike, effectively disrupting the routines of hundreds of thousands of people.

The other option was to call Didier, ask him to brave rush hour, and drive to rue Cadet to collect her. She decided to give the *métro* another chance.

The evening before, Pierre had beckoned to her and Didier. "I want you two to go to Baleville tomorrow morning."

Jeanne's mouth fell open. Why did Pierre want her and Didier to go to Mat's hometown?

"What for?" Didier asked.

"Our main cheese supplier, Monsieur Conchard, wants to showcase his new products. I suspect he may also want to renegotiate the prices."

"Why won't he come here?" Didier asked.

"He doesn't feel like traveling to Paris with an assortment of smelly cheeses in the back of his car . . . and who can blame him?"

"So you want us to assess the new products and negotiate the prices, right?" Jeanne asked.

"It's time you learned to swim on your own, children," Pierre said. "Because in this business, you'll be swimming with sharks."

Jeanne smirked. "You make it sound so attractive."

"I'm glad you see it that way," Pierre said with a wink.

He gave them the necessary instructions and promised to keep his cell phone on. Jeanne agreed to meet Didier in front of his building at nine o'clock the next morning and drive to Baleville in his car. It was eight forty now. Jeanne clenched her fists and edged closer to the track. To hell with good manners—she was a shark in training, after all.

Twenty-five minutes later, she spotted Didier on the corner of his street, glancing at his watch. She waved. He beamed and waved back. And even though Jeanne knew why he was so friendly, she couldn't help warming to him a little.

"I like this look of yours," he said as she sat in the car.

She was wearing low-rise skinny jeans, a mustard-colored cashmere pullover, and a tailored leather jacket that reached the waistline of her jeans.

"You usually come and go from work dressed in the uniform," he added.

"I live next door," she said. "So it makes sense to change at home."

They drove in silence for a little while.

"Have you been in Baleville before?" he asked after they got onto the A13.

"No, never."

"It's a nice town. Only twenty minutes from the sea, but much more affordable than seaside places like Deauville."

"Sounds nice," she said. "Do you know how big it is?"

Hopefully big enough to minimize the risk of running into Mat.

"Ten thousand or thereabouts," he said.

A hundred thousand would've been better, but then again, ten is better than five.

"And it's only an hour and a half from Paris," he added.

Way too close, if you want my opinion.

Didier tapped his fingers on the steering wheel, looking pleased with himself. "If Monsieur Conchard doesn't invite us to lunch, I'll take you to Le Cheval Bleu. It's a nice local restaurant I discovered a few years ago, when I toured the Cider Route with some friends."

"I've wanted to do the Cider Route for years now, but instead I always end up going south," Jeanne said.

"You're from the south, aren't you?"

"Nîmes. My family are still there and some good friends... Where are you from, by the way?" She realized she'd never bothered to ask Didier that basic question.

"I'm from Lille." He smiled. "The Great French North."

She smiled back. *What a strange guy.*

He enjoyed being mean to customers, but he was usually courteous with his colleagues. Now that she thought of it, he'd always been particularly nice to her.

They arrived in Baleville a little before eleven o'clock, parked in front of Monsieur Conchard's shop, and ran inside to avoid getting soaked in the heavy rain. The supplier greeted them, an enthusiastic smile on his face. At twelve thirty they were done. As it turned out, Monsieur Conchard had no intention of a price hike, but only wanted *La Bohème* to order his new cheeses. Immensely relieved, Jeanne and Didier promised to call him within a week with a definitive answer.

"How about lunch? I'm starving," Didier said as they stepped out onto the wet street. Fortunately, the rain had exhausted itself into a drizzle while they'd been inside with Monsieur Conchard.

"How can you still be hungry after tasting twenty different cheeses?" she teased.

"How can you not be hungry?" he retorted.

"If we leave now, we'll avoid traffic, because everyone's having lunch," she offered.

"I'm not leaving without having eaten properly."

Seeing his determination, Jeanne stopped arguing and followed him to his favorite restaurant. As they walked, she tried to form an opinion about the town. It wasn't as pretty as the more touristy places in Normandy, but its half-timbered houses certainly had a lot of charm. And it was provincial through and through even compared to her hometown of Nîmes.

"Jeanne?"

She slowly turned away from the church they were passing, already knowing who it was. She'd recognized his voice. She would have recognized it in a crowd of people shouting her name.

"What are you doing here?" Mat stared at Jeanne as if she were an apparition.

"Meeting with a supplier," Jeanne said before introducing the two men to each other.

"We've met before," Mat said to Didier. "I used to frequent *La Bohème* a few years back, when Rob worked there."

Didier put his hands in the pockets of his jeans. "Can't recall." He turned to Jeanne, "We need to hurry if we want to get a table."

"Where are you guys headed?" Mat asked.

"Le Cheval Bleu—why?" Didier shot Mat a hostile look.

"What a coincidence! That's where I'm going for lunch."

"No kidding," Jeanne said in her driest voice.

"It's the best place in town, and I only go for the best." Mat squinted at her and smiled his crooked smile. "Do you mind if I tag along? We could talk about our common friends and remember the good old times."

Jeanne stole a glance at Didier. He'd folded his arms across his chest, lifted his head, and straightened as if trying to reach Mat's height. His mouth had thinned into a hard line, and even though he remained silent, his body language was loud and clear.

This was a disaster in the making.

Yet some treacherous part of Jeanne's mind was thrilled to spend the next hour in Mat's company.

"Fine. Whatever." Didier tugged at Jeanne's sleeve. "Let's move."

"I'll catch up with you," Mat said. "Just need to make a quick phone call."

Jeanne and Didier were already seated when Mat walked into the restaurant. He exchanged a handshake and a few warm words with the chef and the waiter who rushed to add a chair and utensils to Jeanne's table.

After they ordered, Mat fixed his gaze on Jeanne, staring at her for much longer than was polite.

She shifted in her seat.

"I'm not used to seeing you in jeans," he said by way of apology. "Either of you, that is," he added, turning to Didier.

"Why, did you think I was born in a server uniform?" Didier asked, a muscle pulsing on his jaw.

Mat turned to Jeanne again. "I much prefer your current look to the Gothic stuff you wore outside work a few years ago."

She smiled. "Oh yeah, my Gothic phase."

"Do you still hang out with Goths?" Mat asked.

Jeanne shook her head. "I never did, actually. I was what the Goths call a *poseur*. I loved their esthetics, I copied their dress, but I never shared their worldview."

"Which is?" Didier asked.

"A fascination with all things tragic and morbid," Jeanne explained.

"Was that why you dyed your hair blue rather than black?" Mat asked.

"Yeah," Jeanne said. "I guess it was my touch of rebellion against their rebellion ... I never enjoyed Gothic music, either."

"You used to like Sting," Mat said.

"Still do." Jeanne looked him straight in the eyes. "I'm faithful like that."

Mat swallowed hard and held her gaze. For a few moments, no one spoke. Jeanne and Mat peered at each other, while Didier's face grew tenser and redder by the second. Then, thankfully, their food arrived.

They ate in silence.

"It was nice seeing you . . . guys," Mat said when they finished the meal and stood to leave.

"Take care," Jeanne said.

Didier glared at him and walked out of the restaurant.

On their drive back, Jeanne thought of Mat, noting with satisfaction that her initial excitement was giving way to anger. He had no right to intrude on their meal. He had no right to look at her like that—as if she had mattered to him—or talk to her as if he had cared. He had no right to treat Didier with contempt.

Then she thought of Didier, telling herself he was a solid guy who had enough trust and respect for her to want to be her business partner.

And, possibly, more.

* * *

Chapter Three
November

Cécile climbed into bed next to Mat who looked up from his iPad and smiled. She had a pencil, a highlighter, and a thick binder in her hands.

"Things are looking better for my client," she said.

Given her penchant for understatement, he inferred she expected to win the case. "That's my girl. Would it be premature to announce it during the public debate at the town hall?"

"When's the debate?"

"Saturday. I'm counting on your presence."

"I'll be there. This GMO case will set a precedent in the region, so the judge is taking longer than usual." She tapped her teeth with her pencil. "I should be able to tell you on Friday if you can make an announcement."

"What about the windmills?"

She sighed. "We've got the Government's Environment Pact and the *greater good* on our side, but the plaintiffs' arguments are more... emotionally charged."

"They can't sleep because of the noise and they hate the skyline, right?" He took his glasses off and rubbed the bridge of his nose. "I'll have to take a public stand on this. Sooner or later someone's bound to ask what I think about the windmills."

"Has anyone polled the locals?"

"Mom surveyed a sample of sixty Balevilleans. The opinions were divided, almost fifty-fifty," he said.

"So, what's your stand going to be?" She cocked her head. "You're a Green — you can't turn against wind turbines just because some people find them ugly."

"And noisy. Besides, some Greens are concerned about their impact on wildlife."

"Oh, come on." She rolled her eyes. "A wind turbine kills an average of one bird per year. Fossil fuels kill a *lot* more."

He threw his hands up. "I'm just playing devil's advocate."

"I'll prepare a fact sheet with references to serious studies," she said. "I did tons of research for my case, so it won't take a lot of time."

He leaned over and kissed her on the forehead. "Thanks, baby. What would I do without you?"

"Lose the election?"

"I may lose it anyway," he said.

"Not if you follow my advice." She winked at him. "I want you to become mayor of this town just as much as you do."

"For environmental reasons?" he asked.

"And for private ones, too." She smiled.

He stroked her taut cheek, and his hand slid down to caress her bony shoulder through the fabric of her silk pajamas. He didn't try to bare it. As much as he liked the sight of her dainty frame in her sleek clothes, she was so skinny it pained him to look at her naked. Oh, how he wished she had curves. Not like Jeanne—that would've been too much to ask. He'd be happy with a hint of flesh in one or two strategic places. But Cécile was a calorie-counting, low-carbing, fat-avoiding vegan, which made acquiring said flesh virtually impossible. Once in a moment of drunken honesty, she shared the real reason behind her multiple food restrictions. Cécile hated the act of eating. But she didn't want to explain this to anyone, so she'd come up with all those diets to conveniently invoke at mealtimes.

She had denied her confession vehemently upon sobering up.

Mat kissed her and tugged on her binder. "Put this away," he whispered.

"Mat," she said admonishingly.

"Yes?"

"I have to read all this before the hearing tomorrow."

"Can't you read it first thing in the morning?"

"I won't have the time."

He pulled away a few inches and peered into her eyes.

She looked down at her papers. "Besides, it isn't Saturday yet," she said, her tone reproachful.

He removed his hand from her shoulder and sat up. Christ, she made lovemaking sound like a chore that had to be done on certain days. Like vacuuming or changing the bed linen. Was it what sex was to her—a chore? Was it the real reason why she'd only do it on Saturdays? And only those when she didn't have her period, a headache, or . . . no energy.

Whenever he asked her if she wanted him to do things differently, she'd always say she was happy with his *methods*. But he couldn't shake the feeling she resented their couplings, rare as they may be. Was having sex like eating for her—another bodily function she hated but wouldn't dare admit it? He loved her but, God, how he wished she had a tenth of Jeanne's sensuality!

As he stared unseeing at his tablet computer, he pictured Jeanne in his mind's eye, her out of this world body, her sweet face, her lush lips, and irresistible smile. He recalled every detail of how she looked in her wicked cocktail dress at Rob's party and then in those tight jeans when he'd run into her last month. His pulse picked up.

Great.

Mat clasped his hands over his head. How could Jeanne still make him feel this way, after three years of no contact? The half dozen curvaceous, beautiful women he associated with on a daily basis left him as cold as ice. What was it about Jeanne that affected him like this?

He finally fell asleep after convincing himself that his visceral reaction was residue from his youthful crush. It would peter out. All he needed to do was stay away from her. It would be madness to risk losing Cécile — the woman he planned to marry one day — over a romp with a hot babe he had nothing in common with.

* * *

"I'll have a double this morning," José said. "Haven't slept well."

"A double it is." Jeanne tilted her head to the side. "You do look a little tired."

"That kid on the third floor played the guitar again . . . almost until dawn." José shook his head in despair.

"Is he any good?"

José blinked. "Pardon me?"

"Not that it matters, of course," she said quickly. "He shouldn't disturb his neighbors' sleep."

José gave a tentative nod.

She handed him his coffee and smiled to reassure him she was on his side.

His face relaxed. "I see you hired a new server," he said, taking a sip and nodding in Amar's direction.

"Nothing escapes your notice, José."

"Looks a little too . . . young." He grimaced as he said *young*.

"It'll pass. And it isn't contagious," Jeanne said.

José sighed and drank the rest of his coffee in thoughtful silence.

During the staff lunchtime three hours later, Jeanne caught Amar red-handed: He was about to shove a plate into the microwave.

"Freeze!" she yelled.

He dutifully froze, holding the plate midair while gripping the microwave door with his other hand.

"Now slowly close the microwave, put the plate down, and turn to face me," she ordered.

He turned around.

She shook her head. "Thank God it was me and not Claude who caught you trying to nuke that meat."

"Why?"

"Isn't it obvious? First, if Claude gives you a cold dish for lunch, it's *supposed* to be eaten cold."

"And second?" Amar tilted his head.

"No one ever uses the microwave. It's a firing offense."

"Then why do you keep one here?"

"How shall I explain it..." Jeanne pinched her chin. "You see, every bistro *must* have a microwave oven. Yet, every *good* bistro makes a point of never using it."

"Of course, it's totally obvious," Amar said, deadpan.

"I'm glad we're on the same page." Jeanne nodded, somehow managing not to smile. "So, I'll forget what I just saw, and we'll pretend it never happened, OK?"

"Yes, ma'am."

She turned away to greet Amanda who'd just come in. Her office was around the corner, and she was a regular during lunch at *La Bohème*, eating it at the counter to chat with Jeanne. She once told Jeanne she would have come more often if it hadn't been for fear of running into Lena or Rob. Being the latter's ex, she didn't particularly relish the prospect.

"Do you think you could close the place off after nine on Friday?" Amanda asked.

"Depends on the number of people you're bringing. What's the occasion?" Jeanne asked.

Amanda beamed. "My big promotion. I'm now officially number two in the department."

"We'll close if you can get twenty-five people. Thirty would be better."

"I'm inviting all the colleagues I've worked with directly, which should be about twenty," Amanda said. "And all my friends." She paused before adding, "Which should bring us to twenty-five . . . I hope."

"Are you inviting Rob?"

"No way," Amanda said.

Jeanne gave her a sympathetic look.

Amanda sighed. "I'm not . . . angry anymore. I just don't want to see him, that's all." Then her face brightened. "But I'm inviting Mat and Rob's business partner, Patrick. They're my friends regardless of their connection with Rob."

Jeanne didn't register much after the word "Mat."

I'm going to see him Friday night . . . unless he declines Amanda's invitation.

For some reason she didn't think he would. But what if he brought his girlfriend? Jeanne frowned. She didn't want to see Mat with his girlfriend.

She briefly considered asking Didier to give her a hand during Amanda's promotion bash but decided against it. There was no need to stoke the tension between the two men.

It would be best for everyone if Mat simply didn't show up.

"Is something wrong? You look preoccupied," Amanda said.

"Aside from the universe conspiring against me?" Jeanne shrugged and shook her head. "No, everything's fine."

"How enigmatic." Amanda narrowed her eyes. "But, unfortunately, I've got to get back to the office. We'll discuss this later."

She paid and climbed down from the barstool. "So Friday, right?"

"Right," Jeanne said. "Wine and cheese?"

"You read my mind."

That night Jeanne left earlier than usual. One could pull only so many doubles in a row without a break. Besides, she needed a free evening to reconnect with the people she loved. She hadn't had a meaningful conversation with her parents in a while. Her only communication with her brother over the past months had been a few laconic text messages. And when was the last time she went out with friends? She'd been too focused on work, which was a smart thing to do financially and to keep her mind off Mat.

But the downside was piling into a heap too large to ignore.

As she stepped into the lobby, she spotted the concierge polishing the enormous mirror on one of the walls.

Jeanne approached her and held her hand out. "Hi, I'm Jeanne. My apartment is right there on the ground floor."

The concierge gave her a small smile and shook her hand. "Pleased to meet you. I'm Daniela."

She reminded Jeanne of Lena. Daniela was small, dark-haired, and doe-eyed with something unmistakably East European in her features. She looked to be in her midtwenties. She could have been pretty—but as it was, Daniela wore her hair in the most unflattering style Jeanne had ever seen, hunched her shoulders, and hid her body in shapeless drab clothes.

"I work at *La Bohème* up the street," Jeanne said.

"Oh, I went there a few days ago for a coffee. Nice place."

Her accent was definitely East European.

"Where are you from?" Jeanne asked.

"Romania."

"Daniela, would it be OK if I asked you to take in parcels for me every once in a while?"

"Of course. It's part of my job."

"Great, thank you!"

It was time to wrap up the conversation and let the woman get on with her work. But Jeanne had one more question. "Are you alone in the loge?"

Daniela shook her head. "I have a little boy, Liviu. He's six."

Jeanne nodded.

"But he's a quiet boy. He doesn't make noise."

"I know." Jeanne tugged on her necklace. "Listen, we're next door neighbors now, right? So, if you need anything... or need help, just knock on my door or come over to the bistro. OK?"

"You heard the fight a couple of weeks ago, didn't you?" Daniela asked, biting her lip.

"It was hard not to."

"I'm so sorry about that—"

"You don't need to apologize," Jeanne cut in. "I just want you to know you can reach out to me if... that guy bothers you again."

"He's my boyfriend. He's a nice guy when he's sober. He's good to Liviu, too. He's just going through a rough patch after losing his job."

Jeanne touched Daniela's arm. "I'm sorry, I didn't mean to pry. Welcome to our building, Daniela."

After she walked into her apartment and collapsed on the couch, Jeanne wondered what it was with women like Daniela—and herself— that pushed them toward the wrong men. Daniela's was violent. As for her picks, they were either philandering or already taken. Wouldn't it be wonderful to fall for a nice guy for once? A nice *available* guy.

Someone like Didier.

* * *

The wine and cheese idea had been a stroke of genius, Jeanne thought without false modesty. First, it allowed them to test all the new cheeses they'd ordered from Normandy and quickly gauge which ones were more popular than others. Second, it didn't require the service or even the presence of the chef tonight. Claude had been feeling under the weather all week, so Pierre told him to go home early and watch a comedy. The proprietor, whose *joie de vivre* was indomitable, persisted in hoping depression could be cured by a night off and a comedy. However, he had learned his lesson from Claude's previous bouts and made arrangements in case the chef was a no-show tomorrow.

Mat had come alone.

"Girlfriend too busy again?" Jeanne had asked after they greeted each other.

"Yeah," he said, avoiding her eyes.

She gave a few instructions to Amar, who was helping her tonight, and turned back to Mat. "The cheeses over there are the ones we ordered in Baleville."

"It fills me with immense pride that our products are good enough for refined Parisian palates."

Jeanne smirked and turned her attention to other guests. She spent the next three hours slicing cheese, pouring wine, and taking orders. Mat spent his time talking to Amanda and Patrick. Amanda cruised from one small group to another, joking and laughing and looking the happiest Jeanne had seen her in a long time.

A little before midnight, Jeanne realized that Amanda was the last person left in the bistro, not counting herself and Amar.

So, Mat left without saying good-bye.

Her heart tingled with disappointment, but it was better this way. For everyone.

Amar began to clean up while she went over to Amanda to exchange a cheek kiss. Amanda threw her arms around Jeanne in a bear hug. "Thank you for this lovely evening, Jeanne! Everything was perfect."

Jeanne patted her on the back. "It was a pleasure and ... I think you've had too much wine tonight."

"Why do you say that? Do I look drunk?" Amanda released Jeanne and whipped out a pocket mirror from her purse. "Do I sound drunk?"

Jeanne chuckled. "Neither. It was the hug that gave you away. You don't *do* hugs."

"Oh." Amanda grinned, relieved.

"Let me call you a cab. You shouldn't take the *métro* in this state and at this hour."

Ten minutes later, Amanda was gone and so was Amar. It was time to close up and haul herself home. Jeanne loaded the remaining glasses into the dishwasher and removed her apron. She was about to put on her parka, when someone pushed the back door open and stepped in from the bistro's courtyard.

It was Mat—coatless and shivering.

Spotting Jeanne, Mat sighed with relief and congratulated himself on his perfect timing. Had he waited a few seconds longer, she would've left, locking him in.

"What the . . . ," Jeanne said, stopping in her tracks.

OK. He owed her an explanation. "It got too stuffy in here, so I went out for some air."

"And fell asleep?" She gave him an I'm-so-not-buying-it look.

"I smoked a cigarette," he said, blushing like a schoolboy. "A first in six months . . . And I lost track of time." Another shiver ran through his body.

Jeanne hung her jacket back on the hook. "Come on. Sit by the heater while I make you tea."

"Don't trouble yourself," he said, leaning his back against the blissfully warm heater.

She gave him a shoulder glance. "I won't have a customer catching pneumonia after an evening in my charge."

A few minutes later, she placed two steaming mugs on the table in front of him and sat down. She was unbearably attractive even in the masculine shirt and wide pants of her bistro uniform. He forced himself to look away.

"If you leave in the next half hour, you can still catch the last *métro*," she said. "I suppose you're staying at Rob and Lena's?"

He shook his head. The heater against his back and the tea in his stomach were beginning to warm his blood and relax his muscles. He suspected Jeanne's slightly throaty voice had something to do with it, too. She always sounded as if she'd just rolled out of bed.

The sexiest voice a woman could have.

He lifted his eyes. What was the point in not looking if hearing her speak produced exactly the same effect?

"I'm staying with my dad. He lives in Paris."

"Oh," she said. "I didn't know your parents were divorced."

"It's been ages. But they are on OK terms, making life easier for all of us."

"You've got siblings?"

"Nope." He put his empty mug down. "What about you? Any brothers or sisters?"

"A brother. He's in Nîmes, running the bakery with Mom and Dad."

They remained silent for a moment.

Mat knew he had to thank Jeanne for the tea, collect his coat, and walk out. It was after midnight. She must be tired and wishing he'd just leave so she could finally go home. He racked his brain for a reason to linger.

There was none.

He stood abruptly. "Thank you for the tea."

"You're welcome."

He took a step sideways to get out of the narrow space between the heater and the table, and ended up a mere two inches from Jeanne, who'd risen from her seat in the meantime. They both froze and stared at each other. He swallowed, as his gaze traveled from her mind-blowing lips down to her heaving breasts, and then back up to her warm brown eyes.

He took a deep breath, catching the smell of coffee in her hair. His pulse throbbed in his head.

"I'm going to kiss you," he said. "You may slap me or kick me in the balls afterward, but I must kiss you."

He cradled her head with both his hands to execute his threat. His lips touched hers reverently, lightly, barely grazing them. She let out a soft sigh. He inhaled her head-turning scent and once again brushed his burning lips over hers. He had imagined this moment a thousand times, trying to guess how she would taste. Honey? Chocolate? Mint? But he didn't want to deepen the kiss just yet. He had dreamed of doing this for so damn long. He was going to take it as slowly as he possibly could.

Her lips were soft and warm beneath his as he kissed her with an adoring tenderness he didn't know he possessed. He shifted closer, his hands caressing her shoulders and her back, pressing her to him. The desire that stirred in him was nothing like he had experienced before. It roared like a wild beast and clawed his insides. It demanded to be set free, urging him to abandon all control and invade her mouth, her body, her very soul.

But he wasn't giving in to it. Not yet. He kissed the corner of her mouth, tugged on her lower lip, and nipped it lightly.

She moaned and dug her fingers into his shoulders. "Oh Mat," she whispered against his mouth.

He pulled away just enough to take in her heavy lids, her flushed cheeks, and her heaving chest. She was peering at his mouth, her head tilted up, an unspoken plea in her eyes. She wanted him. Jeanne—the woman he'd craved so desperately, so hopelessly—now desired him, too. He feasted his eyes on her as his shoulders pushed back and his chest expanded.

Does she have any idea what it means to me to see her like this?

Could she guess what it did to him to watch her aroused by his gentlest kiss? To know she desired him, to see her all but begging him to kiss her again?

He traced the outline of her jaw and cupped her nape, delving his fingers into her silky hair. His other hand circled her waist. He held her firmly, preparing to brand her with an entirely different kind of kiss. He was done teasing. The kiss he wanted now would be hot, hard, and messy.

And infinitely intimate.

His phone rang, startling him. It was Cécile's ringtone, which was unusual. When one of them traveled for work, they respected French etiquette and never called each other after ten o'clock. Something must be wrong.

He pulled the phone from his pocket and turned his back to Jeanne. "Are you OK?" he asked Cécile, his voice sounding like a stranger's.

"I'm fine. Sorry about calling, I was just . . . I had this bad feeling, like something happened. Are *you* OK?"

"I'm fine," he echoed her words.

"Are you at your dad's already?"

"Not yet. I'm about to leave."

"Will you please take a cab?" she pleaded. "You must be a little drunk, what with all those wines you've been sampling."

"I will. I promise," he said.

He shoved the phone into his pocket and swirled around. Jeanne was no longer beside him. She stood outside by the entrance, zipping up her parka. She had already pulled the rolling grilles halfway down. He grabbed his coat and rushed out. She lowered the grilles completely, locked them, and bolted away before he could say anything.

* * *

Chapter Four
January

It was a gorgeous midwintry morning, the air bristling with an exotic crispness brought by the northern winds all the way from Greenland. Snow had fallen all night, dressing Paris in a pretty white coat, all prim and virginal, as if the world didn't know better. Christmas decorations still dangled from the wires strung across the streets, a little sad by daylight but a welcome illumination as soon as night would fall.

Jeanne turned away from the window and rubbed her temples. An aspirin was in order if she was going to make it through the morning shift without dozing off in the middle of José's account of his latest rendezvous. She filled a glass with water and swallowed a pill. It should kick in before the first customers arrived.

It had been a rough night. At two in the morning loud voices coming from Daniela's loge woke her up. While she fumbled for the light switch and tried to peel her lids open, Daniela's angry shouting turned into screams of pain. Jeanne pulled a fleece on top of her pajamas and ran out. She knocked on Daniela's door, louder and louder until the voices inside quieted, and Daniela opened the door.

"What's going on?" Jeanne asked.

"Nico—that is, my boyfriend showed up drunk. I'm sorry," Daniela said.

She had a blackened eye and a huge bruise on her arm.

An irate male voice came from inside the loge. "Who are you talking to?" Then a burly red-eyed man shoved Daniela aside and stood in the doorway. "Who are you?"

"I'm Daniela's next-door neighbor. And who are you?" Jeanne asked.

"I'm Daniela's man. You have a problem with that?"

Jeanne inhaled. The guy was scary but she refused to show her fear. "I have a problem with you hitting her."

He looked her over, then turned to Daniela and sneered. "Sounds like you've got yourself a friend. Or maybe she's your special lady friend?" He glanced at Jeanne. "Not a beauty" — he hiccuped — "but so" — another hiccup — "hot."

Nico narrowed his eyes, trying to focus his gaze on Jeanne. His mouth fell slightly open and a small stream of drool trickled down his chin.

Jeanne nearly choked with disgust. "If you don't leave right now, I'm calling the police."

"Really?" He put his hands on his hips and snickered. "And what will you tell them — that you heard lovers bickering?"

"You hit her," Jeanne said. "I'm not blind. And neither are the cops."

Daniela pushed him to the side and pointed at her eye. "This isn't his fault. I fell this morning and hurt myself." She gave Jeanne a pleading look. "Please don't call the police. They'll only add to my problems. Please."

Jeanne shook her head in dismay. How did you help someone who refused to be helped?

She turned to Nico and said as ominously as she could manage. "I'm going back to sleep. And I suggest you do the same." Her gaze fell on his drool again and she winced. "And if you hurt her once more, I'm calling the cops, whether Daniela wants me to or not."

Then she spun around and strode to her apartment, praying he'd do as instructed.

Nico wolf-whistled. "Nice ass."

Jeanne chose to ignore him and pushed her door open.

"Ooh, I'm so scared, I'm trembling," Nico said before Daniela pulled him inside and shut the door.

The rest of the night was quiet, but it took Jeanne several hours to fall asleep again. She thought about the incident and played alternative scenarios in her head. In all of them, she was a lot stronger and stood up to the jerk much more convincingly. In one of the versions, she even punched him in the face and knocked him out. And then said to Daniela, *You're wasting your life with the wrong man.*

Then, somehow, her thoughts wandered to Mat—the wrong man in her own life. She hadn't seen him since their kiss at the bistro, but he'd been ever-present in her thoughts. She'd lost count of her daydreams where he'd show up at *La Bohème* to announce he had broken up his girlfriend because he wanted Jeanne too much to fight it. In other fantasies, he'd knock on her door, tell her the same thing, kiss her, and make love to her.

But it had been almost two months since Amanda's party, and she hadn't seen or heard from him. Not even a note or a text to say he was sorry. Nada. Which meant only one thing—she should stop thinking about him and get real. He wanted her, all right, but he was clearly able to fight it.

And so would she.

In the morning, just before heading to the bistro, she called her old friend Greg.

"Hey, how's my favorite barista doing these days?" Greg asked, sounding happy to hear her voice.

Jeanne told him about Daniela and her violent boyfriend. "Can you help her?" she asked. "Your NGO's there to help people who are in trouble, no?"

"First, I'm in Nîmes, so it's difficult to reach out to someone in Paris," Greg said. "Second, we help refugees and asylum seekers—people who have no one to turn to."

"And how about battered women? Who helps them?"

"I know just the person, as it happens. I'll talk to her and call you back," Greg said.

Jeanne let out a sigh of relief. "You're a darling."

"Let's just hope your friend will be willing to accept help. A lot of women in abusive relationships underestimate the gravity of their situation."

"I know," Jeanne said. "But then again, she seems to be a sensible person. Besides, she has a kid. I hope she'll do it for him, if not for herself."

* * *

The aspirin finally kicked in, and Jeanne inhaled, relieved her head was no longer squeezed by invisible forceps. She turned the coffee machine on, tamped a coffee cake in the filter basket, and poured milk into a steel jug.

"Hey, Amar, come over here. It's time for lesson number . . . what number did we leave off on?"

"Forty-seven? Or was it four hundred forty-seven?" Amar planted himself next to her and dipped the steaming wand into the milk. "I really need my crème this morning."

"So do I," Jeanne said. "But, remember, the main purpose of these two cups is to test the grind. You'll tell me if the grinder needs adjusting after you've had your crème."

"Whoa. This is going too fast. I'm not ready for such a big step." Amar pulled a panicked face.

"Don't worry; I'm not assigning points today. Now, pay attention. You want to heat the milk to seventy degrees, no more. If you overheat it, your crème will taste burned."

She poured the heated milk onto the coffee, creating a perfect froth, handed the cup to Amar, picked up her own espresso cup, and inhaled its full-bodied aroma.

Thank God for coffee.

Didier arrived with bags of fresh croissants from the nearby bakery. He removed his coat and gloves, and offered a croissant to Jeanne. "In exchange for your smile, princess."

"You're mistaken, monsieur. I'm a baker's daughter." Jeanne smiled and took the croissant.

"To me, you're a princess," Didier retorted.

Amar placed his cup on the countertop. "Can I have one, too? I'll smile as much as you want, and you don't have to call me a princess."

Didier glared at him. "If you want a croissant, greenhorn, you have to pay for it. *La Bohème* isn't a charity."

"I'll buy you one if you diagnose the grinder correctly," Jeanne offered.

Didier rolled his eyes. "Still trying to train him? It's a waste of time."

He put a few delicious-smelling specimens on display and packed the rest.

Jeanne turned to Amar. "Don't mind him. He isn't as mean as he's trying to appear."

"I agree—he isn't. He's much meaner than he's trying to appear," Amar said.

Didier tied his black apron around his hips. "When we take this place over, we should refurbish it to make it trendier. The neighborhood is gentrifying at rocket speed. We need to make *La Bohème* attractive for the local bobos."

Jeanne squirmed. What made him so sure it would be *we*? "I agree it needs refurbishment. Badly. And those god-awful flowery tiles definitely have to go."

"I'm glad you agree," Didier said smugly.

"Yes. But... I would keep most of the original fixtures. They give *La Bohème* its identity. And I wouldn't worry about the bobos. This place tends to grow on them."

"Let's not argue about it now, but... wouldn't you prefer to tend a chic lounge bar rather than a bistro counter?" Didier arched an eyebrow.

"I like this counter. Besides, if *La Bohème* became a lounge bar to attract more bobos, we'd lose a good share of our usual patrons. The old people will stop coming. We'd lose clients like José, Madame Blanchard, Monsieur Pascal, the Costa couple, and many more. To some of them *La Bohème* is life support."

Didier rolled his eyes. "Please."

"I'm not kidding. This place keeps them from depression and maybe even from senility. If it becomes too trendy, they'll stop going out."

"They'll go somewhere else. Paris hasn't yet run out of shabby little bistros where they can feel at home."

"Honey, they're *old*. They won't go somewhere else. They depend on their routines, familiar places, familiar faces. They hate change." Jeanne sighed. "They'll stay in their stuffy apartments and... let themselves disintegrate."

"You called me 'honey,' " Didier said with a grin.

"I call everyone 'honey.' "

"No, you don't." He picked up a croissant and pushed it in front of Amar. "Take it and run before I change my mind. I'm happy today."

And he certainly looked it. Jeanne couldn't believe her eyes. The forever sneering headwaiter glowed because she'd called him honey. How weird was that? Over the past few months, he'd shown unequivocal interest in her, without going as far as attempting to kiss her. Clever boy. He no doubt sensed she wasn't ready. Since the end of December, they'd gone out three times and kept it cool and friendly. The latest date had been just last week. They saw a movie and went for drinks afterward. She had a good time.

Jeanne shivered as a gust of cold air whirled through the dining room, and the first customers walked into the bistro. She wiped away her croissant crumbs and went behind the bar. It was time to give her full attention to business. Deciding whether Didier's sudden passion was sincere or a sham to get her to partner with him wasn't a task for today. If it was the latter, he deserved credit for the convincing show. But if he was for real, who knew . . . Maybe she could form a romantic interest in him . . . one day.

She was twenty-seven and longed for a relationship that wasn't impossible, doomed, or complicated. Unlike Mat, Didier was single. Unlike Mat, Didier wasn't above her on the social ladder. His background was similar to hers. He was in the same profession.

But above all, he was *here*. Available and willing.

While Mat was neither.

***

Chapter Five
February

What will I tell her?

Mat had been asking himself that question over and over for the past hour as he paced up and down the hotel lobby, waiting for Jeanne. She had no clue he was here in Copenhagen, stalking her in front of the hotel's reception hall. In fact, hardly anyone knew he was here. When Rob had mentioned a week ago he and Lena were traveling to Copenhagen for the baptism of Pepe's baby, he'd asked if Jeanne was going, too. Rob confirmed, narrowing his eyes at him, as if unsure why it was any of Mat's business.

But Mat was beyond caring. He'd stayed away from Jeanne for nearly three months now, ever since their kiss at Amanda's party. He'd been hoping that time would cure him. As it turned out, time had other plans. His yearning for her had only grown stronger with every passing day until it reached a tipping point. He could no longer bear it. He had to see her.

When Rob told him about the Copenhagen trip Mat had been racking his brain for a reason to turn up at *La Bohème*.

And it just so happened that he had an almost plausible motive to go to the Danish capital himself. He'd been in touch with the Greens in Humlebaek, a small town near Copenhagen twinned with Baleville. They'd discussed some common concerns and exchanged ideas. Before ending their latest phone talk, they'd exchanged nonspecific invitations. From there, telling Cécile he was invited to an important meeting in Humlebaek over the weekend wasn't a complete lie—just an extension of the truth.

Mat glanced at his watch. Nine o'clock. The party would probably go on until midnight, but he hoped Jeanne would pop out at some point to go to the ladies' room. Right on cue, she stepped into the lobby and hurried toward the elevators. She looked amazing in her 50s-style pastel blue dress. Her hair was done up and her mouth painted cherry red. But her face was contorted in pain.

Mat hovered by the elevators for about five minutes, struggling not to bite his nails. Then, on a mad impulse, he jumped into one and rode up to the eleventh floor.

Thank heaven for Scandinavian helpfulness.

The friendly receptionist had given him Jeanne's room number just because he'd asked politely. Something like that would never happen in France, or any other place he could think of.

The elevator came to a halt. Without taking a moment to question the wisdom of what he was about to do, Mat strode over to Jeanne's door and knocked.

"Yes? Who's there?" she said from behind the door.

"It's Mat . . . Will you let me in?"

There was a brief pause, before he heard her shuffle toward the door. When she opened it, she looked unusually pale.

"Are you OK?" he asked, touching her arm.

"I'm fine . . . Just a nasty stomach ache. Must be the oysters." She looked him in the eyes. "What are you doing here?"

"I'm in Denmark for work. Rob told me you were in Copenhagen." He spread his arms helplessly. "I had to see you."

She sighed, turned around, and wobbled to the bed, leaving him stranded in the doorway.

"Come in, if you want," she said as she dropped on her tummy on top of the neatly tucked bed cover. "But I won't be great company tonight."

Mat stepped into the dimly lit room and pulled the door shut behind him. "Shall I get some medicine? I can ask the reception where the nearest pharmacy is—"

"I downed a Coca-Cola from the vending machine. It usually helps. I just need to lie down and wait."

He sat on the bed by her feet and watched her. He couldn't help himself. Her dress wasn't as revealing as the one she had worn at Rob and Lena's party. This one was more girly—cinched at the waist, flared knee-length skirt, and puffy sleeves. The silky fabric draped her curves in a loose, gentle embrace.

Jeanne squirmed, groaned faintly and shifted her position, raising her arms to put them under her head. She looked miserable.

Poor darling.

He turned away, ashamed, because part of him was wondering how much longer he could stand being so close to her, looking at her—and not touching her.

Say something, distract her from her discomfort.

"Would you like me to sing you a song?" he offered.

She lifted her head to give him an amused look. "Depends which song."

"How about *"Frère Jacques"*?

"Seriously?"

"That's the only one whose lyrics I can remember. Kind of."

"Sing away," she said with a sigh.

He began to sing softly. Jeanne closed her eyes, her expression a little more peaceful. Then his hand went to her stockinged foot and stroked it as if acting of its own volition.

She didn't move.

Emboldened by her nonresistance, he stroked the sole and then the elegant arch of her foot, before moving to the other one. Having spent some time on it, his hand slowly climbed to her ankles, and then to her calves. He caressed them lightly, his fingertips gliding over the sheer fabric of her stockings, learning the shape and the feel of her legs. When he reached the back of her knees, just under the hem of her skirt, he finished the song. For a few excruciatingly long moments, he didn't dare move, half expecting her to pull away and ask him to leave.

She did neither, and he tentatively progressed another half inch up her leg. His hand slid under her skirt and pushed it up a little. He continued stroking the back of her thighs, revealing inch after delicious inch, until the hem of her dress barely covered her bottom.

He paused there, just above the lacy edge of her stockings, and took in the full length of her toned legs. Jeanne's legs were a work of art. He had no other word to describe the awe-inspiring sight of her high-arched feet, delicate ankles, athletic calves, and slender thighs. Every curve, every dip in her flesh was breathtakingly beautiful.

Sweet Jesus.

He crawled on the bed, sat on his heels next to her, and rolled her stockings off, taking his time, reveling in every second of that incredibly intimate act. He surveyed her legs again and resumed his ministrations, working his way up from her bare feet. This time, he used both his hands, applying more pressure, involving not only his fingertips but also his palms. He stroked her, making sure to cover every inch while his palms memorized the contours of her flesh.

Sliding down the curve of her calves, he bent down to nibble the tender skin behind her knees and kiss the back of her thighs. She was firm yet soft and painfully, almost unbearably, *right*. Her skin was like the finest, warmest velvet under his lips. And her scent... Oh God, that incomparable, heart-stopping scent.

She didn't move, didn't show any visible reaction to his caresses. But her breathing grew heavy and ragged. It told him everything he needed to know.

By the time he made his way back to the hemline of her dress that he'd hitched up to where her thighs joined her buttocks, he could no longer think straight. With a low growl, he pushed the fabric up to her waist.

And barely stopped himself from roaring his appreciation.

He pulled back a little, and placed his palms on her glorious bottom. She had a tiny butterfly tattoo just above the waistband of her lacy boyshorts. He yearned to catch that waistband between his teeth and pull her panties off. He ached to —

She shifted a little and moaned. But it wasn't a moan of pleasure. It was a plaintive, strained sound of pain.

He blinked a few times and gave her a comforting stroke. "Tummy still unhappy, huh?"

"Yeah."

And all at once, reason returned. His face flamed with guilt. She was unwell, suffering—and he was taking advantage of the situation. He should just talk to her and entertain her until she felt better.

With a superhuman effort, he removed his hands from her, untucked the bed cover on one side and threw it over her.

OK. Now talk. Say something neutral. Something to distract her, and to dissipate the images in his head.

He moved to sit on the edge of the bed so he could see her face. "During my master's study, I spent more time trying to establish the shape of your legs behind your loose bistro pants than writing my course papers."

Neutral, my foot.

Jeanne didn't say anything.

"I made sketches," he continued. "I filled several notebooks with versions of your legs."

She circled her index near her ear in a cuckoo sign.

"In memory serves me right," he said. "Two or three of those sketches are pretty close to the original. Even if my drawing skills are rudimentary."

"No they aren't," she said.

"You haven't seen any of my—"

"I have."

He gave her a quizzical look.

"Pepe and I went to Rob's one night, to watch the World Cup. You were out of town. I went into your room for something... I think we needed an extra chair."

"And you saw my sketchbooks?"

Jeanne shook her head. "No. Even if I had, I wouldn't have opened them. But I saw this feminine nude by your bed. It was drawn on a large canvas, with something like a pencil but thicker and blacker."

"Charcoal," he said. "I drew it with charcoal."

"I knew that woman was me the moment I saw the portrait. I'm not saying it was skillfully done, but you managed to capture something... Something that defines me. Even if I have no idea what it is."

Generosity, he thought. *That's what defines you, Jeanne. All of you — body and soul.*

But he didn't say it.

"When I was working on that portrait," he said instead, "the legs were the most challenging part, because I had to guess. I knew they were long and slender. That much was obvious even through those god-awful pants. But I wasn't sure about their exact shape and fullness, the muscles of your calves, the arch of your feet, the swell of your—"

"You're a perv," she said.

"And proud to be one. So, as for your bottom—"

She propped herself up on her elbows and turned her head to give him a threatening look.

But he wouldn't be intimidated. "I had a pretty good idea of its firmness and roundness, but I wondered about this." He uncovered her and traced his fingers along the curve beneath her buttocks. "Until I finally saw you in that blue bikini when we went to Nice with Lena and Rob."

"And were you satisfied with what you saw?" she asked saucily.

"It blew my mind, baby. Just like now."

* * *

Jeanne's blood ran faster and thicker with every passing minute. It pooled, hot and heavy, inside her lower abdomen, making her forget her pain and her misgivings, along with the reasons why she should send Mat away. His caresses were exquisite, as if some sixth sense guided him, telling him exactly where and in what way she liked to be touched.

As for his words . . . It wasn't the first time a man had raved about her body. In fact, she'd been told she was hot too many times to count. Her ex-boyfriends told her that, at least early in the relationships. Many of the bistro customers told her that. Unfamiliar men on the street told her that. More than a few women told her that. She'd grown to resent compliments—they made her feel demeaned.

But Mat's observations were different. They were earnest, personal, and heartfelt. They were in a league of their own. And she found herself enjoying them.

Right now, his palms smoothed over her buttocks, stroking every inch. Luxuriating in his touch, Jeanne forgot about the dull ache in her stomach until she realized it had gone away. Mat's breathing was heavy as he fondled and rubbed her flesh, but he didn't press his body to hers. She knew he was waiting for a sign from her, for the tiniest invitation to step up a gear. She could just shift her legs half an inch apart or roll over on her back and stare into his eyes—and there'd be no turning back.

Hmm . . . which one would it be?

"Baby, you're so hot," he said.

And suddenly, her desire began to seep out of her body, as though his words had nicked her skin and opened a tiny leak.

He's no different.

Ludo, her ex with whom she'd been for four years, kept telling her that. Even as he slept with other women, none of whom were admittedly as hot as she was. Fred, the cool yuppie she dated after Ludo told her the exact same words. Until it turned out he'd had a fiancée. And Mat had a girlfriend with whom he was in a serious relationship . . . He was no longer the tail-wagging puppy who worshipped the ground she walked on. He had morphed into an entirely different kind of beast.

And she was no more than an irresistibly hot body to him. Just like to the others.

"I'm not well," she said. "The Coke didn't work. I'm going to take a hot bath and try to sleep."

He stopped caressing her, pulled his hand away, and sat there without doing or saying anything. She rolled out of the bed, walked over to the bathroom, and locked the door from inside.

"Jeanne," he said in a gentle voice. "May I please stay here and sleep next to you? I won't touch you — you have my word. I just want to be near you . . . a little longer."

She didn't have the nerve to say no.

* * *

Mat's voice woke her up. "Jeanne... Oh, Jeanne."

She opened her eyes and turned to face him.

He was fast asleep on his back, and his midsection tented the duvet that covered his lower body.

Jeanne couldn't stifle a smile.

He'd kept his word last night and didn't make the slightest attempt to touch her again. They talked for a long time before falling asleep, and all the while, she basked in the heat of his gaze. Oh, how tempting it was to give in! All she had to do to allow him to make love to her was to touch him.

Only she knew better. There would be a price to pay—a high price. No matter how much it affected Mat, she'd have her own burden to bear. Her remorse and guilt to live with.

Mat whispered her name again, still asleep.

She felt her body responding to his hunger. How could it not? The gorgeous male lying next to her craved her in a desperate, fervent way. The way she'd never been craved by anyone in her whole life. It was awe-inspiring and incredibly sexy. It was humbling.

He'd traveled all the way from Paris in the hope of spending the night with her.

But he'd never, not once, hinted he wanted more than a night.

Jeanne got out of the bed as quietly as she could and tiptoed to the bathroom. When she came out, Mat was awake. He lay on his back, his hands clasped under his head, showing off the rippling muscles on his arms and chest.

She tried to look unperturbed.

"Are you feeling better?" he asked.

"Yep."

"When is your flight back to Paris?"

"Tomorrow morning. Yours?"

"Tonight... So what's the plan for today?" He gave her a hopeful look.

"I'm to have breakfast with the gang in thirty minutes. After that, Lena, Rob, and I will do as much sightseeing as we can squeeze into a day. It's my first time in Copenhagen."

I won't spend the day in bed with you, honey.

For a split second, his face fell.

Then he pasted a bright smile on it. "Say hi to the queen for me, and to the Little Mermaid."

He sat up, and Jeanne gawked at the rugged beauty of his naked torso.

With an effort, she looked away. "Are you booked in this hotel?" *Shouldn't you go to your room now?*

"Yeah... I should be going..." He didn't move. "I love your pajama shorts. They're so... short."

"I hope you're more eloquent in your campaign speeches," she said.

"I'd better be." He chortled but still made no attempt to move.

It occurred to Jeanne he might be naked under the blanket, which could explain his reluctance to get out of the bed.

"Um... I'm going back to the bathroom so you can get dressed," she said.

His gaze burned into hers. "Are you seeing anyone?"

"Why is it any of your business?"

"It isn't. I just... I want to know how you're doing."

"I'm doing fine... and I'm dating Didier. Well, almost."

"You're joking."

"No. What's wrong with Didier?"

"What's *right* with Didier?"

Anger swelled in her chest. "I'll tell you what's right. He wants to be my business partner. He finds me competent, great at my job, smart. He's never called me *hot*." She gave him a hard look. "It's refreshing."

"Jeanne, no matter what he calls you, or *doesn't* call you, the guy's a jerk. You can't go out with him."

"Says who? What gives you the right to counsel me on my private life?"

He stared at her, his gray eyes unblinking and a vein pulsing on his strong neck. Then, suddenly, his gaze grew softer, almost pleading. "I may have no right, but a woman like you deserves better than Didier. You . . . a woman like you . . ." He paused, his face contorting in some sort of inner struggle.

Jeanne held her breath. Was he going to say a woman like her deserved *him*? Was he about to tell her he wanted more than one night?

Their gazes locked, hers searching, his conflicted. In the silence that stretched, her heart thumped. She took a deep breath in a hopeless attempt to calm herself.

When he finally spoke, his expression was determined, almost defiant. "I won't deny feeling a little possessive of you, no matter how much I fight it. But it's my problem. It doesn't change the fact that Didier isn't a good match for you."

She exhaled slowly before replying. "Oh yeah? And who's a good match for me? What about you, Mat? Are *you* a good match for me?"

He said nothing, just held her gaze as a flush spread over his cheeks.

Jeanne's nostrils flared. "Or do you expect me to tie a curled ribbon around my neck and offer myself to you just because you find me *hot*?" She spat the last word as if it were an insult.

"Jeanne, I'm not sure why you get so riled up. The way I see it, being hot is . . . awesome." He paused before adding, "I'm saying this from personal experience as a former *toad-eyed* nerd who never got a second glance from you . . . until I became *hot*."

The remark gave her pause. Mat had a point. Her pouring scorn on hotness was dangerously close to hypocrisy. Which she abhorred. But then why was she still so upset at his compliment?

In a flash of clarity, it came to her.

"Tell me, Mat," she said in a much calmer voice. "Would you describe your wonderful girlfriend as *hot*?"

"No," he said without hesitation.

"Thought so. Would you call her *beautiful*?"

He sighed and nodded.

"That's why I get so riled up. It's not the compliment itself—it's the implications." She stared out the window.

He kept silent.

Expelling her breath in a long exhalation, she took a few steps toward him and looked him straight in the eyes.

"Let's say we do it. Say we sleep together. Would your *beautiful* girlfriend be OK with it?"

Mat shook his head slowly, his face crimson.

"Would you even tell her?"

"No."

Jeanne spun around and stomped back into the bathroom. "Get out of my room," she said, pulling the door behind her.

She paused and added before slamming the door shut, "And out of my life."

* * *

Chapter Six
March

February rolled into March with no sign of the winter relenting. Jeanne had never before seen so much snow fall onto the city and refuse to melt. After a week of denial, the Parisian fashionistas swapped their elegant footwear for fur-lined moon boots and resigned themselves to wearing hairdo-ruining knitted hats.

Pierre installed a patio heater next to the main entrance of *La Bohème*. The early morning "coffee and cigarette" patrons hailed the initiative as lifesaving.

On the coldest day in Jeanne's memory, her parents came from the south to stay with her for three days. On the first day, Jeanne took them to see an impressionist exhibit at the Musée d'Orsay. They loved it. The next day she took them to an *avant-garde* art installation at the Petit Palais. They loved the Petit Palais and hated the installation.

On the third and last day of their visit, she took them shopping. Through a combination of persuasion, flattery, manipulation and downright blackmail, the women managed to convince Jeanne's dad to get rid of the "perfectly serviceable" coat he'd worn for twenty years and buy a newer, warmer and much more fashionable one. In the evening, the three of them marked the historic event with a delicious dinner at *La Bohème*.

When her parents left, Jeanne went back to her normal life of working double shifts at the bistro, walking around the apartment in underwear, eating out of a saucepan, and binge-watching her favorite series at night. But there was something to be said for hanging out with Mom and Dad. Something related to the amount of love that permeated the air when those two painfully familiar and infinitely dear people made her pancakes in the morning and hung on her every word, no matter what she blathered about.

Two days after they left Daniela walked into the bistro and asked if Jeanne had a minute for a coffee and a chat.

Must be that SOB boyfriend of hers hitting her again.

"Give me five minutes," she said, gesturing to Amar to stand in for her.

"I've got great news," Daniela said after Jeanne placed two espressos on the table and sat across from her.

Jeanne's raised her eyebrows.

"Nico found a job. It's a six-month contract, but if everything goes well, they'll most certainly renew it."

"Super," Jeanne said.

"He's so excited about it. And he says he'll stop drinking." Daniela paused, sipped some coffee, and then looked into Jeanne's eyes. "If he does, our fighting will stop, too. And... the other stuff. I'm sure."

Jeanne had never seen the concierge looking so happy. Come to think of it, she'd never seen her looking anything but somber. "That's fantastic," she said.

Daniela beamed and looked around. "It's really cozy here. I came by a couple of weeks ago, but they told me you were in Copenhagen. Did you like it?"

"I only had one day to visit, and the weather changed every five minutes. But yes, it's a charming city."

"Like Paris?"

Jeanne shook her head. "Paris is the *belle dame* of Europe. Copenhagen is more like . . . a pretty lass." She winked. "Have you seen *Enchanted*?"

"Of course! It was my favorite movie when I was . . . before things went wrong." Daniela sighed and looked away.

"Remember Giselle?" Jeanne asked not daring to question the concierge about her past.

Daniela turned back to Jeanne and attempted a smile. "So Copenhagen is Amy Adams?"

Jeanne nodded. "And Paris is Grace Kelly."

Daniela's smile broadened. "Got any pictures on your phone?"

"Sure."

Jeanne tapped the screen until she found her Copenhagen photos. "OK. This is the Rosenborg Castle. That's where the queen keeps the crown jewels, in case you were planning the heist of the century."

"It's cute. Like something out of a fairy tale."

Yeah. And so was the couple kissing in the Castle Gardens. Jeanne winced remembering how her chest had clenched in pain on seeing them only an hour after sending Mat away.

She opened another photo. "This is Nyhavn. According to Lena's guidebook, it means 'new harbor,' which I guess it was back in the seventeenth century. It's a bit touristy, but great fun."

"I love that the houses are painted different colors," Daniela said. "If someone tries it here in Paris, the city authorities will descend on them like a bunch of starved vultures."

"No doubt." Jeanne chuckled.

She pulled up another picture. "I forgot the name of this street, but it's in the most popular pedestrian area in town."

"Who's the guy playing the piano?"

"No clue, but he was good. I enjoyed his music." *Until he played the song Mat and I had danced to at Lena's party.*

Jeanne showed Daniela a few more photos, each one awakening bittersweet memories. It had been such a weird day. Physically, she'd spent it with Lena and Rob sightseeing and sampling Copenhagen's food and drink, but her mind used the tiniest pretext to daydream about Mat. The exhibits in the ARKEN Museum reminded her of Mat's love for contemporary art and how he'd once droned on about some undiscovered talent from his hometown. The City Hall building reminded her of Mat's ambition to be mayor of Baleville. But the worst were the people on the streets of Copenhagen. More specifically, the men. By the end of that marathon day, Jeanne could no longer stand the sight of the tall, sandy-haired, light-eyed Viking descendants who looked so different from the average Frenchman.

And so much like Mat.

* * *

How did you avoid someone a month before the wedding when you were the bridesmaid and the someone in question, the best man? Had they lived in different countries—or, better still, continents—it may have been possible. But as it was, Jeanne had no choice but to go to Lena and Rob's for an emergency brunch on the last Sunday of the month. The couple had to find a new venue for the wedding, because the location they'd booked months in advance had fallen through due to a "regrettable misunderstanding."

"It's too late for any Parisian venue," Lena said, placing a steaming coffee pot on the table. "As soon as they hear the wedding is in three weeks, they just laugh at me."

"How many guests are you expecting?" Jeanne asked.

"A hundred and twenty, give or take."

Jeanne wrinkled her nose. "Hmm. That's way beyond what *La Bohème* can handle."

"I know," Rob said with a sigh.

"The worst is that Dad is going to say we should've let him take care of everything." Lena threw her hands up in despair before turning to Rob. "If we eat humble pie, I'm sure he can organize something in Moscow."

Rob gave her a miserable look. "I'm sure he can. And I have no doubt it would be a *grandiose* event. Christ."

Mat swallowed his last piece of toast and wiped his fingers with a napkin. "Everybody, stay calm and eat croissants. I have a plan."

Three pairs of eyes stared at him in hopeful silence.

"After we sign the certificate at the town hall here, get the photos taken and grab a quick lunch, we'll drive to Normandy. The guests can carpool or take the train."

"You think we can get a large enough place there on such short notice?" Rob asked.

"I don't think, I know," Mat replied with a smug smile. "My mom is friends with a priest at Saint-Pierre, a Benedictine abbey not far from Baleville. She talked to him yesterday, and he said he can squeeze you between two other ceremonies."

Lena clapped her hands, and Rob grinned.

Mat raised his hand. "There's more. I talked to the charming hotel near the abbey. The manager is a client."

"And?" Lena looked at him as if he were a messiah.

"It's a go, both for the reception hall and the rooms. You need to travel there as soon as you can, make the payments, and discuss the details."

"We'll go tomorrow," Rob said.

Lena beamed. "You just lifted a ton off my shoulders. Thank you so much, Mat!"

"Don't mention it. That's what the best man is for, after all."

At around two Jeanne stood to leave. "As much as I love your company guys, I'm working this afternoon."

"I need to get going, too," Mat said.

As they walked out of the building, Mat cleared his throat. "May I walk with you to *La Bohème*? It's on my way to the train station."

"That's not where I'm headed," Jeanne said.

"Oh. OK."

"I need to stop by Casa Shop to buy curtains for my apartment," she explained to sweeten the pill. And regretted her charity a second later.

"I know that shop! It's only ten minutes' walk from the *Gare Saint Lazare*," Mat said, perking up. "So we're going in the same direction."

Jeanne shrugged.

They walked in silence for a few minutes.

"How have you been, Jeanne?" Mat asked.

"Great," she said.

"Still going out with Didier?"

"It's none of your business."

"Of course."

A few more minutes passed in silence. Jeanne stole a glance at Mat. He studied the buildings along the street, his lips pressed in a hard line.

"Louis Napoleon had that one built for factory workers." Mat pointed to stately white building.

"How generous of him," Jeanne said.

Mat gave her his crooked smile. "In exchange, the workers were ordered to vote for his majesty's candidate."

"Is it one of the tacks they teach you at the School for Aspiring Politicians?"

"Only these days you're supposed to do it in subtler ways."

Jeanne tut-tutted. "Damn democracy."

Another 500 meters and we part ways.

At the crossing of rue de Rochechouart and rue de Maubeuge, Mat stopped in his tracks and dashed after a scruffy teenage boy. Flabbergasted, Jeanne watched him catch up with the youth, grab his arm, and turn him around.

"Give me that purse," Mat said.

"Easy, man! You're hurting me." The teenager rubbed his arm and handed Mat a tattered purse.

Mat took the purse and returned it to the middle-aged Roma beggar hovering nearby.

"Can I go now?" the young thief asked, trying to wriggle his arm free.

"To do what? Attempt another theft?"

The youth jutted out his chin in defiance.

"I see. Well, you can certainly continue snatching purses," Mat said. "Until you get caught and spend a couple years in juvie."

The teenager rolled his eyes as if to say, I've heard it before.

Mat smirked. "A sweet-faced boy like you, I'm sure you'll have a lot of *fun* in juvie. When they let you out you'll burglarize a dozen apartments. Then you'll go to a *real jail* for a few years. When you're out, you'll graduate to armed robbery—I hear jewelry boutiques are an easy target—until they finally lock you up for a very, very long time."

Jeanne stared at Mat. *Where's he going with this?*

"But I have a better idea," Mat said with a smile that didn't reach his eyes. "Take a shortcut. Skip all the intermediary trouble. Join a serious gang right away and rob Cartier while you're young."

The teenager's mouth fell open.

Jeanne raised her brows in disbelief.

"When you're released after your maximum sentence, you'll still have a few years of relative health to enjoy," Mat said. "Before you sit on a sidewalk vent and beg for a coin. Like the woman you stole that purse from."

The youth squirmed, wiped his nose with his sleeve, and twisted his head to look at the beggar.

Mat let go of him. "Think about it!" he shouted as the boy scampered away.

He walked over to the woman, dropped a one-euro coin into her paper cup, and returned to Jeanne's side.

"Confess," she said as they resumed their walk. "At nightfall you don a red cape and roam the streets of Baleville in search of offenders and lost souls."

Mat smirked and pressed his index to his lips. "Shh."

"Now I understand why you're vying for the mayor's office."

"And why's that?" he asked, a twinkle in his eyes.

"So you can have a legitimate excuse to indulge your interventionist do-gooder tendencies."

"Hmm. I wouldn't put it that way, but you may be right." He gave her a happy grin.

Jeanne's cheeks warmed and her mouth itched to grin back.

She looked away. "You shouldn't have given money to the woman though," she said. "Didier claims it's a mafia system. The women have to hand over their 'earnings' to the clan chief who arranged for them to come to France."

"It can't be excluded."

"So you'd agree it was useless to give her money?"

"No."

Jeanne turned to look into his eyes.

Mat shrugged. "First, Didier's theory won't apply to every case. Second, if she can keep a small share of what people give her, it's fine by me. Imagine the misery where she comes from. Imagine what her alternatives are to make begging in this weather a better option."

"I never thought of it that way," Jeanne muttered and realized they'd reached the Casa Shop.

Finally.

Or was it too soon?

They lingered for a few awkward moments by the entrance until Mat said, "It was great to see you." He gave Jeanne the customary cheek kiss.

She didn't turn her head or move her lips to participate in the ritual. "Good luck with your campaign," she managed in lieu of a good-bye.

Mat nodded and rushed away.

Jeanne lifted her eyes skyward. *Why does he have to be* good *on top of being a hunk?*

As she shopped for curtains, she tried to imagine Mat in a ridiculous comic-book superhero outfit—formfitting tights and all. For more impact, she made said tights bright pink and shimmery.

It worked for three seconds, before her treacherous mind zoomed in on his athletic legs.

And then the bulge between them.

* * *

Chapter Seven
April

The following weeks zoomed by like the TGV train to Marseilles. Mat hardly had a spare minute between his election campaign, day job, and helping with the wedding arrangements.

Then the wedding day arrived. A small crowd of over a hundred people attended the official ceremony in Paris and then drove to Normandy on the congested A13. That they managed to make it to the abbey on time was a minor miracle.

Mat allowed himself to relax only after the last guest took entered the hotel's spacious dining room. He looked around. Everyone appeared a little tired and happy for this chance to replenish their energy depleted by the long day.

He and Cécile were seated at the central table with the newlyweds, Rob's family who'd come from Jura and Lena's from Russia. Lena's maid of honor sat across from them. With her *date*. Or should he call Didier her *boyfriend*? The headwaiter wore a well-cut suit and acted as if he belonged with Jeanne.

And Jeanne... Jeanne was ravishing in a strapless emerald green dress, a silky wrap thrown around her slender shoulders, and her hair pulled back into a loose romantic updo.

For Christ's sake, stop staring at her.

"Did you enjoy the day so far?" he asked Cécile, after he finally peeled his gaze off Jeanne.

"I did. It was a good idea to do it here," she replied with a sweet smile. "By the way, I think you're expected to deliver your speech now."

He collected his thoughts and tapped the side of his wine glass with a spoon.

After everyone quieted and turned to him, he began.

"Dear Lena and Rob, you can pack away your slingshots and relax. I *do not believe* it's the duty of the best man to tell embarrassing stories about the couple in front of family and friends."

Rob beamed and Lena chuckled.

Mat gave them a grin. "Not for lack of material, as you would no doubt agree. But because I'm farsighted. Literally and figuratively."

Half of the table cheered at that, while the other half booed.

"So instead, my dear friends, I'm going to make the most truthful statement I've ever made in public." He cleared his throat. "Lena and Rob, your love is one of those rare, magical things that's impossible to talk about without sounding like a sappy cornball."

Several people giggled.

Mat raised his eyebrows. "You want proof?"

He pulled from his pocket and waved three pages of crossed out notes. "See?"

He turned back to the newlyweds. "But I will say this before I let you guys go back to your meal. Your journey to this day has been long and bumpy. So much, that each of you got very close to giving up at some point. But you didn't. You persevered because what you share is stronger than any obstacle you may face. Your union is based on a love that's brave, pure, and forgiving. That kind of love is the most solid foundation a marriage can have."

He raised his glass and addressed the whole room. "Let's drink to these two generous, dogged, and kind people. Their souls are so full of warmth they radiate the excess of it all around them. And their hearts are so full of love that it gives me hope for humanity. To Lena and Rob. Hip hip hooray!"

Among the hoorays and clinking of wine glasses that followed, Mat stole a glance at Jeanne and caught her staring at him. Her gaze was dark with something intense, something powerful that he hadn't seen before. She looked at him as if he were a hero. Or a Viking god.

Or the only man on Earth.

He swallowed hard, shaken by what he'd glimpsed.

She blinked, stretched her lips into a polite smile and turned to Didier.

Mat's mind raced. *Was it . . . ? Could it be . . . ?*

He didn't dare put his question into words, but for the rest of the evening he couldn't think of anything else. Not even as he held Cécile in his arms while they danced. Nor when he sizzled in guilty jealousy as he watched Didier dance with Jeanne and wondered if they shared a room tonight. Nor when Rob gave him a pat on the back and said, "Nice speech, *mon pote*. Oh, and by the way, you *are* a sappy cornball."

Mat smiled distractedly and, as Rob walked away, he finally allowed his brain to formulate the shocking question.

Could Jeanne have feelings for me?

The notion was both exhilarating and sad. Because he didn't doubt that what he had for her—now as four years ago—was all-consuming, obsessive lust.

Nothing more.

***

Jeanne woke up early, her head pounding and her mouth dry.

Last night was a blur. She'd had too much to drink, tried too hard to smile at Didier's remarks, and resist the urge to look at Mat. Who had stared at her too often to pass for casual interest. But his girlfriend had remained serene and unperturbed. Maybe she didn't notice Mat's scorching looks. Maybe she did, but was too well-bred to make a scene or even show she was affected.

Cécile was a woman of class.

Jeanne smirked. Even Amanda would envy Cécile's polished looks, graceful bearing, and impeccable manners. Everything about her, from her shiny smooth hair and thin nose to her polished voice and long fingers with perfect fingernails, screamed refinement. Screamed quality. She was the kind of woman who would even pee with style and poise. She was the kind of woman a man such as Mat would want for a life partner.

Drop the conditional, hon, Jeanne told herself.

She was the woman Mat *wanted* for a life partner.

Jeanne wondered if Didier had noticed what was going on last night. They still hadn't crossed the boundary between occasional dates and a relationship. She wasn't sure they ever would. It was heartwarming and flattering that he wanted more than a business partnership. But flattering wasn't enough. She didn't fancy him, at least not yet. A month ago, when Didier tried to kiss her, she told him as much. He said he'd wait. She promised herself she'd nurture any embryonic feeling she might develop for him.

But deep inside she suspected Mat was right.

They weren't a good match.

Jeanne showered, pulled on her jeans, and packed her travel bag. The guests were to gather in the hotel's garden in two hours for a copious brunch. After a moment's hesitation, she threw on a sweater, grabbed her book, and headed out to the terrace.

"I knew you'd show up. Not a late sleeper, huh?" Lena greeted her from a lounge chair.

Jeanne slumped down next to her. "What are *you* doing here? Shouldn't you be fast asleep, exhausted from the *wedding night*?"

"Ha-ha." Lena stretched her arms. "I wish I could sleep for a couple more hours though . . ."

"You're telling me."

"Is Didier still asleep?" Lena asked a little too innocently.

"I wouldn't know. We booked separate rooms and spent the night in different beds, if that's what you're trying to establish."

"Good."

Jeanne raised her brows.

"I know he's being super nice to you and all, but . . . I'm not sure he's a good person, Jeanne. The way he treats customers—it's just too mean. He may be one of those guys who turn nasty the moment they think you're in their pocket. He's not a good match for you."

Jeanne's lips thinned. "How come everyone thinks they know who's a good match for me?"

"I'm so sorry, sweetheart, I didn't mean to—" Lena began, her eyes brimming with remorse.

"It's OK. I know you meant well. It's just . . . someone told me the exact same thing not so long ago."

"Mat?"

"Yes."

Lena shook her head. "I noticed the way he looks at you, even with his girlfriend around. It's like a déjà-vu from four years ago. The only difference is that you seem to care this time around." She stared Jeanne in the eyes, defying her to disagree.

Jeanne turned away and began to study the dewy lawn.

"Oh, Jeanne." Lena let out a heavy sigh.

Jeanne shrugged. "What can I say? I've always been good at bad timing."

"Has he said anything to you?"

"No."

Nothing that would give me hope.

Lena took Jeanne's hand in hers. "Please don't repeat my mistakes and get involved with someone who's wrong for you just because you can't have the man you care about. It won't end well."

"I know," Jeanne said.

Lena nodded and reopened her paperback.

Jeanne smiled, grateful for her friend's sense of tact, and opened her own book.

The mood at brunch was cheerful and laid-back. Everyone showed up in casual clothes, looking tired but happy to prolong Lena and Rob's special day. The newlyweds didn't hide their relief that the wedding day hadn't been marred by an *incident* characteristic of gatherings with lots of booze, especially when vodka competed with champagne.

Mat and Cécile came down into the garden side by side, both in pale cotton polo shirts and linen pants. They were a stunning couple. Watching them together hurt so much Jeanne wished she hadn't been Lena's maid of honor so she wouldn't have to sit at the central table. She wished she hadn't been invited to her best friend's wedding at all.

"Did you sleep well?" Didier asked her.

She nodded. "What about you?"

"I didn't."

Jeanne gave him a sympathetic look. "Too much vodka?"

"Maybe. Or maybe something else."

"Oh?"

"I'm a patient man, Jeanne, and I still admire you," he said.

She tensed, waiting for the rest of it.

"But last night..." He lowered his voice to a whisper. "The way you stared at *pretty boy*, encouraging him... I expected better of you."

"You're not my boyfriend," she whispered back.

"But I'm your *date*." He sighed. "I understand the grass is always greener on the other side of the fence. But that's the thing—there's a fence."

She studied her empty plate.

"You're a clever girl. Can't you see what he wants from you?"

She could. The problem was she wanted it, too. Badly.

Wasn't that a hoot?

Didier shook his head. "Get real, Jeanne. I won't wait indefinitely."

You can save time and quit now, she itched to say, but she didn't.

"Will you pass me the butter, please?" Didier asked, raising his voice to normal.

She obliged, avoiding his eyes.

"Tell me, Mat," he said, buttering his toast. "Where exactly do the Greens stand on economic policy? I must admit I don't have a clue. I only follow the parties that *really* matter."

Mat half smiled. "We're in the center. On some issues, we're center left and on others center right, but we're never too far from the golden middle point."

"I would've expected the Greens to be aligned with the socialists," Lena said.

"The European Greens' stance is that environmental politics can't be tied to either the left or the right," Cécile said.

"Well, I'm glad you're not one of those 'champagne socialists' France is famous for," Lena's dad said. "I find their hypocrisy disgusting."

Jeanne felt she had to defend the party she'd always voted for. "I agree our *gauche caviar* can be unsavory, but at least they aren't fascists. If anyone can save Europe from the extreme right, it's the socialists."

"Your feelings are admirable, my dear," Didier said. "But as soon as we buy *La Bohème*, you'll hate them for the taxes they'll be squeezing out of us."

Rob smirked. "Didier has a point."

Jeanne rolled her eyes demonstratively. Of course he had a point. But unlike her parents, she wasn't going to veer to the right the day she became a business owner. At least that was what she hoped.

"Your political activities, it's like a hobby for now, right?" Anton asked Mat. "I suppose in France, like anywhere else, you don't get paid unless you're elected?"

"I'd say my political engagement is more than a hobby. But you're absolutely right—I have a day job. I work for my mom's company."

The older man smirked. "I can imagine how much you long to be emancipated."

"My father is alluding to my refusal to work for him," Lena explained to Mat.

"Oh, I see. Actually, the job is fun and even beneficial for my campaign. We get orders from lots of local businesses and nonprofits, and even Baleville's municipality hired us last year to promote the town in the national media."

"Your address book must be well packed," Lena's stepmom said.

Mat grinned. "I can't complain. So yeah, it's a win-win for me. Besides, I'm free to contradict my boss as much as I want, which is every employee's dream."

The conversation moved to another topic, and Jeanne tried to be her usual feisty self. She nearly succeeded—until she caught Mat looking at her. Her pulse quickened, and she locked her gaze with his for what was, no doubt, indecently long. When he finally looked away, Jeanne felt someone else's scorching look. Cécile was glaring at her, her expression black. It only lasted for a few seconds. Her face became serene again as she turned to say something to Mat.

So, she'd finally noticed what was going on . . . or decided to let Jeanne know she had.

* * *

Mat realized he'd been staring at Jeanne again when his phone buzzed. He glanced at the caller ID, turned to Rob, and whispered apologetically, "Sorry, I have to take this. It's my mom."

"You have to take it because it's your mom or because it's your boss?" Rob teased.

"Good question." Mat grinned.

He strode to the flowerbeds in the middle of the lawn. "Hi, Mom. What's up?"

"Sorry to bother you now, but I need to know if the article is ready," Madame Gérard said.

"Which one?"

"The most urgent one—about the toy shop."

"I emailed it Friday night. Check your spam folder."

"Oh, good," she said. "So, how's the wedding? I hope you didn't lose the rings."

"Mother," he said in exaggerated reproof.

She chuckled. "Oh, before I forget. I ran into monsieur the mayor at Le Cheval Bleu last night. He told me he favored your candidacy over his deputy's."

"Seriously?"

"Well, he was a little drunk, so he may not repeat what he told me for the record, but yes. He said he believed someone like you—young, dynamic, and tech savvy—was what the town needed."

"Cool! Thanks for the news, Mom."

"You're welcome. Do you think you can get him to support you publicly?"

"No. He has to support his deputy. She's from the same party and, well, she's his deputy."

"Too bad."

"It's OK. It's still great to know he thinks I'm what Baleville needs."

Mat returned to the table grinning. Cécile would be pleased to hear the news. He'd better give his full attention to her because so far he'd behaved like a douche.

An hour later, the meal wound down, and the guests began to return to their rooms to pack.

Rob walked around the table and asked Cécile if she could spare Mat for a moment, "to finish off his last best man duties."

"Of course," Cécile said.

Mat smiled, pretending he knew what it was about, and followed Rob to a small patio at the back of the hotel.

"What's the deal with you and Jeanne?" Rob asked as soon as they were out of everyone's earshot. "Are you seeing each other?"

"No. Why?"

"Do you think I'm blind? You've been ogling her nonstop since we got here. And she you."

"So you noticed."

Rob gave him a what-do-you-think look. "I'm afraid everybody did."

"Oh God."

"What did Cécile say?"

"Nothing. Nothing at all. I was hoping she didn't notice . . ."

"Maybe — I don't know her well enough — or maybe she chose to turn a blind eye on it. Whichever it is, you're walking on thin ice."

"Don't I know it."

"Then why don't you . . . avoid looking at Jeanne?"

Mat smirked. "I must have a self-destructive side, like my dad."

Rob tilted his head to the side. "That's a bit too easy, blaming it on your dad."

Mat sucked in his cheeks but said nothing.

"How long has it been going on?"

Mat hesitated before confessing, "Since your engagement dinner last September."

"Holy cow."

Mat smiled. Despite his embarrassment, it was a relief to talk to Rob about it. "The moment I saw her something snapped inside me, and my old crush came rushing back."

"You were profoundly pathetic back then," Rob said.

"Thank you." Mat curled his arms over his head. "You want the whole ugly truth? I crave Jeanne, even as I know it may ruin the relationship with the woman I love."

"So, let me get this straight. You love Cécile but you can't help lusting after Jeanne. Correct?"

"Pretty much, yes. A bit like when you hooked up with Amanda even if it was Lena you loved."

Rob shook his head. "I never felt for Amanda what you feel for Jeanne. I loved her as a friend."

"Are you telling me I should follow my lust?"

Rob gave out a cackle. "I would've said 'follow your heart' if it didn't sound so cheesy."

"You, my friend, are a hopeless romantic. I won't hold it against you."

"And you've become a bit too jaded lately. Must be the politics."

Mat smirked and then his expression darkened. "I like to think I'm driven by a vision, not ambition... But sometimes the distinction gets fuzzy."

Rob nodded.

Mat continued. "As for Jeanne, I have a lot of respect and admiration for her, but... Cécile's the right woman for me."

"Because Jeanne is a baker's daughter?"

"Oh come on, you know me better than that. I'm not a snob."

"Uh-huh."

"Really? You think I'm a snob for preferring Cécile to Jeanne?"

"You tell me."

Mat blinked. "It's not about Jeanne's background. It's about who she is and what she wants to achieve in life. She's a bartender whose greatest ambition is to own a bistro—"

"And it's not how you imagine your future wife," Rob finished for him.

Mat drew in a breath and nodded slowly.

"Then stay away from her."

"I've been trying to."

"Try harder."

Mat held his palms up in frustration. "I lose control when she's around."

"Really? I've never known you to be the addict type."

"I'm not. But with her, I turn into a junkie who'd kill for his fix."

Rob put his hand on Mat's shoulder. "Stay away from her, buddy. She's not as tough as she'd have you think. You could break her." He gave a sad smile and walked away, leaving Mat alone with his thoughts.

* * *

Chapter Eight
May

Didier's remark that *La Bohème* wasn't attracting the local bobos had stuck with Jeanne. She ended up convincing Pierre to start a "happy hour" between five thirty and eight in the evening, serving cocktails at half price. After three weeks the bobo customer stats hadn't budged. But the measure turned out to be a huge success among office workers who now flocked to the bistro en masse for a quick drink and a bite before going home.

Tonight had been no exception. When, around eight thirty, the crowd began to thin, Amar joined Jeanne behind the bar for a short break and a cup of coffee. As they both closed their eyes, inhaling the aroma of their brews, Amanda walked in and headed straight to the bar.

"Working late again?" Jeanne asked.

"I don't mind as long as you serve me one of your vodka Tatins at the happy-hour price," Amanda said.

Jeanne grinned and turned to Amar. "Lesson number one hundred sixty-nine. Don't let friends take advantage of your position. Your motto must be 'Business is Business.'"

"Got it," Amar said.

"And never mind what I charge her for her cocktail. This is a theoretical lesson." Jeanne began to shake Amanda's drink.

When Jeanne was done, Amanda took a sip and lifted her eyes skyward in appreciation. "Ah. I love it. You're the best." She turned to Amar. "Be a darling and fetch me some peanuts."

"I'm off duty," Amar said with a nonchalant shrug. "And business is business."

"Cheeky kid. Anyway, tell me, how come you're working on Fridays? Isn't this the day when all immigrants go to the mosque?"

Amar looked her over and shook his head. "You're one of a kind."

"I know. But, please, enlighten me."

"First, even though my parents are from Algeria, I was born in France, which makes me French—not an immigrant. Second, I'm an agnostic."

"So you don't believe in God?" Amanda asked.

"I didn't say I was an atheist. Agnostics reserve judgment until they can see proof of God's existence or nonexistence. Atheists believe there's no God. To me, they aren't so different from religious fanatics—their philosophy is based on belief, not facts."

"Wow. A Cartesian immigrant, um... immigrant-born Frenchman." She turned to Jeanne. "I'm impressed. If it weren't for your protégé, I could've died now knowing the difference between an agnostic and an atheist."

Jeanne shrugged. "I've been telling the Ministry of Health people they should subsidize us."

Amanda furrowed her brow. "I'm not following. Subsidize you for what?"

"For providing psychotherapy for the price of an espresso." Jeanne sighed. "Now I realize the Ministry of Education should sponsor us, too. For spreading knowledge."

Amanda gave her a dazzling smile. "So what else is up?"

"*La Bohème* is participating in the annual Paris Waiters' Race tomorrow," Amar said.

"That's yesterday's news, my boy," Amanda said with a dismissive wave of her hand. "Is it still you and Didier running?

Amar nodded.

"But hadn't you sustained some kind of injury that made you quit professional sports?"

It was Amar's turn to act surprised. He turned to Jeanne. "Wow. I'm impressed by your friend. She actually pays attention to what people tell her."

Amanda tapped the side of her head. "I can't help it. My brain stores everything I hear or read. Including the most useless and insignificant information. So, what about that injury?"

"It's not a *real* race. Nobody can run with a loaded tray. I'll be fine."

"What about you, Jeanne? Why didn't *you* enroll?"

"With those two participating and Pierre cheering, someone has to mind the shop. I'll serve them chilled beer after they're back."

"Oh come on, can't you leave that chubby waitress in charge? I'm sure she'll manage like a pro."

"Manon isn't chubby," Amar said.

Ignoring him, Amanda looked at Jeanne with dreamy eyes and said, "We could do the American-style pom-pom thing."

"Seriously?"

"What? We're both still young and good-looking. I've always regretted we don't have that tradition in France. I would've made a fantastic cheerleader."

"Maybe you could ask Manon to join you?" Amar said, his face lighting up.

"We're *not* doing it," Jeanne said to Amanda before turning to Amar. "But I'm sure Manon will be there to support you."

"I'll be there, too, supporting *La Bohème*." Amanda beamed.

Jeanne cleared her throat. "Um... Rob is going, too. With Lena."

"You know what? I don't give a hoot. I've decided I'm no longer going out of my way to avoid them. It's too much hassle. It's their turn to do the avoiding."

"Makes sense," Jeanne said.

"So, I'm coming tomorrow. And as a true cheerleader, I've made sure you'll have as many fans as possible along the route."

"You did?" Jeanne asked, a note of concern in her voice.

"Of course. I've been spreading the news for a week now."

Jeanne narrowed her eyes. "In what direction?"

"Oh, everywhere. I told some colleagues at work, my mom, a few friends . . ."

"Who?"

"Karine—you've seen her here a couple of times. Patrick. Mat." Amanda paused, thinking. "I think that's about it. They all said they'd come."

Jeanne smirked. *I'm sure* he *will.*

She tried to work up some righteous anger.

Instead, she grew annoyed with herself for feeling so ridiculously happy about the prospect of seeing him again.

***

"What makes you think you can win against two hundred professional waiters?" Didier arched an eyebrow at Amar.

They were downing their espressos before heading to the Place des Vosges where the Waiters' Race was to start.

Amar shrugged. "My youthful audacity?"

"He's faster than most," Jeanne said.

"That may be the case, but he'll be carrying a tippy tray with a bottle of Orangina and two full glasses on it." Didier turned back to Amar. "You may be the first at the finish line, but if you've broken a glass or even spilled too much Orangina, you're toast."

"I know the rules, thank you," Amar said, giving Didier a low-lidded look.

Jeanne rolled her eyes. "Men. I, for one, am happy both of you are running today. It doubles the chances for *La Bohème*."

"By the way, why did you sign up for this? What's your incentive?" Amar asked Didier.

"Same as yours—Orangina's fat check. Three thousand euros is worth the ridicule."

"Hey, loosen up, man. This thing is supposed to be fun," Amar said.

"We may not have the same notion of fun," Didier retorted.

The entrance door flew open and Pierre walked in, followed by Manon. The young woman wore a yellow wig and pressed a rolled-up white cloth to her chest. When she unfurled it, the cloth turned out to be a hand painted banner that read "*LA BOHEME ROCKS.*"

"Did you make it?" Amar gave Manon a bright-eyed look.

She nodded, a small smile on her round face.

Jeanne glanced at the clock on the wall. "It's time. Go get them, boys! And remember to wear your aprons and bow ties."

Once everyone was gone, Jeanne lost herself in frantic activity. She tended the bar and helped the remaining waiter, Jimmy, during the lunchtime. Whenever she had a moment, she went into the kitchen to give a hand to Claude who'd been alarmingly morose for over a week now. She didn't sit down until around four in the afternoon when things finally calmed down. Her stomach growling, she headed to the kitchen to eat the plate of cassoulet Claude had put aside for her. Halfway through her meal, she heard loud voices coming from the front of the bistro and went to investigate.

The *La Bohème* staff, Rob, Lena, Amanda, Mat, and a few other people were singing "We Are The Champions," taking turns at tapping Amar on the back, and inspecting his medal.

"Our boy won the race," Pierre shouted over the singing as soon as he saw her. "*La Bohème* came first!"

Jeanne opened her mouth to ask Didier about his result—and shut it upon seeing his sullen expression.

"I'm closing the bistro off until seven, and opening our best champagne to celebrate this historic event," Pierre announced.

"Jeanne, you so should've come!" Amanda dropped on a chair next to Jeanne. "There were thousands of people at the Place des Vosges and along the route, everyone chanting and cheering. Great energy. I really enjoyed myself."

"I'm sure I'll hear so much about it I'll end up feeling like I was there," Jeanne said.

Amanda shifted in her seat. "Um... I'm not sure what the etiquette is when customers mix with waiters like this... Do you think I can ask Didier or the chubby girl to get me a glass of sparkling water?"

"How about I pour you some from the tap?" Jeanne offered.

Amanda sighed theatrically. "OK. I hate tap water, but these are exceptional circumstances."

Jeanne handed Amanda her water and then moved closer to Amar, waiting for her turn to congratulate him.

She didn't look at Mat. Not even once.

"I couldn't miss the chance to cheer *La Bohème* during the race," she heard him tell Rob.

Rob rolled his eyes.

She kept not looking at Mat.

Manon hugged Amar and gave him a peck on the cheek.

Amar grinned like a Cheshire cat.

Jeanne still didn't look at Mat.

Lena walked over to Amanda. "Hi. It's good to see you. Really."

Amanda flashed one of her landmark not-quite-reaching-the-eyes smiles. "Yeah, well. I'd hoped you'd figure out it was your turn to take a rain check. I think I've skipped enough events over the past year."

"I was hoping we could stop ... skipping," Lena said.

Amanda shrugged. "I'm not the forgiving type. But I'm willing to pretend I'm OK with being in the same room as you and Rob if you make sure to stay out of my hair."

Lena nodded and left her in peace.

Jeanne kept her gaze trained on Amar.

"Come, I need to tell you something," Lena whispered to Jeanne, heading down the stairs.

Jeanne followed her to the restroom.

"I'm pregnant," Lena said without bothering with an introduction.

Jeanne blinked several times. "Oh. My. God. How far along are you?"

"Three months."

"Wait a minute, so you were already pregnant during the wedding?"

"Yep. Only I didn't know it. I missed my period in March, but I didn't think much of it. My menses aren't regular."

Jeanne gave her friend a bear hug. "I can't believe it. This is huge! How does it feel to be pregnant?"

"It's weird, actually. I'm still having a hard time accepting there's a living creature growing inside me."

"Like in the *Alien* movies."

"Oh no!" Lena grinned. "It's actually a good feeling. Weird, but good."

"You and Rob are going to have a sweet little family," Jeanne said.

"You're next. You caught my wedding bouquet."

"Did I have a choice? You hurled it at me."

Lena chuckled.

When they walked out of the bathroom, Mat was hovering by the door. Lena gave him a small smile and walked past him toward the dining room.

Jeanne followed in Lena's tracks, her head down... until he moved in front of her, blocking her way.

Shit.

Slowly, she looked up.

Double shit.

He was even hotter than she remembered from a month ago.

Must be my imagination.

Mat stared at her in that fierce way that made her knees go weak.

"How's life?" he asked after a while.

"Same old," she said.

They peered at each other for another long moment, and then Mat took a step toward her. His chest rose and fell, and his eyes turned the color of dark slate.

If I don't say anything, he'll kiss me.

It was tempting to let him.

And then she remembered something. She'd thought about Mat last night, but not in the way she usually did. She'd thought about him in connection with Daniela, and that horrible boyfriend of hers. In spite of his new job and promises, the fights hadn't stopped. The concierge denied being battered, even as she wore big sunglasses inside the building. The woman needed help.

And Mat enjoyed helping people.

"I have a neighbor whose boyfriend is violent. I've heard them fight, and I've seen her with bruises several times," she said.

He ceased drawing closer, but he didn't retreat either.

"A friend of mine put her in touch with a Help Center, but it didn't go down too well." She threw her hands up. "I don't know how to convince her to report him. And to jilt him."

Mat took a moment before speaking. "She should learn Krav Maga."

"What in hell is Krav Maga?"

"An extreme form of self-defense. Several martial arts plus a bunch of dirty tricks rolled into a technique that's diabolically effective."

"Wow. Sounds like something I wouldn't mind trying myself. Are you an adept?"

"I've been practicing it for the past two years. In addition to the weight lifting."

"I see."

"If she takes a class twice or three times a week, in a month she'll be able to knock him out."

"No kidding?"

"I'm serious. Besides, it will do wonders for her self-confidence." He smirked. "Remember me four years ago?"

"I thought you were *Cécile's* handiwork," she said archly.

"I'm a multivariate equation." He counted on his fingers. "Cécile's handiwork plus weights plus Krav equals the perfection standing in front of you."

She burst out in laughter. "Why do I have the impression you're only *half* joking?"

He whipped out his phone and scrolled through his contacts. "I know an instructor who gives Krav Maga classes in the 18th, just a few *métro* stops from here. I'll send you his phone and address . . . if your number hasn't changed."

"Still the same." She shifted from one foot to the other. "I've got to go back and congratulate Amar."

"Of course," he said and stepped aside to let her pass.

* * *

"So. Liviu is at a friend's place. I'm free all evening. Where is it you want to take me?" Daniela asked, letting Jeanne into her tiny loge.

"You'll see when we get there."

In the *métro*, Jeanne noticed Daniela eyeing her voluminous backpack with a mixture of curiosity and apprehension. At one point, the concierge opened her mouth to say something but then closed it, shooting Jeanne a haunted look.

She finally spoke when they resurfaced at Château Rouge. "I don't think I can handle another session with a bunch of moralizing old ladies like the ones you set on me last time."

"I'm really sorry about that," Jeanne said. "My friend who recommended them sincerely believed they'd help."

"I'm sure they *sincerely* wanted to. Only they made me feel so . . . ashamed of myself and of my life. I couldn't bear the idea of seeing them again."

"I understand." Jeanne said, feeling her ears burn.

This time we'll try something entirely different.

Daniela adjusted her sunglasses on her nose. "I only agreed to come because you threatened to report Nico to the police." She touched Jeanne's sleeve. "How about we go to the movies? I haven't done that in years."

Jeanne shook her head and halted in front of an incongruous building that said Dojo in Asian-style red letters. She pushed the entrance door open and turned to Daniela. "*Et voilà*. Follow me."

As they made their way through the hallway, Jeanne read the signs on the doors: Karate, Judo, Kung fu, Kickboxing, Ballet.

Really?

The next one said Krav Maga.

She knocked on the door. A few seconds later a big man in his midforties opened the door and ushered them into the large room with padded flooring.

He pointed to the two visitor chairs by a small desk in the corner of the room. "Jeanne, right? And . . . ?"

"Daniela," Jeanne answered for the concierge who looked completely overwhelmed by the turn of events.

"My name's Dominique. Please, sit down," the instructor said. "I've been expecting you. The beginner class starts in fifteen minutes. You can try it after our chat, if you brought the right clothes."

"I have everything we need," Jeanne said, pointing to her backpack.

Dominique delivered a short introduction to his martial art. He particularly stressed how it allowed a smaller and physically weaker person to overpower a larger and stronger one.

"It's great exercise, too," he added in conclusion.

Jeanne opened her backpack and pulled out her checkbook. "I'd like to pay for both of us, for three months."

Dominique gave her a surprised look. "What do you mean? Oh, I see—he didn't tell you. Mat stopped by a few days ago and paid for the two of you. For one year."

Jeanne blinked, processing the information. The class was far from cheap. She'd examined her budget carefully, determining what expenses to cut to free up the funds for it. Mat was no doubt doing well for himself, but even so, a year's fee for two was a substantial amount of money. Especially considering the two in question couldn't even be called his friends . . .

"I'm not sure about this..." Daniela said, interrupting Jeanne's musings. She screwed her face up and glanced at Jeanne then at Dominique.

"Something's bothering you. Will you tell me what it is?" Dominique asked.

"I don't want to beat anyone up," Daniela said.

He smiled and shook his head. "You don't have to. Hopefully, you won't need to. But, believe me, you'll feel so much better knowing that you can."

Daniela stared at him for a moment and then nodded. "OK. Let's do it."

Soaking in her bathtub later that night to relax her aching muscles — including a few she hadn't known she had — Jeanne wondered about Mat's gesture. It was generous, no doubt. But it was also too extravagant. Was he trying to impress her, to make her feel grateful to him so she'd sleep with him?

Jeanne pinched her nose and sank under the water for a few seconds. When she reemerged with a white hat of foam on her head, she told herself Mat wasn't the kind of person to *pay* for a woman's favors. The guy she remembered from four years ago wouldn't have even thought of that.

But then, he was no longer that guy. He'd transformed both outwardly and inwardly into a different kind of man. The kind she'd sworn off after her embarrassing affair with Fred. Jeanne stared at the wall as a bitter, tangy taste spread in her mouth. The truth was this man, the new Mat, didn't have much in common with the geek who used to worship her. Gone were the messy curls and the ugly glasses, but also the vulnerability and the goofiness. He was now a self-confident politician, full of ambition and promise. He was so driven, so sure of the path he'd set for himself.

A path that didn't intersect with hers.

Wasn't it cruelly ironic that she'd waited until this metamorphosis to finally fall in love with him?

* * *

Chapter Nine
June

Mat rubbed his forehead and tried to reason with himself.

Turn around and walk away. Or better still – run.

He didn't move.

He'd been standing in front of Jeanne's building for a good fifteen minutes now, struggling to recover control over his body. But his brain no longer seemed in charge. Mat smirked. He had a pretty good idea *what* had taken over.

Just a glimpse. A quick hello and I'll leave.

Over the past month, he'd thought of Jeanne—her vitality, hearty laughter, sexy voice, and gorgeous body—way more than he should. More than he'd thought about his girlfriend, his work, and the forthcoming municipal elections combined.

Today, having finished his business in Paris earlier than planned, he didn't go to the train station. His feet brought him to *La Bohème* where he hoped to catch a glimpse of Jeanne. Maybe say hi. Maybe even accidentally brush her hand. He was vaguely aware coming here was an uncommonly bad idea. But his traitorous brain refused to list the many reasons why he shouldn't be in Jeanne's vicinity again.

As it turned out, she'd taken the afternoon off.

Mat loosened his tie and took a few breaths. A woman carrying groceries stopped in front of the intercom, keyed in the code, and pushed the entrance door open. Mat rushed in after her. He had no idea on what Jeanne's floor was, but it wasn't a problem. All he had to do was check the names on each door, starting from the ground floor.

He walked past the concierge's loge and smiled. Dominique had told him that since enrolling three weeks ago, Daniela and Jeanne never missed a class. They were beginning to show progress.

The tiny sign over the peephole of the next door read "Jeanne Bonnet."

Mat took a deep breath and rang the doorbell.

She's probably out, he told himself, trying to calm his breathing.

Footsteps approached on the other side of the door. There was a brief pause.

Is she looking through the peephole?

She opened the door and Mat gasped. She was so unbearably lovely in her cotton sundress, her hair tied into a loose bun, and a light blush coloring her cheeks.

He stared at her, spellbound, neglecting to think of an excuse. Forgetting to say hello.

"How did you find me?" she asked.

He blinked, remembering where he was, and why he shouldn't be here. But it was too late for regrets.

"You mentioned some time ago you lived five blocks from *La Bohème*. So I checked the names on the intercoms of all the buildings around the bistro until I found yours."

He'd expected a rebuke but was it *joy* that flickered in her eyes? He didn't dare believe it.

Jeanne schooled her features into a polite smile. "Thanks again for the Krav Maga subscription. You didn't have to do it."

"It was my pleasure." He smirked. "As you know, I get off finding solutions to people's problems. I'm convinced Krav Maga will help Daniela. It's bound to."

Jeanne nodded. "Come on in. I have to leave in about twenty minutes, but I can offer you a cold drink."

He stepped inside. Jeanne reached behind his back and pulled the door shut. As soon as he heard the click, he took her in his arms and pressed her to his chest.

She didn't resist.

He closed his eyes, savoring the moment. God, that smell of coffee in her hair, mixed with her delicate perfume. How he'd missed it! He stroked her tanned shoulders, his thumbs pressing into the smooth warm velvet of her skin. He kissed her forehead, her eyes, her cheeks, and her nose.

"Oh, Jeanne." He repeated her name between the kisses, his voice deep and soft. It felt good to be able to say her name aloud while touching her. His gaze darted to her mouth, but he didn't kiss it, stretching out the sweet torture of anticipation.

Jeanne's arms were now around his neck, and her hands caressed his nape. She closed her eyes and held her face up for his kisses. When she slightly opened her lips and moistened them with her tongue, he knew he was a goner.

With a low groan, he closed his eyes and kissed her. *Really* kissed her. For the first time in his life, he kissed Jeanne the way he'd always wanted to, the way he hadn't had a chance to do until now. His tongue plunged into her mouth and stroked hers. He ran it against the inside of her teeth, her palate, and then sucked on her tongue. She didn't taste of honey or mint. It was something different, sweet, and sultry at the same time.

The taste of paradise.

Jeanne shifted her position, and through the thin layers of their clothing, her taut nipples brushed over his chest. Mat gasped and pulled away a little, afraid he'd embarrass himself like a teenager. He needed a few moments to regain a measure of control over his hunger for this woman, before he could hold her and taste her again.

With a dazed expression, Jeanne opened her eyes. She stroked the back of his head, and a smile touched the corners of her lips. "Let your hair grow."

"I thought you didn't like my curls."

"I didn't. But I wish you had them now."

"It's the new and improved Mat that turns you on, remember?" he teased. "What if the curls triggered your former indifference?"

She smiled a little too brightly. "That's exactly what I'm hoping for."

He suddenly realized how quickly he had grown used to the idea that Jeanne fancied him, that she was unable to resist his touch. It had become a given in his life, a secret source of warmth and reassurance he delved into every time he faced rejection, disappointment, or simply a spot of the blues.

"No chance," he said, gently pushing her toward the wall and bracketing her between his legs.

She leaned into him, her hand sliding to his shoulder. Gripping it, she pulled him even closer. Her other hand remained on his nape, stroking it.

He nuzzled her hair, drawing in the coffee scent. It made his body ache with desire.

I have to take her now, or I'll lose my mind.

He'd wanted her so badly for so damn long. A pang of guilt hit him as the image of Cécile flashed in his brain. But it disappeared as quickly as it came. He grabbed Jeanne's wrists, brought them behind her back, and shackled them with his hands. She was now a prisoner of his legs and hands—of his entire body.

Judging by the look of total abandon on her face, she didn't mind it at all.

He kissed her lips again and penetrated her mouth with one deep thrust of his tongue. The sweetness of it sent a shiver through his body, robbing him of the last traces of restraint. He whispered her name as he slid his palms under her thighs, picked her up, and backed her against the wall.

Jeanne wrapped her legs around his waist and grabbed onto his shoulders. Her voice was deliciously raspy as she said his name. He began to move against her. His right hand slid under her skirt. He rubbed the back of her thighs, stroked her buttocks through her cotton panties, and then went to her core. If he needed more proof of her desire for him, he had it now. Touching her like that nearly sent him over the edge.

"I want you so much," he whispered against her mouth.

Her eyes were glazed when she opened them. "I want you, too."

He stroked her and a tremor spread through his body. "Let me make love to you. Please, let me make love to you."

She peered at him, her face flushed with desire.

Is that a yes?

He pulled out his strongest argument. "Let's get it out of our systems. It's the only way to cure this madness."

He was about to ask if she had a condom when her expression changed. She stiffened in his arms and put her hand on his chest to push him away. Disoriented, he lowered her on the ground and searched her eyes for an explanation.

"You're a fool," she said.

"Why? What did I do?"

"Don't you get it?" Her voice cracked with emotion. "Do you really believe we can *screw* this 'madness' out of our systems?"

She opened the door. "I'd like you to leave now."

He stared at her for a few moments, and then nodded and rushed out without daring to turn back.

* * *

It had been over a week since Claude had given in to his demons and stopped coming to work. He didn't answer or return Jeanne's calls, which worried her a little more every day. On Tuesday she got bad news from Nîmes: Her mom had tripped on the stairs and broken her leg. After talking to her on the phone, Jeanne took the first southbound train and spent two days at the hospital entertaining and distracting her.

Back in Paris, she endured another sleepless night because of Daniela and Nico's fighting.

Then Mat turned up on her doorstep with his ingenious idea to "get it out of their systems."

Jeanne sighed as she emptied the filter basket and began to wipe the coffee machine. Could this week get any worse?

It just might, considering the look on Pierre's face as he approached her, accompanied by Didier.

"Let's finish this morning's conversation," Pierre said.

"OK." Jeanne put her hands on her hips. "You have to fire Thierry."

"Isn't it a bit drastic?" Pierre asked. "Didier thinks highly of him."

Didier said nothing, but a muscle twitched in his jaw.

Jeanne turned back to Pierre. "Amar saw him use the toilet and then go back to the kitchen without washing his hands."

"Amar is lying," Didier spat out. "He's probably trying to get us to fire Thierry so he could bring in some uncle of his."

"I believe him," Jeanne said. "And, by the way, Thierry's cooking isn't good."

"Nobody's cooking is as good as Claude's," Pierre said with a sigh. "But Claude is on sick leave getting treatment for his depression, and we have no idea when he'll return to work. We're stuck."

Jeanne frowned. "We can call at least three other chefs who've filled in for Claude in the past. I don't see why we're stuck with Thierry."

Pierre turned to Didier. "Is he a friend of yours?"

Didier shook his head. "But he was highly recommended by a good friend of mine. I don't believe Amar's tales, and there's nothing wrong with his cooking. I don't see why we should let him go."

He gave Pierre a defiant look.

Jeanne narrowed her eyes at the proprietor. *Decision time.*

Pierre closed his eyes and remained like that for a long moment. When he finally spoke, his voice was firm. "We'll keep him for now."

Jeanne swirled around and marched to the other end of the bar area. She wanted to punch something. Not only did Pierre choose to keep someone who was no good, his decision implied he trusted Didier's judgment more than hers. This was a bad sign. A *very* bad sign.

Jeanne smirked. At least, she had no more doubts about Didier. She'd known for a while she could never be in a romantic relationship with him. Now she could see that a business partnership wasn't an option, either. They disagreed on everything that mattered. In spite of what Pierre hoped and believed, *La Bohème* couldn't be Didier's and hers. It had to be his *or* hers.

And, judging by Pierre's decision about Thierry, things weren't looking good for her.

She needed to focus on something positive.

Has anything good happened recently?

The Krav Maga classes—that was the good thing. And that Daniela wasn't quitting.

Yes, definitely the Krav Maga classes, she repeated to herself, trying to smother another thought that edged its way to her conscious mind. It wasn't even a thought, strictly speaking. There were no nouns or verbs or even interjections in it. It was a breathtaking image, a heady smell, a delightful prickling in her skin ... It was a memory. A memory of something precious and beautiful. Something that had blown her mind away.

Jeanne gave another heavy sigh and finally allowed herself to acknowledge it, to admit how humbled she was by its glory. Yes, it would have been the bright spot of her week, the brightest spot of her entire year ... had it not held as much bitterness as beauty.

Her phone rang. She glanced at the caller ID. Lena.

"How's your mom?" Lena asked.

"Adjusting to her reduced mobility. Luckily, my parents had planned to take some vacation this summer. So now they'll just close the bakery for a month and rent a small house by the sea."

"Sounds like a great plan. I suppose your dad and brother could do with a little rest, too."

"My brother will go hiking in Corsica with his buddies. He's really looking forward to it. What have you been up to?"

"The routine. Translate a few pages, run to the bathroom, vomit, repeat."

"Poor darling! Are you guys still planning on that North Sea cruise?"

"Maybe not. I'm sick enough as it is."

"Isn't your nausea supposed to be gone by now?"

"That's what I keep telling my doctor. Apparently, it can linger beyond the first trimester in some cases. I just hope it won't stay throughout the entire pregnancy!"

"There must be some Russian grandma remedy for it, no?"

"Believe me, I've tried everything. Russian, French, Chinese, Indian — you name it." Lena sighed before adding, her tone brighter now. "Anyway, I didn't call you to whine."

"Of course not." Jeanne grinned. "You *never* call me to whine. That you end up whining is purely coincidental."

"Smartass. I called for a status update on the 'Mat situation.'"

Jeanne's smile slipped. "I wish I could tell you I'm miraculously over him."

"Oh, sweetie."

"Hey, I've been trying a new tack," Jeanne said doing her best to sound light. "The other day I dug out some old pictures from our trip to Nice four years ago, when he was still super skinny."

"Ooh-la-la, he *was* skinny," Lena said. "I used to think of him as 'Mr. Clothes Hanger' before I found out what his name was."

"That's a good one. You should've told me earlier."

"So, what did you do with those pictures? Don't tell me you stabbed his chest with a needle."

"You're full of great ideas today! No, I just looked at that thin toad-eyed guy with wild hair and told myself, *This is who he really is, behind his sleek suits and hard muscles.*"

"Did it work?"

Jeanne bit her nails. "I'm starting to find the guy in those pictures attractive."

"Shit."

"As you said."

* * *

The town of Baleville reelected Mat to sit on the Municipal Council and the Communal Council. But it favored Laetitia Barnier—the outgoing deputy mayor and Mat's main rival—for the top job.

That was three days ago. This morning, the new Municipal Council formalized the citizens' vote by electing Laetitia mayor of Baleville.

When the results were announced, Mat smiled and shook Laetitia's hand. It wasn't too difficult. Despite his conviction that he'd be a better mayor for his town, he'd never stooped to personal attacks during the campaign. Laetitia was unimaginative but upright. He admired her for having played her "benevolent matriarch" card so well.

It was a lot more unpleasant to continue smiling when the Councilors took turns at patting him on the shoulder and saying stupid things like "You're still too young for this job. Try again next time."

The next municipal elections were in six years.

He'd be thirty-three by then and probably married with kids. He'd enjoy more notoriety and influence. With some luck, he might lose his hair and sport dark circles under his eyes.

Would they see him as better mayor material then?

It isn't the end of the world, Mat rationalized on the way home. He still had his PR job that he liked, was reelected Councilor, and would continue his involvement with the Greens. He'd remain active in their pesticides and GMOs regional working group. The members appreciated him and he was eager to do more.

This is just a setback, he told himself, *not the end of my political career*. The whole running for office thing had been a great learning experience, and he'd established a solid foundation to build on over the coming years.

Only . . . why this guilt? And the shame?

"Watch out, you moron!" someone yelled, startling Mat and returning him to reality.

He stopped in his tracks and looked around. He was smack in the middle of a busy intersection surrounded by cars, scooters, and bicycles.

Fuck.

Raising his hands in an apology, he rushed to the sidewalk where he leaned against a wall, loosened his tie, and tried to collect himself. It was there by that wall, his heart racing from his near escape, when he realized what bothered him almost as much as his defeat.

Actually, more.

With sudden clarity, Mat knew why he felt so guilty and ashamed. There was no more hiding from the truth: He hadn't given his campaign all he had, all he could, and should have given. For one simple, embarrassingly banal reason—his obsession with Jeanne.

For the past ten months, he had been consumed by his longing, crushed by his lust for her. He'd lost his drive and sharpness. He'd thought about her all the time—as he shot ads with his mom, sat on the Municipal Council, took Cécile out to dinner... He'd been chronically sleep deprived, but not because of stress or too much work. Every night, he would go to bed with a stack of papers in his hands, full of noble intentions to read a report on organic farming or draft a speech. And then, half an hour later, he'd catch himself fantasizing about making love to Jeanne.

While Cécile would be halfway through her own stack, a highlighter between her teeth, and a look of fierce concentration in her eyes.

Mat took a deep, ragged breath, and resumed his walk.

You brought this upon yourself.

As he pushed open the door to the apartment he and Cécile occupied in a handsome limestone building, he knew she was home. Had she seen his text? She'd been devastated by the results of the public vote, but she'd held onto the crazy hope that the Council pick him in spite of Laetitia's majority. He was going to tell her it was over now. She'd put on a brave face, swallow her disappointment, and say something to comfort him. Like she always did.

"You pathetic, frolicking fool," Cécile spat as soon as he walked into the kitchen.

His jaw went slack. In their two years together, they'd never insulted each other in any circumstance. He'd thought Cécile incapable of uttering an insult.

She strode over, stopped a few inches from him, and gave him a withering stare. "Last summer you were Baleville's golden boy. You had the town eating out of your hand. And you lose to that old cow who has no ideas and no charisma!"

"She's a seasoned politician, and she knows her stuff—"

Cécile shook her head. "She's nothing. She got elected only because you gave up at some point."

"What do you mean, I gave up?"

"It's been a while since your speeches moved or inspired anyone. Your statements lost their punch and your campaign went from hot to lukewarm."

"I didn't realize... I don't know what to say..."

Cecile narrowed her eyes. "I do. It's all because of that woman, that barmaid of yours. She took too much of your energy, too much space in your shriveled brain."

Oh God. She knew.

"I've heard you say her name in your sleep," Cécile continued. "Night after night since last fall. Accompanied by a monumental hard-on."

He couldn't believe his ears. "You've known all this time?"

"Do you think I'm dumb? I *chose* to close my eyes because I believed in your future. I'd invested so much in it... I didn't want to hold up your ascent." She smirked. "But instead of going up, you rolled down. You slipped from the leader I thought you'd become back to your old wacky ways."

He stared at her, a vein pulsing on his neck.

Cécile's shoulders fell and her gaze turned melancholy. She touched his chest. "All this muscle you've gained and all these stylish clothes I've picked for you aren't enough to fool people, Mat. Because people, they know a loser when they see one."

She dropped her hand and brushed past him. "I'm going out for a walk. Can't stand to look at you right now."

He remained planted in the middle of the kitchen for a long while, processing the conversation, adjusting to the new reality. Then he shook his head, as if waking up from a trance, marched into the living room, and began to browse his music collection until he found what he was looking for. It was a new Cyril song about a life-ruining obsession. He'd heard it on the radio a few days ago and purchased it immediately. Because had he possessed any talent for music, he could have written it.

Mat removed his tie, sat on the floor next to his designer stereo, and played the song.

I'm ablaze drowning in the ocean,
I'm adrift pacing in my room,
In my heart only one emotion —
Every
night I

*crave
you,
Like a crazed wolf howling at the moon.*

*You're under my skin —
tattooed.*

* * *

Chapter Ten
July

Thank God, Claude came into work in the morning, ending his sick leave and Thierry's stint at *La Bohème*. Relieved beyond measure, Jeanne made up her mind to restore peace with Didier. She'd propose a truce as soon as the lunch service was over. It wasn't in the interest of either of them to bicker and poison the atmosphere at the bistro. Instead, they should agree to pressure Pierre to make his decision and put an end to this unhealthy rivalry.

She placed two freshly brewed espressos on a tray and handed it to Manon. After she filled some pitchers with water and lined them on the counter, she surveyed the room for Didier.

Speak of the devil.

The headwaiter walked right past her, stopping at the table of a young couple engrossed in their conversation, hands entwined across the table.

"Are you ready to order now?" Didier asked with barely disguised annoyance.

"I'm so sorry. We got sidetracked." The young woman nervously flipped through the menu and turned to her boyfriend. "How about paella?"

"Nah... I'd rather have a couscous," the young man said.

"How do you feel about sushi?" Didier asked sweetly. "I highly recommend it."

The couple exchanged enthusiastic nods, and the man said, "Wonderful idea! We'll go for sushi then."

Didier smiled pleasantly. "What makes you think we have any?"

"But you just said—" the woman began.

"I gave you my opinion about sushi, which is a great dish. I thought we were exchanging views on foreign foods." Didier brushed an invisible speck off the sleeve of his shirt and gave the couple a look of misunderstood innocence.

The young man puffed out his chest. "Rubbish. You misled us deliberately."

Didier picked up one of the menus and held it in front of the man's face. "Had monsieur bothered to read our menu, he would've noticed that it lists none of the dishes we've just discussed. And, in any case, someone your age should know what kind of food to expect in a bistro."

He paused for added drama, then placed the menu on the table, and turned to leave. "Wave when you're ready to order."

He strode toward the bar, propped an elbow on the counter across from Jeanne, and said, "I've been thinking."

"Good for you." Jeanne gave him a bright smile.

"I'm serious, Jeanne. These past months have shown me we can't be a functional couple. But after the way you handled Thierry, I doubt we can even be business partners."

"We can't. I've come to the same conclusion," Jeanne said.

Didier shook his head. "I'm sorry for you. You're going to regret not having seized your chance."

"What makes you so sure you'll have the bistro?"

Didier shrugged. "Pierre is a sensible man."

"Exactly," Jeanne said, giving him a defiant look.

"You won't get *La Bohème*, Jeanne. If I were you, I'd start adjusting to the idea."

She glowered at him.

"I'll be happy to let you keep your current job," Didier said. "You're a fine barista and a decent bartender. But you'll have to ditch your opinions and do as I say."

Jeanne gave him a doe-eyed look. "You're too generous, Didier. Truly, you are. But I'm afraid I'm quite incapable of doing as you say. So . . ."

"I see . . . You want all or nothing."

She nodded.

"You'll have nothing," he said.

It was Jeanne's turn to shrug. "That's OK, as long as I get to keep my opinions."

Didier rolled his eyes and walked away.

You'll have nothing.

Didier's remark reverberated in her head, chilling the blood in her veins. On a self-destructive impulse, she imagined herself in the near future and shuddered at the bleakness of what she saw. Didier had *La Bohème*. Cécile had Mat.

She had nothing.

Fortunately, her indomitable optimism finally kicked in. *Cut this self-indulgent crap.*

She still had a chance—a solid chance—with the bistro. As for Mat, well, he was deeply convinced the *thing* between them was purely physical.

What if he was right? What if she was deluding herself, mistaking attraction for feelings, and lust for love?

She'd called him a fool for thinking they could purge their "systems" of their obsession if they went all the way. But what if he was right? Could she admit for a second they were crazed because the fruit was forbidden? Yes, they'd kissed and fooled around, and it only made things worse. But maybe it was because they never made love, never found release together.

Could sex set them free?

Could Mat have been right about it, and she—a fool?

* * *

Later in the afternoon, Amanda stopped by for a coffee. She was as well groomed and dressed as ever, but her gaze was uncharacteristically dull.

"What brings you here at this time of the day?" Jeanne asked, after they exchanged a cheek kiss.

"Just needed a break. And a good coffee. Can't stand the gunk that comes from our coffee machine anymore."

"A *noisette*, as usual?"

Amanda nodded.

Jeanne began to prepare Amanda's coffee, expecting the customary flood of witty banter. When none came, she glanced at Amanda over her shoulder. "What's wrong?"

"Nothing. Why?"

"You're unusually subdued."

"I'm touched by your concern, but don't worry, I'm fine."

"Boy trouble?"

"No boy, no trouble."

"Work trouble?"

Amanda shook her head. "Still queen of the hill."

Jeanne handed Amanda her coffee. "Your majesty."

Amanda smirked. "What about you? I've seen you staring into the void recently—several times. You never used to do that before. It's about a boy and I must know who."

"Curiosity killed the queen."

"Oh come on, Jeanne. Give me something. I've had a really tough week, if you must know."

Jeanne raised her brows.

"I've worked around the clock and am completely unplugged from the office grapevine. Now I'm running out of juice. I need info that's not related to work."

"Shall I get you my copy of *Le Monde*?" Jeanne asked. "Or you could watch some TV."

"Officially, I don't own a television. It's considered too lowlife in certain circles. And I only read *Le Figaro* and *The Economist*."

Amanda took a sip from her cup. "Ooh, the bliss... Have I mentioned you make the best coffee in Paris?"

"On several occasions."

"Do I know him?"

Jeanne blinked, a little disoriented by the sudden question, then shook her head. "I'm not telling."

"Oh my God. It means I do! Let's see... Didier?" Amanda studied Jeanne's face. "No. OK. The chef? Nah, he's too old and not your type. Oh no! Please don't tell me it's Amar! He's young enough to be your son."

Jeanne snorted. "He's only six years our junior. So there's no way he could be my son. Anyway, it's not him."

Amanda's eyes widened and her mouth fell open. She placed her cup on the counter, cleared her throat and leaned in. "I know who it is. I should've guessed immediately. I remember how he stared at you during my promotion bash. I just didn't think you'd fall for a guy who's already taken..."

Jeanne looked away.

Amanda shook her head. "I've been in Cécile's shoes, as you may remember, and I can tell you it sucks."

"I know." Jeanne rinsed a glass and put it on the drying rack. "I've been in her shoes, too, with Ludo. I left him in the end."

"So you're hoping Cécile will dump Mat? Or he'll dump her for you?"

Jeanne wiped her hands on her apron and refused to answer Amanda's questions or look at her.

"Get real, my dear. Those two are in a symbiotic relationship that goes beyond sentiments. Besides..." Amanda's voice trailed off and she fixed her gaze on her cup.

"What?"

"Never mind. If I say it, I'll risk our friendship... and I can't afford losing a friend right now."

Jeanne flattened her hand on the counter. "I swear on this authentic copper I won't cut you off, no matter what you say."

"OK." Amanda gave her a long sympathetic look. "You're a lovely, funny, sexy woman. But you're no match to Cécile. She's in a different league, Jeanne. And so is Mat."

The next morning, Jeanne got out of bed with a plan hatched during the sleepless night. Quite possibly a stupid plan that would make things only worse, but she hated feeling helpless. So, any plan was better than none.

First, she'd corner Pierre and demand a decision. She might give him three days—a week tops, but no more—lest she explode from not knowing.

Second, she'd call Mat and tell him she had changed her mind. If she really was nothing more than a hot chick to him, then she'd act like one. She wanted him, and she would have him. There was the scary scenario wherein the "curative" sex worked only for him, while she'd end up lovesick and heartbroken because she was a hot chick with a gooey heart.

But she refused to dwell on it now.

She was going for broke, and she'd deal with the consequences later.

Hmm... all things considered, she'd start with the second part of her plan.

Jeanne grabbed her phone and scrolled to his number.

There.

"Jeanne?" He sounded baffled.

"Hi. What's up?"

"I lost the elections last week."

"I'm sorry. I'm sure you'll make it next time."

"Thank you."

Neither of them spoke for a few tense moments.

"Why did you call me?" Mat asked.

"I changed my mind about... your idea. I want to do it."

"Jeanne, I..."

She waited but he didn't finish his sentence. "I'm willing to allow that you might be right about . . . lancing the abscess. Maybe *I'm* the fool, and not you."

"Believe me, the only fool here is me," he said.

"Will you come to Paris and see me one of these days?"

"No."

"But—"

"I made a discovery after my defeat, Jeanne. I realized I'm weaker than I'd like to think. On top of being a fool, as we've already established."

"What are you saying?"

"I've never had a one-night stand in my life . . . I've never desired a woman only for her body. And you . . . you're amazing in every way, Jeanne. If I sleep with you, I'll want more."

Then do it, for Christ's sake! She wanted to shout.

"I'm so sorry. About everything. I wish I could turn back the clock and leave Rob's engagement party earlier . . ."

"I wish you could," she said.

"I'll disappear from your life, completely. I'll stay away from *La Bohème*, from all of Rob and Lena's events, and from Amanda's, too. It's the only way."

"Great plan."

"You'll forget me before the summer's out."

"You bet."

"Take good care, Jeanne."

"No, *you* take care." She spoke slowly, so that her voice wouldn't give away how bitter she felt. "Take *very good* care of yourself and your perfect girlfriend. She'll make you such a fitting wife."

She hung up before he could say anything else.

* * *

Chapter Eleven
August

Jeanne paced the bistro, nearly shaking with apprehension. Pierre had asked her to meet him at seven in the morning so that they could have a quiet talk. She kept urging herself to remain calm and positive. But the past month had been so lousy, she was now primed to expect the worst.

Pierre arrived at five past seven, unshaven and disheveled.

"Bad night?" Jeanne asked.

He nodded and gave her a tired smile. "Judging by your dark circles under, your night wasn't any better than mine."

Jeanne placed two croissants and two cups of coffee on a tray and picked it up. "Backyard?"

"After you."

As soon as they sat at the teak table, she gulped down her espresso and looked the proprietor in the eye. "It's the moment of truth. What's your decision, Pierre?"

He rubbed his chin. "Are you absolutely sure you can't partner with Didier?"

"Positive."

"I see." He nodded slowly. "Then it's yours."

"What?" The verdict was so unexpected she wasn't sure she'd heard him right. "Could you say it again, please?"

"*La Bohème* is yours, Jeanne. I love you like the daughter I've never had. *La Bohème* has always been yours. I was just hoping you could take Didier along—"

Jeanne jumped up from the bench, ran around the table, and gave Pierre a tight hug. When she released him, her eyes glistened with emotion.

Pierre's were downright wet.

He wiped his tears with the back of his hand and blew his nose into a napkin. "This is embarrassing. I'm getting sentimental with age."

"I can't thank you enough—" Jeanne began.

"Wait till you're neck-deep in debt, can't take vacation for a few years, and are forced to learn the art of plumbing. You may curse me then."

Jeanne shook her head. "No chance of that. I'll take good care of this place, and it will be a joy—even fixing the plumbing."

"I'll help you as much as I can for the next few months. But after Christmas, you're on your own."

"While you're sipping a *rosé* poolside in your Baux-de-Provence villa..."

"It's a small house, and I don't think I'll be sipping anything poolside in the middle of winter."

"You should go visit my parents in Nîmes. It's what, a one hour drive?"

"Thereabouts."

Pierre finished his croissant and brushed the crumbs off his protruding belly. "Listen, Jeanne, I know you're planning a major refurbishment, and the place does need one—"

"If you're worried I'll change everything, let me put your worries to rest." Jeanne cut in. "I will change *some* things, but I'll make sure *La Bohème* keeps its soul. It's why we all love it, right?"

Pierre let out a relieved sigh. "That's my girl." Then he sighed again—heavier this time—and stood. "I should go talk to Didier now. And it's going to be a much less pleasant conversation."

You bet.

Jeanne shifted in her seat. "Do you mind if I dash home to call my parents? And my bank. And everyone else I'll be borrowing from. Oh, and I could get some cleaning products or office supplies on my way back..."

Pierre smirked. "Take a look in the supplies closet. I'm sure we're running out of something or other. Scoot now."

When Jeanne returned to the bistro two hours later, Didier barreled toward her, his face red and his right eye twitching. He stopped only a few inches from her and jabbed her with his finger.

His voice trembled when he spoke. "How did you do it? Did you sleep with him?"

Jeanne took a step back. "Sure. Why else would he choose *me* over *you*?"

Didier clenched his fists. His eye twitched so rapidly it was painful to watch.

After a few long seconds he said, "I'm quitting my job."

"You don't have to—"

"You're kidding me? How can I stay here with you as a boss?"

"Please, Didier. Take some time off. You can decide on this later."

"Oh, you're already telling me what to do. Well, my answer is no. I won't take time off. I'm walking."

He removed his apron and handed it to Jeanne. "I give you a year before *La Bohème* goes under. I'll have a good laugh then."

Jeanne said nothing as he turned around and marched out.

Would I have felt this bitter in his place? she wondered. Probably.

Would she have reacted the way he did?

Depends which part.

Asking him if he'd slept with Pierre? She thought not.

Quitting her job? Most certainly yes.

The rest of the day rushed by in a haze. Pierre asked the staff to stay for a few minutes after closing at midnight and announced that Jeanne was going to be the new proprietor of *La Bohème*. He handed everyone an envelope with a good-bye bonus and promised a big party before he left Paris.

After the cheers subsided, Amar said with a lopsided smile. "There may be a God in this universe, after all."

"Wow. What made you a believer?"

"Science. I conducted an experiment. I prayed for Pierre to choose you over Didier, and it happened."

"You may regret that experiment in a few months," Jeanne teased.

"At least I'll have a job for a few more months." Amar countered. "Didier would've fired me on the spot."

Claude smiled—an occurrence as rare as a Yeti sighting—and said, "I hope you won't abolish our coffee breaks."

"Never." Jeanne took his hand and gave it a little squeeze. "I count on you, Claude. Don't you dare quit on me like Didier."

He gave her a quick nod.

She raised her voice, addressing the whole room. "I count on you all, guys. We're in this together."

Everyone looked at her expectantly.

She toyed with her apron strings.

Manon grinned. "Is this all you can come up with for your inaugural speech?"

Jeanne took a breath. "I promise I'll do everything to be a worthy successor to Pierre."

"That's better," Amar said.

"And don't be tardy," Jeanne added.

After a moment of silence, Manon cheered, "Yay!"

Claude smiled once more and went back to the kitchen.

"Great speech," Pierre said, his mouth twitching.

"I thought so, too." Jeanne deadpanned.

***

Mat and his mom had worked their tails off on this account. It was for very big fish—their biggest ever. The founding CEO of a large regional investment bank wanted a PR campaign portraying him as a cultured philanthropist.

According to everything Madame Gérard was able to dig up on him, the man was neither cultured nor a philanthropist—by any standard.

Mat nearly gave up after several days of racking his brain about how to build a public image out of thin air. Then it hit him. He needed a two-step plan: First, turn the CEO into a patron of the arts, and only then sing his praises. Which was why Mat produced a mammoth of a proposal that went far beyond his regular PR strategies.

The first part was a blueprint for a free art exhibit permanently housed in the bank's spacious HQ in Rouen. It included a detailed floor plan, specific artwork, interior design suggestions, and a lot of funky green tech solutions. On a whim, he threw in a life-size dancing T. rex—an extravagant, non-fundable idea by a local artist—as the central piece of the art collection.

The second part was a traditional PR and media outreach plan.

The budget was Pharaonic.

"Do we absolutely need the T. rex?" his mom had asked when she saw the proposal.

They ended up keeping it only because it was too late to redo the whole thing.

Mat submitted the project last Monday, as agreed.

And waited.

Friday morning he received a text from the CEO himself.

Love the T. rex. Let's do it.

Mat's slowly expelled his breath as a huge wave of relief washed over him. It wasn't just because this would be his most ambitious and lucrative project yet. Something much more important had been at stake—his drive and his self-confidence. This order was his first victory after the election debacle. It proved he hadn't lost his mojo.

Mat booked a table at Le Cheval Bleu and sent a text to his mom. A celebration was in order.

Over dessert, Madame Gérard gave her son a long, meaningful look. "Talk to me."

Mat raised an eyebrow. "I've been talking nonstop for the past hour. I thought you were listening."

"Very funny. Mat, what's going on in your life?"

He shrugged lightly. "I haven't given up on politics, if that's what you're asking."

"I'm asking if you're happy."

"Considering the circumstances—"

"To hell with the circumstances! That's not what I'm talking about." She placed her hand over his. "Are you happy with Cécile? Is she the woman you see yourself with in twenty years?"

"I . . . Mom, what is this about?"

"You."

"Why are you suddenly so interested in Cécile?"

"Good question. Could it be because you haven't mentioned her name in weeks?"

The remark gave him pause. "Haven't I?"

She shook her head. "I started to wonder if you were still together."

"Of course we are. I guess I was just overwhelmed by recent events."

"Mat, are you sure she's the right girl for you?"

"Why? You don't like her?"

"I didn't say that. I admire her many qualities. It's just . . . she lacks warmth, and a bit of sincerity wouldn't hurt, either."

"You don't know her."

"Do you? Are you two happy together?"

"We have some issues... but we'll work them out."

"Issues, huh? Do they happen to be named Jeanne?"

Mat nearly jumped at her name. "How do you know about Jeanne?"

Madame Gérard smirked. "Your dad heard you repeat that name when you slept over at his place."

Great. There was no such thing as privacy for sleep talkers. He might as well tell her the truth. At least the gist of it.

"Cécile and I, we're great together in every way except... the physical. And Jeanne... I'm attracted to her, but we have nothing in common."

"How do you know her?"

"She's a waitress at the bistro where Rob used to work."

"I see." Madame Gérard pushed her eyeglasses up. "Mat, I may not be the wisest person on Earth, but I can tell you this: If a couple's chemistry is wrong, sooner or later that couple will fall apart, no matter how well they get along in other ways."

"Mom, I love Cécile. I learn from her, I rely on her. She's so driven, so together."

"I'm sure she is."

"And I'm... I'm not tough enough for politics. I need a woman like Cécile, Mom. When I'm down or demotivated, she tells me to get my act together. She eggs me on and pulls me up."

"Do you believe Jeanne will pull you down?"

"No. It's more that I'm afraid we won't have much to go on once we've finally... done it." Mat's ears and cheeks grew warm. It was seriously weird discussing this with his mother.

"It could happen," she said. "But being with one woman and fancying another isn't so great either, don't you think? How long have you had this crush on her?"

"Since September."

Good Lord, next month would be a year—a whole year since his relapse. He sighed and added, "Not counting the two years in grad school."

"I see. Have you kissed her?"

He nodded.

"Have you done more than kissing?" She stifled a smile.

He wasn't finding the situation amusing at all. "Yes. But we haven't... made love," he said, his face on fire.

She chuckled. "That wasn't what I meant, actually. I was wondering if you'd done any talking. Have you discussed things with her?"

"Not a whole lot, but yes. Why?"

She tilted her head a little in a can't-you-see look. "Were you bored by her conversation?"

Jeanne, boring?

He shook his head. "She's fun to be around."

"Is there anything about her you find objectionable?"

Mat gave his mom a quizzical look. "Define 'objectionable.'"

"Is she vulgar? Unscrupulous? Racist? Smelly?" She smirked. "Is she one of those lost souls that refuse to recycle?"

It was Mat's turn to smirk. "None of the above."

"Then I've got another question. How was the kissing... and whatever else you two did together?"

He couldn't look in her eyes and answer that question. So he turned away from her and fixed a spot on the wall. "Great." He paused, chewed on his lip, and added, "Better than great."

She fell silent for a moment before asking, "When was the last time you saw her?"

"Early June."

"And you still can't get her off your mind?"

He looked into her eyes. What kind of point was she trying to make?

She shrugged. "It's your life, sweetheart." She hesitated.

"Ye-e-s?" he prompted.

She cupped his cheek and smiled. "I'm sure you'll figure this out sooner or later . . . I just hope it won't be too late."

* * *

Chapter Twelve
September

All too soon, summer was over. Between the municipal elections and the exhibit project, Mat had hardly found two weekends to drive to the coast to take a dip in the cool waters of the Channel—once with Cécile and another time with Rob. Vacation plans had been canceled, which suited Cécile just as well, considering all the litigation cases she had to prepare over the summer. So they stayed in Baleville, promising themselves to take a nice long holiday over Christmas and go someplace faraway and exotic.

It would do us good to go someplace faraway.

Mat shut his laptop, turned off the lights, and tiptoed to the bedroom at one in the morning. Lately, he'd gotten into the habit of preparing for bed around eleven, and then working for a couple more hours in the study. That way, he could sneak into bed in the wee hours of the morning without waking Cécile up.

It worked like a charm every time.

Except tonight.

As he lifted the end of the blanket, Cécile stirred and fumbled for the night lamp switch.

"I'm sorry I woke you up," he said.

"You didn't. I couldn't sleep. Must've had too much coffee."

He climbed into bed and lay on his side, facing her.

Touch her, he told himself. But his arm remained motionless by his side.

"Mat, you've been working like crazy on this exhibit project over the past three weeks."

"It'll be less intense once all the contracts are signed and the conversion works begin."

"I doubt it. Are you done with politics?"

"No, of course not. I just . . . I need some time to recover from the defeat, to rebuild my self-confidence."

Cécile sat up and gave him a pointed look. "You should get your priorities straight. While you're 'rebuilding your self-confidence,' opportunities have come and gone. You've already missed the European Parliament elections."

Mat sat up, too. "It would've been unrealistic."

"Maybe. But you can't afford to wait too long. The regional and the cantonal elections are next year. You need to get back in the ring."

He sighed. She was right. As always.

Cécile cocked her head. "You're still hung up on that waitress, aren't you?"

"I haven't seen her since our conversation after the election results."

"I know that. What I don't know is if you're over the whole stupid thing."

He looked down at his hands.

"So sleeping with her didn't help?" she asked.

He stared at her in surprise. "I haven't slept with her. We've ... fooled around, but that was it."

"Then go do it, for heaven's sake! Don't you see how this fixation has been distracting you from the important stuff? From your career, your goals?"

Mat's brows shot up in disbelief. "Wait a second. Slow down. Are you saying you'd be OK if I slept with Jeanne? Are you *giving me leave* to do it?"

"Absolutely. Not only will I be OK, it'll be a good thing for both of us. You'll get what you want and then lose interest in her. And I'll get ... a reprieve."

"What do you mean?"

She sighed. "You know what. Unfortunately, you have needs that . . . overwhelm me."

His mouth curled. "I don't have any *unusual* needs—"

She wasn't listening. "So, please, do have a bit of fun with your waitress. You're welcome to see her every time you're in Paris. Just keep it discreet. I deserve that much."

He suddenly didn't know what to say.

Cécile was looking at him, a benign smile on her face, clearly expecting some kind of gratitude for her grand gesture. But he didn't feel any. What he felt instead was resentment. Yes, he was still mad about Jeanne, and yes, he still craved her. Rejecting her offer a month ago and staying away from her ever since was one of the hardest things he'd done in his life. A real achievement, a feat of self-restraint.

So yeah, he was as desperate for her as ever.

But he didn't want to use her.

He wasn't the kind of man Cécile was casting him to be.

He didn't want to be that man.

* * *

It had been a surreal night. At around two in the morning, Jeanne woke up to yelling, thumping, banging, and other sounds of a fight turned ugly. When Liviu screamed, she ran over without bothering to pull a sweater over her pajamas.

She pounded on Daniela's door. "Open up! Open up immediately, or I call the cops right now!"

To her surprise, Daniela opened the door, looking shaken but unharmed. Giving Jeanne a funny look, she stepped aside and let her enter the loge. The first thing Jeanne noticed was Liviu, rushing in from the kitchen with a glass of water in his shaky hands. He didn't take it to Daniela, but ran around the dining table instead. Jeanne followed him and saw Nico prone on the floor.

He was perfectly motionless.

"Shall I pour it over him?" Liviu asked his mom.

Daniela nodded.

Liviu emptied the glass over Nico's head.

Nothing happened.

"He's breathing." Daniela told Jeanne.

"Did he hit his head?" Jeanne asked, kneeling next to Nico to inspect him.

"No," Daniela said.

Jeanne took his pulse and sighed in relief. He wasn't dead, just passed out.

Thank God.

Then Daniela's reply sank in. "Oh my God. Did you — ?"

Daniela nodded. "When he raised his hand to hit me, I punched him the way Dominique taught us." She chortled nervously. "Turned out to be a little too effective."

"Are you sure he's alive?" Liviu gave Jeanne a doubtful look.

"Positive. Let's see if we can make him come to without calling the firemen," Jeanne said as cheerfully as she could manage and slapped Nico's cheeks.

Nothing happened. She shook him a little, and then slapped his cheeks again.

She went on like that for a few moments, until she heard a faint groan.

Nico opened one eye halfway.

"You did it!" Daniela shouted in relief, rushing to his side. "Liviu, fetch another glass of water, quickly!"

They pulled Nico into a reclining position and propped him against a pile of cushions. He opened his other eye and mumbled something unintelligible.

"Is he drunk?" Jeanne asked.

"Wasted."

Liviu arrived with the water and was about to give Nico another cold shower when Daniela snatched the glass from his hand.

"This one goes into the mouth," she said with a faint smile.

As he drank and looked around, Nico's expression turned from blank to wild-eyed, and then to bleak. "You hit me?" he half asked, half stated, trying to focus his gaze on Daniela.

"Yes," she said, her fists clenched.

He turned to Jeanne. "I'm a b-b-battered man now. Why aren't you calling the cops?" He snorted, mumbled something under his breath, threw his head back, and laughed uncontrollably for a good five minutes.

After he was done, Nico stood up on shaking legs and declared he was leaving.

"Where will you go?" Daniela asked. "The *métro* is closed, and you can't walk to your place like this."

"I'll take the night bus." He wiped his mouth with his sleeve and took a few unsteady steps toward the door.

"Nico, wait! Stay here until dawn. You shouldn't—"

"You're not telling me what I should or shouldn't do," he snapped.

Daniela lifted her chin. "Fine. Go! I don't care if you get mugged or run over."

Nico turned to Liviu. "See you around, kid."

And he was out the door.

When Daniela stopped by the bistro the following afternoon, Jeanne took her aside. "Any news?"

Daniela nodded excitedly. "I called to check on him this morning. He didn't answer. I called again, every fifteen minutes, until he finally picked up around noon."

"Did he get home safely?"

Daniela shook her head. "He blacked out about twenty meters from our building and woke up at the hospital. They're going to keep him under observation for a couple of days."

"How do you feel about all this?"

"That's the weirdest thing, Jeanne." The young woman suddenly beamed. "I feel proud. I landed my boyfriend in the hospital with a small concussion, and I feel proud of myself."

"I can't blame you," Jeanne said with a grin.

Daniela's face grew serious. "As soon as he's out of the hospital, I'll tell him we're finished."

"I'm so glad to hear it!"

"I . . . I may still have feelings for him, but I know they'll pass. I won't have Liviu witness another fight."

She paused and added with a mischievous smile, "Regardless of who batters whom."

* * *

Chapter Thirteen
December

Will I need my city boots in Nîmes?

Jeanne had been pondering the question for five minutes now, a little amused by her own indecision. She hadn't hesitated for a second when she paid all the money she had—and the money she didn't have—for *La Bohème*. Yet now she couldn't make up her mind whether to take her boots to Nîmes. Theoretically, you packed a pair of boots when traveling over Christmastime. In practice, the forecast promised exceptionally mild weather in the south, and even if she ended up going to the mountains with her brother, those high-heeled contraptions would be useless.

That was it—she'd take her hiking boots instead.

Jeanne returned her leather boots to the shoe rack and closed her travel bag. A quiet week with her family was exactly what she needed after this roller-coaster year.

The doorbell rang.

Liviu must be anxious to collect his present.

She rushed to the door and opened it without looking through the peephole.

Mat stood in front of her, in all his tall, manly beauty.

His sandy curls had grown back—not as long and messy as he used to wear them, but long enough to soften the angles of his face.

"Hi," he said.

"Hi."

"May I come in?"

"What are you doing here?"

"I need to talk to you. Please."

She led him to her cozy living room and motioned to the couch.

He removed his coat and took a step to sit down, but stopped in his tracks and turned to face her. "It's over with Cécile."

Jeanne's mouth opened slightly. "What happened?"

He removed his glasses and rubbed the bridge of his nose.

"What happened, Mat?" she repeated her question.

"Cécile gave me permission to sleep with you. She said it would be a relief for her as much as for me."

"Wow. And?"

"And I . . . broke up with her. It's been two months now." He gave Jeanne an unreadable look.

She waited for him to add something, but he just stared at her.

She stared back. "I take it you don't want a woman who doesn't mind sharing you."

"Something like that."

"And you waited for two months before telling me."

"I needed to figure some things out first."

She gave him an amused look. "Have you?"

"Yes."

"Feel like sharing?"

He put his glasses back on. "That's what I came here for. I even prepared a speech, but now I can't remember what exactly I was going to say or in which order." He smiled apologetically. "So, if you don't mind, I'll cut straight to the chase."

"Cut away."

He drew in a deep breath. "Here goes. This thing I feel for you . . . I used to think of it as a weakness. A design flaw. Sometimes, I thought of it as a curse."

"I'm truly flattered," Jeanne said, her mouth twitching.

To her surprise, Mat didn't smile. His expression was so intense that she too grew serious.

"But it isn't a weakness, Jeanne, let alone a curse. I can see it so clearly now. It's a gift. To desire you like this, to love everything about you—body and soul—is a beautiful gift that I was too blind to appreciate."

Wait a second, did he just say "love"?

"In April, when I realized you cared for me..." He swallowed and huffed. "It's amazing how quickly I got used to that idea, as if it were the most normal, ordinary thing. As if it were something I could just walk away from."

He fell silent and searched her eyes.

Jeanne fought to stay calm, not to let herself drown in the gray depths of his gaze. It was so tempting to put her arms around his neck and kiss him. But even as she began to tremble with anticipation, she couldn't—and didn't' want to—discard the resentment she'd cultivated over the past couple of months. She wasn't going to melt into his embrace just because he'd seen his attraction for her in a new light.

He took a step toward her. "This will sound corny, and you may laugh in my face, but I'll say it anyway. You're under my skin, Jeanne, and you're in my heart. You've been there for years."

She blinked a few times and looked away, struggling to remain cool. Did he really think she might laugh at his words? She felt like crying.

Mat threw his head back. "God, it feels so good to finally say these things to you. I want you to distraction. I want you in my life. For the rest of my life. I want your babies."

She swallowed and blinked rapidly, before turning to look away.

"I can't believe it took me so long to see the truth," he said. "You're a rare gemstone. One in a million. I love every single thing about you, Jeanne, — your wit, your looks, your kindness . . . I've never loved anyone the way I love you."

He went down on one knee and pulled a small velvet case out of his pocket.

For the first time in her life, Jeanne was dumbstruck. Mat's unexpected love declaration had been wild enough, but this . . . This scene belonged in her fantasies, not in her living room. She eyed the object in Mat's hand with suspicion, her mind refusing to accept it as reality.

He opened the case. Inside was a magnificent uncut diamond ring.

He looked into her eyes. "Will you marry me?"

Her heart thumped a crazy beat. She couldn't speak.

Mat kept his intense gaze locked on hers until a shadow of panic flickered in his eyes. "Please say something."

"We haven't even dated," she finally said.

"That's easy to fix."

"I . . . I wasn't prepared for this."

"I understand," he said, standing and cupping her face. "You don't need to say anything now. I'll wait. It's only fair."

She nodded. It was, indeed, only fair. And reasonable. She should send him away now, finish packing, and get some sleep before catching her train tomorrow morning. They'd start dating after the Christmas break. They'd take things slow, get to properly know each other . . .

To hell with that crap.

She loved him. Standing before her pouring out his heart was the man of her dreams. She wanted him in every way a woman could want a man. In her bed. In her home. In her life. Hiding this from him might be reasonable. And fair. But who cared about those things in a medical emergency? Because this *was* a medical emergency. Her heart was so swollen with love that if she refused to let it out sometime soon, she feared it might explode.

For a few moments, she basked in his gaze, savoring its ardor and getting drunk on the knowledge that Mat was hers now, completely and unreservedly.

Then she beamed and said, "Yes."

His brow creased. "Yes? As in 'Yes, I'll be your beloved and loving wife'?"

She nodded with a grin.

"Come here." He slid the ring onto her finger.

"It's gorgeous," she said.

"The deal is sealed—you're my fiancée now."

He pulled her close and kissed her. It was so much more than a kiss. Soft and gentle at first, it was a vow to cherish her, a promise of beautiful things to come. Gradually it grew hotter and harder as he devoured her mouth, explored its depths, and bit her lips lightly. It gave her a taste of his hunger for her. A glimpse into what it would be like to let him love her.

Her knees began to wobble, and she drew away a little. His mouth was close, but not touching. Breathing heavily, she fixed her gaze on his lips.

"Jeanne," he rasped.

A flush of desire had darkened his skin. His eyes begged her to renew the kiss, but he didn't move. He was letting her lead the dance.

She stroked his back, feeling his rippling muscles through the soft fabric of his cashmere sweater. Tugging at the hem she said, "Take it off."

He yanked the sweater over his head and dropped it to the floor. The T-shirt came off next. With his upper body stripped, he looked like a true heir to the Norman Vikings.

God, he was beautiful.

She kissed his collarbone, neck, and shoulders. She stroked his back, slowly sliding her hands down to his firm butt. It was arousing as hell to be in control, to discover and explore his body. Soon, she'd let him do the same to her, so she could close her eyes and just feel.

But not yet.

She pulled away again and took off her pullover and bra, but kept her jeans on just like him.

He raked his gaze over her, his face transfixed with longing. "Sweet Lord."

Jeanne undid the button of her jeans, lowered the zipper and peeled off the jeans and the panties. She straightened and said, "Now you."

As soon as he was naked, she took a step toward him, threw her arms around his neck, and pressed her body to his. His muscles were deliciously hard, and every inch of his skin was hot against hers.

Finally.

At last, they were naked together, skin against skin—no distance, no clothing, no barriers of any kind.

She moaned with the pleasure of it.

He growled low in his throat, slid one arm under her knees, and scooped her up. "Which way to the bedroom?"

"First door on your right."

He carried her to the tiny bedroom, lowered her on the bed, and covered her with his body.

An hour later, Jeanne let her lids drop and curled up against him, feeling exquisitely drained, boneless, and sated.

He kissed the top of her head. "Ah. Coffee."

She opened her eyes and propped herself up. "Coffee?"

"That's how your hair smells. I love it."

"Which confirms my theory. You're a perv."

"Want to hear something funny? I didn't drink any coffee all summer. It was part of my getting-over-Jeanne program."

"Wow. You should develop a ten-step tutorial and sell it online." She winked. "Given the success of your program."

He smiled and stroked her hair.

"Will you continue with the politics?" she asked.

He nodded. "I like it, and I believe in what the Greens stand for."

"Will you run for mayor again?"

"Maybe. I may also stand for the cantonal elections or the regionals next year. But only if I'm ready. When I have a clear vision and a strategy."

Jeanne hesitated for a brief moment and then asked, "Will you move to Paris?"

Mat shook his head.

"I can't move to Baleville," she said. "I recently bought *La Bohème*—"

"Jeanne, that's fantastic news! Congratulations. Wasn't it your dream?"

"Yep." She traced his jawline with her thumb. "But how are we going to make it work with you in Baleville and me in Paris?"

"Easily. We're only an hour and a half away. I'll spend half of the week here, provided you have the Internet, so I can work. If not, I'll get a subscription—"

"You're in luck," Jeanne cut in. "The National Barmaids' Association has just issued a memo urging all its members to enter the digital era."

He grinned. "I should send them a thank-you note."

"You can even *email* it."

He smirked, then propped himself on his elbow and stared into her eyes for a long moment. "Say you love me. Say you're crazy about me."

"You know I am."

He traced his finger across her lips. "I need to hear it, Jeanne. Please. I *need* to hear you say it."

She grinned, suddenly giddy. There it was—his vulnerability. The toad eye. He may have become a heartthrob, but deep inside he'd kept the sensitive soul that needed to hear her say she loved him back.

"I love you, Mat," she whispered in his ear. "I love you, I love you, I love you," she said covering his face with kisses. "I'm crazy about you. I want you to be my adored and adoring husband."

He pulled her to him, gripped her hips, and in one swift move, plunged home.

<< <> >>

Like these books? Get another Bistro La Bohème story **free**!

FREE DOWNLOAD

"Sweet, sensual & fun"

To get your **free** novella just copy and paste this link into your browser: bit.ly/alix-freebook

Excerpt from "Winter's Gift?"

(a Bistro La Bohème novella)

What happens when a steely tycoon falls for an elite call girl who won't quit her job?

When Anton and Anna cross paths over the winter holidays, neither can deny that what they share in bed - and out of it - is special. But it threatens the single principle both have lived under for years: Don't lose control.

~~~

Chapter One
Anton

The blonde waves at me again with a coquettish smile on her lips. I turn away and feign interest in the huge painting in front of me. But I can't help wondering if I've met her before—she does look vaguely familiar. Someone must have introduced us at a function or a Bolshoi premiere. If I concentrate, I might even remember her name… Daria. No, Dina. No, definitely, Daria.

Gary prods me with his elbow. "Did you notice the young nymph standing by that enormous landscape?"

"I'm trying not to look at it. The color combination hurts my eyes."

"Well, if I were you, I'd make an effort. Her legs are endless, and I bet you she's naked under that skimpy dress."

"Seriously, Gary?" I shake my head. "What am I, sixteen?"

"No, but you're Moscow's best catch, and she seems desperate for your attention." He winks and singsongs, "A juicy, yummy, low-hanging peach…"

I continue to stare at the canvas. I believe

what I'm looking at is a face. It's green and contorted, and the sign under it says *Number 2: Sadness*. Flanked by two other spasmodic mugs, it forms a triptych titled *Ephemeral Emotions*.

It should have been called *A Group of Constipated Trolls*.

Coming to this vernissage was a mistake. I let the title of the exhibit—*Rhapsody in Blue*—and the reviews lure me here, forgetting that Moscow's art critics would praise anyone who pays them. They'd even call these god-awful daubs "masterpieces of modern art," and their author "Russia's next Kandinsky."

Kandinsky, my foot.

Gary furrows his brow in an effort to concentrate. "I'm sure I've met her before... What was her name, dammit?"

"Daria, wannabe art dealer," I say.

"Of course!" He lowers his voice to a whisper. "She's coming over."

I brace myself for a bout of small talk and a sales pitch. As soon as she's done, I'm out of here.

"Gentlemen," Daria says from behind my back. "It's such a pleasure to see you again!"

"The pleasure is all ours," Gary says.

I turn around, stretch my lips into a semblance of a smile, and nod.

Daria points at the triptych. "What do you think? The artist is a personal friend." She pauses for effect before whispering in my ear, "I could get you a deal on any of these pieces. It's a great investment."

"I'll pass," I say and step back.

"Ah, Anton Malakhov's legendary tough talk!" Daria hooks her arm through mine. "I'm sure I can make you change your mind if you give me ten minutes of your time."

I shake my head and unhook our arms.

She bats her eyelashes. "Forget about these paintings. Why don't we sneak out, find someplace private, and discuss our love of art... and other passions?"

"I have a previous engagement."

She trails her fingers up and down my arm. "Forget about the passions. They're so last century. We could compare our *perversions* instead. What say you?"

Stupid, misguided child, that's what I say. *Go home, sober up, and reflect on your behavior.*

I sigh and shake her hand off me. "I'm not interested."

"I am." Gary's eyes light up.

I open my mouth to say *No, you're not. You're married with children,* but I shut it again before I utter a sound. Gary is one of the handful of people I call friends. All others have eventually used their connection to me for personal gain. Some have done it out of greed, others from jealousy. But not Gary. He may not be faithful to his wife — which, given my history with Stacia I strongly disapprove of — but he's loyal to me. He has been so for almost three decades now, since our nerdy high school days.

And that trumps everything else.

Daria looks him over. "I don't do sidekicks."

I press my lips together to stifle a smile. The "peach" isn't so low-hanging after all.

She turns to me and jabs my chest with her index finger. "As for you, let me tell you something, Mr. Snooty Tycoon. You may be in great shape, but not for much longer. I *know* your age."

I widen my eyes in fake shock. "You do?"

"You're *forty-five*."

She gives me a triumphant look, as if she's just revealed a horrible truth I've been hiding from everyone.

Somehow, I manage to maintain a serious face. "Seeing as you're so well informed, you should know I have a twenty-two-year-old daughter." I pretend to appraise her looks. "About your age, I'd say."

Daria rolls her eyes, turns on her heel, and

storms away.

I glance at Gary's sour countenance. "I'm done here. What about you?"

"I'll stay a little longer."

I begin to make my way toward the exit. As I pass the centerpiece titled *Night on the River Volga*, I can't help wincing.

That's when a clear, exceedingly pleasant female voice says, "The artist should've called this painting *Black Stripe I Drew with My Ruler*. Then, at least, I could give him a point for honesty."

I stop in my tracks, turn in the direction of the voice, and stare. I can't stop staring. My kindred spirit is in her early to mid-thirties, slim, dressed in elegant black pants and a cream cashmere turtleneck. Her brown hair is gathered at her nape into a soft, loose bun. Her makeup is subdued except for the crimson-red lipstick that brings out her flawless skin. The way she's dressed, the way she holds herself and smiles at her giggling friend—everything about her speaks easy elegance and confident wit.

I backtrack to her. "My idea was *Dark and Darker*, but your version is much better."

She nods, and the tiniest smile wrinkles the corners of her gray eyes.

My breath catches. I need to find something

to say quickly, before she turns to her friend. "I wonder how you would dub the entire exhibit."

"Bullshit in Blue," she says without batting an eye.

I burst out laughing.

She laughs too, and it's the most beautiful sound I've heard in a long, long time.

"It's the title that brought me here in the first place," I say. "I love—"

"Gershwin. Me too. Especially *Rhapsody in Blue*."

I grin like an idiot. Not only is she funny and classy, but she also has great taste in music. Anyone who loves jazz does.

"I expected something jazzy from this artist, but what I see here is just..." I pause as I search for a good qualifier.

"Pride, pomp, and circumstance." She winks, and I nearly jump for joy at her apt quote.

My eyes dart to her graceful hands. No wedding band or engagement ring in sight. Excellent. *I'll get her one soon.*

Whoa. Where did that come from? I'll be doing no such thing. I don't even know the woman's name, for heaven's sake. Yet, the image of me slipping a huge rock on her delicate finger refuses to leave my mind.

I don't think I've felt this way about anyone

before. Not even Stacia. When I fell in love with her over twenty years ago, I knew she wasn't like me. Our interests were worlds apart, and we could never agree on anything, big or small. I wish I'd known at the time we didn't share the same values, either. But I was naive and overly optimistic, and I convinced myself we'd work it out.

God knows I tried—for a whole decade.

And now as I look at this woman, I don't doubt for a second we'll get along famously. She looks right, sounds right, even smells right. And from what I've heard so far, I'm sure I'll enjoy her mind as much as I'll enjoy her body.

I hold out my hand. "Anton Malakhov. It's a pleasure to make your acquaintance."

"Anna." She grants me a brief, but intense, joy of her touch. "The pleasure is mine."

I go on to shake hands with her friend without taking my eyes off Anna for a second. There's no point in hiding how much she's impressed me.

Anna. It's a beautiful name... even if a touch too formal.

"Does anyone call you Annushka?" I find myself asking.

"Only my mom."

She smiles, and I debate whether I should

invite her for a drink right now or ask for her number. One thing is certain. I must see her again. In fact, I need to see her as soon as possible, and as often as possible. Preferably, every day.

And every night.

She resolves my quagmire by ripping a page out of her notebook and scribbling something on it. Why am I not surprised she carries a notebook and a pen in her purse? I bet she also has a book or an e-reader somewhere in there. Although I just met her, I feel like I know her. I can see her inner core, her fundamental essence. It shines through.

She hands me the sheet, and I glance at what she's written. There's a phone number, her name, and a meaningless figure under it. I look up at her, about to ask if it's an extension.

"This," she says, pointing her slender index finger at the top line, "is my agent's number. And below is my hourly rate."

My jaw slacks.

The woman of my dreams is a hooker.

End of Excerpt

About the Author

Alix Nichols is an avid reader of chick lit, romance and fantasy, caffeine addict and a badge-wearing Mr. Darcy fan. She released her first romance at the age of six. It had six pages stitched together and bound in purple velvet paper. The book was titled "Eliza and Robert" and featured highly creative spelling. Some words were written in mirror image. Unintentionally.

Decades later, she still loves the name Robert and the genre romance. Her spelling has improved (somewhat) and her books have made the Kindle Top 100 Lists, climbing as high as #1. She lives and works in Paris, France.

Connect with her online:

Blog: http://www.alixnichols.com
Facebook: www.facebook.com/AuthorAlixNichols
Twitter: twitter.com/aalix_nichols
Pinterest: http://www.pinterest.com/AuthorANichols
Goodreads: goodreads.com/alixnichols

Printed in Great Britain
by Amazon.co.uk, Ltd.,
Marston Gate.